"It's be[...]
the edge [...]
picnic tal[...]
the rain b[...]
before the skies really open up."

Before she could stop him, Jack dashed inside the trailer and came back out with a small plastic bag. "For your hair," he said, just as the sky crackled with lightning. A second later, the night exploded with ear-splitting thunder. "Come," Jack said. "We'll make a run for it."

By the time they reached her motorhome, they were both drenched to the skin. "Thanks for a wonderful evening," Ruth said.

"You're a very special lady, Ruth. I'm going to miss you." He put an arm around her wet shoulder and hugged her. A brief, intimate hug. Then he cupped her face in his hands and kissed her.

Ruth felt the warmth of his body as he pressed against her. Then, all too soon, he was gone, running through the rain, back to his own motorhome.

She tipped her head back and let the rain splash against her face, no longer caring that she was soaked. For the first time in her life, she felt totally free, released miraculously from her roles as wife, daughter, mother, grandmother, schoolteacher. She was free . . . at last!

And Jack Colby's kiss still burned on her lips . . .

A KISS
AT SUNRISE

CHARLOTTE SHERMAN

ZEBRA BOOKS
KENSINGTON PUBLISHING CORP.

ZEBRA BOOKS are published by

Kensington Publishing Corp.
475 Park Avenue South
New York, NY 10016

First Printing: August, 1993

Printed in the United States of America

One

For a brief moment the late afternoon sun appeared to be stuck behind the low branches of a cottonwood tree, as if pausing to bask in the cool air surrounding the roaring waters of the Boulder River.

The same towering cottonwood provided a niche of shade for Ruth Nichols as she sat at the picnic table and looked to the riverbank where her son, Tony, was still fishing with his son, Eddie. Another man fished from the bank some fifty feet downstream. He'd been there all day too, and as far as Ruth knew, none of them had caught any fish.

Feeling hot and pleasantly tired, she fanned herself with the brochure she'd picked up when she and Ginny, her eight-year-old granddaughter, had made their third trip up to the campground office to buy fish pellets for a nickel a handful. The air, stirred up by the makeshift fan, felt good against her face.

Retired just two weeks earlier, after teaching for thirty years, Ruth was now comfortably ensconced in a campsite at the Spring Creek Camp & Trout Ranch, three miles from Tony's home in Big Timber, Montana, and eighty miles from her own home in Billings.

The Spring Creek campground lived up to its description in the colorful brochure: a quiet, parklike, shaded setting on the Boulder River. Smaller print listed stocked trout ponds, grassy tent sites, cabins, full hookups, ice, phone, limited groceries, laundry, and sparkling clean restrooms and showers.

It had been Tony's idea to celebrate her retirement by inviting her to camp out with his family for the weekend, and she liked the campsite he'd chosen. It was just a hundred yards from the fast-flowing Boulder River—close enough to hear the restful sound of the water crashing against giant boulders.

The sky-blue and domed family tent was set up on the grass near the rustic sleeping cabin Tony had rented for her and Ginny to share. Flat, round rocks formed a path from the picnic table to the covered porch of the sparsely furnished cabin.

Along the same row of campsites, all shaded by clumps of tall cottonwood trees, were three other sleeping cabins and several recreation vehicles, each site with its own picnic table and barbecue grill.

Ruth turned her head away from the riverbank and stared at the carpet of green grass that surrounded the fishing pond where she and Ginny had spent most of the afternoon. Beyond the wide expanse of lush grass, tents of various sizes, shapes, and colors stood in the shadows of their own trees. There were more than a dozen travel trailers and motorhomes behind the tent area, and still more RVs in another section of the crowded campground.

"I'll be right back, Grandma," Ginny announced as she skipped across the flat rocks.

"Where're you going?" Ruth asked.

"To the cabin. I have to get something. Maybe we can go back up to the pond in a little while."

"Maybe not," Ruth grinned. "Grandma's

all tuckered out."

It was obvious that Ginny enjoyed her self-appointed role of entertaining grandma, because each excursion up to the office had entailed the roundabout tour of the entire campground with Ginny proudly leading Ruth past every tent, travel trailer, motorhome, fifth-wheeler, and sleeping cabin on the grounds before they finally arrived at the pellet-dispensing container, which resembled a gumball machine.

Then with nickels inserted and fish food dispensed into plastic cups, Ruth and Ginny would hike up the grassy knoll to the glittering, clear pond where large trout glinted in the sunlight as they swarmed back and forth, waiting for the next handout. Ginny delighted in tossing the pellets into the pond, two or three at a time, and watching the trout change directions en masse and boil to the surface to snatch the food.

The July heat didn't seem to bother Ginny, but after their last pellet trip, Ruth welcomed the shade and the gentle breeze.

She took a deep breath and wondered why she felt so restless. She loved campgrounds. In fact, she had a big motorhome sitting in her own driveway in Billings that she hadn't moved since the death of her husband, three years ago. And now that she was retired, she had no desire to travel in it alone.

Ruth was supposed to be vacationing in New York right now with her friend, Edith McAllister, also a widow and a retired schoolteacher, but their trip had been postponed because Edith's brother needed cataract surgery. And Ruth had jumped at the chance to camp with Tony and his family instead. She needed this brief respite to recover from the emotional strain of ending her career; the flurry of retirement parties her friends and coworkers had thrown for her.

And now, even though she enjoyed the peaceful setting and the calming pounding of the river, she found it hard to sit still for very long. Maybe it would take time to adjust to a new, more relaxed way of life. Or maybe she'd never get over the feeling that she had to stay busy all the time to keep from feeling old. A silly notion, she knew, but she'd heard the stories about people who retired to a rocking chair, only to give up on life.

In a way, Ruth envied the lone fisherman who sat in a lawn chair downstream from Tony and Eddie. She wished she could just relax and forget about everything for a while, but she couldn't stop the flow of thoughts that bombarded her mind. Snatches of ideas for her retirement years mingled with motherly concerns she felt for her family, and she had a hard time separating the two. When she thought about all the lonely evenings she would be spending in her home in Billings, she quickly shut the image out, before she could start to feel sorry for herself.

At the moment, she was trying to ignore her feelings of guilt. Self-inflicted guilt feelings, she admitted, but disturbing to her equanimity just the same.

Brenda, her older daughter who also lived in Billings, had asked her to babysit this weekend and Ruth had turned her down so she could go with Tony and his family, something she rarely did. And Ruth's mother, Ernestine Murphy, had been indignant when Ruth had called to say she wouldn't be able to take her grocery shopping as she did every Saturday, or to church on Sunday. Ernestine had her own car and if she didn't want to drive, she had plenty of friends who could chauffeur her around. Still, Ruth found the weekend mother-and-daughter rituals hard to break.

So be it, she thought, as she glanced toward the river. She felt a twinge of motherly pride as she watched her son and grandson fishing together. Tony and Eddie wore matching caps, dark blue, with the insignia "Prospector's Cafe, Big Timber, Montana" spelled out in white lettering. They both wore shorts and T-shirts, and while Tony had a slender, muscular build, Eddie, at twelve, still looked long and gangly.

She reached for her new camera, one of those point-and-shoot models with automatic everything, a retirement gift from the principal of the school where she'd taught kindergarten for so long. She'd already used up two rolls of film, one just of Tony's family, the other for what she called her "character studies."

For as long as she could remember, Ruth had been fascinated by people. Over the years, she'd taken dozens of pictures. Her favorite shot today being of an elderly couple who, although they both needed canes, still managed to hold hands as they strolled through the campground.

Ruth walked toward the riverbank, stopping some fifty feet short of the water. She looked through the viewfinder and took a couple of steps to the side. She didn't want Tony and Eddie to look like they had cottonwoods growing out of their heads.

She clicked off a shot and listened for the automatic winder to start. On an impulse, she turned and took a distant profile shot of the lone fisherman who stood at the edge of the water, his pole held in both hands, his taut line glinting in the sunlight as it stretched into the river.

As she strolled back to the campsite, the familiar smell of woodsmoke began to fill the air as fellow campers made preparations for their evening meal. Ruth looked forward to sitting at the table with Tony and his family, watching the glowing lights from lanterns and campfires throughout the park.

Tony's wife, Lynn, moved the ice chest from a patch of shade beside the tent and set it down on the end of the table. Her short blonde hair bounced as she walked. She wore white shorts and a blue print blouse, tucked in at the waist.

"Do you want something to drink?" Lynn asked.

"No thanks," Ruth said. "I think I drank a gallon of water when Ginny and I got back from the fish pond."

"Where is Ginny?" Lynn asked.

"She went into the cabin to get something." Ruth turned and glanced over her shoulder at the small log structure.

"Don't let her wear you out. She'll drag you up to the fish pond as often as you'll let her." Lynn turned and shaded her eyes with her hand as she watched Tony and Eddie.

"I can use the exercise," Ruth said, patting her slightly rounded tummy.

Ginny came out of the sleeping cabin, a small paper sack clutched in her hand. Like the other members of her family, she wore shorts and a colorful top. Her light brown hair was pulled back and tied in a ponytail. As she sat down on the picnic bench, she brushed fine, loose strands of hair away from her face.

"What have you got there?" Ruth asked when Ginny set the sack on the table. She slid closer to Ginny, to get a closer look inside the bag.

"Sparklers. You want to see them?" Ginny reached in the sack.

The cellophane crinkled as Ruth ran her finger over the package. "You'll have fun with these tonight."

Another cooling breeze blew through the camp, bringing with it a flurry of soft white flakes from the cottonwood trees. The ground was already littered with pieces of the white, fluffy substance that had blown from the trees' seeds.

"It's snowing cotton," Ginny squealed as she reached up to catch one of the swirling cotton balls. She held it in the palm of her hand and ran a finger across its soft texture. After scrutinizing it for a minute, she held it out for Ruth to see. "Grandma, is this really cotton?"

"Not the kind you make clothes out of, but it looks like it, doesn't it?"

"Oh," Ginny said, obviously disappointed. She turned her hand over and shook the cotton free, watched it float to the ground.

"That breeze feels good," Ruth commented.

"Grandma, if you're hot, why don't you

wear shorts like the rest of us?"

"I'm too old to wear shorts."

"Are you really?" Ginny looked up at her, a look of concern on her face. "If you're old, why don't you have gray hair?"

Ruth laughed. "I've got plenty of gray hair, mixed in with the dark."

"Oh," Ginny said again, apparently satisfied with the answer.

"Grandma isn't old," Lynn said as she walked over and patted Ruth's shoulder. "You've got a good figure. You'd look good in shorts."

Ginny continued to look at Ruth, a puzzled expression on her face. "Our teacher says that people shrink when they get old. Were you ever tall, Grandma?"

Ruth laughed. "No, Ginny, I've always been five foot, two."

"Ginny, you ask too many questions," Lynn said. She headed for the tent again and emerged a few seconds later with a package of paper plates in one hand, silverware in the other.

"Can I help?" Ruth offered.

"No, I'm just getting things ready. I won't start the fire until the boys are through fishing."

"You know they're not going to catch any fish for dinner," Ginny said, screwing her face into a frown.

Lynn smiled. "That's okay. I've got hot dogs, just in case."

"I don't see why Grandma and I can't go up to the pond and catch five trout for dinner," Ginny whined.

"Because it costs twenty-five cents an inch when you catch them out of the pond," Lynn answered. "As big as those trout are, they would cost four or five dollars apiece."

"Grandma could pay for it."

Before Ruth could offer, Lynn cautioned her with a slight shake of her head.

"Ginny, that wasn't nice," Lynn said. "I already told you that if you want to fish in the pond, you can use your allowance."

"I don't want to spend *my* money on those dumb fish."

"Then don't expect anyone else to."

"Mom, can I light one of my sparklers?" Ginny asked as she fingered the cellophane package.

"Not until it gets dark."

Ginny set the sparklers aside without further protest, as if she'd expected her mother to say that. "Why couldn't we buy some of those fireworks that explode in the sky?" she asked, a slight pout to her mouth.

"Because we're not allowed to shoot them off in the campground. I already told you that, Ginny."

"But today's the Fourth of July. It isn't fair."

"A lot of things aren't fair." Lynn shook her head and smiled before she walked back over to the tent and disappeared inside.

Ginny slid off the bench and carried the sparklers back to the cabin.

"Well, is it going to be hot dogs tonight?" Lynn said as she carried napkins, salt and pepper shakers, and a bag of potato chips to the table.

Ruth laughed. "I guess so. Oh, look, he's got one," she said when she saw the fishing pole bend toward the water.

"Who?" Lynn glanced toward the riverbank. "Oh, the avid fisherman. I was hoping it was Tony or Eddie."

Ruth watched as the man reeled the fish to shore, smoothly tugging back on the pole every time he stopped reeling. His motions were easy, graceful, as if catching fish was second nature to him.

She saw Tony reel in his slack line and set his pole down before he strolled over to the fisherman. The man brought the shimmering fish out of the water, flipping it to the ground with a flick of his wrist. She couldn't hear what Tony was saying because of the rushing roar of the water, but she could see him mouth the words, "That's a big one."

The fisherman was too far away for Ruth to see his features, but she could tell that he was grinning. After the fish had been threaded onto a metal stringer, he cast out again. When he settled back into his folding chair, Tony walked back to his own fishing spot and gathered up his pole and tackle box. He motioned for Eddie to do the same.

"Looks like they're giving up," Lynn said.

Ruth watched Tony walk across the ankle-high grass toward the campsite. It was hard to believe that he was thirty-three years old. Where had the years gone? Tony had been three when she had first started teaching and now her career days were over.

Would she ever get to travel and see the country? Or would she just stick around the house and look for things to keep busy until she wore out? And could she adjust to her new role as a retired schoolteacher? Darned if that didn't sound dull!

She had a sudden urge to hop in her car and drive until she found a quiet mountain stream that she could walk beside, just to see where it led, or a place where she could walk into the woods. She wanted to sit on a stump and listen to the birds, watch the antics of playful squirrels.

Instead, her shoulders sagged as a feeling of quiet desperation settled over her.

Two

Tony had a grin on his face and a slight bounce to his steps as he approached the campsite. On the other hand, Eddie, who followed twenty feet behind his dad, had the walk of an old man as he shuffled through the high grass, his head hung so low that he had to stare at the ground. Or maybe Eddie's walk was that of a young boy who was on the verge of becoming a moody teenager.

Tony leaned his fishing pole against the picnic table, set the tackle box on a corner of the table, and nodded toward the lone fisherman. "Now there's a man after my own heart. That's what I want to do when I retire — fish all day, every day. You know what his ambition is?"

"He doesn't look like he has much ambition," Ruth said.

"Oh, Mom, you'll never understand what fishing's all about. Catching a fish is incidental."

"So what's his ambition?" Lynn asked.

"That fellow wants to fish every lake, stream, and creek in the country before he dies."

"You're right, I don't understand," Ruth said as she stood up and stretched her legs. "Although I have to admit, the thought of seeing all that beautiful country appeals to me."

Tony had a twinkle in his eyes when he smiled. "Mom, you're smarter than I thought. You've got the time to travel now. Go for it."

Ruth thought about the plans she and her husband had made for their retirement years. She still had the desire to roam around the country, but it wouldn't be the same without him.

"Oh that I could," she said, trying to conceal her sudden feelings of despair.

But Tony noticed. Ruth saw the concern in his expression as his smile faded away.

"Hey, don't you remember what you drilled in my head when I was a kid?" Tony chided her. "How many times did you tell me that I could do anything I wanted to if I had the desire? Until I got sick of hearing you say it, that's how many times."

Ruth laughed. "You're right, Tony. So if you get a postcard from me from Timbuktu, don't be surprised."

Tony patted her shoulder. "Nothing you do would surprise me."

Ruth sat down as Eddie wandered up to the picnic table, a hangdog look on his face. He kicked at the loose gravel with his already scuffed Nikes.

"Dad, why can't I have my own tent?"

"You can," Tony said cheerfully. "Just as soon as you earn enough money to buy it."

"It'll take me forever to earn sixty dollars."

"Not if you want it bad enough."

"I want my own Coleman lantern, too."

"Well, you've already got a job mowing Mrs. Fincher's lawn twice a month," Tony reminded him. "Go around the neighborhood and see if anyone else wants some yard work done."

"Yeah, but you told me I have to use that money to buy my own CDs or to go to the movies," Eddie grumbled.

"You can use it for anything you want.

You have to set your own priorities. If you want a tent bad enough, I'm sure you'll find a way to get it." Tony slid onto the bench across the table from Ruth and started sorting through the jumble of lures in his tackle box.

Eddie jammed his hands in the pockets of his cut-off jeans and turned away, headed for the yellow building that housed the restrooms and showers.

The kid broke Ruth's heart as she watched him walk, shoulders drooping. "Tony, why don't I buy the tent for Eddie?" she suggested. "Call it an early birthday present."

"His birthday isn't until November. No, Eddie's got to do this on his own. You remember that saying Dad used to quote all the time?"

"Which one?"

" 'Give a boy a fish, you feed him for a day. Teach him to fish and you feed him for life.' It's the same thing with the tent. If I buy him a tent, or if you do, Eddie'll set it up in the backyard and have four or five campouts with his friends before he loses interest in it. Believe me, I know Eddie. When the novelty of having his own tent wears off, he'll just leave it set up in the yard until it rots in the sun."

"I know. Kids are like that. But I wish he could have his own tent this summer because I know you plan to do a lot of camping."

Tony held up a blue and silver lure and rattled it. "I think I'll try this one in the morning." He put it back in the tackle box and looked at Ruth. "That isn't the point. If Eddie buys a tent with his own hard-earned money, I'll guarantee you he'll take good care of it. It'll last for years."

"I know you're right," Ruth said, "but Eddie's reached the age where he doesn't want to sleep in the family tent anymore. He wants some independence. You were the same way."

"And you didn't buy me my first tent, did you?" Tony challenged.

"We couldn't afford to."

"I know. I spent a whole school year sweeping up floors and washing windows at the drugstore so I could buy my tent before summer. I was thirteen when I got it. It was a Saturday, a week before Amy was born. I'll never forget that day."

"I remember," Ruth said as her mind

24

drifted back in time. "You counted your money every day and the minute you got that last five dollars from the drugstore, you insisted that I drive you to Sears immediately. Never mind that I could barely fit behind the steering wheel."

"That's right." Tony raised the tackle box off the table, leaned over, and set it on the ground. He winced when he straightened up. "I'm stiff," he said, rubbing his upper arm. As if on cue, Lynn walked up behind him and began massaging his shoulders.

Ginny came out of the cabin again, carrying her package of sparklers. She hopped across the flat rocks to the table, then sat down, and scooted over next to Ruth.

"Yep, I felt pretty grown up that day," Tony said. "You'll never know how proud I was when I carried the tent out of the store, knowing it was all mine."

Ruth smiled. "The box was almost as big as you were and you wouldn't let anyone help you with it. You had a stubborn streak a mile long."

"He still does," Lynn said in a teasing tone.

"Oh, you're telling your tent story again." Ginny sighed with an exaggerated show of boredom. "Are you trying to teach Grandma about saving her money so she can buy something she really wants?"

"I guess I am," Tony said with a straight face. "Now that Grandma's retired, she has to be very careful about how she spends her allowance, just like you do."

Ginny sat there for a minute, a puzzled look on her face. Then she cocked her head and looked up at Ruth. "Grandma, do you get an allowance?"

Ruth laughed. "Sort of, except at my age I think they call it a fixed income."

"What's a fixed income?" Ginny asked.

"Something you won't have to worry about for a long, long time," Lynn said. She dropped her hands from Tony's shoulders and sat down next to him.

Ginny picked up the package of sparklers and ran her hand over the cellophane. "Is it going to be dark soon?"

"In about half an hour, Ginny." Tony's expression became serious. "Mom, I don't want to deprive you of the joys of being a grandmother, but I hope you can understand that I'm just trying to instill the same values in my two children that you and Dad gave me. I want Eddie and Ginny to grow up to be independent, responsible adults."

"And you're doing a good job. Both of you."

"I'll tell you what. If Eddie can save enough money to buy the tent, and you still want to help him out, you can get him the Coleman lantern."

"That sounds fair enough," Ruth agreed.

"I want a tent, too," Ginny piped up.

"Then start saving your money," Lynn said as she stood up. "I'd better get the fire started so we can eat."

Tony stood up, too. "Ginny, why don't you and Grandma go up to the pond and catch a couple of trout for dinner?"

Ginny beamed with excitement as she scooted off the bench. "Come on, Grandma, hurry up. I don't want to fish in the dark." She tugged on Ruth's hand, then stopped abruptly and frowned. "Do I have to pay for the fish?"

"No, that wouldn't be fair, would it?" Tony reached for his wallet. "Eddie and I got skunked out there today, but I was supposed to provide the fish for dinner, so it's my responsibility to pay for them."

He gave Ginny a ten-dollar bill and she

automatically passed it over to Ruth. When he handed her his fishing pole, she clutched it in both hands, glancing up to make sure the tip of the pole wouldn't get tangled in a nearby tree branch.

Ruth grabbed her camera from the table and draped its cord around her neck so she wouldn't drop it.

"It won't take us long to catch two fish," Ginny said proudly as she and Ruth headed for the pond.

Ginny was right. It didn't take long.

They stopped in at the campground office to inform the managers that they wanted to fish in the pond. Dick Patton, the friendly owner, grabbed a metal stringer off a peg on the wall and followed them out the door, snatching up a plastic bucket before they headed up the grassy knoll.

Ginny insisted on fishing all by herself, but she lacked the strength and expertise to cast, and the bright orange and gold lure merely plopped into the water close to the edge.

Ruth stared down into the clear water and watched the wide school of fish swarm toward the colorful lure. The first trout to reach it took the hook.

"I got one! I got one!" Ginny squealed.

Mr. Patton reached over and jerked the pole back to hook the fish, then assisted Ginny in her efforts to reel it in.

Ruth raised her camera and shot three pictures of Ginny catching her first fish.

With quick, easy movements, Mr. Patton separated the hefty fish from the hook, threaded a loop of the stringer into the trout's mouth, and lowered the flopping fish into the bucket.

Then he helped Ginny cast out again, and with his strength behind her, the lure splashed into the middle of the pond. The trout, still swimming back and forth at the edge of the pond, reversed directions in a shimmering mass and darted toward the lure.

The fish line tautened within seconds as a greedy trout snagged the hook and ran with it.

"I got another one," Ginny yelled.

Again, Mr. Patton helped her drag in the trout. He removed the hook from the fish and leaned the fishing pole against the back of a slatted wooden bench.

"You want to watch me clean them?" he

asked Ginny when both fish were on the stringer.

"Yuuuck." Ginny wrinkled her nose in disgust. "Grandma, I'll need that money now. I have to go pay for the fish," she said, taking on her grown-up ambiance.

Ruth hid her amusement as she dug into the side pocket of her dark slacks and brought out the neatly folded ten-dollar bill.

"Thank you," Ginny said as she took the money from Ruth. "I'll be right back." She hurried across the grass, trying to keep up with Mr. Patton as he headed for the fish-cleaning table at the side of the office building.

Ruth picked up Tony's fishing pole and walked to the edge of the pond, the camera hanging from the neck strap. Fascinated by the graceful movements of the silver-flecked fish, she stared into the water and saw the reflection of the overhead gray clouds that were tinged with the orange-red color of sunset.

The trout, about fifty of them in the particular school she was watching, swam in silent unison beneath the surface of the water, changing directions simultaneously in a smooth, flowing swirl of motion. It was as if they were individual parts of a sculptured, animated mobile, held together by invisible wires, and pulled along effortlessly by the head trout.

Did fish play follow the leader? And if they did, how did they know who the leader was? Did they merely follow the first fish who darted away from the pack, or was there some mysterious pecking order that she wasn't aware of?

These were the things Ruth was thinking about when she saw the long shadow fall across the surface of the shimmering water.

"Evenin', ma'am.

Startled by the voice, Ruth looked up and saw the man approaching from the direction of the river. It was the same man who had been fishing all day downstream from Tony and Eddie. She saw that he had a stubble of a beard and figured that he hadn't shaved for days. His white T-shirt and red walking shorts were stained and wrinkled, as if he'd slept in them.

"Hi," she said with a polite nod of her head.

He doffed his grimy fishing cap and smiled, returning her nod.

Ruth noticed the gap where his two top front teeth were missing. His hair, dark brown and silvered at the temples, was long and straggly, matted flat against his head, giving him an unkempt look.

She reminded herself that her hair didn't look all that good with the dampness from the heat destroying what little curl she had left in it. That's why she'd chosen to wear her little white hat that resembled an old-time seaman's cap. She hadn't bothered to put on fresh lipstick since she left home that morning and she knew she'd eaten it away.

But those things didn't matter to her. She was camping and not trying to impress anyone, especially this man who looked like an old reprobate.

"That's the cheatin' pond, lady."

How rude, Ruth thought. She didn't like the insinuation that she was cheating by catching fish in the pond. And she certainly didn't like to be called "lady."

When she saw the mischievous twinkle in his bright blue eyes, she decided he wasn't so old. He was just a bum. Still, the insinuation in his remark irritated her.

"I beg your pardon," she said with a hint

of indignation in her voice.

"No use wasting your money fishin' the pond, ma'am. Not when there's plenty of fish out there in the Boulder, free for the catchin'."

"I wouldn't have the patience to sit there long enough to catch one."

"I did." He grinned like an idiot as he held up his fish, which was still attached to the stringer. The trout was slightly larger than the ones Ginny had caught.

"Hold it a minute." Ruth leaned over and gently placed Tony's fishing pole on the soft grass. She straightened and raised her camera to her eye. Here was her chance to photograph a real character, one who fit her idea of what a diehard fisherman should look like.

The man struck a pose, his fishing pole and tackle box in one hand, the fish held up in the other. He smiled proudly as Ruth clicked off two quick shots.

The fisherman lowered his stringer. "You ought to learn a little patience, if that's what's bothering you," he suggested.

"I have no trouble with it," she replied coldly. Where did this stranger get off telling her what she should do?

"Sit a day with a pole in your hand and you'll learn more about yourself than you care to know." With that, he turned and walked away, heading for the tent area, or the trailers beyond.

At the same time, Ruth saw Ginny come around the side of the office, carrying the cleaned fish in a plastic bag. "Come on, Grandma, let's go," she called, not bothering to walk up the hill. Instead, she started down the gravel path back to the campsite.

Ginny was halfway home by the time Ruth gathered up Tony's fishing pole and walked down the grassy hill. The sun had dropped below the horizon and the darkening clouds had already lost their pink glow.

Coleman lanterns glowed brightly across the campground. Ruth breathed in the comforting smell of campfires as she walked along the gravel path, haunted by the stranger's words.

Was he real? Or just a figment of her imagination? Was he some sort of mystical spirit that had been sent down from above to show her that she needed to find out who she really was, besides just a retired schoolteacher?

Of course Ruth knew the man was real,

but she believed in the wisdom of an old saying she'd heard her father quote over the years. "When the student is ready, the teacher will appear."

Sometimes she liked to believe in such things as spiritual guides. And this was one of those times.

Three

Ruth Nichols didn't mean to slam the phone down, but she was upset.

Upset with herself, more than anything else. Once again she had allowed herself to fall victim to her mother's clever manipulations. She wouldn't mind if her mother really needed her help, but Ernestine Murphy had completely recovered from the broken hip she suffered two years ago, and although she was seventy-seven, she was perfectly healthy, and perfectly capable of driving her own car to her bridge club that afternoon.

"Learn to say no," Ruth told herself as she stood alone in her bright, airy kitchen, her hands covered with sticky bread dough.

What had started out to be a quiet morning had already turned into another one of those chaotic days that would be eaten up by taking care of other people's needs instead her own.

It had been that way ever since she retired, nearly three months ago. Here it was the beginning of the Labor Day weekend and she couldn't believe she'd frittered away the entire summer. She hadn't even taken a vacation, except for that brief Fourth of July camping weekend.

Ruth wiped her gummy hands with the paper towel she'd grabbed when the phone rang. At the sink, she gazed out the kitchen window as she washed her hands.

Brittle oak leaves scuttled across the road like skeletal crabs, pushed along by a gentle breeze. It had been a hot, dry summer in Montana, and although the first day of autumn was still more than two weeks away, some of the leaves would never blaze with their usual vibrant fall colors. They had dried up and blown away before they had a chance to shine.

That was the way Ruth Nichols felt about her own life as she watched the small parade of dried leaves rattle across her lawn and settle in clusters around the oversized tires of her motorhome. She'd let the summer slip away without making any plans for her future. If she wasn't careful, she just might dry up and blow away too, before she had a chance to enjoy her retirement.

She turned off the faucet and tried to sort out the thoughts that had kept her awake in bed the previous night before she'd finally fallen into a fitful sleep.

She knew she had to sell the motorhome. It sat on the far edge of her driveway like a huge white elephant. It was the first thing she saw every morning when she opened the bright yellow curtains above her kitchen sink, and the last thing she saw every evening before she closed the curtains against the approaching darkness. The expensive motorhome was a constant reminder of the good times she'd shared with her late husband, a reminder of the leisurely trips she and Henry had planned to take as soon as she retired.

She dried her hands with a paper towel. Why did everyone always call her at the worst possible moment? She was in the middle of making bread, and her mother's call was the third time the phone had rung while she was wrist deep in the kneading process.

The first call, a short one, had been from Brenda, her thirty-two-year-old daughter, who had asked if she could drop the kids off and leave them overnight so she and her husband could have a night out. "Time to ourselves," as Brenda had put it.

And what about me, Ruth thought. Don't I deserve some time to myself? Why did her family make so many demands on her time now that she was retired? Why did her mother make it so hard to say no? Why did her mother pester her continually to sell the house and move into a dinky efficiency apartment similar to the one *she* lived in, eight blocks away? And why did Brenda try to match her up with men like Norman Rogers, the stuffy professor at the college where Brenda worked as a secretary in the business office? Sometimes she wondered if her family had formed a conspiracy to keep her occupied so she wouldn't be lonely.

The second call, much longer and obviously charged to her calling card number, was from her younger daughter, Amy, who was twenty and just about to start her second year of college at Missoula, Montana.

Amy had chatted for at least five minutes before she got to the point of her call, which was to ask for a small loan. She said she hadn't been able to save enough money from her summer job to pay for her textbooks for the new semester and still make her car payment.

Ruth had promised to send her a check for five hundred dollars, knowing full well that Amy wouldn't be able to pay the money back right away, as she'd promised. Ruth didn't care so much about the money, but she wanted to teach her daughter to be independent.

She pushed the window open and drank in the heady scent of the late-blooming flowers blended with the fresh smell of the pines. A neighbor's puppy yapped pathetically and Ruth, knowing that the owners were at work, had the urge to go over and comfort the lonely pup. And from somewhere down the block, she heard the happy, squealing voices of young children and concluded that they were playing in the small plastic swimming pool she'd seen in a front yard.

She stared at the woods across the street and was grateful that she and Henry had

had the foresight, nearly thirty years ago, to buy five acres of forest land instead of just a single plot to build their house on. Her property, which included the wooded lot across the road and a wide expanse of dense foliage and trees on either side of the house, was worth a lot now. Over the years she'd had several offers for the land across the street, but she'd never sell it. As long as she held on to the land, nobody could chop down those trees and take away her little piece of serenity.

Ruth had never been one to suffer from bouts of depression, not even after Henry died. She didn't see herself as particularly strong or independent, but she was confident that she could take care of herself. When life dealt her a rough blow, she merely rolled with the punches, facing any obstacles head-on. Things she couldn't change, she accepted. She went on with her life.

Usually the sight of the peaceful woods soothed her and brought her out of the grumps, but this morning she couldn't shake the restless feeling that tugged at her nerves. Part of her temporary doldrums stemmed from the fact that everyone around her was excited about the beginning of the new school year, and for the first time in thirty years, she wouldn't be a part of it. She'd figured that much out before she went to bed last night.

It had been late last evening, after a day spent taking care of others, before she'd had a chance to sit down and read the paper. She had kept Brenda's kids all day because her babysitter called in sick. And she'd made two trips to her mother's apartment, once in the morning to look for, and kill, the "huge" spider that lurked in the bathtub, and again in the afternoon to help her mark the hemline of a dress she wanted to shorten.

For weeks now, the newspaper had been running "Back-to-School Specials," but when she'd read the paper last night and realized that the ads had switched to "Labor Day Picnic Specials," the impact of her situation had hit her like a searing gust from a blast furnace. She had nothing to look forward to as she always had at this time of year.

No lessons to prepare. No cute pictures to tack on the schoolroom walls. No neatly-printed name tags to make for her new, bright-eyed kindergarten students. No books to select for the special reading class she taught for the older slow learners.

Even though she'd signed up as a substitute teacher for the coming school year, she felt left out. Rejected. As if she were the only girl in class not invited to the prom.

Ruth turned away from the window and tried to ignore her feelings of melancholy. She had no reason to let her spirits sag. She had her family, good friends, and a lovely home that was paid for, the mortgage-burning celebrated ten years ago.

Of all the rooms in the big, rambling house, the spacious kitchen was her favorite. She'd designed it herself and called it her country kitchen, but the long, open room with windows across the front of the house was actually a combination kitchen, dining, and family room.

She smiled as she remembered how she'd tested Henry's patience as she'd changed the floor plans at least a dozen times before she got it just the way she wanted it. And at the last minute, as the contractor was ready to begin work, she'd made one final change. She'd added a breakfast nook in the front corner of the kitchen area, sacrificing cupboard space in order to have a wide formica ledge around the top of the booth and a big window above it so she could look out at the woods during meals.

The dining area held an oval oak table with the extension leaves removed, four oak chairs with padded seats, and a china cabinet against the wall filled with the good dishes she seldom used.

She spent most of her evenings in the far end of the room in one of the two Wedgwood blue recliners, or at one end of the comfortable sofa, her feet tucked under her as she read a book or made notes for the journal of her family's history she was writing.

A flagstone fireplace, with built-in book shelves on either side covered the far wall. It was a double fireplace and led into the formal living room on the other side of the wall. A television set perched on a high table in the corner near the fireplace, slanted so it could be seen from the kitchen. She didn't watch a lot of television, but she kept it on every evening for company.

Lost in thought, Ruth leaned against the kitchen counter, which served as a partition between the kitchen and the dining area. She looked over at the back-to-back, waist-high book shelves that separated the dining area from the family room. She stared at the mementos displayed on the shelves and was filled with pleasant memories of raising her three children.

She glanced over at the two old school desks she'd purchased when the school officials bought new ones. The desks had hinged lids that opened and inside the tray, she stored crayons, marking pens, and sheets of plain white paper. When she thought about the hours of entertainment the desks provided for her grandchildren, she decided she'd better get back to her baking.

She reached over and flicked on the radio. She turned the dial until she found her favorite easy-listening station. Elevator music, Amy called it.

Strains of Floyd Cramer's piano rendition of "Make the World Go Away" floated across the room. A slow smile came to her lips. How appropriate. Just make the world go away for a little while.

The bread dough had already risen. She punched it back down, breathing in the sharp, sweet aroma of the yeast as she kneaded it again. As usual, the familiar pungent odor brought back happy childhood memories of coming home from school to a house filled with the smell of fresh-baked bread, pie, or cookies.

Ernestine Murphy, a marvelous cook in her day, had given in to microwave ovens and convenience foods much more quickly than Ruth had. Now if Ernestine craved something sweet, she bought it at the bakery.

Ruth patted the dough into a round, smooth ball, covered the stainless steel bowl with a clean dishtowel, and set it aside for the dough to rise again.

With that done, she snatched her big black purse from the counter, slid into the breakfast nook booth and took a minute to write the check for Amy. She wrote a quick note and stuck it in an envelope with the check, then stuffed the envelope into the side pouch of her purse so she wouldn't forget to mail it.

Ruth was a great list-maker, something Brenda teased her about all the time. Before she got up from the booth, she turned sideways, glanced over her shoulder at the white formica ledge behind her and grabbed the notepad she kept beside the telephone. She scanned the list of "THINGS TO DO TODAY" and drew a line through the quickly-scribbled notation, "check for Amy."

With pen still in hand, her mind ran through the way her day was shaping up. She jotted down "new crayons" and under that, "video store—movie for kids." And then she added "check out motorhome."

While the bread dough was rising, she got up and walked on out to the motorhome, noting that the neighbor's puppy had finally given up its noisy plea for companionship.

Feeling suddenly dwarfed by its size, Ruth surveyed the thirty-four-foot Coachman. The original from-the-factory paint, creamy ivory with cocoa-brown trim, was still in good shape, still polished to a fine sheen from the wax job Glen Amos had given it when he took the motorhome into his RV shop last November to winterize it.

The memories flooded in on her again when she thought about Barbara Amos, Glen's wife. Barbara was the school librarian at the elementary school where Ruth had taught, and they had been good friends for more than twenty years. Barbara was a real character and Ruth knew she was going to miss working with her on the special learning-to-read classes that Barbara had instigated at the school. And she'd miss the delicious, homemade cinnamon rolls Barbara brought in for the teaching staff every Friday morning.

Ruth planned to take Glen up on his offer to help sell the motorhome. He'd sold the Coachman to them more than eight years ago and after Henry died, Glen had told her he could get a fair price for it whenever she was ready to sell. Well, she thought, she was ready.

As she reached for the door handle, the colorful magnetic map that was stuck to the side of the motorhome caught her eye. Actually, it wasn't a map, but an outline of the United States, a jigsaw puzzle, with the states she and Henry had visited filled in with the proper shapes in bright blues, reds, greens, and yellows.

Not even a third of the United States was filled in, and the kit had even come with the extra shapes of Alaska and Hawaii if needed. Obviously, the shape of Montana was set in place, and in the western half of the country: Idaho, Washington, Oregon, California, Arizona, New Mexico, Colorado, and Wyoming. Somehow they had skirted around Nevada and Utah, missing them entirely. And then there were the states they'd gone through to get to Florida the last summer before Henry died. Besides Florida, that summer they had added Texas, Louisiana, Mississippi, and Alabama.

She would have to remove the map before she sold the motorhome. A new owner would have no use for her memories.

The motorhome seemed so big from the outside, but when she stepped inside, it became a cozy home with all the luxuries of an expensive apartment. She was amazed that after all these years, the Coachman still had that brand-new-car smell about it.

A quick stroll through the motorcoach assured her that everything was clean, from the double stainless steel sinks and the inside of the oven and microwave to the dinette tabletop and the sparkling small bathtub and shower. In the other part of the split bathroom, which held the toilet and sink, she opened the mirrored medicine cabinet and saw a package of disposable razors she'd forgotten to remove the last time she'd scrubbed.

She went on back to the rear of the coach where a queen-sized bed was bolted to the floor. She brushed a wrinkle from the bulky comforter. She would leave the comforter and the matching drapes. They matched the beige, brown, and salmon-pink color scheme of the rest of the decor.

She opened a nightstand drawer and found one of her old bathing suits. That she would throw away. She didn't wear bathing suits anymore.

As she walked back through the motorhome, she realized that she'd have to remove all the dishes, silverware and pots and pans that she and Henry had bought especially for traveling. Or, she supposed, she could leave them for the new owner.

She didn't want to think about a new owner.

As she passed between the beautiful sleeper sofa and the two matching comfortable chairs, she ran her hand along the top of a chair, taking comfort in the soothing velvety feel of the fabric. She didn't want to sell the motorhome, it held too many happy memories.

She slid into the plush driver's seat at the front of the coach, rested both hands on the steering wheel, and like a child, pretended she was driving.

Her nerves began to tingle with excitement at the thought of actually taking off, by herself, for a long, leisurely vacation. Could she really do it . . . if she wanted to?

Four

The package of frozen round steak on the counter reminded Ruth that she needed to start the beef stew and get it in the Crockpot before she left to pick up her mother.

Naturally, she'd told Brenda to bring the kids over to spend the night, but that meant she'd have to call Norm Rogers and warn him that her grandchildren would be there when he came for dinner. Norm wouldn't like it. He'd never been married and had very little tolerance for normal rambunctious youngsters. But that was his problem and if he decided to cancel, she wouldn't be disappointed.

She should have sold the motorhome when Henry died three years ago, she thought, as she walked to the cupboard and brought out two cans of beef broth for the stew. Now that she'd finally retired at the age of fifty-five, she'd never use the Gypsy again. It just wouldn't be the same without Henry.

The Gypsy. She remembered the excitement she'd felt on that day eight years ago when she and Henry bought the beautiful, brand-new Coachman. They'd driven it home, slowing to a snail's pace when they got to their own street, giving the curious neighbors every chance to notice it.

After spending a good chunk of their savings to purchase the plush recreation vehicle, they'd christened it with a bottle of champagne, naming it The Gypsy because it represented the kind of wandering lifestyle they'd planned for their early retirement years. But Henry never made it to retirement. He died of a heart attack while still working as a loan officer at the bank. She'd kept the motorhome after Henry died so her grown children could use it. But that was just an excuse, and she knew it. Tony lived eighty miles away in Big Timber. He loved to camp out with Lynn and the kids, but he preferred roughing it in his own well-worn tent. The thought of either one of her daughters vacationing in the motorhome amused her. Brenda, the head-strong one, was too busy working at the college and raising her own family to stray very far from home. And on the rare occasion when Brenda did take a vacation with her brood, she insisted on the comforts of a luxury hotel, firm in her notion that a woman who cooked and cleaned for her family all year long, shouldn't have to perform those mundane chores when she was on vacation.

And then there was Amy, the dreamer of the family, who spent a fortune on makeup so she could have that "natural" look. Amy had no desire to use the motorhome. Her interests were limited to boys, shopping malls, and, after college, the pursuit of a high-paying job so she could afford a fancy car and a condo on some exotic, faraway beach.

Ruth set the cans of broth on the counter next to the steak and reached for the phone. She dialed the first three digits of Norm's number, stopped abruptly, and pressed the button down to cut off the connection. With a great deal of satisfaction, she gently placed the receiver back in its cradle and pushed the phone back to its resting place above the breakfast nook.

She didn't owe Norm an explanation, or an apology. After all, he'd invited himself to dinner. Actually, he'd called the previous night and invited her to dine with him at a nice restaurant. She'd accepted his invitation, but before their phone conversation ended, Norm had twisted things around, saying that he'd prefer to spend a quiet evening at home with her if she didn't mind fixing a simple meal.

She knew what a quiet evening with Norm would be like. During dinner, he would carry on a boring, one-sided conversation on the state of the world's economy and politics. After dinner, instead of watching her favorite Saturday night sitcoms, they would sit at opposite ends of the couch, silently sipping coffee while they watched an hour or two of PBS so he could reevaluate his position on world affairs.

Their individual ideas of a simple meal didn't coincide either. She had suggested barbecued steaks, baked potatoes, and a tossed salad.

"How about something you can just throw in the Crockpot and forget about?" Norm had countered. "Like that good beef stew you made the last time I was over there. Stew and a slice or two of your delicious homemade bread will be plenty for me. Surprise me with something special for dessert."

Ruth snatched up the package of round steak and shoved it back in the freezer section of her refrigerator. "Why don't you surprise me and bring dessert with you?" she said aloud as she rummaged through the freezer for something easier to fix. She'd go ahead and bake the bread, but she wasn't about to spend the next hour cutting the meat into small squares and trimming the fat off before she browned them, or peeling potatoes and carrots, chopping onions and celery.

She dug out a package of frozen hot dogs. Hot dogs, macaroni and cheese, and Jell-O. That's what her grandchildren, Hank and Lori, liked best. And she'd make chocolate chip cookies instead of messing with the complicated pecan, chocolate-drizzle cheesecake she'd planned to fix for Norm.

She returned the cans of broth to the cupboard, then set all of the ingredients for cookies on the counter.

She had just finished stirring the chips into the batter, and was spooning drops of it onto a cookie sheet, when the phone rang again. Annoyed, she set the spoon down and turned the radio off before she answered the phone.

"Hi, Mom," said the familiar voice.

Ruth smiled. "Tony. How are you?" She pictured her son sitting at his wide, cluttered desk in the study of his home. Tony was tall and handsome, as his father had been, but he'd inherited her dark hair and easygoing disposition. He also shared her love of the outdoors and had followed in her footsteps as far as his choice of careers: He taught high school English. She could almost see Tony running his hand through his hair when he spoke.

"Lynn and I are taking the kids camping tonight," Tony said after they'd exchanged greetings. "One last hurrah before school starts next Tuesday. Actually, school has already started for me. I've been busy with teachers' meetings all week. But you know how that is."

"I remember."

"You're going to miss teaching, aren't you, Mom?"

Did it show in her voice? "Yes, I'll miss the children, but I certainly won't miss the daily routine," she said with more conviction than she felt.

"I hear you. Anyway, we'd love to have you drive over and camp with us. What do you think?"

"Oh, I wish I could. It sounds like fun." Ruth slid into the booth.

"We're packing up now. You could meet us at the campground. It wouldn't take you more than an hour and a half. You could be here by the time we get set up."

"Where are you camping?" Ruth didn't know why she asked. She couldn't go anyway.

Tony laughed. "Practically in our own backyard. We're going to that same campground on the Boulder River where we all camped last July. Three miles from beautiful downtown Big Timber."

"The one with the fishing ponds. I remember."

"That's the one. Eddie wants to try out his new tent and since it's Labor Day weekend, we didn't want to risk the heavy traffic going to Yellowstone."

"Eddie got his tent? Well, bless his heart.

58

When did he get it?"

"Yesterday. He bought it with the money he earned from mowing lawns all summer. He's pretty proud of himself."

"Well, you tell him I'm proud of him, too. And tell him I'll buy him the Coleman lantern I promised him."

"I will. Now Ginny wants her own tent. She's eight years old, going on sixteen, and still afraid of the dark. Which reminds me, I've reserved one of those little rustic cabins for you and Ginny again. So don't worry, you won't have to sleep on the hard ground."

"I wouldn't mind sleeping on the ground. Although, with these creaking old bones of mine, once I got down, I might not be able to get back up."

Tony laughed. "You're not old, Mom, you've just let yourself get soft this summer. So, can you come over?"

"I'd really love to, Tony, but I can't. I've got to take Mother to her bridge club this afternoon and I promised Brenda I'd keep her kids tonight."

"How about Brenda driving Grandma to her card party and Grandma taking care of Brenda's kids?" Tony suggested.

"Oh, sure." Ruth knew Tony was kidding. She could hear it in his voice. "Somehow I just can't quite picture Mother actually taking care of Hank and Lori. She'd be gibbering in less than an hour."

"Yeah, I know," Tony laughed. "Grandma doesn't do windows and she doesn't do grandkids."

"I'll probably be the same way in another twenty years when I get old and cranky."

"No you won't, Mom. You've got a built-in affinity for babies, little kids, and lost puppy dogs."

Ruth thought of the neighbor's lonely puppy and laughed. "You're probably right. Why don't you go ahead and get the lantern for Eddie so he can have it tonight? I'll send you a check."

"I can if you want. That would please him."

"So, are you and the kids all set to go back to school next week?" Ruth asked.

"The kids are, but I'm not so sure about myself. The summer went by too fast."

"What ever happened to that trip to New York you and Edith McAllister were planning to take?" Tony asked.

Ruth had almost given up on the trip to

New York. Every time she and Edith set a tentative date for the trip, one or the other of them had to cancel.

"We had to postpone it again. With any luck, we still might make it in time to do our Christmas shopping for the grandkids at F.A.O. Schwarz."

"I'll go with you. Just name the date." Tony paused. "Mom, are you doing all right? I worry about you."

Ruth heard the concern in her son's voice. "Not to worry," she said in a light-hearted tone. "I enjoy every minute of my life, even when it's hectic."

"If you were smart, you'd bring your motorhome over here and camp out for a month by yourself. Let Grandma and Brenda fend for themselves. Then maybe they'd appreciate you. I'm serious, Mom. I could come over and drive the motorhome back here for you."

"I can drive the motorhome myself, thank you, but I've decided to sell it. What do you think?"

"If you're not going to use it, it's a good idea. It must cost a bundle to keep it up."

"More than I like to think about. I thought I'd talk to Glen Amos at the RV shop. I think he might be able to sell it for me."

"Glen's a good man. He'll do right by you. He should be able to get you thirty or thirty-five thousand for it."

"That's the price range he mentioned the last time I talked to him about selling, but with the economy such as it is, I may have to settle for the lower figure."

"Still not bad, considering it's paid for. Does Brenda know you're planning to sell it?"

"I haven't told her yet."

"I wouldn't want to be in your shoes when you do. She'll fight you on it every inch of the way. She'll try her best to talk you out of selling it."

"Let her try. Won't do her any good."

"You know how she feels about it. She considers the Gypsy a shrine to Dad's memory, and to sell it would be sacrilegious. She expects you to keep the motorhome in the family forever."

"Then let her shell out a thousand dollars a year to keep it."

"A thousand dollars?" Tony exclaimed. "I didn't know it was that much."

"Figure it out. I have to keep the insurance up whether I drive it or not; the license renewal costs three times as much as my car; and I have to have it winterized every year so the water pipes don't freeze up."

"And de-winterized in the spring," Tony added.

"Then I had to put six new tires on it last April. They were rotting away from sitting in the sun all the time."

"I guess that's why I stick to a tent," Tony said with a chuckle. "No pipes to freeze. And absolutely no chance of a flat tire."

Ruth laughed, "Maybe I should just trade the Gypsy in for a tent."

"It's not a bad way to go."

Ruth heard a car pull into the driveway. She slid across the soft vinyl seat and peered out the window above the U-shaped breakfast nook. "Brenda just drove up," she told Tony as she scooted back across the padded seat. She listened for Brenda's footsteps on the breezeway that separated the house from the two-car garage. "Do you want to talk to her?"

"No, just tell her howdy. And remember, Mom, stick to your guns about selling the

Gypsy. Don't let her intimidate you."

"I won't, Tony."

"I mean it, Mom. When you tell Brenda you're selling the Gypsy, she'll try to make you feel as guilty as sin."

"I know. I can handle it."

What she didn't tell Tony was that she already felt as guilty as sin. She wasn't just selling the motorhome, she was selling her memories. And more painful than that, she was selling all her longtime dreams for the future.

Five

Brenda was already in the kitchen. She'd given her usual two quick raps on the door, called out, "Just me," then opened the door and stepped inside before Ruth could get there. "Oh, you're on the phone."

"Just finished. Tony called." Ruth felt herself tighten up. Just once, couldn't Brenda respect her privacy enough to wait until she opened the door instead of barging in?

No, Brenda probably never would, Ruth thought. Brenda was family and she'd been letting herself into the house ever since she moved out twelve years ago. And Ruth had never told her not to.

"What's Tony up to these days?" Brenda touched the package of frozen hot dogs, as if to see if they were really cold. She sidled on down the counter and felt the side of the stainless steel bowl. She raised a corner of the dishtowel and sniffed the bread dough.

"He and the kids are getting ready to go back to school," Ruth said.

"Isn't everybody?" Brenda sighed. "Oops, sorry," she said, turning around to look at Ruth. "I know how touchy you are about not going back to teaching this year."

Ruth's resentments faded away when she saw Brenda's sheepish look. "Not at all. While the rest of you are slaving away, I'll be on some exotic island, sipping rum and Coca-Cola. Or maybe I'll take a cruise and meet some dashing young man who'll sweep me off my feet."

"That's what you should be doing, but it'll never happen," Brenda said with a knowing smile. At five-foot eight, she was six inches taller than her mother, and slim enough to look good in her tight jeans. She had pulled her hair away from her face and held it in place with a red bow. Red and white earrings dangled from pierced ears, swinging when she turned her head.

"Actually, Tony called to invite me to camp with his family tonight," Ruth said as she put the phone back on the ledge.

"Oh, lucky you," Brenda said sarcastically. Then a look of panic crossed her face. "You're not going, are you?"

"No, I promised to keep your kids, remember? By the way, where are they?" Ruth asked as she stood up.

"At home with Danny. I'll bring them over later this afternoon. I came to take you shopping with me. I want to get a new dress for tonight."

"I can't go, Brenda. Mother called and I have to chauffeur her to her bridge club this afternoon. I want to finish my baking and clean the house before I go."

"Ooooh, chocolate chip cookies," Brenda said when she glanced at the counter across from the one that held the thawing hot dogs and the rising dough. She automatically scooped a wad of cookie batter out of the bowl with her finger and stuck it in her mouth.

"Stop that." Ruth gave Brenda a teasing slap on the wrist as she walked past her.

"Why don't you use a cookie mix? It's easier than making them from scratch."

"Making them from scratch is the only way to make good cookies." Ruth dipped a rounded spoonful of batter from the bowl and pushed it onto the cookie sheet with her finger.

Brenda stepped back, giving her mother room to work. "You're such a perfectionist, Mother. Cookies from mixes might not taste as good as homemade, but they save a lot of time."

"I've got plenty of time."

"You're stubborn, too."

"I'm a Taurus. I'm supposed to be stubborn." Ruth dished up another spoonful of batter. She was accustomed to their easy banter, but this morning it annoyed her. Everything annoyed her. "Have you got time for a cup of coffee?"

"Just a quick cup. Then I've got to dash." Brenda poured her own coffee, slid into the breakfast nook on the seat at the far side of the booth, so she was facing the room. "I don't see why you cater to Mama Murph's every whim. She'll run you ragged if you let her."

"I know," Ruth said, her back to Brenda as she worked with the cookie batter. She wanted to tell Brenda that she was guilty of the same thing, but she bit her tongue. "She said her bad hip is bothering her so

68

much she's limping again."

"That's bull and you know it." Brenda stared out the window as she talked. "Grandma just loves to be fussed over. If she was really hurting, she'd be sitting in the doctor's office instead of running around town. Her only problem is that she's so tightfisted she won't use her own gasoline if she can get you to run her around."

"Brenda, that's not nice to say about your grandmother."

"Well, it's true. I love Mama Murph, but she's still a miserly old woman."

"We all have our faults." Ruth glanced over her shoulder at Brenda.

"And why do you have to clean house?" Brenda looked around the room, raised her arms in a gesture of amazement. "It isn't dirty. Your house is never dirty. That's all you've done all summer, clean your house and spend hours at the library reading to the kids in the Book Worm Club."

"The library's summer reading program is important to me, Brenda. If I can get the preschoolers interested in books by reading to them, then my time's well spent." The book check-out rate for children in kindergarten through sixth grade has tripled this summer."

"Touché," Brenda said. "So, getting back to my original question, why do you have to clean your house when it's already clean?"

"Norm Rogers is coming for dinner. I just want to dust and run the vacuum." Ruth slid the cookie sheet into the oven. She poured a cup of coffee and slid into the booth across from her daughter. "Tony thinks I should take my motorhome over to Big Timber and stay in the campground for a month."

"You're not going to, are you?" Brenda looked at her mother, concern obvious in her expression.

"No, although it sounds mighty tempting. I've decided to sell it."

Brenda had just taken a drink of coffee and nearly choked as she jerked her head up, a shocked expression on her face. "No! You're not serious." She looked into Ruth's eyes, as if searching for reassurance.

"Dead serious." Feeling extremely uncomfortable, Ruth took a sip of coffee.

"You can't sell the Gypsy," Brenda protested. "It's part of the family."

"Brenda, I don't need it anymore," Ruth said. "I know you want to keep it in the family but it just sits out there in the driveway gathering dust and cobwebs. You have no idea how much it costs me just for the privilege of parking it in my own front yard, and I can think of a dozen things I'd rather spend my money on."

"But I thought you wanted to keep it so we could all take a trip together some day," Brenda pleaded.

"It'll never happen," Ruth said with a sigh. "You don't like to camp out."

"Not in a tent, but I think it'd be fun to go somewhere with you in the motorhome when the kids get a little older."

"A little older?" Ruth challenged. "How much older? What's wrong with right now?"

"You know Hank and Lori. They bicker and tease each other all the time." Brenda looked upward and shook her head. "God, if I had to be cooped up in those tiny quarters with my two little monsters constantly underfoot, I'd get cabin fever."

"Tiny quarters? That motorhome is thirty-four feet long. The kids would spend most of their time playing outside."

"And if it rained?" Brenda shook her head again. "Believe me, Mother, that motorhome isn't big enough for me and the kids. Dan wouldn't mind so much because he's got more patience than I do, but I couldn't handle being confined with my kids whining and fighting all the time."

Ruth got a whiff of the sweet smell of warm chocolate; the cookies would be done soon. She took a quick sip of her coffee, then got up to prepare the next batch.

"A little discipline might help," she suggested as she began dropping the batter onto a clean tray.

The minute she said it, Ruth wished she hadn't. She was breaking her own cardinal rule of not interfering with the lives of her grown children. She glanced over her shoulder and saw that Brenda had crossed her arms, a sign that she was irritated.

"Mother, you know that the way I raise my children is not a topic open for discussion," Brenda said with a hard, cold edge to her voice. "When they're in your home, you set the rules. Other than that, Dan and I decide what's best for them."

Brenda was a good and loving mother,

Ruth knew, but she found it easier to give in to her kids' demands than to take the time to establish a sense of responsibility in them, the way Tony did with his children. But Ruth didn't dare compare Brenda's method of raising children to the way Tony handled Eddie and Ginny. That was already a touchy subject between Brenda and Tony whenever the family got together.

Ruth slid the final spoonful of dough onto the cookie sheet. "If there was any chance that you'd use the motorhome in the next year or two, I'd gladly keep it," she said.

"It would be at least five years before I'd even consider it," Brenda said with a loud sigh.

The oven timer buzzed, shutting off Ruth's other thoughts for the moment. She grabbed a pot holder from a hook near the stove and opened the oven door. A swirl of hot air rose from the oven, carrying with it the sweet aroma of hot chocolate.

"Smells good," Brenda said from her seat.

"Yes, it does." Ruth had a weakness for anything chocolate and she knew she'd have to fight her urge to consume half a dozen cookies before lunch. She removed the hot cookie sheet from the oven, set it on a cooling rack, then quickly slid another tray into place and shut the oven door.

"I was just trying to explain that the kids would spend most of their time playing outside," she said. "That's the fun of camping. Fishing in a lake, hiking up a trail, collecting pine cones or seashells. You and Tony used to love to camp out."

"I remember camping out in the tent, and as I recall, it was fun. But I didn't know any better then," Brenda said as she toyed with her coffee mug. Then she looked across the table at her mother. "Do you realize that I never set foot in a motel room until we had to drive to Colorado right before Grandpa Nichols died? I was fourteen years old and thought only rich people stayed in motels."

"So you grew up thinking we were poor?" Ruth challenged, struggling to keep her emotions in check. "You felt deprived?"

Brenda grinned. "Not really. Tenting was fun. Okay? And at least I got enough experience sleeping on the hard ground to know that I prefer a soft bed. Don't worry about it, Mom. Tony likes to camp out. One out of three isn't bad."

"Well, I don't want you to think we were poor, because we weren't. Your dad and I worked very hard and we saved our money until we could afford the things we wanted. Young couples today buy with credit cards and end up with staggering payments they can't afford."

"Times have changed, Mother."

"I know. You're part of the Now Generation. It's buy now and pay later. It's no wonder our economy is in such a mess."

"Don't blame the lousy economy on me," Brenda argued. She sat up straighter, as if to do battle. "Danny and I have never abused our credit cards."

Brenda cocked her head and looked at Ruth, then smiled. "Mother, if I didn't know better, I'd think you were suffering from PMS."

"We didn't have PMS in my day and I managed just fine, thank you. Next you'll be saying I'm co-dependent."

"Well you are co-dependent," Brenda teased.

"That's ridiculous."

"Face it, Mom, you're a real people-pleaser." Brenda grinned and reached over and patted her mother's arm.

"Does that make me mentally unstable by your modern standards?" Ruth said sarcastically. "And, what's wrong with trying to please the people you love?"

"Not a thing unless you allow them to run your life." Brenda continued to smile as she ran her finger around the rim of her empty coffee cup.

"Don't worry, I know when to say no. You don't see me fixing beef stew, do you?"

Brenda frowned. "What the hell is that supposed to mean?"

"It means I'm not going to let Norm Rogers dictate what I fix for supper. He can eat hot dogs and Jell-O like the rest of us."

Brenda's hand shot to her forehead as she rocked back in the booth and laughed. "You're feeding Norman Rogers hot dogs? I can't believe it. And with my two little monsters running around, that should really make for a romantic evening."

Ruth cringed at the thought. "There's

nothing romantic about Norm. We're friends, nothing more."

"Really? I assumed you and Norm would get married some day. You've been dating him for four or five months now."

"We don't date," Ruth stated emphatically. "I'm merely his companion when he has to attend those boring college faculty functions. We have absolutely nothing in common."

"But, Mom, Norm's a nice man. He's an immaculate dresser . . ."

"A finicky dresser who wouldn't be caught dead in blue jeans or a T-shirt."

"True. But he's always polite. He's intelligent. . . ."

"And dull as mud."

"Maybe so, but I'd think twice before tossing him aside. He's got status at the university, and tenure. He's a well-respected professor."

"He's too old for me, too set in his ways." Ruth put both hands on the table, a gesture she hoped would end the conversation.

"He's only sixty-five," Brenda argued. "At your age, what difference does ten years make? If you two got married, he could give you all the security you need."

Ruth shot Brenda a look. "I *have* all the security I need. Remember, I worked for a living all these years. In addition to the investments from the proceeds of your father's life insurance policy, I've got good retirement benefits of my own."

"Okay, so you have financial security, but what about your emotional security?" Brenda tipped her head and looked her mother directly in the eye.

"My emotional state would be fine if you'd quit trying to marry me off."

"The long evenings must get lonely for you," Brenda persisted.

Ruth laughed. "Not that lonely. The only thing Norm wants in a companion is a housekeeper, a cook, and someone to play nursemaid when he's sick. No thanks, that's not what I had in mind for my old age. Norman Rogers isn't my type, so quit trying to play cupid."

"And just what is your type?" Brenda said with a coy smile. "What kind of a man would you like to marry?"

"None. I'm not in the market for a husband, or a boyfriend, for that matter. I plan to enjoy my freedom without having to account to anyone else."

"Then let's just say a companion. What kind of a person would you like to spend your time with?"

Ruth saw the mischievous twinkle in her daughter's eyes and knew they were back to their bantering.

"What are you going to do? Go out and scout up a man for me?"

"Sure. Tell me what you want. Just a minute, let me get the pad," Brenda said as she turned around in the seat.

"Brenda, that's stupid."

Brenda tore off the top sheet where Ruth had doodled. She dug a pen out of the coffee-can pencil holder and poised it above the tablet. "Begin," she said.

Ruth played along with her. "Okay, bring me someone who's adventurous, someone who likes to do things spontaneously," she said as Brenda began to jot down notes. Ruth smiled and shook her head, knowing Brenda was teasing her. "Find someone who isn't afraid to climb a mountain or swim a stream, or follow a country road on a whim just to see where it leads. And, of course, someone who likes to travel as much as I do. Is that good enough?"

Ruth was relieved when the oven timer buzzed. She got up and tended to the cookies.

"Sure," Brenda said as she tore off the sheet. She made a big show of stuffing the note into the back pocket of her jeans. "And as long as you're dreaming the impossible dream, how about tall, dark, and handsome?"

"Oh, no," Ruth said. "I wouldn't want a man who constantly needed his ego stroked. As long as he had a good sense of humor, I wouldn't care what he looked like."

"Good. I'll go out and interview some ugly men. Meanwhile, I've got to dash off in all directions." Brenda stood up and gave her mother an affectionate pat on the shoulder. "Don't worry, Mom, I'll find you a man who will traipse all over the country with you."

"I don't need a man for that. I could drive the Gypsy across the country by myself and be perfectly happy. And if you don't get off my case, that's just what I'm going to do."

"You wouldn't," Brenda laughed. "Not in that big rig. Not by yourself."

"You want to make a small bet?" Ruth challenged.

Brenda begged off. "No, you'd be stubborn enough to try it just to prove you could." She snatched three warm cookies off the tray and headed for the door.

"I just might," Ruth said. "I just might hop aboard the Gypsy and drive until I run out of road."

Six

Ruth got out of her silvery blue Cutlass, her mail and key chain clutched in one hand, her purse and a rented videotape in the other. She brushed loose strands of hair out of her eyes and reminded herself to make a hair appointment for the following week.

She'd let her hair grow all summer and now she had to use the curling iron every morning to keep it looking nice. She had a few gray hairs mixed in with the brown, but she refused to have her hair dyed like her mother did. She'd get a hair cut and a permanent and that was all.

A noisy bird squawked nearby. Ruth turned around in time to see a jay dive-bomb a pair of squirrels who were chasing each other through the woods across the street from her house. She smiled and hoped she'd never get in such a financial bind that she'd be forced to sell that extra lot.

She looked through her mail as she walked toward the house. Besides the usual junk mail and a couple of first-of-the-month bills, there were two magazines and a letter from her brother's wife, Mary. Mary never bothered to put her return address on her letters, but even without her reading glasses on, Ruth recognized Mary's hastily scrawled handwriting and the San Diego postmark.

The quarterly, obligatory letter from Ross, she thought. But Ross never wrote the letters himself. He left that chore to his wife.

Ruth didn't have to read the letter to know what it said. Mary's letters were always the same. In the first few paragraphs, Mary would brag about her family, her children and grandchildren, and the perfect weather in San Diego. The rest of the letter would be filled with Mary's complaints about her life.

Inside the house, the aroma of freshly

baked bread wafted through the warm kitchen. Ruth dropped her purse, her car keys, and the rented video on the edge of the counter. She reached over and grabbed a cookie off the plate where she'd stacked them, and took a bite. She took another cookie before she walked over to the sink with her mail.

When both cookies were gone, Ruth tossed the junk mail in the wastebasket under the sink, and carried the rest to the breakfast nook.

She was already seated in the booth when she remembered her reading glasses. She had reached that point in her life when, without her glasses, she couldn't read anything as small as newsprint.

She got up and walked over to her purse, snatching just one more cookie as she did. To avoid further temptation, she set the plate of cookies in a cupboard before she opened her bag.

She dug out the small black case that held her reading glasses. Next to it, the brown case in her purse held her driving glasses.

Sticking the last piece of cookie in her mouth, she unfolded the flap of the black leather pouch. It was empty. Her glasses weren't there.

She glanced around the counter and then tried to retrace her steps in her mind. She walked over to the breakfast nook and patted the stack of mail, the notepad, the table itself.

The eternal search for her glasses, she thought with a big sigh. Brenda had nagged her to get one of those strap things, but Ruth didn't like the idea of wearing her glasses around her neck like an elderly librarian.

Stop and think, she told herself. Where had she been when she'd last used them? At the post office when she wrote a check for stamps? In the video store when she'd made her selection for a movie for her grandkids?

And then she remembered when she'd last used her glasses. In the car, after she'd bought a magazine. She'd put them on to read a short article.

She headed out to the car, praying that her glasses would be there. She squinted against the sudden glare of the late-morning sun as its reflection bounced off the glossy surface of her waxed hood and hit her square in the eyes.

She had just reached for the door handle when she heard the smooth whine of an engine as a car slowed down nearby. She looked up and saw the familiar red, shiny Porsche pulling into the vacant parking space between her car and the motorhome.

It wasn't unusual for her good friend, Meg Rodecker, to drop by for coffee, but Ruth wished she'd called first this time so she could have saved her a trip. She just didn't have time today to sit and listen to Meg's current gossip.

Ruth glanced at her watch and saw that she had only ten minutes left before she had to leave to pick up her mother and deposit her across town for her bridge club. She leaned against her car, giving Meg room to park.

Meg's tinted window slid down and Ruth saw that her friend had dyed her hair an even brighter shade of red.

"Ready to go?" Meg grinned, making no move to get out of her car.

Ruth stood there with a blank expression on her face. What had she forgotten now? "Go where?"

"To the library," Meg said. "The Friends of the Library monthly meeting. The bring-your-own-lunch business meeting, except we decided not-to-bring-our-own-lunch and eat out afterwards. The Book Worm Club awards presentations directly following the business meeting." She waved her hand in front of Ruth's face, as if to snap Ruth out of her trance. "Does any of this ring a bell?"

"Oh, my God," Ruth said. "Is that today? I thought it was next Saturday." She clapped her hand to her mouth, horrified that she could forget something so important.

"It's today. The memory goes when you get to be our age." Meg raised her hand high enough for Ruth to see the diamond-studded watch on her wrist. She checked the time and opened her car door.

"I can't make it," Ruth said.

"Yes, you can. It's 11:35. You've got just ten minutes to change your clothes and comb your hair. We can still get to the library by noon." Meg got out of her Porsche and clapped her hands, two quick claps. "Now, hop to it."

Ruth saw that Meg was wearing a summer print dress and heels. The dress looked simple enough, but Ruth knew it was expensive. Meg didn't buy cheap clothes. She had inherited a fortune from her wealthy father and since she and her husband didn't have any children, Meg didn't have any qualms about spending her money on nice clothes.

"No, I mean I can't go to the library, period." When Ruth thought of all the things she still had to do that day, she wanted to collapse. How did she get herself into these situations? "I have to leave in a few minutes to drive my mother clear across town. That's an hour, round trip. There's no way I could get back over here before one o'clock."

"Then I don't see that we have a problem," Meg said in her usual cheerful voice. "You go on and do your thing with your mother and I'll meet you at the library. We can still have lunch afterwards, can't we?"

"Yes, I guess we can."

"Then, get to it," Meg said as she eased back into the shiny sports car. "I'll see you there."

After Meg left, Ruth almost headed toward the house, then she remembered why she was outside. She opened her car door and quickly found her glasses, hidden from sight under the magazine she'd left in the passenger seat to take to her mother.

As she walked back to the house, she promised herself that she'd be more careful with her reading glasses in the future. But she'd made that vow dozens of times before and it hadn't changed her way of doing things one iota.

As she slid into the booth for a second time, she reached around and grabbed the silver letter opener out of the decorated coffee can, a gift from one of her students, that served as a pencil holder.

She stuck the bills in a slot in her small file organizer, then put on her glasses and glanced at the magazine covers. One was for elementary school teachers, which she quickly pushed aside. She had no reason to read it now.

The other magazine cover, done in full color, displayed a new travel trailer nestled among giant redwoods and green foliage. Ruth didn't know why she continued to renew her subscription to *Trailer Life* every year; maybe because it gave her something to dream about.

She thumbed through the slick pages of the magazine and glanced at the advertisements for new motorhomes, travel trailers, and fifth wheelers. She couldn't help but notice the pictures of happy couples with their recreation vehicles, a painful reminder that she was alone.

She was about to set the magazine aside and read Mary's letter when a quarter-page advertisement caught her attention.

"OZARKS FALL FESTIVAL," the header read. She went on to read the smaller print.

Caravan through the Ozarks where the trees are ablaze with color. September 29—October 7. Headquarter in Branson, Missouri. Six-day caravan with overnight stops in Eureka Springs, Arkansas, and the Mark Twain National Forest. Return to Branson for three fun-filled days of fishing and sightseeing. Includes tickets to Silver Dollar City, two country music shows, and an unforgettable boat trip to see the spectacular fall colors from Lake Taneycomo. Call or write for brochure.

Excitement surged through her. Could she drive the motorhome that far, by herself?

A spark of enthusiasm began to ignite her almost-extinguished dreams. It would be nice to take one last vacation in the motorhome before she sold it. The trip would give her a chance to see a part of the country she'd never seen, to meet the kind of people she liked to be with. And she wouldn't be alone; she would be with other campers.

Ruth glanced up at the large school clock on the kitchen wall and saw that it was time to leave.

The clock, an exact replica of the one that had hung in her kindergarten class for so many years, had been a retirement gift from her fellow teachers. The gift card had read, "Take time to think of us."

She pushed the magazine, and her dreams, momentarily away. She slit open Mary's letter with the letter opener.

The first paragraph of the letter stunned Ruth to the core. Her face flushed as she sat up straight in the booth, not believing what she'd just read. As she read through the beginning paragraph a second time, her shock quickly turned to anger.

"Dear Ruth. Ross and I are so pleased that you will be driving Mother Murphy to San Diego for a visit later this month. It was so kind of you to offer to do this for Ross's mother, but now that you're retired, what better way to spend your free time?"

"I can think of a lot of things I'd rather do with my time," Ruth said aloud. Seething inside, she went on to the next paragraph.

"Mother Murphy says that you can only stay for three weeks . . ."

"Three weeks!" Ruth shouted. She went back and read that part of it again, her stomach churning with rage.

". . . but after you arrive, maybe we can talk you into staying through Thanksgiving. Wouldn't that be fun?" Mary had drawn a little happy face at the end of the line.

"No, it wouldn't be fun," Ruth snapped. There was no way she would be away from her own family at Thanksgiving.

She continued reading. "You and Mother Murphy can share the double bed in our spare bedroom. And please don't worry about food. We'll have plenty to eat here. Mother Murphy says you're thinking about selling your beautiful house and moving into a small efficiency apartment close to her. Ross and I had no idea that you were going through such tough times financially. Sorry to hear about it." Here, Mary had drawn a little sad face.

And with each sentence she read, her anger grew.

"We look forward to your visit and hope you will decide to stay longer. Please let us know as soon as possible what day to expect you here in beautiful San Diego."

"Don't expect us at all," Ruth muttered through clenched teeth.

"By the way, Ruth," the letter continued, "while you're here, we want you to meet a dear friend of ours. Clarence

Tidwell is a scholar on ancient history and has written several textbooks on the subject. He is retired and about your height, so you two have a lot in common."

Even though she was hopping mad, Ruth had to laugh at Mary's logic. Since when did being retired and short make two people compatible?

In parenthesis, Mary had added: "Clarence is financially stable, so if you two hit it off, he could be the solution to your money problems." Mary had drawn another one of those dreaded happy faces. Ruth wanted to strangle her.

The letter ended with, "Sorry this letter is so short, but will fill you in on the news when you and Mother Murphy arrive."

Ruth slammed the letter down. She took her glasses off and set them on the table, then covered her face with both hands.

How could her mother do this to her? How could she take her for granted like that? Why couldn't Ernestine have had the courtesy to at least discuss the trip with her before she made plans?

She wouldn't go to San Diego, no matter how much her mother begged. She loved her brother Ross, but there was no way she'd spend even one night with that whining, bossy wife of his.

Furious, Ruth whirled around and reached for the phone on the ledge behind her.

No, she decided, she wouldn't call her mother. This was one time when she wanted to confront her Highness, Ernestine Murphy, face to face. Ruth would wait until she took Ernestine home after the bridge club was over, when her mother would have no choice but to sit and listen.

She grabbed her purse from the counter, dug out her car keys, and started out the side door, then hesitated. She marched over and snatched the RV magazine off of the table. She stuck her glasses on and flipped through the pages until she found the ad for the Ozarks caravan.

She dialed the number, and waited for an answer.

"Please send me your brochure as soon as possible," she said to the voice that answered. And then she gave all the necessary information.

From now on, Ruth vowed, she was going to please herself.

Seven

Ruth breathed in the smells of spicy Mexican cooking as she placed her napkin in her lap. She sat in a corner booth across from Meg, pleased that she'd made it to the library in time to meet Meg for lunch.

A pig-shaped piñata hung above the U-shaped booth. Ruth's gaze drifted from it to the black velvet painting of a graceful bullfighter in full regalia above Meg's head. The wall itself was rough-stuccoed and painted white to resemble adobe.

Raphael's, still celebrating the first month of its grand opening, was charming and Ruth was glad Meg had chosen this place to eat.

For the first time that day, she started to relax. At least something was going right for her, she thought, as she studied the menu. She loved Mexican food, but hadn't tried the new restaurant because of her aversion to eating out alone.

"Oh, before I forget," Meg said as she lowered her menu and looked over at Ruth. "Scot's joining us for lunch. He should be here any time now." She glanced toward the door.

In one fell swoop, there went Ruth's good mood. Whatever good feelings she'd had were suddenly gone.

She really didn't dislike Meg's husband, but she always felt very uncomfortable in his presence. It hadn't always been that way. In fact, both Meg and Scot had been her close friends for many years.

Ruth thought back to her high school days when she and Meg had both planned to become teachers. Meg married after one year of college and dropped out of school to go to work as a secretary. She divorced a year later, but kept on working to pay off the enormous debts her no-good ex-husband had accumulated.

Meg hadn't married Scot until she was thirty-two, a year after her parents died in a tragic car accident, leaving her with a healthy inheritance. Meg and Scot had moved away from Billings before Ruth ever got a chance to know him.

Meg had kept in touch by letter, so Ruth had been aware over the years of Meg's desperate desire to have children. But it had never happened. Meg had had two miscarriages and finally got too old to bear children.

When Meg and Scot returned to Billings ten years ago, Ruth and Meg had renewed their close friendship. Henry had gotten Scot a job at the bank, and until Henry died three years ago, the two couples had been a happy foursome. They had camped together, shared holidays, and had been there for each other through good times and bad.

And, both Scot and Meg had helped her through the difficult times when Henry died. A month later, the president of the bank had chosen Scot Rodecker to fill the vacancy created by Henry's death. Scot was promoted to the position of Senior Loan Officer, the title Henry had held for more than fifteen years.

Meg and Scot had remained her closest

and most trusted friends for a while.

But all that changed the night Scot propositioned her at a New Year's Eve party—just two short months after Henry died.

Ruth had mentioned the incident to Meg, and she never would, but she'd never forget how shocked she'd been that night. She'd never forget the feeling of betrayal she felt, the disgust. From that night on, Ruth had avoided Scot whenever possible. And after the hectic morning she'd had, she was in no mood to face him now.

Meg ordered a margarita. Ruth stuck to coffee. She still had a long drive to pick up her mother.

"How's your book coming?" Ruth asked as she set her menu down, trying to ignore her feeling of apprehension. It was the same question she asked Meg every time she saw her. Several months ago, Meg had mentioned that she wanted to write a book like *Peyton Place* about Billings, Montana, and the subject had become a running joke between them.

"Not very good," Meg said. "Not

enough scandalous things happening around this town."

The waitress came up to the table carrying a tray. She wore a black and red Spanish dress with rows of ruffles around the hem and the sleeves. She put the drinks in front of them, then set a basket of tortilla chips and a bowl of salsa in the middle of the table.

"Hi. I'm Maria and I'll be back to take your order in a few minutes."

After Maria left, Meg spoke again. "If you were a real friend, you'd help me dig up the dirt. We could write the book together."

They both laughed. "Sorry, Meg. I've got more exciting things to do."

"Like what?" Meg teased.

"Like cleaning all the light bulbs in my house."

"That wouldn't surprise me a bit if you actually washed your light bulbs." Meg took a sip of her drink, then held it up. "Now that's good. Want a taste?"

"No thanks," Ruth said. She watched the steam rise from her coffee.

Meg took another drink of her margarita before she set the bowl-shaped glass down. She brushed her locks of red hair back away from her face with her hand, a show of mock defiance. "Well, if you won't help me write the great American novel, I guess I'll have to stick to writing travel articles for the magazines. But I still think we could make a fortune with a raunchy little book." Her bright blue eyes had a mischievous twinkle to them.

"As if you needed the money," Ruth said with a smile. She dipped a chip in the salsa and took a bite.

"Well, I've got to have something to do with my time, or I'd go crazy. I don't have any kids or grandchildren to keep me busy and Scot insists on having a gardener and a cleaning lady, so what's left for me to do? You don't know how lucky you are to have grandchildren, Ruth." Meg took another drink of the margarita, then set the salt-rimmed glass to the side.

Ruth felt a pang of guilt. She reached over and touched Meg's arm. "I wish things could have turned out differently for you, Meg."

"Oh, I'm no longer bitter about not being able to have children. I'm happy, but I live my life in monotone. It's a straight line with no ups and downs." Meg fiddled with her glass, then took a long drink.

"I never thought of it that way." Ruth sipped from her coffee mug and got lost in her thoughts.

"That's why I do volunteer work at the library and at the hospital," Meg said. "That's why I write those travel articles. Scot and I can afford to travel around the world if we wanted to. But writing the articles gives me a reason to visit new places, instead of just vacationing there."

The waitress approached, pad in hand. "Can I take your order now?" she asked, pencil poised above the tablet.

Meg ordered another drink instead of lunch. Maria stuck the pad in her pocket and walked away.

It surprised Ruth that her friend had ordered another drink. She glanced over at Meg's glass and saw that it was almost empty. Something wasn't right.

Ruth knew that Scot could put his drinks away and although it had been a long time since she'd had lunch or dinner with them, she couldn't remember Meg ever taking more than one drink before a meal.

"Is there something you want to talk about?" Ruth asked. She munched on another tortilla chip.

Meg looked puzzled. Then she smiled. "No. I've been doing all the talking and I haven't let you tell me what's going on in your life."

"I'd rather listen," Ruth said.

"You know, Scot comes from a big family and I'm an only child," Meg said with a wistful look. "I think not being able to have children was harder on him than it was on me. And, I think the realization that he'll never have grandchildren has finally hit him."

"What makes you say that?" Ruth wondered if Scot was having an affair with some pretty young thing. It wouldn't surprise her at all.

When Maria brought the second margarita, Meg picked up her first drink, tipped the goblet up and drank what was left before she handed the glass over to the waitress.

"Are you ready to order now?" Maria asked.

"Not yet," Meg said. "We're waiting for my husband."

"So what's going on?" Ruth urged after Maria was gone.

"Nothing really. It's just that Scot seems restless lately, but then, so am I. We're together all the time, but we seem to be growing apart, if you know what I mean."

"Not exactly," Ruth said.

"It's hard to explain." Meg stared down at her drink, as if in thought. She took another sip before she spoke again. "I think Scot's going through a mid-life crisis. He's just different somehow."

"In what way?"

"Oh, I don't know. Little things. He's quieter at home, not as much fun as he used to be. He doesn't talk about work anymore, like he used to. He's irritable. He drinks too much most of the time." Meg looked over at Ruth. "I know, so do I."

"Is he abusive?" Ruth asked.

"No. He yells at me sometimes, but

he's never hit me. I know he's under a lot of pressure at work right now. He mentioned something about a big audit, but that's nothing unusual for a bank."

"I wouldn't think so." But Ruth wondered. She'd never heard Henry complain about the routine bank audits when he was a loan officer. But Henry had been easygoing and hadn't complained about many things.

"Do you know that Scot and I have been married for twenty-three years and we've never spent a single night apart? Maybe we're just bored with each other. Do you suppose?" Meg smiled.

"I think all couples get bored with each other at some time or other during their marriage."

"Probably so, but Scot and I don't communicate anymore. I get the feeling that something's bothering him, but when I ask him about it, he just clams up. I think it would do us both good if we got away from each other for a few days."

"I'm taking a vacation in my motorhome in a couple of weeks. Why don't you go with me?"

"Where are you going?"

"To Branson, Missouri."

Meg's face brightened. "Really? I've heard a lot about Branson lately. I guess it's really growing into a country music center. I've been thinking about writing an article about it, if I can come up with a new angle."

"Then go with me. I could use the company," Ruth said.

"I'd like to, but I don't want to leave Scot alone right now. It's like we're on a sinking ship, desperately clinging to each other for comfort. Doesn't make sense, does it?" Meg smiled and reached for a tortilla chip.

Ruth smiled, too. "It's a standing invitation."

"Thanks. Oh, here comes Scot now," Meg said as she slid to the middle of the booth.

Ruth felt herself tense.

"Well look who's here," Scot said as he strolled up to the table. "My two favorite girls. Can I buy you lunch?" He slid into the booth, leaned over and gave Meg a quick kiss, then settled in directly across from Ruth. "Good to see you again, Ruth. It's been a long time."

Ruth could barely look him in the eyes. "Yes it has."

Maria scurried over to the table, her ruffles flouncing, and set a menu in front of Scot. "Would you like something to drink?" she asked.

"Double Scotch on the rocks," Scot said.

"Do you want to order your food now?" Maria asked, rather timidly.

"You gals go ahead and order," Scot said. "I'll take a look at the menu."

Even though she'd lost her appetite, Ruth ordered a combination plate. Meg ordered the same.

While Scot studied the menu, Ruth and Meg talked about the library club and the awards presentation. When Maria brought Scot's drink, he set the menu down and took a healthy swig.

"Are you ready to order, sir?" Maria asked.

"No, I think I'll unwind for a few minutes first."

"Flag me down when you're ready."

Maria picked up two of the menus, and left the one Scot had set aside.

"Sorry I'm late," Scot said. "I got tied up at the office."

"We're glad you're here to pick up the tab," Meg said in a teasing tone that sounded forced.

Ruth studied Scot's face for a minute and was surprised at how much he'd aged since she'd seen him some six months before. He had a lot more gray in his hair and deep creases across his forehead. His pale gray eyes seemed to have faded and jowls had formed on either side of his jaw.

Scot Rodecker no longer looked like the swaggering, cocky man he'd been when he'd propositioned her so soon after Henry's death.

Maybe she'd been too harsh in her judgment of him, she thought. After all, he'd been very drunk that New Year's Eve, and he probably didn't even remember what he'd said to her. He probably didn't have any memory of touching her breast in the hallway. And he probably didn't remember that she had slapped him and walked away.

And as much as she hated to admit it, she knew darn well that part of her resentment toward Scot had to do with the fact that he had taken Henry's place at the bank. She also knew that it was irrational thinking, but that's how she felt.

She knew that as a bank officer, Scot had access to all of the information contained in her financial records, and she didn't like that either. It was none of his business if she wanted to send her daughter a check for five hundred dollars, or if she wanted to buy a new dress, or a new car. It was none of his business how much she had invested in bank certificates, or how much she received monthly from her retirement benefits.

She was being paranoid, and that too was a matter she was trying to deal with. Scot had been privileged to all bank records for the past ten years, ever since he first started working there as a junior loan officer. And nothing had really changed since Henry died.

Ruth felt her face flush with shame for her unkind thoughts when she remembered how helpful Scot had been in getting all of her joint accounts changed over to her name after Henry died.

She knew Scot didn't give a darn about how much she spent for groceries or anything else. It was just that if he wanted to, he could read her life's comings and goings like a book. She considered it an invasion of her privacy.

She had already decided what she would do with the money from the sale of her motorhome. She would open a savings account in Big Timber, where Tony banked, and eventually start a college trust fund for each of her grandchildren.

When Scot caught her staring at him across the table, she quickly turned her head toward Meg, hoping he hadn't noticed the flush in her cheeks.

"So, how was your meeting at the library?" Scot asked as he turned to face his wife. He downed half of his drink.

"Good," Meg said without elaborating.

"Who read the most books? And how many did he read?" He directed his question to Ruth as he raised his drink to his lips and stared at her over the rim of the glass.

Ruth didn't like the way he looked at her. His gaze was too smug, too suggestive. Or was she reading something into it that wasn't there?

"It was a she," she stated with a cold edge to her voice. "A fourth grader named Tracey. She read sixty-four books."

The conversation came to a dead halt and Ruth was grateful for the Spanish music being piped into the room. She stared up again at the bull fighter painting just so she'd have someplace to look.

"How's the audit going?" Meg asked.

"The auditors are still there," Scot said. "I wish to hell they'd finish up and let us get back to a normal routine." He rotated his glass around in his hand and stared at the swirling ice.

"How much longer do you think it'll take?" Meg asked.

Ruth noticed the brief glare Scot directed at his wife.

"How should I know? They're getting paid by the hour so they're taking their sweet time about it. They promised to be out of our hair by Monday, but we'll see." He took a drink, swallowed. "So were the kids excited?"

"Yes, they were," Meg said.

Then the awkward silence came between them again. Ruth could tell that they were having a problem finding something to talk about, but as far as she could see, Meg was just as guilty as he was of making no attempt to communicate.

She was relieved when the food was finally served.

"Can I take your order now, sir?" Maria asked.

"Another double," Scot said, holding out his empty glass.

"Anyone else?"

"I'd like another margarita, please," Meg said.

Ruth saw the dirty looks exchanged between the couple and knew that the drinking had become a problem in their marriage. She hoped that was all there was to it.

She toyed with her food as she listened to the feeble attempts at conversation. She saw the flash of anger that flicked in and out of Scot's pale gray eyes whenever Meg said something that displeased him. She noticed the way Meg flipped her soft red hair away from her face in defiance.

She saw the way Scot watched Maria walk away from the table, his focus on the smooth red fabric that covered her behind, and how Scot ogled the two young women in tight jeans as they were seated in the next booth.

All men look at pretty girls, she told herself. It was part of their nature to do so. But Scot didn't seem to look at these women with admiration and fantasy, as other men did. There was something sick, or maybe morbid in his expression.

If Scot hadn't strayed from his marriage bed, Ruth decided, it wasn't because he didn't want to. He had a respectable job and a wealthy wife, and he was too spineless to risk losing either one of them. He wasn't a strong, self-confident man, as she'd once believed. He was an insecure wimp.

Ruth had suspected that Scot Rodecker was a ne'er-do-well when Meg had first met him, and she'd never had any doubt that Scot had married Meg for her money.

By the time she finished her meal, Ruth decided that she'd been right about her original assessment of Scot Rodecker. There was something unwholesome about the man. She had sensed it the first time she'd met him. And she was convinced of it now.

Ruth realized that the heavy drinking was not the problem. The drinking was only the end result of the real trouble brewing within the marriage.

Her heart went out to both of them, but she knew that this was one time she couldn't do anything to help. They'd have to work through their own problems or their marriage would fall apart. Maybe the marriage had fallen apart before it began. Maybe it was never meant to be.

Eight

Ernestine Murphy sat in the passenger seat, looking very much like a geriatric Barbie doll. She dyed her hair black to cover the gray, but the short, curly hairstyle looked like a wig. In an attempt to conceal the wrinkles in her face, she wore makeup that was too light in color, which, in turn, caused her lipstick to look too red, too stark, against her pale, pasty complexion.

Her straight back rested against the dark blue of the seat in Ruth's Olds Cutlass. At only five feet tall in stocking feet, Ernestine insisted on sitting on a thick pillow to improve her view of the road.

She had complained of a terrible pain in her hip and leg all the way over to her friend's house earlier, and as if to prove her point, she'd made a big show of limping up to the house when Ruth dropped her off. And when Ruth picked her up after the card party, Ernestine had limped to the car.

Ruth had offered to take her mother to the doctor, or to the hospital, but that wasn't what Ernestine Murphy wanted. She wanted sympathy and attention.

Ernestine had buckled her seat belt for the return trip home, but only after protesting, as she always did, that the restraining strap would wrinkle her good dress. And Ruth knew that her mother's knit dress wouldn't wrinkle easily. It was made of soft, silver lamé with rich gold threads woven into the delicate fabric.

Ernestine wore three gold chains around her neck, dangling gold earrings, and a large, flashy rhinestone dinner ring on her right hand. On her left hand, she still wore her plain gold wedding band, even though she'd been a widow for nearly twenty years.

The only concession Ernestine made to her endeavor to dress with a fashionable flair was the pair of plain, black orthopedic shoes she'd been forced to wear ever since she broke her hip two years ago.

All the way home, Ruth listened patiently as Ernestine bragged about her wonderful friends and about the lovely refreshments the hostess had served after the card games.

Ruth didn't broach the subject of the proposed trip to San Diego until she stopped her car in the parking lot of her mother's apartment complex.

"Mother, I need to talk to you," she said after she shut the engine off.

"Oh, I already know the good news," Ernestine said, her thin lips broadening to a smile. "Brenda stopped by and told me you're going to sell that useless motorhome. I'm glad you've finally decided to take my sage advice."

"That isn't what I wanted to talk to you about." Ruth rested both hands on the steering wheel and looked straight ahead.

"I've tried to warn you for a long time that you've got to start watching your pennies now that you don't have a regular paycheck coming in," Ernestine continued, as if she hadn't heard Ruth. "You're too young to collect Social Security and it's going to be rough for you financially for the next few years. Mark my words."

"That isn't why I'm selling the motorhome."

"The reason doesn't matter," Ernestine said with a haughty air about her. "You take that money you get from the sale of the motorhome and invest it. Put it in a CD immediately. Before you're tempted to squander it."

"Mother, I know how to handle my affairs." Ruth struggled to keep her voice calm and even.

"Not so you'd notice," Ernestine snapped. "You're always talking about flying off to New York with that friend of yours and flying doesn't come cheap. As far as I'm concerned, it's nonsense to waste good money on fancy hotels and expensive restaurants. When the vacation is over, it's over, and you have nothing to show for your money."

"I'd have the memories." Ruth sighed, realizing that there was no way to reason with her mother.

Ernestine unbuckled her seat belt and

119

brushed imaginary wrinkles from the front of her dress. "Speaking of vacations, Ross and Mary have invited me to San Diego for a short visit and I told them you'd be more than happy to drive me out there. I thought we'd leave two weeks from tomorrow, after church. It'll be a nice little vacation for both of us."

"And that isn't a waste of my money?" Ruth challenged. She turned and faced her mother.

"Oh, this is different. This is family." Ernestine clutched her black pocketbook with both hands as it rested in her lap. "Don't worry, Ruth. I plan to pay for my share of the food and motel bills on the trip."

"And what about the gasoline?"

Ernestine frowned at her. "Well, it's your car and I just assumed you'd pay for the gas. But if you can't afford to, I suppose I could pay for half."

"Mother, I'm not driving you to California. I've got other plans."

"But you have to," Ernestine insisted. "I promised Ross."

"You should have consulted me before

you made any promises."

"Well," Ernestine huffed. "I certainly didn't think that was necessary. After all, you're my daughter and I thought you'd be happy to do me a small favor. Especially now that you have more time than you know what to do with."

Ruth ignored the crude, insensitive remark. "Mother, common courtesy should have told you that it wasn't right to make plans that involved me without checking with me first."

"Well, maybe I was wrong in not mentioning it before, but I hope you can understand how important my visit to Ross is. I have to go see him and that's all there is to it."

"Then you'll have to fly out to San Diego. Or take a train."

"You know I don't trust airplanes, and with my broken hip, a long train trip is out of the question."

"Then you'll just have to cancel the trip or find someone else to take you."

Ruth saw her mother's shoulders sag and recognized the sign. Ernestine was about to change tactics.

"Please, Ruth, you can't let me down," Ernestine pleaded, her voice suddenly weak and whiny. "I'm depending on you. You're the only one who can take me. This will probably be my last chance to see my only son before I die."

Ruth steeled herself against her mother's manipulative tactics. "I'm sorry, Mother. I can't drive you to San Diego."

"Give me one good reason why not," Ernestine demanded as she sat up straighter.

"I told you, I have other plans. I'm leaving for a vacation in the Ozarks in a couple of weeks."

Ernestine glared at her daughter. "So that's how you're going to squander the money you get from the sale of your motorhome," she accused. "I knew it. I just knew you couldn't hold on to that money."

"I'm driving the motorhome to Missouri," Ruth said in an even tone. "I'll sell it when I get back."

"Why you can't drive that huge thing by yourself. Who's going with you?"

"Nobody. I'm going by myself."

"I'll be darned if you are. No daughter of mine is going to drive across the country by herself. Decent women don't travel alone. Besides, it's far too dangerous. I won't hear of it and that's that."

Ruth felt her face flush with controlled anger. "I'm going to the Ozarks and nobody's going to talk me out of it."

Ernestine opened the door and got out of the car.

"We'll talk about this later, Ruth," she said in a huffy tone. "You'll change your mind before I'm through." She slammed the door and marched toward her apartment building.

"No I won't," Ruth said softly to herself as she watched her mother walk away without any trace of a limp.

Nine

It was already 5:30 when Ruth pulled into her driveway, her shoulders sagging from the emotional strain of the confrontation with her mother.

Brenda drove in a few seconds later and parked her car in her usual spot between the tall motorhome and her mother's blue Cutlass.

"Talk about perfect timing," Ruth said as she walked around to the driver's side of Brenda's car.

Little Lori broke into a big grin when she saw her grandmother. She waited impatiently while her mother helped her unfasten her seat belt, then scrambled out of the car and raced to Ruth.

"Grandma, I get to go to school in three more days." She held up three pudgy fingers. The fact that she had not lost all of her baby fat was evident by the way she filled out her new outfit, bright pink shorts and a blouse that was patterned with pink and neon-green dinosaurs. Her twin braids were still neat, evidence that Brenda had just finished fixing her hair.

"I know, sweetheart." Ruth gave her a hug.

"Lori, come back and get your suitcase, and close the car door," Brenda called.

Lori dashed back to the car as Hank got out of the back seat with his overnight bag.

"Hi, Grandma," he said. Hank was slim and wore faded jeans, a new shirt with a surfer on the front, and scuffed sneakers.

"You got a hug for Grandma?" Ruth urged, knowing that, at seven, Hank was going through a shy spell about such things.

Hank brushed back a strand of dark brown hair and gave her a quick hug. "I brought a new game for us to play tonight," he said.

"So did I, Grandma," Lori said as she ran back, her miniature suitcase in her hand. "We get to play my game first, don't we, Grandma?"

"No way Lori," Hank said. "Your game is dumb."

"No it isn't, Hank. You're just a big baby."

"You kids quit your bickering," Brenda scolded from the driver's seat.

"Don't worry, Brenda, I came prepared. I rented 'The Little Mermaid' today."

"Yeah," Lori cried, jumping up and down, clapping her little hands.

"Lori, you're a jerk," Hank said.

"Am not."

"Quiet, kids. Mom, I just decided what you need," Brenda said as she cocked her head and studied her mother's face.

"What's that?"

"You need a makeover."

Ruth laughed and ran her fingers through her longer-than-usual hair. "You don't like the way I look? I'm getting a permanent next week."

"No, no, not a permanent. Have your hair cut short and have it styled so it just falls in place naturally when you brush it. You'd look cute in short hair."

"Cute? Women my age don't look cute."

"Yes they do. And buy some jeans, some T-shirts."

"I'm too old to wear jeans and T-shirts."

"That's stupid. Everybody wears jeans

126

these days. You'd look sexy in Levi's."

"I don't want to look sexy."

"You're old-fashioned."

"Maybe so, but I am what I am and if people don't like me, then that's their problem."

Brenda sighed with obvious disgust. "Hey, Mom, I just want you to go modern, try something different. You've worn that same hairstyle for as long as I can remember."

"I didn't know it offended you," Ruth said sarcastically.

"It doesn't offend me, it's just that you look like every other woman your age. Get out of your rut. Do something for yourself for a change."

"Oh, I plan to. Very soon," Ruth said with a smug smile.

Lori tugged on her pantleg. "Hurry up, Grandma."

Hank pulled Lori away. "You're rude, Lori."

"No I'm not, Hank. You're rude." Lori turned around and tried to shove him. When he ducked away, Lori chased him around the front yard, trying to punch him with her tiny fist.

"Kids, stop that," Brenda called, then

looked back up at Ruth. "What do you mean? You've got that look in your eyes and I know you're up to something wicked."

"Nothing wicked. I've decided to take a trip in the motorhome before I sell it, that's all."

"What kind of a trip? How far?"

Ruth smiled proudly. "In two weeks, I'm pulling up stakes and heading for Branson, Missouri, in the Ozarks."

"You're what!" Brenda poked her head out of the car window, a startled look on her face. "Is Edith going with you?"

"No, I'm going by myself."

"Mom, you're not serious, are you?"

"Quite serious. And I'm very excited about it, too, so don't take the wind out of my sails."

"You can't do that, Mother. What if you have mechanical trouble along the way?" Brenda argued. "The Gypsy's been sitting there for so long, you don't know what shape it's in. Anything could happen."

"I'm going to have Glen Amos check it out before I leave town."

"No, no, no," Brenda muttered as she stared down at the ground. Then she looked up at Ruth with an expression that showed that she wanted to reason with her mother. "Look, Mom, I think it's great that you want to take a vacation, but I don't like the idea of you making the trip alone. Can't you find someone to go with you?"

"I don't want anyone to go with me. I'm signing up for a caravan, so once I get to Branson, I won't be alone. I'll be with other people who share my interests."

"Yeah, old fogies," Brenda snorted.

"Probably. I figure most of them will be retired people who want to do a little traveling before they get too old."

"Come on, Grandma," Lori nagged impatiently as she ran back to Ruth, escaping Hank's taunting. "I want to watch 'The Little Mermaid.'"

"Lori, Grandma and I are talking," Brenda hollered.

"I'll be with you in a minute, Lori." Ruth patted her granddaughter on the head. "Brenda, there's nothing more to say. I've made up my mind. I'm going to take one last trip in the motorhome before I sell it. I really thought you'd be happy for me."

"But that's so far to go by yourself. Think of the problems you could run into."

"This is something I really want to do, so

it won't do you any good to try to discourage me."

"You're stubborn." Brenda tucked her head back into the car and started the engine. "We'll discuss this later."

"I'm sure we will. Have a good time tonight." Ruth waved and turned away, and walked up to her house.

Inside, Ruth started the videotape and, when the children were settled into the two recliners at the other end of the room, strolled back to the kitchen area and started a fresh pot of coffee.

She had already changed out of her comfortable, faded jogging suit and put on a tailored, pink pants suit. The only jewelry she wore was a pair of pearl clip-on earrings. And, like her mother, she still wore her diamond wedding rings even though she was a widow. She just couldn't bring herself to take them off.

She went to the cupboard and grabbed a box of macaroni and cheese mix which she could prepare in a hurry. She had planned to make the casserole dish from scratch, but was running behind schedule. Norm Rogers had said that he wanted to eat at precisely six o'clock so he could watch some program on

PBS at 6:30.

Ruth wanted to use paper plates and eat at the breakfast nook, as she usually did when the grandkids were there. But she compromised and counted out four of her everyday ceramic plates instead of getting out the good china.

She had just reached for the paper napkins when she heard a car outside. She glanced out the window and saw Norm's beige car pull into the driveway. Darn, why did he have to be early tonight?

Ruth opened the kitchen door and stepped out onto the breezeway. She wanted to catch Norm before he headed for the front door, as he always did. She didn't feel like walking around to the living room to let him in.

"Hello, Ruth," he said when she opened the breezeway gate. "How are you this evening?"

Ruth studied him more closely than she had before and decided she'd been right in her assessment of him.

Norm was tall and thin and walked with a slight stoop to his shoulders. He wore dark brown slacks and a white dress shirt, open at the collar. He carried a neatly folded sport jacket over his arm. A pen and a small, leather appointment book jutted out from the clear plastic liner in one shirt pocket. His reading glasses, encased in a black leather pouch, stuck out of the other pocket. He was almost bald, but had a fringe of short gray hair around his head. His shuffling walk made him appear older than sixty-five.

"I'm fine. Come on in," she said, leading him toward the kitchen door.

"When are you going to get rid of that expensive yard ornament out there?" he said, nodding toward the driveway.

Ruth glanced back over her shoulder. "What yard ornament?"

"That motorhome. It's an eyesore. If you're not going to sell it, you should put it in storage before your neighbors start complaining."

How dare he call her prized possession an eyesore. A knot of anger formed in the pit of her stomach and she instinctively pulled away from his touch when he smiled and patted her on the shoulder.

"My neighbors are polite enough to mind their own business," she said, doubting that he got the point. She went on into the house, wishing that he'd go back home. She was in no mood to put up with his wimpy, self-centered ways.

"I smell the homemade bread," he said as he followed her inside. "Smells delicious."

Ruth observed him as he scanned the counter until he spotted the loaf of bread. She saw his attention shift to the far end of the room where the television was on. And, she saw the jerk of his head, the startled look on his face, when he noticed Hank and Lori there. She also noticed the dark shadow of irritation that crept into his expression.

"I didn't know your grandchildren would be here tonight," he said, the annoyance evident in his voice. "You should have told me."

"I didn't know they'd be here when you called last night," Ruth said without offering an apology.

"You could have called me today."

"I was busy today. Can I take your jacket?" She reached for the sport coat, but Norm pulled his arm in closer to his thin body.

Norm noticed the box of macaroni and cheese. He frowned and squinted his eyes as he scanned the length of the long counter again.

"Where's the Crockpot?" he asked, a hint of reproach in his pale blue eyes.

"Oh, I didn't make beef stew," Ruth said, too cheerfully. "You said a simple meal and I took you at your word."

Norm backed up a couple of steps, edging toward the door. "Perhaps this isn't a good night for me to be here. You're obviously preoccupied and if your grandchildren are going to tie up the television, I won't be able to watch my show on PBS."

"You could watch the television in the living room," she suggested, amused by his discomfort.

"No, I don't want to interfere. We'll just reschedule dinner for tomorrow night."

"I'm busy tomorrow night," Ruth said, even though she had no plans.

"I'm afraid that's the only night I have free for a while. Once school starts next week, I'll be quite busy, as you know." Norm pulled the thin appointment book out of his pocket and thumbed through it. "Let's see, we're having a faculty dinner in three weeks to welcome the new professors. I'd like you to go with me."

"Oh, I won't be here then. I'll be on my way to Missouri."

Norm looked at her. "Oh, do you have relatives there?"

Ruth realized that Norm knew very little about her family, nor did he care. He knew Brenda, of course, because she worked in the business office at the college where he taught, and she'd been the one to introduce them.

"No, I don't know anybody there. I just want to take a vacation by myself in the motorhome."

A scowl lined Norm's forehead and it was a minute before he spoke again. "Why, you can't do that."

"Why can't I?"

"Because you're a woman. A very short woman, I might add, and that motorhome is far too big for you to handle by yourself," he said.

"I've driven it before."

"Maybe so, but only when your husband was with you. I don't mean to sound disrespectful, Ruth, but you're a very small person, helpless in the event of trouble."

"I can take care of myself." Ruth's dander was up, but she was also taking some sort of perverse pleasure in their verbal exchange.

"Regardless, respectable women don't venture out on their own. They don't vacation by themselves. Not unless they're looking for trouble." Norm tipped his head and stared at her, as if he were questioning her morality.

"Let's say I'm looking for a good time."

"Don't you know what kind of shiftless degenerates pass through those camp-grounds?"

"My kind of people," Ruth said, stifling the urge to laugh.

Norm's pale eyes widened at her remark. "Quit being so insolent, Ruth," he demanded "You're not listening to a thing I say."

"I'm listening," she said. And quickly losing any respect I might have had for you, she thought to herself.

Norm shifted weight and smiled briefly with thin lips, obviously satisfied that he was in control of the situation again. "I'm trying to be a friend, Ruth. Aren't you aware of the dangers out there? Or do you just live in your own tiny world?"

His last remark finished it for her. This was her house, her kitchen, and she didn't have to stand there and listen to his insults. "Norman, I'm leaving on vacation soon and I won't be back in time for your faculty dinner," she said firmly. "I suggest you find someone else to accompany you."

Norm raised his hands, as if to stop her from saying anything more. "Well, it's obvious that you won't listen to reason. So, for your own sake, Ruth, I forbid you to go," he said, as if his word was final.

Ruth struggled to keep her temper under control.

"I think you're right, Norman. I don't think this is a good night for you to be here."

Norm backed out the door without another word.

After Norm left, Ruth collapsed in the breakfast nook to compose herself.

If she'd had any doubts about going through with the trip to the Ozarks before, she certainly didn't now. She could put up with the well-meaning concerns of her family, but no man, especially that stuffy, spineless Norman Rogers, was going to tell her what she could or couldn't do.

A minute later, Ruth nearly jumped out of her skin when the telephone rang directly behind her.

She didn't want to talk to anyone else tonight. Not her mother, not Brenda. Not anyone.

She let the phone ring four times before little Lori climbed out of the recliner and ran to the kitchen.

"Grandma, the phone's ringing," she announced proudly, then ran back to her movie.

Ruth finally picked up the receiver. "Hello," she said without her usual cheerfulness.

"Hi, Mom."

Ruth was startled to hear Tony's voice. She assumed he was camping. Worried that something had happened for him to call again so soon, she reached for her notepad to take down any information he might give her.

"Is everything all right?" She held her breath, dreading his answer.

Tony laughed. "Everything is fine here, but I guess there's plenty of trouble brewing at the old homestead. Brenda just tracked me down and called me out here at the campground. I'm supposed to talk some sense into that stubborn little head of yours."

Ruth's body went limp with relief that there'd been no accident, but at the same time, she felt the pangs of betrayal. "Don't waste your breath, Tony. I've had so much free advice today, my ears are burning. I'm going to the Ozarks and that's final. Don't try to talk me out of it. It won't do you any good."

"Hey, Mom! Hold on, Mom," Tony shouted in the phone to get her attention. "I just called to tell you that I think it's a terrific idea for you to take part in that caravan. You'll love the Ozarks. I wish I were going with you."

"But I thought Brenda . . ."

"Brenda's a busybody. Follow your heart. Isn't that what you've always told me?"

"Oh, Tony, you've made my day," she sighed. "There is justice after all. You're an angel."

"I do have one word of advice about taking that trip across country by yourself, however."

Ruth heard the stern tone in Tony's voice and her heart sank. "I don't think I can take any more advice today, but what is it?"

"I'd get the hell out of town as soon as possible. Before Brenda and Grandma have a chance to declare you mentally incompetent."

Ten

With the last of the perishable foods neatly arranged in the small refrigerator, Ruth stood in the middle of the motorhome and wondered if she'd forgotten anything. Her comfortable, new walking shoes made only a whispering sound as she walked across the gleaming, gold-flecked linoleum floor of the compact kitchen.

The new-car scent followed her as she padded across the thick beige carpet, making her way toward the front of the coach. As she passed the sofa she noticed that she'd left her new flashlight on one of the throw pillows. She picked up the flashlight and found room for it in the enclosed storage section of the stationary end table that sat between the two swivel chairs.

While she was there, she checked to make sure both chairs were locked in position, then tested the small television set to see that it was securely bolted to the top of the end table.

Still nagged by the feeling she'd forgotten something, which was not an unusual state of mind for Ruth these days, she eased into the driver's seat, her hands perched on the steering wheel. After driving a car for so many years, the steering wheel, tilted to an almost flat, horizontal position, felt strange to her.

Like an airline pilot, she sat there for a moment and went through a final mental checklist before she started the engine.

Her food was put away. Her clothes hung in a neat row in the narrow closet. A dozen new paperback books were stowed away next to the first aid kit in an enclosed storage bin under one of the dinette seats.

She'd brought along her most recent photo album so she could look at the pictures of her family if she got homesick. The thick album was in a dresser drawer with her sweaters.

The motorhome, she knew, was mechanically sound. Glen Amos had spent two whole days going over it and had checked everything and anything that could give her problems on the road.

She glanced over and confirmed that the new *Rand McNally Road Atlas* and her *Trailer Life* campground directory were in the passenger seat. Other maps, along with important documents, her address book, and her reading glasses, were in the glove compartment. Her driving glasses, still in their leather case, were in the black, plastic console between the seats.

Satisfied that everything was in order, she sat up straight, fastened her seat belt, then slipped her driving glasses on. The seat was as far forward as she could get it. She shifted slightly to a more comfortable position, then turned the key in the ignition. A smile came over her face when the engine started up with a soft humming sound. Glen's expert tuning, she knew.

As Ruth stared out through the wide windshield, she felt her legs suddenly go weak, as if the strength had been zapped from her muscles. The joyous anticipation she'd experienced for the past few days suddenly turned to nerve-wracking apprehension.

Could she really handle this big rig by herself? Or was she a fool to even try? She took a deep breath and forced herself to relax.

She eased the motorhome out of her driveway and onto her quiet street. A few minutes later, she turned onto a busy four-lane street. As she eased the vehicle into traffic, the long motorhome seemed to take on the proportions of a gigantic whale in a fishbowl. She glanced in her rear view mirror and nearly panicked when she saw the encroaching traffic behind her.

Two cars zipped by her on her left. Her natural instinct was to shy away from the passing cars, give them plenty of room. But she didn't have any room to spare, not unless she wanted to drive up onto the crowded sidewalk. Fighting the feelings of trepidation that rose up in her throat, threatening to strangle her, Ruth concentrated on keeping the Coachman on a straight path in the right lane.

Normally, she paid no attention to the noisy din of city traffic, but when she had to stop for a red light at a busy intersection, the sounds invaded her senses. The honking of horns, the constant noises of passing cars, it all set her nerves on edge.

From her high driver's seat, she glanced

down at the young driver of the red sports car beside her, wishing he would quit revving his motor as he waited impatiently for the light to change.

She looked back over her shoulder, a quick check to see if everything was riding all right, and was immediately panic-stricken by the mere length of the motorhome as it stretched out behind her, all the way back to the rear bedroom. Her heart fluttered. She took a breath and the air wasn't there. She felt like she was drowning in her own fear.

How could she think she could easily handle something this big in traffic? How had she managed to make it this far without clipping another vehicle? What would she do if she hit a big metropolitan area at the wrong time of day and got tangled up in the nightmare of commuter traffic?

She had an overwhelming urge to turn around and go back home. Or maybe she could drive the eighty miles to Big Timber and hide out at the trout pond campground for a month, as Tony had suggested.

No, she told herself, she wasn't a quitter. She was a survivor and she could handle whatever obstacles were thrown in her path.

At least she hoped so.

When the light finally turned green, Ruth held her breath while she made a right turn at the intersection, hoping she wouldn't swing too wide, praying that she wouldn't cut the corner too sharp, either. She maneuvered the Coachman through three more blocks of traffic before she reached the Interstate.

As she entered the freeway, heading east, she pulled the visor down to block off the mid-morning sun. Once she was a few miles away from the bustle of the city, she began to relax as she settled into the familiar rhythm of driving.

The divided highway stretched out ahead of her, glimmering in the sunlight like twin water canals cutting their way through the landscape. On both sides of the road, tall, green pines stood stark against the dead, brown grasses of the rolling hills. When she looked up at the white, billowy clouds against the wide expanse of blue sky, Ruth understood why they called this Big Sky Country.

The sparse traffic was well spread out and Ruth felt none of the tension she'd experienced earlier while driving in the big city. A feeling of eager anticipation flowed through her as she thought about her trip.

A big truck passed her. She felt the impact from the tunnel of air as the eighteen-wheeler rolled by, but she didn't mind. There was plenty of room on the road for both of them.

Tall boulder bluffs began to appear at the side of the road and long after she'd passed them, the highway curved through miles of rolling fields, some brown and fallow, others green with winter crops. Cattle grazed on the land and ponds glimmered in the sunlight. The huge, round bales of hay that dotted the landscape were turning dark with age. Occasionally, Ruth spotted a farm-house nestled amid shade trees, tucked way back in the hills. The cotton-woods closer to the road hadn't yet begun to turn color.

A sudden gust of wind hit the side of the Gypsy. Surprised by the abrupt jerk of the motorhome, Ruth automatically gripped the steering wheel tighter. She glanced out the window and saw the tall treetops swaying wildly, the green leaves flapping, as if taking flight.

The wind didn't let up. The strong gusts

came in waves, pounding against the long, flat side of the Coachman as she drove. A tumbleweed blew across the road ahead of her, barely missing her rig. She slowed down and tried to keep the motorhome on an even keel.

Ruth was about to pull to the side of the road and wait out the windstorm when she spotted the blue highway sign. "REST AREA—One mile ahead." She took some comfort knowing that there was a safe place for her to stop soon.

Determined to make it to the rest area, Ruth sat up straighter in the driver's seat as the motorhome continued to shake and sway from side to side as each new gust of wind bounced against it. As she drove, she noticed other motorists were fighting the same battle.

She slowed down to twenty-five miles an hour. She fought the steering wheel and struggled to keep the motorhome on a straight path. Even so, one powerful gust of wind blew her into the other lane and it was an effort for her to bring the unwieldy motorhome back in line.

Out of the corner of her eye, she saw a dust devil spinning across an open field on her right. She turned her head and watched in horror as the swirling cloud of dust took a sudden turn and headed straight for her motorhome, pushed along by the blustering wind.

Ruth clutched the steering wheel with white knuckles. She didn't know whether to slow down to a crawl and let the miniature whirlwind pass in front of her, or speed up and try to outrun it. She had no time to do either.

The mass of fine, dusty particles skipped across the dry land, sucking up more dirt and sand from the parched ground as it picked up speed and volume.

Ruth braced for the brunt of the assault. As the whirling column of dust and grit rushed toward her, Ruth instinctively ducked and turned the steering wheel. The motorhome swerved to the left, crossing into the other lane. She quickly jerked the wheel the other way and overcorrected. Weaving over to the blacktop shoulder, the motorhome was on a crash course with the rapidly approaching whirling dervish.

Ruth knew she was losing control of the vehicle and she was afraid that if she got it rocking too much, it would tip over on its side. She forced herself to calm down and take charge of the situation.

She turned the steering wheel only slightly to the left this time, which brought the motorhome back on the road. She then turned the steering wheel slightly to the right to keep the Gypsy on a straight course as she slowed the vehicle down so it was just barely rolling.

Ruth stiffened and waited for the impact. She heard the rush of wind. She held her breath and prayed.

Then at the last minute, the dust devil switched directions, just barely missing her. It skirted the edge of the road, then doubled back to the open fields, dancing away like a carefree nymph.

A swirl of dust remained in its wake. Ruth had brought the Gypsy to a rolling stop in the middle of the road by the time the blinding mass of gritty dust washed over the motorhome. For a minute, she couldn't see anything except the brown cloud. She heard the sand pelt against the side of her motorhome. But the dust storm had no strength behind it and Ruth knew there wouldn't be much damage.

She eased the motorhome over to the

wide shoulder and stopped. Her knees felt like rubber, but it wasn't until she shut off the engine that she began to shake. She put her hands in her lap, willing them to stop trembling.

She looked out the window and an eerie feeling came over her when she realized that the road was deserted. She was grateful that there hadn't been any vehicles close to her when she was weaving all over the road, but now, she felt a terrible pang of loneliness.

The wind regained its strength and began to pound the side of her motorhome again. She sat there, unable to move, as the Coachman swayed back and forth.

She wished a highway patrolman would come and lead her to safety. She knew she had to drive on to the rest area where there would be other people around, but she couldn't face driving in the wind again.

She was so frightened, she wanted to cry. She wondered if the trip was worth the stress.

For the second time that day, she wanted to turn the motorhome around and drive back to the security of her house in Billings.

And she was only twelve miles from home.

Eleven

The smell of dust hung in the air. Ruth sank back in her seat and fought the urge to drive back to Billings and abandon her vacation plans. She took off her glasses and looped them over a finger as she cupped her head in her hand and tried to compose herself.

There was no sound except that of the howling wind. And when she closed her eyes, there was no perception of movement except for the gentle rocking back and forth, as if she were sleeping in a Pullman on a slow-moving train.

After a few minutes, Ruth sat up straight and slipped her driving glasses back in place. When she looked out through the dust-laden windshield, she was surprised to see the little blue sign up ahead. "REST AREA—Five hundred feet." After her harrowing experience with the dust devil, she hadn't realized she was so close.

Although she dreaded driving even that short distance in the fierce wind, she knew it would be better to be with other people at the rest area than to be stranded alone on the road. She started the engine and pulled onto the highway.

When she finally reached her destination, she slowed down and turned right, guiding the Coachman between the high curbs that lined the entrance to the parklike rest area. She heard a metal thunk and assumed a rock had blown against the side of the motorhome. She cursed under her breath and hoped the rock hadn't damaged the paint, or left its mark in the form of a dent.

Following the signs, she eased the motorhome to the left to park in the wide area designated for truck and recreation vehicle parking.

A dozen or so passenger cars were parked near the brick restroom building of the nicely landscaped rest area. In the area reserved for eighteen-wheelers and long recreation vehicles, there were already three big trucks, another motorhome, and four travel trailers attached to their tow vehicles.

Ruth brought the motorhome to a smooth stop alongside one of the big trucks. She turned the ignition off and set the emergency brake.

With her knees still shaking from the frightening incident with the dust devil, she sank back into the upholstered seat and just sat there for a moment, relieved to be off the road. The Coachman continued to shake and rock with each new gust of wind.

Before she slid out of the bucket seat, she reached over and moved the black plastic console box out of her path, sliding it over in front of the other seat.

When she stood up and stepped through to the carpeted area of the living room, she felt the full impact of her stress. Every muscle in her body ached and she felt like she didn't have enough strength left even to walk across the room.

She walked back to the kitchen and peered out the window. Dried dead leaves blew across the parking lot and she saw the broken tree branches that littered the grassy area around the covered picnic tables.

There were no people at the scattered

tables, but she did see one couple leaning into the wind as they made their way to the restroom. Another man was using the pay phone, his shirt flapping like a wind-blown flag as he kept his back to the strong gusts. He was probably a trucker reporting to someone that he wouldn't be able to make his delivery on time.

Curious about the damage the rock had caused to the side of her motorhome, Ruth waited at the window until the wind died down. Then she walked around the end of the counter and unlocked the aluminum door.

When she opened the door, she was startled to see that the metal step was already extended.

Like a flash bulb going off in her brain, Ruth now knew what had nagged at her mind before she left home.

"Damn," she muttered under her breath. How could she have been so careless?

When she'd done her last-minute packing that morning, she'd locked the step down in its extended position so she wouldn't have to mess with it while she carried several heavy boxes to the motorhome. When she'd finished packing, she'd forgotten to set the switch back to automatic, so the step would glide down into an extended position whenever the door was open and then slide up whenever the door was closed. It was a stupid mistake.

"Damn," she said again when she saw that the step was tilted at an odd angle. She realized then that the motorhome hadn't been hit by a wind-blown rock. The sound she'd heard when she drove into the rest area was the step banging into the high curb as she'd cut her right-hand turn too sharp.

She reached over and flipped the switch on the wall beside the door. The motor whined but the step stuck fast in its extended position.

"Shoot," she said as she lowered herself to the ground, avoiding the step completely.

A gust of wind whipped through her short, dark hair, causing the fine strands to stick out in all directions. She had taken Brenda's suggestion and had her hair styled so that it just fell into place after a quick blow-dry. But, right now she didn't care about her hair. She just wanted to get the step back into place before she started up

155

again. As low as the step was to the ground, she knew she'd risk knocking it further out of alignment if she hit so much as a bump in the road.

This had happened to her once before. Not with the motorhome, but when she and Henry had owned a small travel trailer. Henry had been driving that time and as he pulled into a remote camping spot in the woods, where there were no designated camp sites, he hadn't seen the foot-high tree stump that was hidden by tall grasses. Ruth remembered what a struggle it had been to maneuver the metal step back into place.

She tugged on the metal step, and pushed and pulled it every which way. But the step didn't budge. She changed positions and sat down on the hard, dusty, blacktop of the parking lot, knowing that her light blue slacks would get dirty. If she could just get the right leverage on the step, she figured she could snap it back in place.

She put all the muscle she could muster into her efforts to push the corner of the step up into its proper position. But it didn't do any good. The step didn't move.

She was concentrating so hard on trying to straighten the step, she didn't notice the man who walked up beside her until he spoke.

"Do you need some help, lady?"

Startled, Ruth looked up and saw the tall man hovering above her. He smiled down at her, a smile that was too easy, too quick, she thought. When she saw that he carried a crowbar in one hand, a pang of sheer terror shot through her body.

She fought the urge to scream, the urge to roll under the Coachman to escape a brutal attack from the crowbar he was wielding.

Finally realizing that most of her trepidation stemmed from the fact that her mother and Brenda had drilled too many horror stories into her head in an attempt to discourage her from taking the trip, Ruth shook off her fears.

With her knees still so wobbly from fright that she didn't know if they would support her, she stood up, catching a whiff of the well-groomed stranger's pleasant-smelling aftershave.

A sudden gust of wind ruffled the man's neatly styled hair. His hair was dark brown with enough gray at the temples to give him a distinguished look. His clean-shaven face was rugged, but not particularly handsome.

There was something vaguely familiar about the stranger, but Ruth couldn't place him, not even when she looked into his deep blue eyes. He wore a blue chambray shirt, rolled up at the sleeves, faded Levi's that hugged his slender build, and scuffed Hush Puppies.

"Thanks anyway, but it's too windy to try to fix the step right now," Ruth said politely.

She really needed his help, and he looked like he had the muscles to straighten the step by himself, but she reminded herself that she was in a rest area, not a campground, and somehow that made a difference. Besides, she didn't like being called "lady."

She didn't see the small dust devil swirling through the parking lot until it reached her. She closed her eyes tight, and covered her face with her hands. But not in time. Sand blew into her eyes and felt like sharp slivers of glass slicing into her eyeballs. She batted her eyes, trying to clear the grit as the miniature whirlwind danced away.

The stranger smiled at her again, exposing pearly white teeth that were perfectly straight. "You're right, ma'am, It's too damned windy right now."

Ruth didn't like to be called "ma'am" either. "Thanks for offering," she said. She shielded her eyes from another blast of wind, then turned to go back inside.

"I won't be going anywhere for a while," the man said. "Not with this wind knocking my rig around. Maybe I can fix that step for you before you pull out."

"Maybe." Ruth turned to face him again, wondering what kind of a rig he was talking about. Was he an over-the-road trucker, or a camper like herself? He seemed pleasant enough, but he was a stranger and she had all of her guards up.

"Are you traveling alone?" the tall fellow asked casually as he nodded toward her motorhome.

Ruth hesitated. She didn't want this stranger to know that she was alone, but she knew it must be pretty obvious. If she had an able-bodied man traveling with her, she wouldn't be trying to fix the step herself. She faced him again and looked into his eyes, searching for some ulterior motive for his question. The man was just being friendly, she decided, and she didn't want to be rude.

"I am right now," she said, hedging on her answer. "But, I'm meeting up with friends along the way."

"Where are you headed?"

It was another casual question, the kind she expected from people who crossed paths at rest areas or campgrounds. Still, he was a stranger, and she didn't want to offer any information about her plans.

"To the Ozarks," she said, knowing that the Ozarks covered a broad area, including the corners of three states: Arkansas, Missouri, and Oklahoma.

"I'll bet you're going to Branson," he said with a knowing twinkle in his eye.

Ruth frowned. "Why would you say that?"

The wind gusted around them, sounding like a roaring river of air. They both ducked their heads.

When Ruth looked up, she saw that the man was staring at her and it unnerved her.

He smiled. "You look like the type who likes country music. I hear they've built six new music theaters there this year."

"Have you been there?" Ruth asked. She really didn't want to carry on a conversation with this man, but she allowed her curiosity to take precedent over caution and common sense.

"I go there every year to fish," he said, running his fingers through his hair. "In fact, I'm heading out that way after I spend a week fishing the Cache la Poudre near Fort Collins, Colorado. Which route are you taking? Interstate 90 to Sioux Falls?"

"I'm not sure yet," Ruth said, refusing to give him any more information.

"That'd be an easier route for you," he persisted. "You wouldn't have to drive this rig through the mountains."

"I'll think about it," she said. "I'd planned to make it to Sheridan tonight, but I'm thinking about driving back to Billings and getting this step fixed. It's only twenty-five miles."

"No need to do that. I think I can help you snap it back in place. The same thing's happened to me more than once."

"I appreciate your offer," Ruth said politely.

"The name's Jack Colby," he said as he extended his hand.

Jack Colby. The name didn't ring a bell. Neither did his appearance, except maybe for his blue eyes. There was a familiar mischievous twinkle to them when he smiled.

Despite her reservations, Ruth shook his hand, just because it was there. She noticed that his handshake was firm, not limp like Norm Rogers. "It was nice to talk to you," she said, deliberately not giving her name.

"Well, I admire your spunk, ma'am. Not many women your age would be brave enough to wrestle a rig that big by herself. Especially not someone as tiny as you are."

Ruth didn't know whether to be offended or not. What did he mean by that remark? Did he think she was a foolish, little old lady? Or was he just being honest and speaking his mind?

Jack Colby smiled and Ruth wondered if he was just teasing her.

"Not brave. The motorhome is easy to drive." She turned and reached for her door handle.

"Well, if you get bored while you're waiting for the wind to blow itself out, you can come over to my trailer for a cup of coffee. I've got a whole thermos full. It's the green and white Prowler over there." He pointed to a small trailer attached to an old, beat-up, white Chevy Blazer.

Before Ruth could answer, another gust of wind hit them. Jack Colby turned and leaned into the wind as he walked back to his trailer.

Ruth watched him go and noticed the fishing poles jutting up inside the back of his Blazer. She found herself somewhat relieved to know that he was a fellow camper.

Back inside her motorhome, Ruth settled into the padded dinette booth across from the kitchen counter. She thought about the stranger and wondered why he seemed so familiar.

She didn't recognize his face. She was pretty sure of that. Maybe it was the twinkle in his clear blue eyes, or his easy smile. No, she knew several men with blue eyes and pleasant smiles. It was more than that. It had to do with the irritation she felt when he had called her "lady" or "ma'am." But who had called her that before? She couldn't remember.

And there was something about his reference to fishing that struck a chord of recognition in her mind. How many fishermen did she know, besides her son, Tony?

And then she remembered where she'd seen him before. And if her memory was right, she thought she had a picture of him in her photo album.

She walked back to the bedroom, opened a drawer, and pulled out the photo album, then she sat down on the edge of the bed and opened the book.

She turned the pages, glancing at pictures of Brenda's family at a summer barbecue, of Amy, proudly standing beside her red Mustang before she went off to college. She saw the pictures of Henry and her vacationing with Meg and Scot Rodecker, and laughed at a picture Brenda had taken of her with Norm Rogers when they were all dressed up to go to a college faculty dinner. They looked like a couple of pompous dolts.

And then she found the picture she was searching for. It was among those of her Fourth of July camping trip with Tony and his family. She studied the picture of the uncouth fisherman in his grimy cap and wrinkled clothes, his hair straggly and matted. She noticed the stubble on his un-shaven face. She saw his infectious smile, but the man in the picture had two front teeth missing. Maybe they weren't the same man. But when she saw the twinkle in his bright blue eyes, she was sure of it.

Jack Colby was the shabby, shiftless, be-whiskered fisherman she'd seen fishing from the banks of the Boulder River when she'd camped with Tony and his family at the Big Timber campground on the Fourth of July.

She laughed when she saw what she'd written underneath the picture. "An old reprobate."

Ruth couldn't help but notice the picture of herself, taken that same day. It happened to be on the same page. She was amused when she saw that silly little hat she'd worn, with its floppy brim pulled down to shade her eyes. Her hair was long, and just as straggly as Jack's had been.

How could she have been so quick to judge him that day at the fishing pond when she had looked pretty awful her-self?

She wondered if Jack had recognized her when he'd offered to fix her step, hoping that he hadn't. Probably not. He would have mentioned it.

She couldn't believe it. Jack Colby, now clean shaven and neatly dressed, was the same man who had smiled at her when he passed the fishing pond where she'd been fishing with Ginny. He'd only spoken to her briefly that day, and she couldn't remember their conversation, but she'd never forget one particular comment he'd made. She remembered his exact words vividly.

"That's the cheatin' pond, lady," he'd said.

The crude remark had irritated her then. And, as she conjured up the long-ago incident in her mind, it irritated her now.

Twelve

Despite the continuing wind, Ruth decided to walk over to the public restrooms, to stretch her legs more than anything else. The wind always made her nervous, but with the constant swaying of her motorhome, she found it impossible to concentrate on the romance novel she'd started to read.

She set the book on the table and picked up her purse, making sure she had her keys before she ventured out. Once outside, she reached up and checked to be sure her door was locked. She wasn't taking any chances.

Before she headed toward the small brick building, she walked around the motorhome to see if the dust storm had done any damage. When she got around to the other side, she saw that a fancy, red conversion van had pulled in next to her. An elderly couple walked toward the van. The man held on to the woman's arm, as if to keep his frail wife from blowing away.

Ruth felt them staring at her as she ran her hand across the smooth surface of the motorhome. The Gypsy was covered with a film of gritty dust, but as far as Ruth could determine, the paint hadn't been damaged.

"You driving that big motorhome all by yourself?" the man asked when Ruth looked his way.

"Yes," Ruth said.

The woman looked to be in her late seventies, or early eighties. Her hair was gray and tightly curled, evidence of a recent permanent. Ruth didn't see a single hair out of place and figured the woman must have used half a can of hair spray before she'd ventured out in the wind.

"Oh, my, you shouldn't be traveling by yourself," the lady said in a raspy voice.

"Clara, maybe that's the way she likes to travel. You shouldn't be telling her what to do," the balding, round-bellied man said in a loud voice to his wife. He tilted his head down and looked at Ruth over the rim of his glasses. "Where do you hail from?"

"Billings."

"Did she say Billings?" the woman asked,

cupping a thin, bony hand to her ear. She wore a tailored, pink pants suit, much like the one Ruth wore, except hers was spotless.

"Yes, Clara. Billings."

"Oh, then you're almost to home," the woman said.

Ruth saw the relief in the older woman's expression. "Actually, I'm just starting out," she said.

"We're from Portland, Oregon," the man said with obvious pride. "Where're you headed?"

"To Missouri, if this wind ever lets up." Ruth glanced up at the blowing trees.

"Well, I'll be darned. We're headed that way ourselves," the old man said. "We're gonna tour the Ozarks and see the fall colors again."

"This is our second year," the lady added proudly. "You wouldn't believe how pretty those hills are this time of year with all them trees."

"I guess I'll find out for myself," Ruth said. "I'm joining a caravan of campers out there and according to the brochure, we should see some pretty country."

The woman turned toward her husband. "You don't suppose it could be the same trip we're taking, do you?" she asked.

"I don't know. Are you going to the KOA Kampground in Branson?" the gentleman asked.

"Yes, I am."

"Then, we must be signed up for the same tour," the man said with a broad grin. He ran his hand across his balding head.

"Well, isn't it a small world after all?" the lady commented. The wind gusted around them and she grabbed at her hair with both hands.

Ruth noticed that the woman's thin, bony fingers were stiff and arthritic, her pale blue eyes faded and listless.

The man stepped forward and extended his hand. "My name's Letterman. Bill Letterman, and this is my wife, Clara."

Clara nodded at Ruth.

"I'm Ruth Nichols," Ruth said. She started to offer her hand, but pulled it back when she realized it was filthy from running her fingers across the side of her motorhome. She looked around for something to wipe her hands on. Not finding anything, she dusted her hand off on her light blue slacks, knowing the pants were already dirty. "I guess I'll be seeing you two down the road," she said as she shook the man's hand. "It'll be nice to know someone when I get to Branson."

"Yes," Clara agreed. "Bill and me can watch over you when you're there and make sure you're safe. My goodness, you must be afraid to travel alone. Maybe you can park right next to us."

"Now, Clara, don't be tellin' the nice lady how to run her life," Letterman said.

"Well, somebody's got to watch after us women," Clara said with a tone of defiance.

Ruth wanted to tell Clara that she didn't need watching over, but the wind swelled up around them just then and the roar was deafening. They all ducked their heads down and covered their eyes.

"I sure hope this wind stops soon," Bill Letterman said when the gust was gone. "We've got reservations in Cheyenne tonight and that's a far piece from here. Are you going through Cheyenne?"

"I'm not sure yet," Ruth said. "But I won't make it that far today. Now, you two better get back in your van before you blow away."

"Yes," Letterman agreed. "Nice to meet you, Miss Nichols. We'll see you in Branson, if not before." He turned and opened the door for his wife.

"I sure hope Shoji's still there," the little woman said as she fumbled for the padded hand grip on the inside of the door.

"What's Shoji?" Ruth asked.

"She's talking about Shoji Tabuchi," Bill explained. "He's a Japanese fiddler."

"He's a country music star," Clara said indignantly, correcting her husband.

"A Japanese fiddler playing country music?" Ruth said. "That's hard to imagine."

"Oh, he's good, really good," Bill said. "You've got to see him while you're there. We're hoping that's one of the shows included in the tour package."

"And, what about John Paul Cody out at Waltzing Waters?" Clara said. "They'll make your toes curl."

"Clara! Watch your tongue," Bill said in a teasing voice.

"They?" Ruth said when she realized that Clara had only mentioned one man's name.

"Twins," Clara declared with a flicker of life in her tired eyes. "The most handsome twins I ever did see."

"She's just trying to make me jealous." Bill Letterman winked at Ruth as he helped his wife up into the high van. She held onto the hand grip until she was settled in the seat.

"Don't let her fool you, though. Clara's big heart throb is Andy Williams and when she heard he'd opened his own theater in Branson this year, she got so excited, she was flyin' all over the room. I had to sit on her to calm her down."

Clara grinned. "That's right. Bill and me have been married for sixty-one years and I'd leave him in a minute if Andy would give me the nod," she said just before her husband closed the door.

"See you down the road, Miss Nichols." Letterman waved and walked around to his own side of the van.

Ruth waved back and smiled when she turned away. As she walked across the parking lot, she stooped to pick up a couple of pieces of paper and a plastic cup that had blown in the wind. She carried the items to the trash can and disposed of them, her small contribution to the ecology. Dead leaves and twigs littered the sidewalk and the grass-covered grounds.

Ruth strolled briskly toward the red brick building, her stained polyester slacks clinging to her legs as she walked. She wished she'd worn the Levi's she had bought for the trip. But she was still too self-conscious to wear jeans, like the younger women did.

The wind didn't seem as strong when she returned to her motorhome a few minutes later, her purse straps clutched tightly in her hand. She was restless and anxious to get on the road again, but she wouldn't venture out until she was sure that she wouldn't have to face the strong winds she'd battled earlier.

She glanced over and saw that Jack Colby's green and white travel trailer was still parked in the same spot. It didn't really matter that he was still there, except it told her that it was still not safe to travel. She looked up at the trees and saw that they were still being whipped around by the wind. She would have to wait it out, just like everyone else was doing.

Once she was inside her coach, Ruth locked her door and walked around the kitchen checking each cupboard to see how everything was riding. Satisfied that she had done a good job of packing, she got a map out of the glove compartment and picked up the campground guide from the passenger seat and carried them back to the dinette table.

She grabbed a box of crackers from one of the cupboards, removed an apple from the refrigerator, and slid into the dinette seat to study the map. She wasn't really hungry, but once she started driving again, she didn't want to stop until she was settled in a campground.

She opened the map and spread it out across the table as she bit into the apple. Sheridan, Wyoming was a little over a hundred miles away, and although she could easily go that far, she decided to stop in Hardin to see if she could get the step repaired. If so, maybe she'd go on to Sheridan that afternoon. It all depended on the wind.

She checked the campground directory and saw that there were two campgrounds listed for Hardin, only one for Sheridan. There were also several National Forest Parks included in the Sheridan listing, but they were all forty or fifty miles off the Interstate and Ruth didn't want to stray that far from the main highway on her first day of travel.

She stood up and pulled a spiral notebook out of an overhead cupboard. She sank back in the seat and began making notes of exit numbers and brief directions to the three campgrounds.

For the next thirty minutes, she alternated between pacing the floor and studying her maps. She had to make a decision about the route she would take. She didn't know whether she should follow her original itinerary and swing down through Denver, where she would pick up Interstate 70 to Kansas City, or to stay on Interstate 90 to Sioux Falls, as Jack Colby had suggested. After her scare with the dust devil, she wasn't sure she was up to driving the motorhome through the mountains.

Every once in a while, she glanced out the window above the table to see if the wind had stopped, to see if anyone had left yet. From inside the motorhome, she couldn't see Jack Colby's travel trailer, but she didn't need to. By keeping an eye on the nearby eighteen-wheelers, she would know when it was safe to get on the road again. When they moved out, so would she.

As time dragged on, she heard an engine start up, and when she looked out, she saw it was a passenger car that was leaving. Cars handled better in the wind because they didn't have the long, broad side for the wind to bounce off of.

She peeked out at the second car that left a few minutes later, but after that, she didn't bother checking when she heard the humming of a car motor. She would recognize the sound of the motor of any of the bigger rigs, and she wouldn't leave until they did.

Another twenty minutes passed before she heard the rumble-roar-whine of a big truck engine starting up. She quickly slid out of the dinette seat and walked to her door. The minute she opened it, she could tell by the renewed activity outside that it was time to leave. She stepped outside and tested the air for herself. There was still a strong breeze blowing, but it was nothing like the grinding wind she'd driven through earlier.

She glanced across the parking area, expecting to see Jack Colby's travel trailer.

It was gone. And for some strange reason that she couldn't understand, she felt disappointed that he had already left.

She smiled and shook her head.

So much for Jack Colby's generous offer to help her with the step.

Thirteen

Back inside the motorhome, Ruth locked the door, then flexed her stiff shoulder muscles before she slid into the driver's seat. She fastened her seat belt and slid her prescription sunglasses in place.

She turned the key in the ignition, cocked her head to listen for the purr of her motor. The whining roar of the nearby truck blotted out all other sounds and she couldn't tell if her engine started. She gave up and waited for the big truck beside her to pull out before she started her engine.

The eighteen-wheeler picked up speed slowly as it headed toward the freeway entrance. She eased the motorhome in line behind the truck and was relieved when she was finally on the Interstate again.

The divided highway stretched out ahead of her, curving with the contour of the land.

Tree-dotted hills rose up gently on either side of the road and a few miles down the way, they leveled off and dipped to shallow valleys. Cattle grazed on the slopes and Ruth wondered what kept them from tumbling down the hillside.

She kept the motorhome at a steady pace, five miles an hour below the speed limit. Traffic picked up for awhile as other cars and truckers got back on the road from their various stopping places. Some of them passed her and others held at a steady speed way behind her.

Twenty miles down the road, she saw the sign for Exit 495, the exit for Hardin. She took the off ramp and soon spotted Highway 47, where she knew the campground was located. She drove through the small town, but saw no evidence of an RV repair shop. She turned around and looped back through the town, more comfortable with the narrow, two-way street than she'd been when she'd first left Billings. She decided to get back on Interstate 90 and look for a repair shop ahead.

Shortly after she left Hardin, she crossed the Bighorn River and after that, the highway curved to the south. Fifteen miles down the road she passed the Custer Battlefield. Ruth tried to read the marker as she drove by it, but a truck passed her just then and she couldn't take her eyes off the road long enough to read the sign.

From that point on, Ruth knew, the towns were few and far between. The land itself was equally deserted, with fewer trees and flatter ground. There was still an occasional herd of cattle and the watering holes, the small farm houses way off the road.

After an hour of driving through country that all looked the same, Ruth began to sag in the seat as weariness set it. She pulled off at one of the few small towns and bought a Coke to keep her alert.

Before she got back in the driver's seat, she checked her campground directory and memorized the directions from the Sheridan exit to the KOA Kampground.

She started her engine and a quick glance at her gas gauge told her that she still had plenty of fuel.

By the time she reached the Wyoming border, she wondered if she had the stamina to go the next twenty miles to Sheridan. She crossed the Tongue River and kept on going.

When she reached Sheridan she pulled off Interstate 90 and into the nearest service station. A young attendant came out and offered to pump her gas, even though it was a self-service station. He wore jeans and a maroon shirt with the name Dustin embroidered in white thread just below the station's emblem.

"Shouldn't you be in school?" she asked the boy, who looked to be about twelve or thirteen, the same age as her grandson, Eddie.

The boy grinned. "It's a holiday. They're having a teachers' meeting, so I get in an extra day of work. I'm saving up to buy a car when I turn sixteen."

"That's good."

The boy finished pumping the gas. "I'll get those windows for you," he said. He trotted to the office, grabbed a small step stool and set it down in front of her motorhome. He cleaned half of the wide windshield, dragged the stool over with his foot and began on the other side.

Ruth watched him clean the glass. When Dustin lowered himself from the step stool, he paused long enough to wipe both sets of double headlights before he moved the stool around back and cleaned the rear window.

As Ruth watched the boy, she thought about how hard Eddie had worked all summer to buy his tent, and how proud he was when he finally bought it.

"That's $19.82," he said after checking the pump.

She paid by credit card and while Dustin was in the office doing the paper work, Ruth fished a ten-dollar bill out of her wallet and folded it in half twice. She signed the charge slip and passed the clipboard back to him.

"Thank you. Have a nice day." Dustin gave her the receipt, returned her credit card.

"Thank you." Ruth handed him the folded bill.

Dustin stared at the money, his eyes widening, then he tried to give it back. "We're not allowed to accept tips," he said. "But thanks anyway."

Ruth smiled and thought of her grandson. "Oh, that isn't a tip. That's for washing my windows. Thanks. You did a good job."

She saw the puzzled look on the young boy's face, as if he were trying to figure out her logic. When she saw a smile begin to form on his lips, she turned and walked back to her motorhome.

"Thank you," Dustin called out as Ruth opened the high door on the driver's side and pulled herself up. She eased the Coachman out of the driveway, feeling good that she'd helped the boy. It was the same with her family, she realized. She felt good when she did things for them. It was only when they'd come to expect it of her that she had begun to feel the resentments build.

She followed the distinctive KOA signs along Decker Road, out into the country, grateful that the campground was only a half mile away.

When she finally eased the motorhome to a stop near the office and shut off the engine, she drew in a deep breath and felt her body go limp with relief. She checked her watch. It was just a little after three in the afternoon, but she felt as if she'd been driving for twenty-four hours straight.

She dragged herself out of the seat, picked up her purse and headed for the office. Although the campground wasn't full, she was surprised to see so many recreation vehicles already in camp. They were in neat rows throughout the grass-covered grounds, with several tents scattered around the edges.

The KOA office was like so many others Ruth had seen over the years. The check-in counter was to her right as she walked in the door. To her left were three short rows of back-to-back shelves, stocked with "limited groceries," as her campground directory referred to the mini-stores.

A young mother, with two young children in tow, stood in a middle row, trying to settle an argument about which box of cereal to buy.

The tall, aluminum case in the corner had the word "ICE" written across the front in large blue letters. Along the far wall were three glass-enclosed display units. The first held row after row of canned soda which would sell for exorbitant prices. The second unit held items that needed to be refrigerated: milk, cheese, eggs, lunch meat, hot dogs, margarine, bottles of expensive fruit juices and mineral water, all in limited quantities. The third glass case was full of ice cream bars, small cartons of ice cream, and TV dinners for those fortunate enough to have microwave ovens in their trailers.

There were two identically dressed women behind the counter, one a pretty, young blonde, the other, a middle-aged woman.

The younger woman stood at the cash register, ready to ring up the sale even before the harried woman with the two young children had made her selections.

When the young mother asked if they had any Oreo cookies, the blonde left her post to help find them.

"Hi, do you need a campsite?" asked the middle-aged desk clerk as Ruth stepped up to the counter. At Ruth's nod, the woman automatically reached for the check-in form and picked up a pen. The name tag above her pocket stated that she was Cathy Bender.

"Yes, a pull-through, if you have it," Ruth said.

Cathy pushed the tablet across the counter and asked Ruth to fill in her name, address, and license plate number.

Ruth had forgotten about that part of checking in; she no longer remembered her license plate number. She excused herself and dashed out to the motorhome, repeating the numbers until she got back to the office where she could write them down.

The young mother and her bickering children came out of the office door with their purchases just as Ruth was going back in.

When she finished filling out the form, Ruth pushed it back to the clerk.

"Do you need full hook-ups?" the clerk asked.

"Yes, please."

Mrs. Bender made a small check mark in one of the boxes on the form. "What kind of a vehicle are you driving?" She leaned to the side and looked out the window, as if to see for herself.

"A motorhome," Ruth said. "A Coachman." The clerk had already checked the proper box by the time Ruth finished speaking.

"Are there just two of you?" Ms. Bender asked routinely.

"Just one." Ruth hated the question, but she knew it was one she would be asked at every campground across the country.

The insensitive question brought back memories of the feelings of loneliness she'd experienced soon after Henry died, when she'd had the urge to eat out at one of her favorite restaurants. The question at the restaurant was worded differently but it had the same implications. "A table for one?" the hostess had asked.

For Ruth, the hardest part of eating alone was watching cheerful, nicely dressed couples being seated and then trying to ignore them while they shared a meal and intimate conversation.

It got to the point where she didn't eat out alone anymore. If she wanted something special from one of the restaurants, she'd order it

186

to take out and eat it later in front of her television set.

"Have you got a dog?" Cathy Bender, asked, continuing the routine of the check-in process.

"Not any more," Ruth said, suddenly smiling. She brought her hand up to cover her mouth, hoping the pleasant clerk wouldn't notice her idiotic grin.

Cathy Bender noticed. "Did I say something funny?" she asked.

"No," Ruth laughed. "When you asked if I had a dog, it reminded me of something that happened a long time ago."

Cathy Bender relaxed her officious demeanor and smiled. "Care to share it with me? It's been one of those days and I could use a good laugh."

"Oh, it was just something silly that happened one time when my husband and I were checking into a campground."

"Well?" she said, waiting.

"My husband and I seldom argued, but we'd had a rough day of driving," Ruth explained. "Mechanical problems, miles of road construction, the usual things you face when you're traveling. We tried to cover too many miles that day and we were both irritable by the time we reached the campground."

"Most folks are tired and irritable by the time they get to us," Cathy said with a knowing smile. "That's why we try to keep a happy face."

"Well, Henry and I had a little squabble just before we got to the campground and with my stubborn streak, I refused to go into the office with him," Ruth said. "When Henry came out laughing a few minutes later, he told me what happened." Ruth paused.

"Which was?" Mrs. Bender urged.

"When the desk clerk asked Henry if he had a dog, he was still miffed at me and he told her, 'Just the bitch in the front seat. Does she count?' "

Cathy Bender laughed.

Ruth continued. "The desk clerk was so accustomed to getting a stock yes-or-no answer to the question, she only heard what she expected to hear. She told Henry, 'Well, just keep her on a leash.' "

"That's funny," Mrs. Bender said. "Did your husband explain?"

"No. Henry was so amused at her reply, he just said, 'I'll do that, miss,' and walked away. Henry died three years ago and this is the first time I've driven the motorhome since then.

Either it's not as easy to drive as I remember, or the wind threw me for a loop."

"Well, you've got more guts than I do," the clerk said as she handed Ruth a trash bag and a map of the campground with Ruth's site circled in red. "I know a lot of women are driving those big motorhomes these days, but I'd be scared to death to try it."

Ruth smiled. "It isn't so bad unless you have to drive through a windstorm."

Mrs. Bender laughed. "I couldn't even stand up when that wind hit today so I can imagine what it was like for you. This is your campsite," she said, tracing the red line on the map with the end of her pen. "You're in row three, space fifty-four."

"Thanks." Ruth paid the fee.

"There's a nice little barbecue place called The Chuck Wagon at the south end of the campground," Mrs. Bender said as she handed Ruth a flyer. "They specialize in buffalo meat, if you're interested."

"I think I'll pass," Ruth said as she wrinkled her nose.

"Not my favorite food, either, but I hear it's really good. Have a nice stay."

By the time Ruth left the office, the tension in her shoulder muscles was gone and she was in a better mood. After she got the motorhome into her campsite and hooked up to electricity and water, she decided to try to fix the step again.

Armed with a hammer and crowbar, she sat down on the plastic bag she'd spread out on the hard, rocky gravel. She knew her hair was disheveled, her clothes wrinkled and stained from working on the step at the rest area, but she didn't care. When she was through, she'd take a shower and put on fresh clothes.

She pounded the side of the step with the hammer, but it didn't move even a fraction of an inch. After several attempts and more frustration than she could handle right then, she tossed the hammer to the ground. She picked up the crowbar and shoved it in a crack between the step and the metal bar that held the step in position.

She pushed the crowbar up with all the strength she could muster, grunting with the effort. The step moved ever so slightly, the metal squeaking. She was encouraged and pushed harder. But when she released the pressure, the step fell back to its awkward tilted position.

If she only had more strength, she thought she could slide the step back in place. She glanced around the campground, looking for some strong man to come to her aid.

She was surprised to see Jack Colby's green and white travel trailer parked on the second row over from her. She thought he'd be long gone out of the area by now and headed for Fort Collins.

She was even more surprised when she noticed Jack heading toward his trailer with a pretty young blonde by his side.

Ruth didn't move. She watched them until they went inside his trailer. Jack hadn't mentioned that he was married, but why should he? And what difference did it make? She barely knew the man.

Still, she felt a twinge of jealousy. Not jealousy, she realized. It was envy that she felt. Jack Colby had someone to share his travels with and she didn't. It was as simple as that. It was a normal reaction for someone in her position.

She tried the crowbar again, without success. She glanced over at Jack's trailer just in time to see Jack and the blonde come back out. The young blonde headed toward the tent area and Jack walked straight toward Ruth's motorhome.

Ruth quickly lowered her head, hoping he hadn't seen her and was merely walking up to the office. She tried the crowbar again, putting more strength into her upward thrust. The step moved a little more this time, but she couldn't apply enough pressure to get it over the hump.

"You need some help, lady?" Jack said when he reached Ruth's side.

She stood up, crowbar still in her hand. She wondered if he had recognized her from the Big Timber camping trip two and a half months ago. She doubted it. She was sure she hadn't made much of an impression on him that day by the trout pond. If it hadn't been for her irritation with him for calling her lady, she certainly wouldn't have recognized him.

"No thank you, Mr. Colby."

"It's just Jack, ma'am. Mr. Colby was my father. I'd be glad to help you." He reached for the crowbar.

"I can manage, thank you." Ruth drew the crowbar back away from him.

"Suit yourself, lady." He shrugged his shoulders and turned away.

"It's Ruth, not Lady," Ruth said sarcastically.

Jack whirled around and grinned at her. "I was wondering if you were ever going to get around to telling me your name. I told you mine right off."

"You never asked," she said in a quiet voice. Ruth melted under his easy smile, remembering how he'd had that same mischievous smile the first time she met him at the rest area.

"Ruth. Have you got a last name?"

"It's Ruth Nichols."

"Pleased to meet you, Ruth Nichols." He stuck out his hand and, for the second time that day, they shook hands.

"Nice to meet you again, Jack Colby." Ruth smiled at him.

"Well, Ruth Nichols, I won't insult you by offering my help again. I know you women libbers want to be independent, but sometimes you've got to admit that you need a man around. I'll be here in the campground until early tomorrow morning. You know where I am if you need me."

"I won't need you," she said coldly, offended that he had labeled her a women's libber.

"Man, you got a stubborn streak in you, lady." He turned and walked away.

Ruth regretted her words the minute Jack was gone. She really did need him. At least she needed his strong arms. Why did she have to be so darned stubborn? Why couldn't she have just accepted his help with aplomb?

Well, he wouldn't be back and unless she could find someone else to help her, she might have to eat humble pie.

She whacked the broken step with the crowbar. The step didn't budge, but seemed to defy her with a silent, stillborn malevolence.

Fourteen

The sudden commotion just outside her motorhome brought Ruth right up out of the sofa where she was curled up reading a book. After refusing Jack Colby's help in fixing her step earlier, she'd been too embarrassed to go outside and work on it again. She'd left the tools where they lay and retreated to her motorhome, where she'd been ever since.

The soft upholstery gave way to the weight of her arm as she leaned over and peered out through the sheer white curtain behind the couch. She would pull the heavy drapes after it got dark, but for now, the thin curtains gave her the privacy she wanted while still allowing her to see outside.

She'd taken a shower in her divided bathroom, blow drying her short hair with the aid of a brush so that it fell into place naturally. She was glad now that she'd taken Brenda's advice about getting her hair cut short because it was easier to handle than a tight, new permanent. She wore clean clothes, navy blue, permanently-pressed slacks and a pink, tailored blouse.

A man's loud curse startled her. But when she saw that he was trying to back his travel trailer into the graveled site next to hers, with his rather plump wife guiding him in, she had to laugh.

She and Henry had gone through the same thing back in the good old days when the campgrounds didn't have pull-through sites. They used to get a kick out of watching the weird hand signals the women used to direct the recreation vehicles into place. And, almost as much fun, had been watching the befuddled expressions on the faces of the frustrated husbands who were doing the backing.

Ruth didn't know what she'd do if she had to back the motorhome into a designated camp space. Panic, probably. Or drive on to another campground. She knew it was harder to back a travel trailer because the driver had to worry about two vehicles instead of just one, and he had to remember to turn the steering wheel in the opposite direction from where he wanted to go.

Still, Ruth didn't relish the idea of backing her motorhome into a site, even with her over-sized rearview mirrors to guide her. That's why she always asked for pull-throughs.

She'd been reading her romance novel, when she heard the commotion, and the paperback book was still in her hand. She placed a bookmark between the pages, and closed the book.

Ruth set the book down and turned around to face the window. She rested her arms on the back of the sofa and leaned closer to the window, knowing that the people next door couldn't see her through the curtains.

A big hulk of a man sat in the driver's seat of the beat-up Chevy truck, his head swinging from side to side, as if he were watching a tennis match, as he constantly checked both exterior rearview mirrors.

"I can't see you, dammit!" he yelled through his open window.

Ruth pushed into the back of the sofa, leaning even closer to the window, and giggled. It was no wonder the man couldn't see his chubby wife. She stood near the rear of the twenty-four foot trailer, off to the side. So far off to the side that she had all but disappeared into the row of tall bushes that separated the two sites. She waved her hands frantically, using some mysterious hand signals that nobody would be able to interpret.

"Where are you, Emma?" the driver shouted as he stuck his head out of the window and looked back.

"I'm back here, Roy." Emma waddled out of the bushes, but kept her distance from the trailer, obviously afraid that she'd be run down if she was anywhere near the backing up rig.

"I see you now. Let's try it again." Roy dragged his head back inside and, looking like a bulky wrestler, eased the truck a full car-length forward, pulling the trailer with it.

Roy had a full beard and to Ruth, he looked like the type who would be more comfortable driving a big Harley motorcycle.

Roy stuck his head out the window again and turned to look over his shoulder, apparently to get his bearings and to see where his wife was standing.

As he started to back up, Emma began gesticulating, pecking the air with her finger, pointing toward the trailer. Her other arm shot straight up as she pointed to the sky.

"What in the hell is that supposed to mean?" Roy shouted as he eased the rig backwards.

Ruth giggled self-consciously and quickly covered her mouth, even though she knew the rugged driver couldn't see her. Yes, she remembered those days of backing a trailer onto that narrow strip of concrete or gravel that was known as an RV pad.

"More to your right. More to your right," Emma called out frantically over the roar of the truck's engine. "You're too close to the bushes."

"What's overhead? Am I going to hit a power line or a low tree branch?" Roy stopped the Chevy truck with a jerk and looked back at Emma.

"No. No. You're fine."

"Then why in the hell are you pointing up in the air? Am I supposed to be bird-watching while I'm trying to park this friggin' rig?"

Ruth snickered to herself and felt her stomach jiggle as she tried to keep from laughing out loud.

"I'm just trying to get your attention, Roy," Emma shouted in a petulant tone.

"Well, you got it," he grumbled sarcastically.

As the trailer inched back, Emma brought the thick of her arms down against her sides, keeping her hands up in front of her. She began rolling her hands around in quick circles, as if she were performing simple aerobics for the elderly.

Ruth supposed the quick, circling hand gesture meant for Roy to keep backing because that's what he was doing. From what she could see, the man seemed to be hitting his mark.

Suddenly, Emma stopped flexing her wrists and turned to face the side of the trailer. With her arms stiff, she raised them straight above her head, then brought them down again, repeating the movements over and over again. Ruth decided that if the fat woman were holding bright orange flashlights in each hand, she'd resemble the fellow at the airport who guided incoming planes to the right terminal.

"More to your right. More to your right," Emma cried.

Ruth heard the loud crunch, obviously at the same time Roy did, judging from the way he slammed on the brakes and lurched forward in his seat.

"Damn!" she heard him exclaim.

Ruth pressed her head against the curtained window and strained to see what happened.

"Emma, what'd I hit?" Roy yelled as he stuck his head out the window again. "Emma, where in God's creation are you?"

Ruth saw Emma disappear behind the trailer and reappear a minute later.

Emma waddled up and stood next to the truck's open window, glancing all around. "Don't yell," she said in a hushed voice. "People will hear you."

"What'd I hit?" he insisted, not bothering to lower his voice.

"You didn't do much damage," she said, apparently trying to calm her husband down. "You just bumped that little yellow post."

"What little yellow post?"

"The one where you plug into the electricity." Emma pointed to the back of the trailer.

"Oh, great. That's just great."

Ruth saw the frustration on the man's face and she'd bet anything he was using every bit of willpower he had to keep from screaming out every obscenity he knew.

"It's nothing to worry about, Roy, so settle down. You just bent the post a little bit, that's all. And you scraped off a little bit of the yellow paint. The post is made of wood, so I don't think you did any permanent damage to it."

"And what about the trailer?"

"There's just a little streak of yellow on the back bumper, but we can clean that off."

"Thanks a lot, Emma. You're a big help."

"Well, I can't see both sides of the trailer at once," she whined.

"Then why in the heck don't you stand behind the trailer so you can?"

"Because I'm afraid you'll back into me."

"Right now, I'd like to," he said, shaking his fist at her.

Ruth got the impression that the big man was all talk. She doubted that he would hurt anyone.

"Oh, Roy, don't say that." Emma said with a coy smile that showed her crooked teeth. She gave his fist a playful slap.

He stuck both hands on the steering wheel and shook his head.

Ruth eased back away from the window slightly. The couple and their unwieldy rig were not more than fifteen feet from her motorhome and she didn't want to risk them seeing her silhouette through the thin curtain.

"I'm just trying to be helpful," Emma said

"Then help me," Roy said. "Do something."

Emma turned to face her husband. "Remember what that salesman told you about turning the steering wheel real slow."

"That's what I'm doing, dammit!"

"He said to turn your wheel just a little at a time until you know where you're going," she said. "You'll get the feel of it, Roy."

The full-bearded driver let out a big sigh. "We'll have one more go at it and if it doesn't work this time, Emma, I swear, I'll just drive away and leave you standing there."

Ruth was so engrossed in the misadventures of the couple that she jumped a foot when she heard the loud knock on her door.

Still kneeling on the sofa cushion, faced the wrong way so she could stare out the window, she whirled around and untangled her legs as she stood up.

She couldn't imagine who would be knocking at her door. A camp employee, probably. But why?

She glanced down at the carpet, located the white moccasins she'd kicked off earlier. One of them was at the front end of the couch, and the other had landed upside down at the foot of a recliner chair, across from the sofa.

She quickly gathered up the scattered moccasins, dropped them on the floor beside the couch so she could slip into them before she answered the door.

She looked at the door, wondering who had knocked. It had to be someone from the office. With bad tidings? A message from home? An emergency?

A wave of anxiety coursed through her as she thought of her family back home. She wished now that she'd taken Brenda's advice and had a car phone installed in the motorhome.

Fifteen

Ruth stared at the door, fumbling to get the soft shoes on all the way.

A louder bang on the door, more insistent this time, made her heart skip a beat. She dreaded the thought of bad news and prayed that nothing had happened to any of her family.

Hurrying to get to the door, she half limped, dragging the moccasin across the thick, beige carpet with her toes.

It couldn't be a message from home. Nobody knew where she was. She hadn't even called Brenda yet, as she'd promised to do every day while she was gone. Or had she mentioned that she might stay in Sheridan the first night of her trip? She couldn't remember.

Ruth glanced at her watch. Five-thirty. Brenda would probably be home from work by now. Brenda was to be her contact point for the rest of the family, so if anybody was calling with bad news, it would be Brenda.

As she reached for the door handle, she heard Roy bellow at his fat wife again. Forgetting her momentary worries, Ruth shook her head and grinned.

Her smile hadn't faded away when she opened the door and saw Jack Colby standing there. Her emotions got all tangled up inside. She was stunned to see Jack at her door, glad to see him, in fact, and at the same instant, she went weak with relief that it wasn't a campground employee delivering a message from home.

I have to stop jumping to conclusions, she told herself. If she wanted to worry about her family, she could have done that at home.

"Well, you seem to be in a better mood than you were an hour ago," Jack said, returning her smile.

"Oh, I've been watching those clowns next door trying to back their trailer onto the pad," she said in a hushed voice, even though she knew the frustrated couple were on the other side of the motorhome and couldn't hear her.

"They're all balled up. I laughed all the way over here." He raised his hands, palms up. "Hey, it's free entertainment. What more could you ask for?"

Jack still wore Levi's but it was obvious that he'd showered and shaved before changing into a clean, short-sleeved, dusty-burgundy shirt. The embroidered patch above his left shirt pocket showed a fish jumping out of water.

The green and yellow trademark patch looked instantly familiar to Ruth, and when she thought about it, she recalled seeing the same exact insignia on the glossy cover of a thick catalog on her son's cluttered desk at his home. In fact, if she remembered right, Tony had a shirt just like Jack's, except Tony's was a dusty-blue color.

"It is free entertainment," Ruth agreed, smiling again. "I get a kick out of watching the funny hand signals the wives use to guide their husbands in. And the fellows never seem to understand what the gestures mean. It's as if they're talking two different languages."

"They are," Jack said. His stance was casual as he stood on the grass with his feet apart, the palms of his hands resting on his back at the waistline, his fingers probably tucked into tight back pockets.

"You'd think someone would standardize the hand signs," Ruth commented. "Like the Navy carriers do for guiding airplanes aboard. Can you imagine what would happen to our fleet of planes if the sailors had to depend on someone like that gal next door?"

"It would be disastrous." Jack grinned.

Ruth started to go outside to talk to Jack, then remembered the broken step. "No, I haven't fixed the step yet."

"I didn't mention it." Jack brought his hands around front, held them up, as if to show that he wasn't guilty. "That's your business."

"I'm going to wait until I get to the next big town," Ruth said as she stared down at the awkwardly twisted step. "I'm afraid if I put too much pressure on it, I'll break it."

"A wise decision." Jack's blue eyes twinkled when he glanced down at the step and smiled, as if he knew something she didn't. "Do you always wear your shoes on the wrong feet?" He crossed his arms, nodded toward her moccasins.

Ruth looked down at her shoes. No wonder she'd had so much trouble slipping into them in her hurried effort to answer the door. No wonder they felt so tight. She was immediately embarrassed, knowing that he must think she was a helpless, befuddled, little old lady.

"I guess I put them on backwards," she said sheepishly. She leaned down, quickly pushed the heels of the moccasins off her feet, and switched the shoes around, sliding her feet into them the right way. "That's what happens when someone stops by and I'm not expecting them."

"You got a cellular phone in there?" He nodded toward the motorhome.

"No. Why?"

"I've got one in my Blazer. I could have called and let you know I was coming over," he teased.

"So, what brings you knocking at my door?" she asked casually as she eased down out of the motorhome, careful not to put her weight on the step. No way was she going to invite this man inside.

"I was wondering if you might be wandering up to the office any time soon."

Puzzled, Ruth frowned. "Why do you ask?"

"I'm out of coffee and I thought you could save me a trip if you're going up there anyway." Jack let his arms drop to his sides.

"I have to go up and call my daughter in a little while," Ruth said.

"Good. Would you mind getting me a can of coffee while you're up there? Folger's, if they have it." He fished a five-dollar bill out of his pocket and held it out.

His request irritated her more than she wanted to let on. What did he think she was, the camp errand girl? If he was too darned lazy to walk up to the store himself, why didn't he send that pretty blonde wife of his?

"What'd you do, break a leg?" She said it in a teasing way, but she meant the sarcasm her words conveyed.

"No, I'm real busy right now," he said. "I've got some things I need to get done before it gets dark."

"And you think I'm just sitting here twiddling my thumbs?" She cringed at her own rudeness.

It went against the grain for her to refuse someone who asked for her help, but since Brenda had labelled her a people-pleaser, a co-dependent, Ruth had made an effort to see that people didn't take advantage of her generous nature.

She was trying to change her ways, but she found old habits hard to break.

"If you're too busy, forget it," he said politely. "I just thought you might be going up to the store. I know how women like to browse."

That was a sexist remark, Ruth thought.

Ruth saw the hurt look in Jack's eyes and wondered if she was being too harsh in her attitude toward him. After all, he hadn't asked her to walk up to the office. He had merely asked her to buy him a simple can of coffee.

Besides, she usually took pleasure in helping other people. It was her nature. And maybe Jack's wife wasn't feeling well. She didn't know. She didn't know anything about Jack, except that he was willing to help others, as evidenced by his offer to fix her step on two separate occasions. In that way, they were probably very much alike.

"I'll go on up and call my daughter now," she said after she glanced at her watch. "I'd be happy to get your coffee."

"Where does your daughter live?" Jack asked.

"In Billings."

"Oh, not too far away. Are you on your way to see her?"

Ruth hesitated. "I've just come from there," she said.

"Where do you call home?"

It was another innocuous question, but Ruth still had her guard up because she didn't know how she felt about Jack Colby.

"What is this, the third degree?" she asked without a smile.

Jack stepped back and held up his hands, as if surrendering. "Hey, I didn't mean to pry. Most campers like to brag about their families, as much as they like to talk about their travel adventures."

Ruth couldn't believe she was being so callous to this man she barely knew. He'd done nothing to deserve her rudeness. "You're right. People who camp are always friendly." She took a deep breath and looked into his clear blue eyes. "Forgive me, Jack. It's been a rough day and I guess I'm a little irritable."

"I understand. No explanation needed."

Ruth smiled, finally. "I'll go get your coffee." She snatched the money out of his hand.

"Thanks. I appreciate it." Jack strolled to the front of her motorhome and stood beside her picnic table as he glanced at the couple next door.

Ruth raised her leg high and managed to get inside the motorhome without putting her foot on the step. She retrieved her purse from the plush carpet in front of the passenger seat, checked to be sure she had her keys, then locked the door on the way out.

"I'll be right back, assuming I can get ahold of Brenda," she told Jack. He was watching the couple who were still trying to park their trailer.

"No hurry," Jack said in a hushed voice. "That poor fellow still can't get it right."

Ruth walked up to see for herself. "Do you want me to deliver the coffee to your trailer?"

"No, just leave it on your picnic table. I'll pick it up later."

The office was straight through the campground from where Ruth was parked, with two rows of campers in between, but she went the long way around, walking along the narrow blacktop. She didn't want to cut through the camp and disturb anyone's small slice of privacy.

And as she walked, she began to have doubts about herself. She wondered if she was still allowing other people to manipulate her. Or was she becoming too obsessed by the whole darned thing? One thing she knew for sure. She was happier when she was just being herself, faults and all.

Sixteen

A squirrel scurried across the paved road just ahead of Ruth and scrambled up the trunk of an oak tree, finding refuge in a fork of high branch. Making her way up to the office, Ruth paused in the middle of the road and looked up just as the frisky animal sat up on its haunches, as if daring her to catch him.

"Skirl! Skirl!" squealed a small, towheaded boy who ran across the grass from one of the travel trailers that lined the road. He stopped short of the pavement and pointed to the high tree branch. "Skirl. Skirl," he told Ruth.

Ruth smiled, but before she could talk to him, the excited boy ran back to the travel trailer, apparently to tell his parents of his discovery.

Continuing her leisurely stroll to the office, Ruth nodded at an older couple who were already cooking their evening meal on the barbecue grill that was furnished as part of their campsite. They were camping in a small pop-up trailer.

Ruth said hello to several campers along the way, stopped to chat briefly with others, and at one point, she stepped off the pavement and onto the grass to allow two sleek motorcycles to pass by. The matching motorcycles towed small matching trailers that were slightly bigger than large luggage carriers on wheels.

The two couples on the motorcycles, all wearing glistening helmets, smiled and nodded at Ruth, acknowledging her courtesy.

When Ruth finally rounded the corner, after passing by two more rows of tents and trailers, the office came into view. A long line of recreation vehicles, at least six or seven of them, stretched out on the wider road in front of the office building, as their owners checked in at the office. Ruth remembered that this was the time of day when most travelers pulled off the road in search of a place to camp. She was glad she'd arrived early enough to get a pull-through site.

As she neared the office, the pleasant smell of campfire wood smoke was replaced by the stench of exhaust fumes from the line of vehicles that had been left with their motors running.

Before Ruth entered the office to buy the coffee for Jack, she stopped at one of the two public pay phones on the far side of the building. She dialed Brenda's number and heard the staccato buzzing tone that told her Brenda's line was busy.

She went on into the crowded office and found the coffee Jack wanted on a shelf near the frozen food. When she passed by the freezer case, she fought the urge to buy a chocolate-covered ice cream bar.

Instead, she wandered along the short isles of canned goods and food staples, exchanging pleasant greetings with two other women. Even though she had plenty of food in her motorhome, she was looking for something easy to fix. After her hectic day she didn't feel like cooking.

Nothing appealed to her and after her second time around the short rows of shelves, she gave up and went to stand in line with three weary travelers who were still waiting to check in. The others had already left.

When she dialed Brenda's phone again, ten minutes later, the call rang through. Her large, black purse hung by its straps from her free hand. Sticking out from a side pouch was the paper sack with Jack's coffee and his change.

"Hi, Brenda," Ruth said after her daughter answered.

"Mother. I've been so worried about you. Thank God you called. Are you all right? Where are you?"

"I'm in Sheridan. Why are you worried? I told you I wouldn't call until early evening."

"I know, but the winds were fierce here today and I knew you had to get hit by them, too."

"I did."

"Wasn't it hard to drive the motorhome in the wind?" Brenda asked.

Ruth smiled. "Of course it was hard to drive in the wind, but give me credit for pulling off the road until the worst of it passed."

"Sheridan," Brenda said. "That's about a hundred and thirty miles from here. You didn't get very far."

"I'm lucky I got this far. For every mile I drove forward, the wind blew me back two miles," Ruth laughed, purposely keeping her tone lighthearted. "It's a wonder I didn't end up in my own backyard."

"Isn't it dangerous to drive that big motorhome in the wind?" Brenda asked, the concern still evident in her voice.

Ruth sensed a nervousness in Brenda's voice that couldn't be attributed to her concern over the wind.

"Yes, it's dangerous," she said. "That's why I spent part of the day parked at the rest area with all the other big rigs and passenger cars that pulled off the road."

"So, tell me all about your trip. Have you met any interesting people yet?" Brenda asked in a more cheerful, chatty voice.

"Brenda, it's my nickel so I'll save the details for a letter. Interesting people? Well, a couple of big, burly fellows on motorcycles just drove into the campground as I was walking up to the office to call you," Ruth said, knowing she'd get a rise out of Brenda. "They should liven things up tonight."

"Oh, no, Mother! You mean the campground owners allow them to stay there?"

"I guess so." Ruth tried not to laugh. She turned and watched the last of the travel trailers pull away from the parking lane in front of the office, grateful that she no longer had to breathe in the smelly exhaust. "As long as they pay their camp fee, I guess they're entitled to a campsite, like everyone else."

"Well, you lock yourself in and don't go out after dark," Brenda ordered.

Ruth laughed. "Actually, the fellows looked pretty decent, and so did the women with them. They were riding expensive bikes, like that one Danny's been drooling over. I think Danny said that fancy motorcycles could cost more than my new Cutlass did, so I doubt that they'll be needing to steal from me."

"Mother, don't scare me like that."

"Well, you asked about interesting people," Ruth reminded her. "Brenda, is something bothering you?"

"It's been a bad day. I'm harried. I still work for a living, remember?"

Ruth didn't push the issue. "Well, to put your mind at ease, I did meet an elderly couple at the rest area who are on their way to Branson. They'll be with me on the caravan through the Ozarks and they promised to watch over me."

"Oh, thank God." Brenda's sigh came over the phone line. "So, have you found that special man yet?" she teased. "I know that's why you took a vacation."

"I'd never tell if I had. So, how are things at home?"

Ruth felt a pang of anxiety when Brenda hesitated before answering.

"There's a problem," Brenda said, her voice low, her tone serious.

Ruth could picture her daughter twisting the telephone cord around her finger, as she did when she was upset.

"An emergency?" Ruth held her breath, waited for an answer.

"Not the kind you think."

Ruth wondered if Brenda was avoiding a direct reply. "How do you know what I'm thinking? If there's a problem, I want to know about it."

"Mom, I don't want to talk about it right now."

Ruth felt the butterflies start in her stomach.

"What is it, Brenda?" Ruth demanded.

"Mom, I can't tell you now. I don't want to spoil your vacation."

Ruth felt like she'd been clubbed in the chest. She took a deep breath and nearly strangled on her own fear.

Seventeen

The thoughts in Ruth's mind tumbled over and over, and fear was the thing that always surfaced first.

She forced herself to think more logically. If there'd been a death in the family, heaven forbid, or an accident, or even a serious illness, Brenda wouldn't withhold such information just so her mother could enjoy the rest of her vacation.

Also, Brenda tended to blow unpleasant situations out of proportion and become panicky over things that had simple solutions.

"Brenda, you're ruining my vacation right now. Now, what's bothering you?" she demanded.

"Well, I didn't want to tell you until you got home, but as soon as you get back I desperately need you to babysit.

223

Full time," Brenda added.

"Babysit?" Ruth felt a flood of relief, which was instantly replaced by a feeling of irritation that Brenda was making such a big deal out of something that seemed so trivial. "I don't understand."

"Dolores, my babysitter, called this afternoon and said she couldn't be at the house when the kids got home from school today. She's pregnant, I just found out, and she's developed some complications. The doctor ordered her to bed."

"You didn't leave the kids home alone, did you?" Ruth felt the straps of her heavy purse cut into her arm. She clamped the phone between her shoulder and chin, and quickly slid the straps down.

"No. I had to leave work and go on home. I called Mama Murph to see if she could come over and watch the kids today, just from the time they got home from school at four, until I got home at five-thirty. She wouldn't do it," Brenda grumbled. "I asked her to stay with the kids for a lousy hour and a half and she refused, the old bat."

"Brenda! She's your grandmother."

"She's still an old bat. I wouldn't ask her to do another thing for me if my life depended on it."

"Brenda, settle down."

"I'll probably get fired," Brenda said in a pouty voice.

"You won't get fired, Brenda. You had an emergency situation. Surely your boss will understand."

"What am I going to do, Mother?" Brenda whined. "I'm desperate."

It broke Ruth's heart to hear her daughter in such anguish and she felt a twinge of guilt because she wasn't there in Billings to help her out when she needed her.

On the other hand, she wished Brenda could be more self-confident about her abilities to solve her own problems. Ruth knew from experience that Brenda, once she put her mind to it could accomplish anything she wanted to.

"It isn't the end of the world, Brenda," Ruth said as she shifted weight. "You'll find another babysitter."

"I guess I'll have to until you get

home."

"Don't depend on me to babysit full time," Ruth said firmly as she stared out across the busy campground. She couldn't see her motorhome from there. There were too many camp vehicles, tents, and trees in between. "I'll be able to help you out once in awhile, but not on a permanent basis."

Brenda laughed. "I know, you're on vacation and you don't want to think about the problems at home."

"That's right. I'd better get off the phone now and get back to my life of leisure," she joked. "Give Hank and Lori a hug. Tell them I miss them."

"I will. Don't forget to call me tomorrow afternoon and let me know where you are."

"I won't forget, Brenda. I've got a little red ribbon tied around my finger to remind me."

"Sure you do, Mother. Talk to you tomorrow."

Ruth took the same path back and strolled leisurely along the road, thinking about her family as she nodded and smiled at the campers she passed by.

Maybe she had spoiled Brenda, as Ernestine claimed. And maybe she'd catered to Ernestine's every whim, as Brenda accused. Had she deprived Brenda of her independence by being there when she needed her? Had she done the same to her mother? And where did Ruth draw the fine line between helping those she loved and not helping them so they would be happy, healthy, independent individuals?

Ruth didn't know the answers. Nor did she know the solution to ending the petty resentments that existed between her mother and her daughter. As if it were any business of hers in the first place. If Brenda and Ernestine wanted to pick at each other like bickering children, then let them fight it out between themselves and leave her out of it.

When she walked by the couple in the campsite next to her motorhome, she saw that they had finally maneuvered their travel trailer into place. As the woman poured black charcoal briquettes from a big bag into the barbecue grill, her husky husband sat at his picnic table, a beer in hand. Happily established in their own little parcel of land for the night, they were ready to enjoy life.

They both waved and said hello to Ruth as she passed by. She smiled at them and returned a friendly greeting before walking over to her motorhome. She, too, was ready to put aside her problems and enjoy the evening.

As she passed directly in front of her motorhome, she looked up at the wide, gracefully curved windshield and remembered the warm feeling she'd felt when she looked into her rearview mirror as she pulled out of the service station. She had seen the broad grin of the young boy who was watching her leave, the ten-dollar tip still clutched in his hand.

The reflection of white, billowy clouds drifting across the blue sky filled her entire windshield. Ruth glanced up to the sky and wondered if the gathering clouds would bring much-needed rain to the parched land.

The faint odor of gasoline came to her on a current of air as a cooling breeze stirred through the campground. Ruth noticed the tiny piece of blue paper towel that was caught in the rim of a headlight. She picked it off with her fingernails, then walked along the side of her motorhome to check her gas cap, even though the weak scent of gasoline had blown away with the breeze.

She tested the gas cap with her hand, and caught the faint smell of gas again. The cap seemed to be tight. She squatted down and looked under the motorhome and saw no wet pebbles that would indicate that she had a leak in her gas tank.

With a sense of relief she remembered that her husband had never filled the gas tank to the brim when he got gas just before stopping at a campground. He had explained that gasoline expanded in the heat of day and could leak slowly around the gas cap because of its safety valve. Ruth didn't quite understand such things, but she accepted the fact that the motorhome, at least that side of it, had been sitting in the hot sun for more than two hours.

Satisfied that the boy named Dustin

had over-filled the gas tank in his eagerness to please, she strolled back up to the front of the long coach, looking forward to a quiet evening.

When she walked around to the other side of her motorhome, she was startled to see Jack Colby sitting at her picnic table. He stood up and smiled.

She removed the paper sack from the side pouch of her oversized purse and handed it to him. "Here's your coffee. The change is in the bag."

"Thanks, I appreciate it." Jack set the sack on the table and nodded toward the campsite on the other side of the motorhome. "Well, they finally got parked, but you missed a good show."

"You stayed here and watched them?" she said, fighting back the resentment that began to fester inside. The term male chauvinist pig came to mind.

"Yes. I couldn't tear myself away." Jack leaned against the end of the table, so casual she wanted to hit him.

She clenched her teeth.

"I thought you were too busy to run up to the store," she reminded him.

"I *was* busy," Jack said. "Very busy."

"Sure, real busy. Watching the circus next door." She stiffened and turned away, dug her keys out of her purse.

Jack laughed. "That describes it perfectly."

"Well, if you'll excuse me, I'm very busy myself," she said coldly.

She unlocked the aluminum door, opened it and automatically climbed up the double metal steps into her living room, not bothering to turn and say goodbye.

Jack Colby was like everyone else she knew. He was too self-centered to realize that he'd taken advantage of her generous nature.

She was trying to change her life and she was darned if she was going to be manipulated by anyone, especially by someone she barely knew. From now on, she'd be more careful about who she talked to and if anyone made an unreasonable request for her help, she'd turn away and run like hell.

Eighteen

It wasn't until she was inside her motorhome that Ruth realized what she'd just done. She spun around, dropped her purse onto the counter and stared down. The step wasn't tilting anymore.

Puzzled, she went back outside, testing each step with her weight. Once on the ground, she leaned down and examined the metal unit. The steps were as straight as they'd ever been. Pleasantly surprised, she turned around and smiled at Jack. But he was already walking away.

"Jack, you fixed my step," she called out.

Jack Colby turned around slowly and grinned. "Like I said, I've been busy. Real busy. Try it out," he said as he strolled back over. "I got the step back in place but I don't know if it will go up and down."

Until he came up and positioned himself right beside her, she didn't realize how tall he was. At five foot two, she stood eye level with the mass of his shoulder.

Ruth reached inside and flipped the wall switch near the door that controlled the step. She stared at the step, but it didn't move.

"You've got your door open," Jack said.

"Oh, I forgot." She closed the door and the step slid smoothly up into its slot under the door. She opened the door and the step came back out. "It works. How did you manage to fix it?"

"It's all in the wrists."

"Oh, thank you so much. I could kiss you."

Without thinking, she dashed up and gave him a big hug. His arms settled around her back as he drew her close to him. She buried her head against his chest and lingered there, suddenly needing the comfort of his strong arms. Not because he had fixed her step, but because she didn't know who she was anymore.

She caught a whiff of his aftershave and realized that she was still in the security of his comforting embrace. She felt a flush of heat rise from her neck and creep into her cheeks.

Embarrassed, she backed away. "Sorry about that. I'm so glad to have that step fixed, I just got carried away."

"I'm not complaining."

Ruth saw the teasing curve to his smile, the playful twinkle in his eyes. But there was something else there, too, something deep in his eyes that made her heart rise up in her throat. It wasn't exactly a look of sadness. It was more of a longing for what might have been, as if he wanted to hold someone for longer than just a brief thank you.

Or was the look in his eyes merely a reflection of what was in her own heart?

"How much do I owe you, Jack?" She straightened her shoulders and took on a more impersonal air.

"Don't insult me by asking." He smiled

and there was no trace of melancholy in his expression. "I was just helping a friend in need. I'm sure you'd do the same for me."

"If I could, I would." She tried the step again, then turned to Jack, hands on hips, an accusing look on her face. "That's why you sent me to the store, isn't it? So you could fix the step."

"You're a stubborn lady and too proud to ask for help. How else was I going to get you away from the motorhome long enough to fix it?"

"And here I thought you were an egotistical clod for asking me to do your bidding," she joked.

"Maybe I am."

"Maybe you are. Seriously, Jack, you don't know how much I appreciate your help. How can I ever thank you?"

"Well, for starters, you could have dinner with me tonight." He smiled and cocked his head, waiting for her reply.

Her heart skipped a beat at his invitation, but then she remembered the blonde she'd seen entering his trailer earlier. "What do you think your wife would say about me having dinner with you?"

"Not much, I reckon. We seldom talk to each other since we were divorced twenty-five years ago. If it weren't for our daughter, we'd never speak to each other."

Ruth heard the bitterness in his voice. "I'm sorry. When I saw you with that woman, I just assumed . . ."

"What woman? Oh, the one who borrowed a hammer from me so her husband could pound their tent stakes in? I reckon she wouldn't mind if you and I had dinner together, either, since I don't even know her."

Ruth felt foolish. "I guess I jumped to conclusions."

"Does your mouth taste of foot?"

He smiled and Ruth felt all giddy inside.

She suddenly felt very comfortable around Jack. She liked his openness, his natural self-confidence, and there was something about the innocent look in his clear, blue eyes that told her she could trust him. And yet, her sense of morality dictated that she could not get involved with a man she barely knew. Not that

236

sharing a meal was getting involved, but it was a first step that could lead to other things if she didn't stop the entanglement before it got started.

"I think I'll have to pass on your dinner invitation, Jack. It's nothing personal."

Jack smiled. "I know. Your mother taught you not to go anywhere with strangers."

"Yes, she did."

"Well, I respect your wishes. In fact, I think you're a smart lady. It seems like we've always been friends, but I realize that we've only known each other for a few hours and you don't know anything about me. I could be a monster, for all you know."

"I doubt that."

"I hope you don't think I was trying to move in on your privacy, because I wasn't. It's just no fun to eat alone. I enjoy your company and I thought it would be nice to have someone to talk to during dinner."

"I understand," Ruth said simply, not trusting herself to tell him that she felt the same way about eating alone.

Jack picked up the sack with his can of coffee. "Well, you're going to miss a great meal."

"Really?" She smiled. "You wouldn't be trying to get me to change my mind, would you?"

"No. I wouldn't want to pressure you into doing anything you didn't want to," Jack said seriously.

"I appreciate that."

Jack laughed. "Actually, I don't feel like cooking tonight so I thought I'd wander over to the Chuck Wagon barbecue shack at the far end of the campground and get some roast buffalo."

"Buffalo? Is that your idea of a great meal?" Ruth laughed, too.

"I take it you don't like buffalo meat."

"I've never tried it."

"Then you don't know if you like it or not. They've got other things, too. Chicken, steak, barbecued ribs."

"Don't tempt me."

Ruth didn't know how she felt about Jack, but she was so accustomed to having other people trying to run her life, it was a refreshing change to be around him. He didn't push her. He didn't try to talk her into doing anything she didn't want to do. Maybe that was part of his charm. Maybe that was why she felt drawn to him.

"Thanks for getting the coffee for me." He turned and started to walk away.

"And thanks for fixing my step," she said, sorry to see him go.

"You're welcome," he said over his shoulder.

Confused by her ricocheting emotions when she was around him, Ruth watched Jack walk across the thick grass. She took a deep breath and tossed caution to the wind.

"Jack?"

He stopped and turned around.

"I've changed my mind," she said. "I'd very much like to have dinner with you tonight. I don't like to eat alone, either."

Jack walked back to her, a big grin on his lips. "I'm pleased."

"It'll be fun."

"Do you like wine with your meal? I've got a bottle I've been saving for a special occasion."

"I'm not much of a drinker, but a glass of wine sounds good tonight."

"Why don't we get the food to go and bring it back and eat at my picnic table?" he suggested.

"Sounds good," she said, glad that they would be eating outside. Somehow, that helped to assuage the pangs of guilt she was feeling about sharing a meal with a stranger. Eating at a picnic table seemed less intimate, and therefore, more acceptable than sharing a meal within the cozy confines of Jack's trailer. "I'll need a few minutes to freshen up."

"Do you want me to go on over and get the food?"

"No, I'd like to walk over there with you."

Jack glanced at the gleaming gold watch on his wrist. "Then I'll be back in about fifteen minutes. *Hasta lueqo.*"

"Until later," she said, repeating the phrase in English. It was one of the few Spanish phrases she knew.

Ruth watched him walk away, reminding herself that this was not a date. This was companionship. This was two lonely people sharing a meal. Although, when she thought about it, she doubted that Jack was a lonely man. He seemed too comfortable with himself to be lonely.

Back inside her motorhome, she had second thoughts about what she was doing. What would her family think if they knew she was having dinner with a stranger? Tony wouldn't say anything, even if he didn't approve, and Amy probably wouldn't care, but her mother and Brenda would have an absolute fit.

And then she thought about Meg Rodecker, her wealthy friend who wrote travel articles to keep from getting bored.. Ruth thought about Meg's continual search for something scandalous to write in her Peyton Place novel about Billings.

Ruth laughed when she looked at her own situation through Meg's perspective. Here she was, on her first day of her trip, her first day away from home, and she was already planning to have dinner, and wine, with a man she'd spent no more than five or six minutes with since she met him, a total of maybe ten minutes if she counted the brief encounter at the long-ago fish pond in the campground in Big Timber.

Meg would have a field day with this juicy tidbit of gossip.

And, for the first time in her life, Ruth didn't really care what other people thought. She planned to enjoy every minute she could with the mysterious stranger.

The thought of such an unexpected brief liaison gave her a feeling of delicious wickedness, a warm rosy glow. She could feel the flush of triumph suffuse her cheeks. It was as if she had overcome a major obstacle in her path, had thrown off the shackles that had bound her to convention all of her adult life.

There was no feeling like it, nothing even close to it. She felt tall and strong, young and beautiful, like some enigmatic woman who had emerged from a dark shadow, graceful as a swan, cool and self-assured, only to stand proudly in a luminous pool of light brighter than the brightest sun.

It was a feeling she wanted to capture,

to hold in her heart so that it would carry her through this night and all the days and lonely nights to come.

Nineteen

The smell of woodsmoke hung in the air. Dusk had come early that night because of the low, gathering clouds overhead. Individual sites across the darkening campground were marked by the glowing light from bright camp lanterns or the softer saffron light filtering through the curtains of trailers and motorhomes like spun gold or delicate copper.

Jack had already turned on the lights in his travel trailer, which was still hooked up to his old battered Blazer. The wide awning that extended out from the trailer had provided shade in the late afternoon for the single folding lawn chair and the small TV tray table beneath it. When Ruth had first noticed the chair, she'd pictured Jack sitting in it, staring out at the distant, snow-capped Big Horn mountains. At least that's what she would have done.

A Coleman lantern sat at the far end of Jack's picnic table, spilling its shadowy light across the blue, plastic tablecloth and spreading out to light the grassy area around the table.

"It's going to rain tonight," Jack said as he glanced toward the dark slate sky. He stood up, gathering up a handful of used paper napkins, and the various Styrofoam containers that had once held roast buffalo, barbecued chicken, baked beans, and coleslaw.

"I hope so," Ruth said. "I love the sound of rain pattering on the roof of my motorhome." Holding her empty goblet by the stem, she twirled it around slowly, watching the way the glass sparkled when the lamp light got caught up in the intricate pattern of the cut crystal. "Styrofoam and good crystal. I guess they go together." She laughed and set the goblet down on the table.

Jack smiled. "Wine should always be served in good crystal, except when you're drinking it around a swimming pool or on a sandy beach. Call me eccentric, but I enjoy the finer things in life."

"I do, too, but I don't drag my good china and silverware out except at Thanksgiving and Christmas."

"Well, don't feel bad. Wineglasses, yes, but I use a lot of paper plates in the trailer. When you eat alone, they come in handy."

"I know. I use my share of them and I eat more TV dinners than I care to admit. I don't like to cook just for myself. It seems a waste, I guess.

"How long have you been a widow?" Jack asked.

The question surprised her because she couldn't remember mentioning that she was a widow. Then she saw him looking over at her hand, she glanced down and saw the solitaire diamond of her ring glittering in the lamp glow.

"Three years." Without realizing what she was doing, Ruth began turning her wedding band slowly, then dropped her hands to her lap.

"It was a good marriage, wasn't it?" Jack asked.

"Yes, it was," she said.

"That's all I wanted in life: a good marriage, someone to grow old with. But I guess it wasn't to be." Jack sighed and glanced up at the darkening sky. "We could get a real storm out of this weather front."

As he turned his head to look out at the sky,

the glowing light from the lantern bounced off the gray hairs at his temples and silvered them. The same light caught in his bright blue eyes just long enough for Ruth to see the brief flash of wistfulness before he changed the subject.

The sadness she saw in his eyes tugged at her heart and she wondered if he had any idea that, she too, dreamed of having someone to share her retirement years with.

"I'll settle for a gentle rain," Ruth said.

"So, how'd you like the buffalo meat?"

"It was better than I thought it would be, but I'm glad I ordered the barbecued chicken. It was delicious. Thanks so much."

"*¿Quieres un otro trago de vino?*" he asked.

Ruth laughed. "You lost me there. I don't understand much more than *gracias* and *buenos dias.*"

"Would you like another glass of wine?"

"*Sí, señor,*" she grinned.

"*Eso es para una mujer muy amable,*" he said as he poured the dark red wine into her goblet. "For a nice lady," he repeated.

"*Gracias.*" She picked up the delicate crystal glass and took a sip.

"*De nada.*"

"You're welcome, right?"

247

"Sort of," he said. He held his glass up to the light, then took a drink and sighed. *"Chef d'oeuvre."*

Ruth laughed. "And what does that mean?"

"It's French for masterpiece. As far as I'm concerned, the more expensive imported wines can't touch the quality or taste of Gallo's burgundy."

"Ah, the man speaks both Spanish and French," Ruth teased. She tasted the wine again.

"Oui. Italian and Tagalog, as well. I've always been fascinated by languages and I've been lucky enough to visit some foreign countries where I picked up the lingo."

"Oh, a world traveler."

"Sure. Paid for by the government. I was in the Navy. *"Mabuhay. Ekaw ay ang magandang dalaga."*

"What language is that?"

"Tagalog. I was stationed in the Philippines for three years. It means 'Long may you live, beautiful lady.' "

"Very nice. How long were you in the Navy?"

"Thirty long years. I joined when I was nineteen and retired five years ago, when I was forty-nine. And if you can add in your head, you'll know that on my next birthday, in October, I'll reach the ripe old age of fifty-five."

Ruth would have guessed him to be a few years younger than she was. She did some quick figuring in her head; he was only about six months younger. She laughed. "You're still a young pup," she said. "I've already reached that ripe old age."

Jack gazed at her, as if studying her face. "I don't believe it." His hands flew into action as he used sign language to say something.

"You know sign language, too?"

Jack smiled, "I have a love of languages. Before that, I said that you are too young to be old." He repeated the words again with his hands.

Ruth was amazed at how comfortable he was using sign language, how quick his fingers and hands moved through the gestured words. It was evident that he had spent as much time learning sign language as he had the foreign tongues.

"I'm impressed," she said. "I suppose you also read braille."

"Have you got a book written in braille? I'll show you what I can do." He laughed, then.

"Actually, I can't read braille, but it's on my list of things to learn."

"Thank God you're not perfect. I was beginning to feel like a dummy. After teaching kindergarten for thirty years, I'm afraid I'm not as worldly as you are."

Jack looked at her and smiled.

"I figured you were a teacher."

"Why? Do I look like one?"

"No. You have a quiet, reserved quality."

"In other words, I'm dull."

"Not dull. I've seen some pretty brazen women in my time and it's nice to meet a decent woman for a change." Jack gestured with his hands in sign language and translated at the same time. "You are not dull and you are not dumb. You are a nice lady. Your husband was a very lucky man."

Ruth felt her cheeks flush and was glad that at least part of her face was in shadow. "Thank you, kind sir, but you don't know anything about me."

"Yes, I do. If you taught kindergarten for thirty years, I know that you like children and you must have the patience of Job."

"True."

"I also know that you're stubborn as all get out," Jack continued. "And I know that you

250

gladly do things for other people, but you have trouble accepting help from others." He sipped from his glass and looked at her over the rim of the goblet.

"Right on both counts." Ruth laughed nervously, suddenly uncomfortable under his gaze.

Jack set his glass down and stroked his chin as he stared at her. "You've settled into a lifestyle routine that's as comfortable as your old bedroom slippers and your robe."

Ruth laughed just as she was raising her glass to take a drink and as the goblet tilted, the wine sloshed, but didn't spill. "You've been peeking. I do wear old slippers around the house, and a robe that should have been tossed out years ago. But, they're comfortable."

"I'm sure you went through hell when your husband died, but you're a strong woman. You made the necessary adjustments and went on with your life because that's what you had to do. Now you are satisfied with the status quo of your life and you don't want anyone coming in and making waves. You constantly fight changes in your lifestyle."

How could he know these things? Could he see into her mind? Could he tell what was in her heart and soul? Ruth shifted her weight on the hard bench. Even though she'd already learned that Jack was a keen observer of human nature, it unnerved her to be scrutinized by him, especially because he was hitting every nail on the head.

"What makes you say that I fight changes in my life?"

"You never tried buffalo meat before, did you?" Jack said with a grin. "If you weren't afraid of changes, you might have tried it a long time ago."

The tension faded away as Ruth grinned. "How can I fight logic like that?"

"You can't."

"Old habits are hard to break, but now that I'm retired, I'm making changes in my life," she said, not knowing why she felt the need to defend herself. "I'm doing things I never dreamed I could, like driving across the country in the motorhome by myself."

A jagged, lancing bolt of lightning streaked the dark sky to the south, followed ten seconds later by the distant rumble of thunder.

"Did you see that?" Jack asked.

"Yes, we'll get that rain tonight," she said, grateful for the change of subject. "So, you think I should stay on Interstate 90 to Sioux

Falls, South Dakota, before I head south," she asked, dragging the open atlas toward her.

"It's up to you, but it would be an easier route and if you've never been through South Dakota, you'll see some pretty country."

She looked down at the page that displayed the map of South Dakota. "I think I will go that way," she said. "I've always wanted to see Mount Rushmore and the Badlands and I've allowed plenty of traveling time. I don't have to be in Branson until next Monday, the twenty-eighth."

"You're on a schedule?" he asked. "I assumed you were on vacation."

Ruth grinned. "I am on vacation. I've signed up for a caravan through the Ozarks to see the fall colors. The tour starts on Tuesday, the twenty-ninth, and I want to be there the day before."

Another streak of lightning illuminated the night sky. Jack watched the sky until the thunder rolled through the darkness.

"*Ay de mí,* I may have to skip fishing the Cache la Poudre for the time being," Jack said. "The mountains create their own weather and with a storm brewing, that part of the Rocky Mountains, the Medicine Bows, could get hit hard."

"I hope we don't get the wind again. If we do, I'm staying put."

Two lightning streaks lit the sky almost simultaneously. The thunder that reverberated through the night air seemed closer.

A few drops of rain fell on the picnic table, one of them splashing into Ruth's goblet.

"Here it comes," she said. She quickly folded the atlas and pushed it over to Jack, who was already gathering up the notepad and the unopened bags of chips and cookies.

As Jack carried the things to his trailer and set them down just inside the door, Ruth grabbed her purse from under the table, stuffed her camera and flashlight inside it, and shoved the purse back under the table where it would be protected from the few raindrops that were falling.

While Jack was at the trailer, he flipped on the outside light.

He dashed back to the picnic table, carried the two wineglasses to the small table under the trailer awning, and set them down. "Don't want to dilute the wine," he said.

"No, we wouldn't want to do that," Ruth laughed.

Jack picked up the Coleman lantern carefully and turned the knob that shut off the lamp's fuel supply. The bright glow of the lantern faded slowly. The exterior light was not as bright, but was enough to light the area.

"Do you want to go inside?" Jack suggested. He removed the jug of water and the tablecloth from the wooden table and put them inside his trailer.

"No, I'd better get on home before it starts pouring," Ruth said. She felt uncomfortable with the thought of being in the intimacy of his cozy trailer. She held her palm out and tested for rain. A couple of raindrops fell on the shoulders of her blouse and a few more fell on the table as she stood up.

Jack looked up to the sky. "It's not raining here yet," he said after a minute. "That's blowing in from the south. Do you want to sit under the awning for awhile?"

"Yes, that would be nice. I like to sit out and watch the weather."

"Go ahead and sit down. I'll get another chair."

Ruth picked up her purse, heavier now with the camera and flashlight inside, and set it beside the chair before she sat down. Facing the south, she watched the lightning etch silver lace across the black sky. For just an instant, the whole campground lit up as bright as daylight and without the bright light from the lantern, the storm seemed more ominous.

A loud crack of thunder startled her. The thunder continued to rumble like falling tenpins and she knew the rain wasn't far away. She looked around and saw other campers scrambling around, putting things away and climbing into the security of their recreation vehicles, or ducking into dry tents.

Jack unfolded the lawn chair that he'd dug out of the back of his Blazer and set it down on the other side of the small table. He raised his wineglass to the sky. *"Va a llover mucho. Hace mucho ruidoso."* Then in English, he said, "It's going to be a dilly of a storm."

"Were you out at sea a lot when you were in the Navy?" Ruth asked.

"Quite a bit," he said. "When I was aboard the Nimitz, we were out at sea three or four months at a time. Once we were gone for seven months and had to spend Christmas at sea. That was rough on everybody. But every three or four years we alternated between shore duty and ship duty, so it wasn't so bad."

"I suppose that was hard on your wife, having you gone so much."

"Not really. She knew I was career Navy when we married and she liked that life. For the first three years of our marriage, we were very happy. She wrote me every day I was gone, sent me cookies. You know, the kind of things women do for their men when they're out at sea.

"I know."

"It wasn't until after our daughter, Jennifer, was born that things changed between us. My wife just couldn't cope with the stress of raising our little girl, even though I had shore duty at the time and was home every night to help her. My wife and I were divorced when our daughter was two years old and I got full custody of Jenny."

Ruth heard the sigh and knew it must be painful for Jack to talk about the breakup of his marriage. He hadn't looked at her once while he was talking, but had stared out into the darkness, watching the jagged lightning slash across the sky.

"It must have been hard to raise her by yourself, especially with you gone so much of the time."

"It wasn't easy, but I got a lot of help along the way. Navy families stick together and whenever I had sea duty, I was able to leave Jenny with the wife and children of one of my shipmates. But when I was home, I took care of her. And I think I did a damned fine job of raising her. She's beautiful. She's bright. She's got a wonderful sense of humor. But, you know what it's like to have a daughter."

A flash of lightning lit the sky and Ruth saw the look of pride on Jack's face. "I've got two daughters, and a son," she said. "They're all different, but I'm proud of all of them. How old is your daughter?" she asked.

"Jenny's twenty-seven, and as independent as they come. I think you'd like her, Ruth. She's a teacher."

"She is? What grade does she teach?"

"I don't know. The elementary grades, but she also teaches a special education class for older children."

"So do I, or I did," Ruth said. "I taught the slow learners to read. Where does Jenny live?"

"In Springfield, Missouri."

"That's close to Branson, isn't it?" Ruth asked.

"It's about forty miles north of Branson. I'm heading out that way to see her sometime in the next few weeks, and I've got a business deal I've got to check out in Kansas City while I'm out there. But I'm going to get in as much fishing as I can on my way across country."

"Do you work?" Ruth asked, her curiosity

piqued by the mention of a business deal.

"Not so you'd notice it," Jack said with a grin. "I live a simple life so I don't need much money. Did you know that it costs less to live full time in campgrounds than it does to maintain a home?"

"No, but it wouldn't surprise me."

"My Navy retirement benefits are enough to carry me through life. But, I do need to get a new tow vehicle. My Blazer's about to fall apart."

"Where do you live?"

"Wherever I am." Jack took a drink of wine, set the glass down on the small folding table and leaned back in his chair. "I live full time in my trailer."

"Don't you have a home somewhere?" She heard the soft splattering of raindrops on the overhead awning and looked up.

Jack stood up and went to the edge of the canopy, held his palm out and glanced up at the dark sky. "The rain is on its way," he said, then walked back over to the chair and looked down at Ruth. "I have a little fishing shack near Livingston, but I'm hardly ever there. My ambition in life is to fish every lake, stream, and creek in the country before I die."

Ruth then remembered camping out last

July in Big Timber with Tony and his family. That day, Tony had mentioned the same thing about Jack's ambitions in life. She still found it hard to believe that the unkempt man she'd seen fishing the banks of the Boulder had turned out to be Jack Colby.

"Livingston, Montana?" Ruth asked as she retrieved her purse from the ground and stood up. "I'd better get home before the skies open up."

"Yes, Livingston, Montana. I have to maintain a residency somewhere so I can license my vehicles and pay taxes to Uncle Sam. I wish you didn't have to go. I've enjoyed talking to you."

"It has been fun, hasn't it?" Ruth walked to the edge of the awning and looked out at the picnic table. It was dotted with dark wet circles where a spattering of raindrops had fallen. "Livingston isn't too far from where I live."

"Where's that?"

"Billings."

"Oh, I thought you said your daughter lived in Billings."

"You have a good memory. I think it was way back at the rest area when I mentioned that Brenda lived in Billings."

"It was. When you're in the Navy, you learn to listen to what people are saying."

"Yes, I live in Billings. My daughter and her husband and their two small children live there, too. And so does my dear little old mother," she sighed.

"And you're running away from home," Jack said in a teasing manner.

The rain started to come down, gentle at first, slowly filling in the dry spaces around the damp spots that already stained the picnic table.

Ruth laughed. "I guess I am. And speaking of running, I'd better make a dash for it."

"I don't have an umbrella, but let me get you a plastic bag to hold above your head."

Before Ruth could answer, he ran inside the trailer and came back out with a small plastic trash bag.

"Thanks," she said as she took the bag. "I don't need it for my hair, but I'll wrap my purse in it." She dug her keys out before she slid the oversized shoulder bag inside the bag and folded the end over to secure it.

"Do you want another bag for your hair?" Jack asked.

The sky crackled with lightning and a second later, the night exploded with an ear-splitting boom of thunder.

Ruth jerked and ducked her head instinctively. "That was close," she said. The rain began to fall hard and the picnic table now shimmered in the soft light with a glossy sheen. The smell of wet grass and earth rose up in the heavy air. "I've got to go."

"I'll walk you back to your motorhome."

"You don't need to do that. I'm not that far away, just two rows over." With her keys clutched in her hand and her protected purse held close to her body, she hesitated, prepared to make a run for it.

"I insist." He grabbed her arm. "Come on, let's go. We'll cut straight through."

They made a dash for it and Ruth could feel the soggy grass under her moccasins as they ran between two travel trailers. A dog barked from inside one of the trailers. Someone pulled a curtain aside and peered out, spilling a shaft of light across the wet ground.

The rain came down in sheets and peppered her face, soaked her hair. When they got to the stretch of road in front of her motorhome, she slowed to a walk and caught her breath. The black pavement glimmered in the light of the lamp at the end of her row.

By the time they reached her motorhome,

they were both drenched to the skin. Her dark, soaked hair was straggly and plastered to her head, and so was Jack's. She unlocked her door, opened it and reached inside, flipped a light switch. Her drapes were already closed and only a pale orange light filtered through them.

"Thanks for a wonderful evening," she said.

"You're a very special lady, Ruth. I'm going to miss you." He put an arm around her wet shoulder and hugged her. A brief, intimate hug.

His words hit her as she realized that she'd probably never see Jack Colby again. "I'll miss you, too."

"Maybe we'll see each other down the road someday."

"Maybe so."

Jack leaned over and gave her a quick kiss on her damp cheek. He said something in sign language, but in the rain, didn't bother to translate. He turned away and hightailed it for his own trailer, ducking his head down. Ruth heard the dog bark again as he ran back between the two trailers.

Ruth stood there in the driving rain and watched him until he disappeared from sight. "Let it rain. Let it rain. Let it rain," she said aloud as she paraphrased the song lyrics that ran through her head.

She tipped her head back and let the rain splash against her face, no longer caring that she was soaked. For the first time in her life, she felt totally free, miraculously released from her obligations as daughter, wife, mother, grandmother, and schoolteacher.

She went on inside her motorhome, not caring that she left a trail of small puddles on her carpet from her dripping clothes.

She stood in the living room for a minute, wondering what would have happened if she'd gone inside Jack's trailer to get out of the rain. Her body trembled, not from the cold of being damp, but from the thought of her near romantic encounter with a man she barely knew.

Twenty

Ruth slept later than she had in a long time. When she cocked open one eye and saw the face of the bedside clock, she rolled over as if to avoid the nagging glow of the digital numerals. This was a morning to languish in the warm bed, to savor the breaking dawn in its comfort. A morning to recall the pleasantness of the evening before, to relish each moment of her newfound freedom.

She found herself paraphrasing Robert Frost. "Freedom," he had written, "is working easily in harness." She chuckled to herself as she paraphrased Frost in her mind: "Freedom is dawdling easily in harness." This morning, she vowed, she would dawdle. The road could wait. It would still be out there and she could always make up time if she got behind in her schedule.

What was time, anyway? Something man-made, a constriction. A harness. Well, this was her harness and she could just lie in bed and laze away a few more minutes, an hour, if she felt like it.

She reached over and pushed aside a curtain, looked at the majestic Big Horn mountains, so gray and muscular in the feeble dawn light, their snowcapped peaks like ermine beacons in the soft darkness. It was sweet to lie there and feel the comfort of those ancient mountains, standing like guardians over the city of Sheridan, like stolid sentinels waiting for the sun to kiss their snow-flocked mantles.

She left the curtain open, propped her pillow up, and watched the shadows lighten on the campers, watched in rapt fascination as the rising sun poured gold into the eastern sky and tinged the few long strands of clouds that floated high above like remnants of cotton batting. After the rain, the sky looked scrubbed and clean; it was already beginning to turn a pale blue.

But her gaze drifted and she looked again at the angry red glow of the digital clock. She almost threw one of the pillows at it, but would not allow even such a mild violence to spoil her mood. She burrowed deeper into the bed and wriggled her toes, stretched her legs underneath the covers just to feel the strength in her body, to devour the thrill of being alive on such a beautiful, no-hurry morning.

Later, she arose, without looking at the clock again, almost defiantly ignoring it, and slid her feet into slippers, shawled herself in her robe and went to the bathroom. She took a shower, grateful for the hot water after the first dashing cold spray that made her jump inside her skin. She emerged, sleek as a seal, and toweled herself dry. Leisurely, she dried her short hair and dressed for the road before making up her bed. She took her time smoothing out the wrinkles in the bedspread and fluffing up her pillows.

But, by seven o'clock she was ready to leave the campground.

A decent, civilized hour, she thought. Several rigs had already pulled out, but she wasn't in a race. Let them have the road, let them stare into the rising sun and burn their eyes as they climbed the hills toward their various destinations.

She still felt the glow from the evening before when she'd shared dinner and conversation with Jack Colby. He had planned to head out before dawn that morning. He had almost four hundred miles to go that day to reach Laporte, and he wanted to drive on up and fish the Poudre before dark.

As she unhooked her water and sewer hoses, she thought of her decision to end a lovely evening while it was still perfect. She was glad they'd said their farewells in the rain last night. She couldn't face saying good-bye to him in the reality of the morning light, her face naked without makeup, revealing every wrinkle, every flaw, her hair tangled like a schoolgirl's.

After a final check of her motorhome and campsite, Ruth settled into the driver's seat, fastened her seatbelt, and slipped her driving glasses into place.

She pulled out of the park slowly and drove back to the intersection where she'd gotten gas the night before. When she passed the service station, she automatically checked her gas gauge. The red needle was right on the full mark, not above it, as it sometimes was. Maybe Dustin hadn't over-filled her tank after all.

Ruth leaned toward the dash and flipped the switch on the auxiliary gas tank. Just to check, she thought. The needle slowly rose on the dial until it stopped—a tad above the F. She toggled the switch back so that the engine drew fuel from the main tank.

"Odd," she said to herself, then put the puzzle out of her mind.

Back on the Interstate, she left sleeping Sheridan behind. Off to her right, the early morning sun had finally reached the peaks of the snowcapped Big Horns. She saw a snow fence along the way, a reminder of the long, lonely winter nights to come.

There were just a few clouds to the east, their undersides glowing salmon in the golden light. The closer hills had no trees, just a few clumps of bushes, a dappling of fragrant sagebrush.

The divided highway curved along the contour of the land. She saw mule deer grazing. They lifted their heads as she passed, their enormous ears flickering as they gauged every sound. Scattered antelope, with five or six in a bunch, grazed peacefully on the tawny short grass that mantled the gentle hills; cattle shared the vast open spaces, fat and awkward in contrast to the graceful antelope.

She saw the green highway sign that told her she was sixty-eight miles from Gillette,

Wyoming. She passed Crazy Woman Creek and saw a radiant display of sunlight, streaming to the earth in shimmering shafts through a vagrant cloud that had drifted over the Big Horns. The effect, as the light fanned out, was like being in an enormous chapel, a hushed wildwood church. Sprayed light seemed to come from a hidden, divine source, descending to the earth in vibrant rays.

Later, she noticed that more clouds had ventured from beyond the eastern face of the mountains, billowed up from hidden recesses deep in the Big Horn chain. Soon, the sun was hidden by the billowy white clouds that had dark bottoms, huge thunderheads, explosive with the promise of more rain. She no longer needed her prescription sunglasses, but kept them on anyway.

She drove on tirelessly, her hands firm on the big steering wheel that made driving such a big rig so easy, and saw the rugged gullies breaking up the land. She wondered what it would be like to take a covered wagon across the country, like her ancestors had.

The land was rugged, stark, and, though disfigured, strangely beautiful. Desolate, she thought, like the dark paintings of Max

Ernst. It was like being on a deserted planet, devoid of life. But, there was something compelling about the ravaged hills, with their deep, crooked arroyos and rugged ridges. She had to force herself to keep her eyes on the road.

Ruth settled back in the plush, comfortable seat. The Coachman pulled the hills easily and seemed to flow with the contours of the highway. She found herself experiencing what she had come to call "road rapture," dangerous after eating a full lunch when she grew sleepy, but thrilling when she was alert. It was like being a part of the motorhome, part of the land and sky, vibrant with life and the road stretching out forever and ever, like a magic carpet to enchanted kingdoms, a curving yellow-brick road that lulled the senses, put the driver into a kind of euphoric state that was almost sensual. At such times, Ruth felt she could drive for hours without stopping and never become weary or bored.

"Oh, damn," she said, jolted out of her euphoric state of mind.

A large sign broke the spell: ROAD CONSTRUCTION NEXT 7 MILES.

"Why do they have to work on these roads

during the height of the tourist season?" she asked aloud.

TWO LANE TRAFFIC NEXT 7 MILES, the next sign proclaimed.

Ruth sighed, and slowed her speed to conform to the warning of the next sign she saw.

She became aware of her surroundings once again as she was jounced over the rough road, wheeling through the dust thrown up by giant construction vehicles. A sign said: GIVE 'EM A BREAK with the word "Break" crossed out and BRAKE painted in above it.

She halted when a flagman raised his stop sign paddle and spoke into a walkie-talkie. She glanced at the drivers in the oncoming vehicles as they passed, feeling strangely self-conscious, trapped there while they were running free for the open road.

Finally, the flagman turned his sign until it read SLOW and the line of cars, pickups, campers, motorhomes, and eighteen-wheelers lurched into a crawl over bumpy, gravel-strewn ground.

She saw the Powder River, slate gray beneath the scudding thunderheads that seemed destined to join up and brood a violent storm before the morning was over.

Traffic halted just before the bridge once again, and she saw swarms of deerflies trying to invade her motorhome.

Later, she passed Dead Horse Creek and wondered if the waterway earned its name from horses that had been stung and bitten to death by the clouds of deerflies.

The land changed again, became more hospitable with sagebrush and grass. Prairie, she thought, the Great American Prairie. Beautiful. Once considered a wasteland by government bureaucrats.

As she neared Gillette, the hills became gentler. They seemed to roll and flow in a quiet undulation, invisible, but powerful, somehow muscular. Glancing idly at the dashboard, she looked at the gas gauge and felt instant alarm.

"That's funny," she said.

The needle showed that her main tank was more than half empty. Alarmed, she tapped on the gauge. The needle jiggled, but did not move upward to the F at the top. It was only about a hundred miles from Sheridan to Gillette. She knew she shouldn't have used that much gas in the distance she'd traveled. She shrugged, knowing she still had plenty of gas until she reached Gillette.

But, she felt a tightness in her shoulder muscles. There were clusters of nice homes on both sides of the Interstate and she knew she was coming into the edge of Gillette. When she spotted an off ramp, she turned off and found a gas station. She filled her tank, stretched her legs, bought hot coffee and a sweet roll, then climbed back into the seat and strapped on her seat belt.

"Easy on, easy off," she said, smiling, as she flowed back onto the Interstate.

Beyond Gillette, the road dissected the land, a double ribbon of concrete. Cattle and sheep grazed on both sides of the road. She saw a shepherd's pickup with a camper shell, parked atop a hillock. In other times, she knew, sheepherders lived in lonesome shacks or small trailers with smokestacks. They burned wood for heat and cooking. A lonely life, she thought, and slower than any she could imagine. The sheep looked like a wooly tide that scarcely moved.

Ruth crossed the Belle Fourche River, a reminder that French fur trappers had passed through a hundred and fifty years ago and left a sign of their Gallic presence. The locals pronounced it "Belle Foosh" she knew, from listening to the radio, which she had turned on for company as she left Gillette behind. She glanced at the road signs directing tourists to Moorcroft and Keyhole State Park.

After passing Moorcroft, she noticed that the land changed again. Stands of tall pines bristled on the hillsides, green and stately. Then the landscape became barren for awhile as the road climbed. Yet, when she rounded still another curve, there were the pines again, thicker than before.

She sliced through rolling hills, with woods on both sides of the road, and comely valleys below their slopes. The radio began to crackle with static, and rather than find another station, Ruth twisted the knob and shut it off. Blessed silence filled the cab of the motorhome.

As Ruth neared Sundance, the soil suddenly turned red and she wondered if that was because the earth was filled with iron ore. She passed another snow fence on the left side of the freeway, a ragged stagger of wooden slats bound with wire as a buffer against windblown snow blowing off the hillside and drifting onto the highway. Bluffs towered above the red soil and she was reminded of the color of the earth in New Mexico.

She glanced apprehensively at the sky again. The clouds had darkened the sky, filling it from horizon to horizon with elephantine herds of thunderheads. In the distance, she saw a jagged flash of lightning stab downward. Seconds later, she heard the rumble of thunder.

As she approached Sundance, she began to see cars and semi-trucks, campers and motorhomes coming toward her with their lights on. Beyond, she thought she could see the peculiar haze that a rainstorm created, as if shreds of clouds had been left dangling after dumping their moisture. She was driving straight into bad weather.

"Nice name, Sundance," she said, finishing off the last of her sweet roll, washing it down with a swallow of coffee that had grown cold.

She passed the town without really seeing it, then saw the familiar blue sign announcing a rest area ahead. Her left foot had gone to sleep and knowing that the South Dakota border was just a few miles ahead, she thought it might be time for another stretch, to get her circulation going again.

She shook her left foot, felt the toes tingle as blood invaded the capillaries. Her glance strayed to the gas gauge again as she neared the rest area. She stiffened in her seat as she saw the needle's position.

"That can't be," she said, as jagged lightning laced the sky to the east. She felt the motorhome shudder as a powerful gust of wind struck the side. The steering wheel tried to spin from her grip, but she held on and steadied the vehicle.

Ruth's gaze fixed on the gas gauge once again as peals of thunder shattered the silence inside the motorhome.

The needle quavered at the quarter-full mark and as she watched in fascinated disbelief, fell even lower.

She drove right on by the rest area, knowing that she didn't dare stop until she reached a service station.

Ruth sniffed the air inside the motorhome. There was no smell of gasoline, but she knew now that something was wrong.

Terribly wrong.

Twenty-one

Before Ruth could summon her tangled wits about her and figure out why she'd used over half a tank in only 65 miles, the storm struck with full fury.

Wind lashed at the motorhome, buffeting its flat sides until Ruth had to wrestle the steering wheel to stay on course. Rain spat at the windshield, then drenched it opaque before she could turn on the wipers. She heard the wind howling past the rearview mirrors, squealing in the window cracks. She switched on her lights as the road ahead danced with needles of rain.

She passed cars pulled off to the side of the road as she climbed a steep hill. Then, she heard a sound that startled her, brought her heart leaping into her throat. Hailstones suddenly drummed a steady, ominous tattoo on the motorhome's roof and side panels. The highway turned a snowy white. Her stomach roiled as she felt the rear wheels slide sickeningly on the icy road as she cleared the hill.

The apron on the side of the road was too narrow for her to pull off safely. Dim headlights streamed toward her as huge 18-wheelers shot down the hill, pummeled by a fierce tailwind, while she could feel the Coachman's engine strain against the ram of the gusting headwinds.

Sporadic bolts of lightning etched jagged lines of quicksilver in the black sky. Thunder boomed, rattled the windows, echoed inside the motorhome.

Ruth felt the big rig sway as powerful windgusts hammered it from all sides. The needle on the gas gauge continued to fall at an alarming rate. When it was hovering over the E, she switched to the auxiliary tank. The engine missed a beat, then caught as fresh gasoline flooded through the carburetor.

With relief, she noted that the gauge now read full, and she knew the auxiliary tank held thirty gallons. More than enough to reach Spearfish, the next town, she reasoned.

Ruth turned on the radio again, twisting the knob to bring in a weather report. She found a station on the FM band that was reporting local weather. But, something else in the report perked her attention.

"The storm generated hail to the east, but snow to the south. Interstate highway twenty-five is closed between Buffalo and Casper. Motorists are advised that the storm is moving southward, toward Cheyenne, where another storm is already causing heavy rain and strong winds."

Ruth wondered if Jack had heard the broadcast, or if he was stuck somewhere on I-25. He had said something about visiting his daughter in Springfield. Perhaps he might turn back and head in that direction. She felt a tingle of excitement surge through her veins.

How silly, she thought. Even if he came this way, our chances of meeting up on the road would be slim to none. She tried to shake off the thought, but it lingered on as the storm continued to rage.

The big duals on the rear of the motorhome crunched over the hail in the road. Ruth knew she had to keep going at a steady pace. If she spun her wheels, she

MORE PASSION AND ADVENTURE AWAIT... YOUR TRIP TO A BIG ADVENTUROUS WORLD BEGINS WHEN YOU ACCEPT YOUR FIRST 4 NOVELS ABSOLUTELY *FREE*
(AN $18.00 VALUE)

Accept your Free gift and start to experience more of the passion and adventure you like in a historical romance novel. Each Zebra novel is filled with proud men, spirited women and tempestuous love that you'll remember long after you turn the last page.

Zebra Historical Romances are the finest novels of their kind. They are written by authors who really know how to weave tales of romance and adventure in the historical settings you love. You'll feel like you've actually gone back in time with the thrilling stories that each Zebra novel offers.

GET YOUR FREE GIFT WITH THE START OF YOUR HOME SUBSCRIPTION

Our readers tell us that these books sell out very fast in book stores and often they miss the newest titles. So Zebra has made arrangements for you to receive the four newest novels published each month.

You'll be guaranteed that you'll never miss a title, and home delivery is so convenient. And to show you just how easy it is to get Zebra Historical Romances, we'll send you your first 4 books absolutely FREE! Our gift to you just for trying our home subscription service.

BIG SAVINGS AND FREE HOME DELIVERY

Each month, you'll receive the four newest titles as soon as they are published. You'll probably receive them even before the bookstores do. What's more, you may preview these exciting novels free for 10 days. If you like them as much as we think you will, just pay the low preferred subscriber's price of just $3.75 each. *You'll save $3.00 each month off the publisher's price.* AND, your savings are even greater because there are never any shipping, handling or other hidden charges—FREE Home Delivery. Of course you can return any shipment within 10 days for full credit, no questions asked. There is no minimum number of books you must buy.

GET
FOUR
FREE
BOOKS
(AN $18.00 VALUE)

ZEBRA HOME SUBSCRIPTION
SERVICE, INC.
120 BRIGHTON ROAD
P.O. Box 5214
CLIFTON, NEW JERSEY 07015-5214

could yaw off the road and skid down a slope to disaster. And if she braked too hard, the same thing could happen.

The hailstones seemed larger, seemed to strike with more force. She prayed that none broke her windshield. Cords of ice began to form at the edges of the glass where her wipers didn't reach. She turned on the de-icer as the windows fogged up.

Shivering, Ruth turned on the heater. She tried to settle her senses, senses that were being bombarded on every side by thunder, hail, and screeching winds. She could feel the tenseness in her arms, the stiffness in her shoulders as she fought the wheel against the wind, the icy slick road.

"How far is Spearfish?" she asked aloud, knowing there would be no answer. Every road sign was blurred as she passed it, and even with the defogger on, it was still very difficult to see. Visibility was, she guessed, at a hundred yards, perhaps less when the wind blew the hail hard against the windshield.

She felt like a pilot flying blind. But even a pilot had instruments that could guide a plane through fog, snow, or rain. All she had were her gauges and they were useless for navigation.

She glanced at the gas gauge again, out of habit, expecting to see the needle still on the full mark.

In two miles, she had used up almost a quarter of a tank.

Was it the wind? Her speed? What was wrong? Was her gauge out of whack? A thousand questions clamored in her mind, and a thousand bells sounded a warning. She knew, with a sudden sinking feeling, that there was nothing wrong with her instruments. She was losing gasoline at a rapid rate. But how?

She had never used the auxiliary tank before, but she knew her husband, Henry, had. She had watched him switch over many times, with never a bit of trouble. She knew Glen Amos had filled both gas tanks when he'd checked over the motorhome before she left on her trip.

Was her speed a factor? Perhaps, in struggling against the raging storm, the motorhome burned gasoline at a frightening rate. Was that possible? She felt bewildered, lost, confused.

"Don't panic," she told herself. "Just keep driving for as long as you can."

If she ran out of gas, there was always the CB. She could call for help. She looked at the CB, debated whether to turn it on or not. No, she decided. She didn't really need it yet and she couldn't stand to hear the truckers' constant profanity. Yet, in an emergency, it was a lifeline.

The storm continued to batter Ruth's motorhome as she blindly drove through the hail. She kept an eye on the center line and the line at the edge of the road. She could see just far enough ahead to avoid colliding with a stalled vehicle.

She looked at the speedometer. She was only going 40 miles per hour, at times dropping to 35. It still seemed too fast. Yet, if she went any slower, there was the danger of her tires slipping on the ice when she climbed the hills.

The needle on the gas gauge continued to drop.

A sign loomed up out of the murky assault of hail and rain spattering her windshield. WELCOME TO SOUTH DAKOTA, it read. Ruth breathed a sigh of relief. She knew Spearfish, the closest town was just ten or twelve miles from the state border.

South Dakota. At last. Ruth felt some of the tension drain from her shoulders. But, there was still a squeezing knot in her stomach that she had not noticed before.

She breathed deeply, willing the discomfort away and felt better almost immediately. As if to echo her positive thoughts, the hail stopped. There were still hailstones on the road, but these gradually diminished. The rain slackened a few moments later, and she saw a roadside sign that said: Spearfish, S.D., 10 Miles.

Suddenly, Ruth realized she'd never been in South Dakota before. I must remember to add the shape of South Dakota to my map of the United States, she thought, incongruously. She smiled with satisfaction, then looked at the gas gauge again.

"Oh, no!" she exclaimed.

Unbelievably, incredibly, the needle hovered just above the empty mark.

Ruth's jaw muscles tautened as she pressed her lips together in consternation. She could feel her stomach knot up again. She hammered a fist on the steering wheel as if to punish the motorhome for burning all that gasoline. But, the needle stood on the E and she began to feel the strain of driving. It felt as if only her will could keep the big, lumbering vehicle going. She seemed to be moving at a crawl as cars, trucks, other RVs, passed her relentlessly.

She was afraid to push down on the gas pedal and found herself pushing on the steering wheel, urging the Coachman to gain speed without consuming fuel.

The long hill before the turnoff to Spearfish seemed interminable. Finally, she reached the off ramp and turned the wheel to the right.

"Gas station, gas station," she chanted, but to her chagrin, she saw none close by. Instead, the road curved downward into the town. Surely, she thought, there'll be one within a block or two. She kept looking at the gas gauge. The needle had passed the E mark and was lying there at its bottom point. The needle did not move at all.

She drove block after block down what had to be Spearfish's main street, but there wasn't a gas station in sight. The streets were still wet from the rain, but she saw no signs of hail.

"Unbelievable," she murmured.

To add to her dismay, she entered a construction zone. The street was torn up on both sides, the businesses blocked off with yellow sawhorses, rope, and reflectors. The ground was muddy, and puddles of water stood in some of the excavations. Young men in yellow hard hats, wearing blaze orange vests, waved her through. Finally, two blocks ahead, she saw a Mini-Mart sign on the right-hand side of the boulevard.

The engine coughed. Ruth gripped the steering wheel in panic and pushed the gas pedal to the floor. The engine caught and the motorhome lurched forward. But, the engine began to sputter and she knew she must be driving on fumes.

When she reached the Mini-Mart on the corner, she flipped on her right turn signal. She turned the steering wheel, praying she could get to a pump before she ran out of gas.

The big rig jumped the sloping curb and glided to a stop next to a line of pumps. Ruth shut off the ignition quickly and sat there, taking in deep gulps of air, waited until her hands stopped shaking. She opened the door and stepped down onto the smooth pavement.

As she walked around the front of the

motorhome, she smelled gasoline. She leaned down, saw a stream of fuel shooting downward from her engine. The gasoline made a puddle, then spread rapidly into a volatile, explosive pool.

And, the pool kept getting bigger.

She ran the few feet to the Mini-Mart store, pushing aside a man who had opened the door to exit it.

"There's gasoline pouring out of my gas tank," she yelled.

The three people behind the counter stopped what they were doing and one of them began barking orders as Ruth hurried back out to her motorhome.

As Ruth stood there staring at the puddle of gas, a young girl in the yellow and red Mini-Mart uniform came dashing out of the store carrying a bucket and a small, plastic shovel.

"Step back," said the young store clerk. She began to shovel an absorbent material that looked like kitty litter onto the growing pool of gasoline.

"I don't dare fill my tanks," said Ruth, "but I've got to get that leak fixed. Is there a mechanic close by?"

"I don't really know," said the girl. "Ask

Joe, the manager." She nodded toward the store and continued spreading the absorbent material over the spilled gasoline.

Ruth dashed back inside the convenience store and found the man who had barked the orders. He was coatless, wearing a white shirt and tie, and dark pants.

"Looks like you've got real problems, lady," he said to Ruth.

"Oh, I'm so embarrassed by all this." Ruth put her hands to her flushed cheeks. "I don't suppose you have a mechanic working here."

"No, sorry, miss."

"I don't know what to do," Ruth said, feeling helpless. "Are there any mechanics close by?"

"There's one two blocks away," the manager said as he reached for the phone on a ledge behind the counter. "I'll get him on the phone for you."

The man set the phone on the counter, dialed a number, and spoke briefly to someone on the other end of the line.

"Here," he said, handing the phone to Ruth.

"Hello," she said into the mouthpiece. She looked out through the large pane of glass, but couldn't see if the gas was still spouting from her engine. But, the girl was still out there, hunched over as she fought to keep the gasoline from spreading.

"What's your problem?" asked the mechanic.

Ruth told him.

"I can't get to it until this afternoon. Can you bring your RV up here? I work at the Standard station."

"No, I can't put gasoline in it. It just runs out."

"Well, I can't get to it anyway. I'm real busy."

"But, you've got to help me," she begged. "At least come down and look at it. Maybe you can find the leak and put a clamp on it."

There was a long pause.

"I'll try to run down there, but I can't give you much time. I'm really swamped."

"I would deeply appreciate it," said Ruth. "I'll pay you for your time."

"Be there shortly," said the mechanic, hanging up the phone.

Ruth handed the instrument back to the store manager and sighed with relief that help was on its way.

"What did he say?"

"He's busy, but he's going to come over and see if he can help me out. I'm really sorry about this. I know I'm blocking your pumps and I've made a mess out there."

"No problem."

The girl came back in the store, carrying the empty pail.

"I think it's still leaking," she said.

"I really appreciate you helping me out," Ruth said to both of them. "I'm so sorry."

Ruth turned from the counter, walked outside to her motorhome. She didn't know what to say. The people were so nice, all of them. She felt like a fool.

Ruth leaned down, saw the gas was still leaking, although not as fast. More like a steady drip. She walked to the rear of her motorhome and stood there for a minute, looking up and down the busy street for some sign of the mechanic.

She paced back and forth, walking clear out to the curb to look for the mechanic again, then strolling back to her motorhome in frustration. She hated the stares of other motorists who drove into the other lane, filled their tanks, and left without saying a word to her.

Finally, a pickup, with the legend "Pete's Standard Station" emblazoned on its door, drove into the gas station and pulled up in front of Ruth's RV. A young man got out and strode toward her motorhome. She walked up to him.

"Are you the mechanic I spoke to?" she asked.

He bruskly nodded, sat down, and turned over on his back and slid underneath the Coachman. He brushed away some of the gasoline-soaked absorbent. She squatted too and looked underneath.

The young man reached up with both hands, twisting his body into a different position.

In a moment, he slid back from underneath the motorhme.

"Looks like a busted fuel pump," he said. "I tied a knot in a loose hose."

"Will that stop the leak?"

"For a while. You'll need to have that fuel pump checked out before you drive much farther."

"Can you fix it?"

"Like I told you, I'm swamped. Probably couldn't get to it today." She faced the young man, who appeared to be in his late twenties. He was clean-shaven, thin, with close-cropped brown hair and light blue eyes.

"Oh, dear," said Ruth. "Is there anywhere I can get a fuel pump installed?"

"I'd suggest going to MotorSports. They're a big outfit and they've always got four or five mechanics on hand. They should be able to help you out."

"MotorSports? Where are they?"

The young man gave her directions.

"Do you think I have enough gas in my tank to get there?" Ruth asked.

"You can put a gallon or two in. It should hold for awhile."

"How much do I owe you?"

"Nothing. Wish I could have been more help." He stuck a pair of pliers into his hip pocket, got in his pickup, and drove away.

Afraid to put more gas into her tank, Ruth held her breath and kept her eye on the numbers on the gas pump as she pumped in exactly one gallon. Leaving the pump handle poised in her tank, she squatted down and looked under her motorhome. The smell of spilled gasoline was powerful, but she couldn't detect any new leaks. Still nervous about her situation, she pumped in one more gallon. She placed the pump handle back in its slot, then went inside to pay for her gas.

"Did you get it fixed?" the manager asked as he took her money.

"No, but the fellow recommended another mechanic. I'm sorry I caused such a mess out there. If you've got a broom, I'll sweep it up."

"No, you've got enough problems as it is. We'll take care of it. Good luck."

Ruth was glad to pull out of the driveway and away from the embarrassment she felt. She turned right and several blocks away, she found MotorSports. As she walked toward the office, she saw that there were six mechanic stalls, four of them already filled with cars in various stages of repair.

She stepped into the coolness of a tiny office. Just beyond the counter was an inside door, painted the same beige color as the walls. While she stood at the counter and waited for someone to appear, she glanced around and saw the slatted wooden bench near the front door, the three hard plastic chairs, and a stack of dog-eared magazines, evidence of other customers who had waited for their vehicles to be repaired.

A tall, slender man with a full dark beard stepped through the door behind the counter. He wore a shirt with the company emblem on it. A patch below the emblem had the word DAVE embroidered on it.

Ruth explained her problem.

"Let me grab my tools." Dave went through the back door into the shop area and came back a few minutes later, a heavy tool belt in hand. "Let's go have a look at it," he said, a serious look on his face.

The mechanic took long strides across the parking lot, his heavy boots crunching across the gravel. Ruth had to walk fast to keep up with him.

The bearded man hunkered down, rolled over on his back, and pulled himself under the motorhome, the back of his shirt scraping across the hard gravel. It didn't take him long to make his diagnosis.

He slid out from under the rig, stood up, and dusted his hands off. His expression was still serious.

"You need a new fuel pump," he said.

"Can you put one in?" Ruth asked, her

hopes high.

"Sure can. If we've got it in stock. You wait here. I'll go up to the parts store and see if we've got one."

Ruth tried to remain calm, but the tension mounted after she saw the mechanic disappear inside the parts store. She stood in the hot sun, watching the door for him to come out again.

Finally, she went inside the motorhome, just to get some shade. While she was there, she dug out the packet that contained the extra states for her map of the United States. She sorted through the colorful plastic shapes until she found the one for South Dakota. It was bright yellow and had a strip of magnet on its backside.

After she put the packet back in a kitchen drawer, she carried the small piece of plastic outside and jiggled it into the space allowed for South Dakota on the map, which was still attached to the side of the motorhome. When she was finished, she stood back and admired the map, sad that Henry couldn't be with her.

When she turned around, she saw the tall, lanky mechanic walking her way. His expression never changed and she couldn't tell if his news was good or bad. She said a silent prayer.

He shook his head just before he got to Ruth.

"We don't have that model in stock."

Ruth's heart sank. She knew she couldn't drive on to the next big city. She was stuck for God only knew how long in Spearfish, South Dakota. And now, she began to feel the pressure of getting to Branson on time.

Twenty-two

Ruth ran her hand over the smooth plastic of the outlined map of the States near the door of her broken motorhome and wondered if she would ever add any more states.

"What am I going to do?" she asked the mechanic. "I can't drive any farther in the motorhome the way it is,"

The bearded man finally smiled. "I called a big auto parts shop in Rapid City. They've got the right model. I went ahead and ordered one and they'll deliver it when they make their daily delivery run this afternoon."

"Oh, that's great. Do you have any idea what time they'll deliver it?"

"About 3:30," Dave said. "The driver always gets here at the same time."

"Oh," Ruth said, disappointed that it wouldn't be earlier.

"Once I get the new fuel pump, I can install it in about a half an hour. Get you back on the road by 4:00 or 4:30."

Ruth glanced at her watch and saw that it was 11:30. That meant a long, four-hour wait for the part to arrive. "I'll gladly wait," she said, grateful that the man could help her.

"You're welcome to wait in our shop office, but we've got a nice little city park in town if you'd rather drive over there. It would be better than spending the day sitting around here."

"How far away is the park?"

"Just a few blocks away. There's a city campground next to the park if you want to stay overnight."

Ruth looked at the bottom of her motorhome. "Can I drive it that far?"

"Yeah, I put a clamp on the hose. You won't have any problem." The mechanic gave her directions to the park, pointed her in the right direction, then strolled back to the stall where he was working on a red car with its hood up.

Remembering that she'd seen a Taco Bell

next door to MotorSports when she'd turned into the driveway, she walked over, ordered tacos, beans, and a burrito to go, and carried the white sack back to her motorhome.

She had no trouble finding the city park. She eased the motorhome off the road and parked on the wide shoulder directly in front of it. A blue passenger car with California license plates, and clothes hanging from a pole across the back seat, was parked several car lengths ahead of her. An elderly couple sat at a picnic table near the car, eating lunch.

When the mechanic had mentioned the city park, Ruth had conjured up an image of a square block of land furnished with swings, a slide, and a climbing bar. But this park was huge and shaded throughout with tall, full trees that were just beginning to turn color.

She noticed construction work going on at the far end of the park. From the number of orange graders and other road equipment, and the chunks of cement on the ground and rising up in the air, it looked like a new bridge, or a new road over a bridge.

Ruth opened the window above her sink to let some fresh air in, and stared out at the park where several people were eating at scattered picnic tables. There were plenty of vacant tables, but she felt too self-conscious to carry her white sack of Mexican fast food to one of them where she would have to sit alone.

She retrieved the sack from the passenger seat and picked up the road atlas. She suddenly felt very hungry as she carried it to the dinette booth. She slid into the seat, reached over and wound open the double windows next to the table, and felt a cool breeze on her face. She bit into one of the small tacos and stared out at the parking lot across the street.

As she dug her fork into the container of refried beans, she tried to ignore her worries about the motorhome. But that wasn't the only thing that was bothering her, she realized. She felt out of touch with everyone. So alone. She missed her students, she missed her family, and missed being with Jack Colby. She wondered if Jack had made it through the bad weather before they closed the roads to the south. Had he spent the day fishing near Fort

Collins? Or had he changed his plans and headed toward Springfield to see his daughter? If so, he'd probably be clear across the state by now.

After she finished eating, she opened the atlas to the page that displayed the state of South Dakota and studied the route she was taking across the state.

Rapid City was about forty-five miles up the road and that's where she planned to take a twenty-mile side trip to see Mount Rushmore. And beyond that was the city of Wall, where she wanted to stop and see the Wall Drugstore, which had been advertised on a billboard she'd seen as "The World's Largest Drugstore." She also wanted to take the side road that would lead her through the heart of the Badlands. She knew from brochures she'd picked up along the way that it would be a hauntingly beautiful drive.

She turned the map sideways and traced her finger down a line in the mileage chart. Sioux Falls was 349 miles from Rapid City, a full day's drive. Maybe she shouldn't take the time to make the sidetrips. She had to get to Branson in time for the caravan and she didn't want to risk further delays if she had more car trouble or ran into foul weather.

A quick look at her watch told her that it was not even one o'clock yet. More than two-and-a-half-hours to go, she thought. She got up, checked her bag to make sure her keys were inside, then slid the wide strap over her shoulder. On her way out the door, she grabbed the white sack of trash and after checking to make sure her door was locked, she carried the sack over to a nearby trash can and dropped it in.

Ruth watched as two brawny, young men got up from a table and walked across the street to the matching pickups that bore a power company emblem on their side panels. Part of the construction crew, she decided.

She strolled through the shaded park, stopping to read every word on several historical markers, pausing to watch squirrels scamper from tree to tree, sitting a spell on a bench and watching the birds, taking the time to talk to a couple her age who were just leaving their picnic table and said they were on their way to see Mount Rushmore for the very first time.

In her rambling, she stumbled across a

stream at the back edge of the park. When she saw a man fishing from the banks, she turned away, wishing it had been Jack.

She didn't know how many times she'd looked at her watch during the long afternoon, but when she checked it again, it was only 2:30. One hour and counting, she thought.

She waited for another fifteen minutes and then couldn't wait any longer. As she wound her way back through the small town to MotorSports, she wondered if her new fuel pump would be there on time. Or would it come at all? Maybe they didn't have the right part after all, or maybe the delivery man from Rapid City had forgotten to bring it along on his daily run to Spearfish.

She knew it did no good to worry and she finally forced the negative thoughts out of her mind as she pulled into the large gravel parking lot. She parked in the same space where she'd parked earlier and checked her watch. It was 2:45. With her keys in her hand and her purse straps slung over her shoulder, she strolled over to the stall where the bearded mechanic was still working on the little red sports car.

"I thought I'd come back in case the fuel pump came in early," she explained.

"Nope, it'll be 3:30," Dave said as he looked up from his repair work on the car, "Pete gets here at the same time every day. I can set my clock by it."

"You have a nice city park here," she said to hide her disappointment. "I'm glad you suggested it."

Dave set his screwdriver down someplace inside the maw of the engine compartment and turned to Ruth. "I'm glad you came back early. I'll go ahead and take the old fuel pump off and when Pete gets here, it won't take me long to put the new one in. Don't worry, miss, we'll get you fixed up."

Ruth smiled and felt some of the tension go out of her shoulders. After the mechanic drove her motorhome into an empty stall, Ruth went back to the Taco Bell and got a cup of coffee, sitting down at a small table where she could watch the traffic driving by out front.

Even after her coffee was gone, she forced herself to sit at the table. At 3:15, she finally got up, strolled across the restaurant's blacktop parking lot, and walked to the curb near the side of the parts store.

She stood there for several minutes, watching the cars and trucks come to a stop at the signal on the corner. The noise of the heavy traffic, the squealing of tires, the honking of a horn, set her nerves on edge.

Finally, when the strong exhaust fumes got too much for her, she walked around to the front of the automotive parts store and settled on an old-fashioned slatted wooden bench next to the store entrance.

At 3:25, a red pickup drove up and parked. Ruth watched carefully as the driver got out. But he didn't have a package with him. He just walked into the store empty-handed.

A station wagon pulled in a couple of minutes later. Again, Ruth watched the driver. It was a woman, and when she walked to the back of her wagon and opened the rear door, Ruth got her hopes up. The blonde woman reached into the back of her station wagon, brought out a dirty, oddly-shaped piece of metal, and carried it into the store. Ruth didn't know what the greasy thing was, but she knew it wasn't her new fuel pump.

There was no mistaking the delivery

truck when it finally arrived, two minutes late, according to Ruth's watch. It was a white pickup with "Special Delivery, Rapid City" printed on the side of the door. The uniformed driver carried a clipboard in one hand as he walked to the back and lifted a cardboard package out of the truck bed. The package looked too small to hold a fuel pump, but then, Ruth had no idea how big a fuel pump was.

Ruth stood up. "Is that a fuel pump?" she asked as he walked toward the door.

"Sure is."

Ruth waited outside while the man made his delivery and as he was leaving, she saw the mechanic walking up from the shop.

"It won't take me long," he assured her, "You'll be ready to go in half an hour."

The mechanic was right and Ruth was back on the road shortly after 4:00, after stopping to fill her gas tank at a different gas station. She couldn't face the embarrassment of going back to the MiniMart.

She wanted to get a few miles under her belt before she stopped for the night, but once she got back on the Interstate, the weariness of the day's stress hit her. Her shoulder muscles ached with a need to be rubbed, but she didn't dare take even one hand off the big steering wheel.

The landscape changed after she left Spearfish, and Ruth began to notice the wide swath of dark evergreens that followed the contours of the hills.

The cars and trucks coming toward her in the far lanes all had their sun visors pulled down to shut out the late afternoon sun. Ruth was glad she was headed east. She'd rather face into the sun in the early morning when she was fresh, than to drive into the sun and fight the glare in the afternoon when she was tired.

Her intentions were to drive as far as Rapid City before she started looking for a campground. Rapid City, she knew, was a jumping off place for several tourist attractions, including Mount Rushmore, the Black Hills National Forest, Rushmore Cave, and the Badlands. She wondered if the busy campgrounds in Rapid City would already be full this time of day.

Ruth really didn't care where she stayed that night, and that was one of the things she liked about this gypsy way of life. But if the campgrounds in Rapid City were already full, she knew she'd have to drive on another hour or so in search of someplace to stay. She couldn't face the thought. She began to watch for billboards announcing closer campgrounds.

Ruth wanted nothing more than to find a campground and settle in for the night. She just wanted to be someplace where she could feel at home.

Twenty-three

The rolling hills on both sides of the road were covered with thick forests of dark green pines. She knew from studying her atlas that she was driving through the edge of Black Hills country and wondered if the area had earned its name because of the appearance of the land. The trees were such a dark shade of green, they made the hills look black.

When she saw the sign for Piedmont, she turned off the Interstate and followed the signs to a campground. She checked in at the office and as she drove to her campsite, she looked around at the other recreation vehicles that were scattered among the trees, hoping that by some chance Jack Colby would be there, but knowing that he wouldn't be.

The campground, she saw, was not as

rigidly organized as most of the places she'd camped at over the years, and she liked the arrangement. The main camping area consisted of a huge circular field of grassy lawn, with the designated campsites spaced out all around the rim of the circle. A children's play area, with swings and slides, was at one end of the inside circle of lush grass and at the other end, several picnic tables were clustered together under a common roof to accommodate large groups of people traveling together.

Ruth found her assigned site and was glad to see that there were no other people or rigs around her. She didn't feel like making conversation with strangers.

She stepped out of her motorhome and stretched her tired muscles, massaging them with her hands. She glanced around at her surroundings, establishing in her mind, her territory for the night. She had a nice picnic table, shaded by a tall oak tree that was beginning to show its colors. And she had a magnificent view of the hills that ringed the campground.

She'd noticed the tree-covered mountains as she drove in, but it wasn't until she stood outside her motorhome and really looked at them that she was struck by their awesome beauty. The light from the late afternoon sun skimmed across the hilltops and brightened the sides of the thick, dark pines.

She stared up at the hill just beyond her motorhome and saw that it looked oddly nude compared to the more distant mountains that were lush with greenery. The nearby hillside was covered with boulders and low scrub brush. The only stands of trees were on the very top of the hill.

When she noticed the path up the hill, she had the urge to put on her walking shoes and hike up to the top. It was a challenge, but she wondered if she was up to climbing that far.

When she walked around to the other side of the motorhome to hook up to the water and electricity, she noticed the telephone pole at the edge of the road. She glanced up and saw that there was a street lamp near the top of the pole. She knew that her site would be well-lit that night and that gave her some comfort.

After she completed the chores of hooking up, she went back inside and rummaged through the refrigerator for something easy to fix. The sandwich she made from lunchmeat and cheese looked dull and unappetizing, but she didn't feel like cooking. She fixed a glass of instant iced tea, grabbed a package of potato chips, and sat outside at the picnic table.

When she glanced up at the nearby hill, she saw a young couple start up the uneven dirt path. Ruth watched in fascination as the man seemed to walk straight up the side of the hill. The girl, obviously less sure of herself, picked her way through the brush and rocks that were part of the path, reaching out at times for a healthy bush to help pull herself up. When they had made it three fourths of the way up the hill, the couple stopped and sat on a wide, flat rock. Looking down over the valley that held the campground, the young man pointed to the distant hills. The girl turned to look, and smiled.

Ruth could only imagine the grand view they must have from their high position. Before she was through eating, she watched the young couple make their way down the path. Again, the young man walked down with the ease of a mountain goat, turning every so often to extend a helping hand to his more cautious partner, who, more often than not, was in a squatting position as she descended.

No longer able to resist the challenge of climbing the mountain, Ruth started up the slope- a few minutes later, her pocket bulging with the keys to her motorhome. She wanted her hands free so she could take pictures with the camera hanging around her neck.

She'd changed into her walking shoes, but didn't bother to change from the navy blue slacks and peach-colored blouse she wore.

The first part of the hill was a gentle slope, but halfway up, when the path became steeper, Ruth found herself grasping for the limb of a low bush to give her a handhold, just as the girl had done before.

Before she had gone another two feet up the slope, she was practically crawling on hands and feet, hunched over like an old woman, holding onto sturdy bushes when she could, grabbing a solid rock when there were no bushes to hold on to. She stopped and caught her breath, clutching at a thin stalk of weed to steady herself.

She hoped nobody in the campground was watching her, but she knew that everyone below had a perfect view of her struggle if they chose to look that way.

She glanced up at the path ahead, wondering if she should turn around and go back down to level ground before she got herself into a situation that she would later regret.

The flat rock where the young couple had been sitting was only another six or seven feet up the slope. The path didn't look too bad, certainly no worse than what she'd already climbed. And that's as far as Ruth wanted to go. She wanted to sit on the rock just long enough to look around at the panoramic view and take a few pictures while she was there.

She picked her way up the path, testing each new rock or uneven piece of ground with her foot before she put her full weight on it. She never rose to an upright position during her climb, and in her awkward, bent posture, she saw nothing but dirt and rocks, and sticks and stones, and her small black camera that hung straight down from its straps. She didn't allow herself to glance at her back trail.

By the time she was within easy reach of the big, flat rock, she began to experience the exhilaration of her venture. She placed her foot on a flat section of ground, but when she thrust her body upward to take her final step, the dry dirt beneath the heel of her shoe gave way, causing a mini-avalanche of loose dirt and tiny pebbles to slide down the hill.

If she'd kept her wits about her and leaned forward so that her weight was on the ball of her foot, she wouldn't have had any trouble keeping her balance. But she panicked and grasped the closest thing at hand, a thin stalk of a withered bush. The dry, brittle branch broke off in her hand. She lurched back, fighting to keep her balance.

She teetered back and forth, horrified by the feeling that she was falling backwards. She threw herself forward and frantically grabbed for another bush. This time the bush supported her weight without breaking or pulling out of the ground.

Ruth held on for dear life, afraid to move.

Up so high, she was in a world of silence. No voices drifted up from the campground. The only sound she heard was the rapid pounding of her heart pulsating in her ears. She struggled to calm herself.

Finally, she got up the nerve to turn her head slowly. The flat rock was to her left, still within easy reach. She studied it for a minute and when she saw a place where she could get a good handhold on it, she let go of the green bush with one hand and reached over to the rock.

When she had a good grip on the solid rock, she released her hold on the bush entirely and grabbed the rock. Taking short, shuffling steps, she pulled herself over to its ledge and eased herself down until she was sitting on the edge. Carefully moving her hands around, she slid over the rough surface until she was sitting in the middle of the flat rock.

When she finally looked down, she was petrified. There was nothing there except thin air and the valley way down below her.

Her breath caught in her throat as she was suddenly overcome by the sensation that she was going to tumble down hill. There was nothing to hold her back. She gripped the rock so tight, she thought her fingers would turn numb.

She wished she was still down on the ground where it was safe. If she had realized how steep the hill was, she never would have climbed it.

She was afraid to look down again. Afraid to close her eyes for fear of losing her balance. She wanted to cry. She wanted to be back in the safe surroundings of her motorhome.

Twenty-four

Ruth looked straight out at the Black Hills around her, awestruck by their shadowy beauty. She was surprised to see a portion of the sun still wedged in the V between two rugged hills. When she'd looked to the west from the campground before she'd climbed up the steep path, the sun had already disappeared behind the tree-flocked mountains.

Although it was not as frightening to look straight ahead as it was to stare down at the small valley way below her, Ruth couldn't really enjoy the magnificent view. She was too numb with fear.

After sitting rigidly for a minute, she let go of the rock with her right hand and looked down at her camera as she pressed it against her chest and slid the lens open, one-handed. She slowly brought the camera up to her eye, aimed it at the distant hills, and clicked off a shot.

She listened as the camera went through the grinding hum of its automatic winding cycle, then turned slightly and pressed the button again. She felt dizzy when she lowered her head until the campground appeared in the viewfinder. She took another shot and then let the camera fall back against her chest.

She knew she had to get down off the steep hillside right away, before she fainted from sheer panic. The sun would soon disappear completely and she was afraid that darkness would come quickly.

She eased back over to the edge of the rock and looked down at the steep, rugged path. She had a sick feeling in the pit of her stomach. How could she get down? Crawl down backwards like a baby, holding onto the bushes again? Slide down on her bottom, hoping that she wouldn't get going too fast?

She took a deep breath and tried to quiet her pounding heart. She tried to think logically. She had gotten herself into this precarious predicament and now she knew she had to get herself out of it. There was nobody around to help her.

"Jack Colby, where are you now that I need you?" she said aloud. But she was glad Jack wasn't there to see her.

She turned to glance up the hill and felt like her body was wobbling back and forth, as if she were going to fall out into space. She clutched the rock with both hands, steadying herself.

The path up to the tall, slender trees at the top of the hill didn't seem as treacherous as the trail that led back to the bottom. Knowing that she'd have to look down if she took the lower path, she made her decision. Uphill, that's the only way she could go to get down off the mountain.

She didn't know if she'd get herself into worse trouble by going uphill, but at least there were slender trees and she'd have something solid to hold on to once she got there. If she was lucky, she could find an easier way to get back down. And if everything else failed, she'd scream her lungs out, hoping that someone down below would hear her.

She braced herself and tried to put the

paralyzing fear out of her mind. She scooted off the flat rock and slowly made her way another two feet up the trail, not daring to stand up, clutching the firmly planted bushes along the way as if her very life depended on it.

When she saw that the last few feet weren't as steep, she dropped to her knees, prayed, and crawled up like a baby, scrambling as fast as she could go. Sharp rocks dug into her knees, sending shoots of pain to her brain. But she didn't care. She just wanted to reach a safe haven.

When the ground leveled out at the top, she crawled to a nearby tree, not standing up until she could actually touch its bark. She wrapped her arms around the slender trunk, pulling herself up, and finally got up the nerve to look down at the valley below. The people moving about in the campground looked like little dolls and the motorhomes, travel trailers, and tents looked like toys.

Hanging onto the tree with both arms, she looked out at the panoramic view. The sight of the distant mountains was breathtaking and while standing at the tree for security, she took several more pictures.

Still panicky about getting back down before it turned dark, she made her way through the trees on the level ridge, ducking the low branches. A buzzard circled overhead, drifting silently on a down current of air. The sound of her shoes crunching through the carpet of brittle leaves seemed too loud, unreal. She longed more than anything else to hear human voices.

As she came to a clearing at the edge of the stand of trees, she was startled by what she saw. Stretched out ahead of her was a gentle, grass-covered slope that led down to the office and the far edge of the campground, just opposite from where her motorhome was parked. She noticed the path of trampled grass leading down the hill, evidence that there were other adventurous souls who had climbed up to the top.

She strolled easily down the gentle slope, standing upright as she followed the path of trampled grass. It wasn't until she was safe at the bottom that she began to tremble. Her knees going weak with relief.

She stood there for several minutes, taking deep breaths to regain her composure. She brushed at the dirt on her dark pants, but when she looked down at them, she knew they'd have to go into her laundry bag.

It seemed odd to stand on level ground again and she felt suddenly shorter than she was. It was as if she'd been aboard a big ship and still had her sea legs when she stepped ashore.

Before returning to her motorhome at the far end of the campground, she strolled along the circular road and headed toward the pay phone near the office. She noticed that the young couple who had climbed the steep hill earlier were walking toward her.

"Hi," she said with a nod of her head as they got close.

"I agree with you," said the young woman in the red blouse. She smiled and gave Ruth a knowing look.

Ruth frowned. "Agree with me about what?"

"That hill is a lot steeper than it looks," the girl said sheepishly. "I was scared out of my mind when I was up there."

"You watched me?" Ruth asked.

"Watched and sympathized." The girl giggled self-consciously.

The young man, who had a muscular

build beneath his green T-shirt, rolled his eyes and shook his head, as if he thought they were both crazy.

Ruth ignored him. "Well, if you want to try it again, there's an easy path clear up to the top, just around the curve in the road back there." She pointed toward the grassy slope.

"No thanks," said the pretty girl. "We're on our honeymoon and although I'm on cloud nine, I plan to keep both feet on solid ground." She looked up coyly at her new husband and looped her arm around his.

"I can't say as I blame you. Congratulations to both of you."

After they were gone, Ruth walked on to the pay phone. She didn't need her calling card to place a call because she'd committed the number to memory, but she wished she had her purse with her. Her mouth tasted of dry cotton after the strenuous climb up the hill and she wanted to buy a Coke out of the machine.

She dialed Brenda's number and the call went right through on the first try.

"Mother, I've been worried about you," Brenda said after they exchanged greetings.

"It's almost seven o'clock."

"You shouldn't worry. It's not always convenient for me to get to a telephone when I'm on the road." The truth was that she'd forgotten all about calling Brenda until she'd seen the pay phone after she got down off the hill. But, she didn't tell Brenda that.

"Well, we saw the freak snowstorms they had near Denver on the evening news and I was worried sick that you got caught in them. I could just see you stranded in your motorhome someplace, freezing to death, or worse yet, being in an accident because of the slippery roads."

Ruth laughed. "You've got a vivid imagination. I didn't go that way."

"You didn't? Where are you?"

"In South Dakota. In a little town called Piedmont. I did get into a brief hailstorm this morning, but it blew over."

"Well, I'm glad to know you're safe."

"So am I," Ruth said with a big sigh. She was relieved to have some sense of normalcy back in her life.

"What does that mean?"

Ruth heard the note of concern in Brenda's voice. "Nothing. I just got back from an exhilarating hike up a mountainside and it's good to be back on level ground, that's all."

"In other words, you were scared to death," Brenda teased.

"You know me and my fear of heights. I had a few anxious moments up there, but the view was worth it." She stared out at the campground and saw the newlyweds sitting at a picnic table near a small tent. "So how are things at home?"

"Fine, I guess. About the same."

"Did you find a babysitter?"

"Not yet, but I stayed home from work today, so I didn't need one."

"Surely you could have found someone to watch the kids," Ruth said.

"It wasn't that. I didn't feel good this morning. Probably due to the stress of not having a sitter I can depend on."

Ruth knew Brenda was trying to make her feel guilty, but she was determined she wasn't going to be manipulated into watching over Hank and Lori on a full time basis when she returned to Billings.

"Brenda, have some faith. You'll find someone."

"I know. So, how's your vacation going?"

"Great. I had to have a new fuel pump put in today, but other than that, the Gypsy's running fine."

"Where are you headed next?"

"Straight across South Dakota, but I may take a side trip to Mount Rushmore. Depends on my mood when I get there."

"Well, just don't go climbing up Mount Rushmore to get a better look at the presidents."

"Think of the pictures I could get from up there."

"Yeah, like a closeup of Lincoln's beard or Washington's nostrils."

"On that gross note, I'll say good-bye. Are you feeling all right now?"

"Yeah, I'm fine. It was probably just a touch of the flu."

"Take care of yourself and give my love to everybody."

"Same to you and don't forget to call tomorrow evening."

After Ruth hung up, she dug her keys out of her pocket and walked in a straight line to her motorhome, cutting across the grass instead of following the road that circled the camping area. It was still light out, but the bottoms of the scattered clouds were already beginning to take on the salmon coloring of sunset.

Back inside the Gypsy, she fixed a glass of ice water and took a long slow drink to quench her thirst, then added more water to the glass and carried it out to the picnic table so she could sit and watch the sunset.

She saw that several more campers had come in since she left to climb the mountain, but none of them were camped next to her. She was grateful for the privacy. For some reason she couldn't explain, she felt self-conscious sitting alone at her table. The closest rig was a shiny new fifth-wheeler which was parked several spaces away, on the other side of her motorhome.

The puffs of rosy-bottomed clouds drifted across the sky. They held no threat of rain.

Ruth found herself thinking about Jack Colby again, wondering where he was, wishing he were with her to share the sunset, as they'd shared the rain the night before.

When she heard the hum of a motor, she looked out at the circular road, hoping for just an instant that it would be Jack. Instead, she saw a small white car driving her way. The car pulled into the space next to her and came to a stop on the grass several feet away from a picnic table. A tall, slender, gray-haired woman about her age got out of the car, walked around the campsite, looked around, then got back in the car and pulled forward so the back end of her car was almost even with the edge of the table.

Ruth expected to see the woman's husband drive up within minutes in a fancy motorhome. She figured the man had probably stopped to get gas and sent his wife on ahead to secure a campsite. So much for her privacy, Ruth thought.

She watched idly as the woman opened her trunk and began setting things on the table. A flat, green Coleman stove, a Coleman lantern, a white and blue cooler, a big flashlight, a clear plastic box that looked like it contained cans of food, and a similar box that appeared to hold dishes and various sized jars and plastic containers. Ruth realized that these were not items the woman would carry in her car if she had a husband who was following in a motorhome.

No, Ruth thought, this middle-aged woman was traveling alone. A kindred spirit.

The lady opened the lid on the cooking stove. She glanced over at Ruth, nodding a greeting. "Hi. How are you?" she called out.

Curious about the woman, Ruth got up and strolled across the grass. "What do you do, sleep in your car?" she asked.

"Yes. My back seat folds down into a bed. As tall as I am, it's a little cramped, but I don't mind."

"Not a bad way to travel," Ruth said, thinking how much simpler it would be to drive across the country in a car.

"I love living in my car when I'm on vacation. I carry everything I need with me: my food, two coolers, and a cook stove. I always stay at campgrounds where I've got a hot shower and bathrooms, and since I don't need electricity or water, it's a lot cheaper than a site with hookups. My family thinks I'm crazy, but it's a great life."

Ruth noticed that the woman was very well organized, with all of the food and dishes and utensils neatly arranged in the two clear plastic tubs. "And you can go anywhere in a car," she said. "That's the problem with the motorhome. There are some places I just can't go. And I always have to find a big parking lot at a store or a restaurant, even if it's a fast-food place, or I can't stop."

"I know," the woman said with a smile. "That's why I prefer a car." She dug a saucepan and a small bottle of propane out of the cardboard box. She set the pan on the table and screwed the bottle into the tip of a metal arm of the stove.

Ruth watched in fascination. "Where are you from?" she asked.

"Tulsa, Oklahoma. My name is Louise Stewart."

"I'm Ruth Nichols from Billings, Montana. Where are you headed?"

"To Wyoming. I'm going to backpack through the Rockies for four days."

"By yourself?"

Louise laughed. "Heavens no. I wouldn't try it alone." She withdrew a small container from one of the ice chests, opened it, and spooned what looked to be beef stew into the saucepan. She looked up at Ruth. "I prepare enough food at home for the first few days on the road. It's easier that way. No, I'm not going alone. I'm meeting some other backpackers from the Sierra Club. We use the buddy system. We never go hiking into the wilderness unless there are at least two of us going, but there are usually six to ten people in our group."

"You mean you carry a backpack?"

"A heavy backpack," Louise said as she looked over at Ruth. "We park our cars and carry all the supplies we'll need for several days — food, cooking utensils, some water and a water purifying kit. By the time you add a sleeping bag and a small tent, the load gets pretty heavy."

"That sounds like fun, but I don't think I could do it," Ruth said. "I had trouble going up that little slope over there." She pointed to the hillside.

The tall woman laughed. "I think I'd have trouble with that myself. It's straight up and down. Well, not really, but there's no place to zigzag across the terrain, like we do up in the mountains. Since I've been hiking with the Sierra Club, I've learned to take the path of least resistance."

"How long have you been backpacking?" Ruth asked.

"For five years. My husband left me when our three children were little," she said as she chopped up some fresh celery and dropped it into the stew. "So I spent most of my life working full time and raising the kids by myself. When they were all grown and out on their own, I just sort of rattled around the house, not knowing what I wanted to do."

"I know what you mean," Ruth said. "My three kids are grown and I just retired from teaching school, so I'm trying to adjust. That's why I decided to go off by myself."

Louise sighed. "Not much fun traveling by yourself, is it?" She picked up a box of wooden matches, took one out and struck it on the side of the box. She leaned over the Coleman stove and held the lit match over a burner. When a circle of blue flames appeared around the burner plate, she blew out the match.

"Not really," Ruth said. "But I enjoy meeting new people along the way." She felt a cool breeze against her face and looked up at the darkening sky.

Louise set the saucepan on the burner and covered it with a lid. "Sometimes I think I'd like to have a traveling companion, just to have someone to talk to, but traveling alone has definite advantages." She looked across the table and smiled. "I can come and go as I want to, and I don't have to defer to anyone else."

"That's right." Ruth laughed. "So, how'd you get started in backpacking?"

Louise lit the Coleman lantern and in the bright glow of light, the evening seemed suddenly darker than it actually was. "Five years ago I felt so listless and useless, I finally went to my doctor to see why I was always so tired."

"He must have had a miracle cure," Ruth said, amazed that this woman, who was about her own age, had so much vitality.

A bright glow spread over the area. Ruth looked back over her shoulder and saw that the street lamp above her motorhome had just come on.

Louise glanced up at the light, too. "Oh, good, we've got a security lamp," she said. "Actually, the doctor couldn't help me. There was nothing wrong with me except sheer boredom. But while I was in the waiting room, I picked up a magazine and read an article about the Sierra Club. I wrote down the address, sent for their information, and within two weeks, I was a member. I've been hiking and backpacking with them two or three times a year ever since."

"It sounds like a good life."

"And it's not very expensive. I have to travel on a budget, but my car gets thirty-four miles to the gallon, so that helps."

"I only get eight miles to the gallon! The motorhome is a gas hog."

"Eight miles to the gallon? That's rough." Louise lifted the pan lid and stirred the food with a wooden spoon.

Steam rose from the pot and the aroma of the stew drifted over to Ruth. She thought about the dull sandwich she'd eaten earlier and promised herself that she would start cooking real meals for herself.

"It's rough on the pocketbook," she said.

"Last year I went to Oregon to backpack with ten other members of the Sierra Club. I was gone two weeks and the entire trip cost me three hundred dollars, including food, gas, campground fees, and incidentals. That's about twenty-one dollars a day."

Louise lifted the lid again and then turned off the burner. She set out a bowl, a napkin, and silverware.

"Well, I'd better get back and let you eat."

Louise sat down at the table and began spooning the stew into the bowl. "It's been nice talking to you. Have a good trip."

"You, too," Ruth said as she turned away and walked across the grass to her motorhome.

Inside the Coachman, she turned on the lights and walked through the motorhome, closing all of the drapes and mini-blinds as she went. While she was in her bedroom, she got her nightgown out of a drawer and set it on the bed.

She walked back into the living room and turned on the television that was bolted to the table between the two recliners. After turning the dial, she discovered that she only got two channels and she wasn't interested in either one of them.

She clicked the television off and reached for her book, but she didn't feel like reading either. She decided to go to bed and get a good night's sleep so she could get an early start in the morning.

She changed into her nightgown and crawled in between the cool sheets, pulling the covers up, then reached over and turned off the lamp on the bedstand next to the bed. The room was bathed in a warm, rosy haze as the light from outside filtered through her thick mauve drapes.

She snuggled down into the covers and basked in a glow of contentment.

But sleep didn't come easy. Her thoughts drifted back to the night before when she'd experienced the same feeling of contentment after spending a pleasant evening with Jack Colby. She wondered where he was tonight, and if he'd thought about her since they parted company in the rain. She wondered if she'd ever see him again.

Something he'd said puzzled her. He'd mentioned that he had a business deal in Kansas City. He was retired with a good pension, she knew, so what kind of business did he have in Kansas City? He'd said that he needed a new tow vehicle and it was in the back of her mind that the business deal had something to do with getting the extra money to buy a new Blazer.

Was he taking a job? Was he opening a

small business? Was he investing in land? And what difference did it make? For all she knew, he could be a drug dealer in need of quick cash. No, Jack couldn't be involved in anything illegal, she thought, hating herself for even thinking such a thing.

But the only thing she definitely knew about Jack Colby was what she felt in her heart. She wanted to be with him. She wanted to wander around the country with him and explore places she'd never seen. But most of all, she wanted him as a friend.

Twenty-five

The layers of clouds looked like a huge gray sea as they stretched out across the sky, ringing the horizon. Overhead, the sky was clear and bright blue. A hot air balloon floated high in the air, its bright colors stark against the dull gray of the cloud bank as it caught the rays of the early morning sun.

Even before Ruth got to Rapid City, she had decided not to take the side trip to see the presidential monuments at Mount Rushmore. It would cost her another day of travel time and as it was, she wanted to make up the driving time she'd lost during the past two days.

The freeway rose above Rapid City like a long elevated bridge, spanning across a sea of houses and trees, shopping centers and parking lots. From Ruth's vantage point, the cars and trucks that moved through the city looked as if they were following a maze.

After she left the busy metropolis behind, the hills she saw were barren, the fields fallow. As she steered the motorhome with both hands, she glanced out the wide windshield and watched the clouds link up, then separate again as they were stirred up by a high wind.

The green and white billboards advertising Wall Drugstore became more frequent along the side of the road. "Wall Drug—See the Pharmacy Museum," said one sign. "Wall Drug—5¢ Coffee," announced the next billboard. Still another read, "Wall Drug—Free Coffee and Donuts for Honeymooners."

The countryside became more rugged, deeply gouged, and she knew she was nearing the Badlands. Way off to her right, a long, cumbersome train chugged slowly uphill, pushed along by three separate engine cars that spewed black smoke from their smokestacks.

She pulled off at the exit for Wall and followed the signs that directed her to the public parking area, which was a block and a half away from the famous drug-store. When she eased the motorhome into the huge, paved parking lot, she saw that it was already jammed with cars and recreation vehicles bearing out-of-state license plates, and two chartered tour buses from Minnesota.

Avoiding the cracks in the sidewalk, she followed two elderly couples who were headed the same place she was. Always couples, she thought, feeling like a fifth wheel.

She expected to see a lot of tourists in Wall Drug, but when she walked through the entrance, she was surprised by both the enormous size of the building and the vast number of people who meandered through the aisles looking at the novelty items that were for sale.

She plunged right into the midst of the crowd and walked toward the back, searching for the area where she could get a cup of coffee for a nickel. She read the overhead signs that directed people to other rooms of the gigantic drugstore, including a cafe and a snack bar.

This was a place where she could spend

a whole day and be perfectly happy. She wished she could visit the pharmacy museum in one of the back rooms, but didn't want to take the time.

Even though she hated crowds, she had to fight the urge to stop and linger and look for souvenirs for her grandchildren. She made a quick loop through several of the rooms, bumping into preoccupied tourists who turned suddenly in the crowded aisles without paying attention to where they were going.

She followed the signs to the cafe, but when she got there, she saw that the room was already full and people were lined up to be seated. She walked on and finally found the snack bar, which was near another front entrance to the store.

There was no room to sit down at the counter or at the small tables around the snack bar. But she didn't care. All she wanted now was to get a quick cup of coffee, just so she could say she'd been there.

It took her five full minutes to wait her turn in line before she finally reached the counter. The uniformed girl behind the counter, who looked like she had a permanent smile pasted on her face, took her order for one black coffee. The clerk turned her head and called the order back to another employee, who filled a white Styrofoam cup with coffee, then carried the cup to the counter. The clerk with the smile slid the cup across the counter. Ruth picked it up and handed the girl a nickel.

Carrying the small, white cup, Ruth wandered over to a far wall to get away from the crush of people around the counter. She faced the wall and began reading the inscriptions on the postcards and photographs that were tacked to it. She soon realized that all of the cards and pictures were from previous customers and that each one told how far the writer had traveled to visit Wall Drug.

Ruth sipped the hot coffee and scanned the wall that was literally covered with postcards and various sized pictures.

One snapshot showed a grinning, elderly couple holding a hand-printed sign between them that read, "Greetings from the Parkinsons in Columbus, Ohio, 1188 miles from WALL DRUG."

Another picture showed a young couple and a smiling, dark-haired boy who looked to be about twelve. All three were wearing bathing suits and they stood with the ocean in the background. Their sign was attached to a four-foot stake that had been planted in the soft sand. The greeting on the photo said, "Hi from Janet, Steve, and Ryan Gimlin, from sunny Miami Beach, Florida, 2125 miles from WALL DRUG."

A picture higher on the wall was of a couple, the man wearing a Navy uniform, and two small tow-headed children. Their sign, propped up near their feet, said, "Jerry, Colleen, Tanya, and Randy Wilhite send greetings from San Diego, California, 1543 miles from WALL DRUG."

Evidently this was the thing to do if you visited Wall Drug, Ruth thought.

Fascinated, Ruth sipped her coffee and walked along beside the cluttered wall. She saw several photos from foreign countries, all of them listing high mileage figures. She wondered if the foreigners knew the actual mileage, or whether they were guessing by how the crow flies.

Realizing that she was wasting too much valuable time, Ruth took a last long drink of the cooling coffee and dropped the cup in a trash can on her way out of the store.

Back on the road, after filling her tank with gas, she resisted the urge to take the loop through the Badlands. She knew it would be a beautiful drive, but she could see enough of the rugged country from the Interstate to imagine what it would be like. Besides, she had the rest of her life to explore the places that interested her. She didn't have to do it all on this trip.

As she drove, she noticed a sign for an 1890s town and a few miles down the road, she saw an advertisement for the Badlands Petrified Gardens. Both were near Belvidere, South Dakota. Local tourist attractions, she thought. Each town had its own. She wished she could take the time to see the Petrified Gardens.

She drove on without stopping at the next rest area. She wanted to make Sioux Falls before she stopped for the night, and even farther if she could. It was about 360 miles to Sioux Falls from the campground where she'd spent the night. The way she drove, slower than most drivers, that meant a long, nine or ten hours of driving.

When she passed Murdo, she saw the

road sign that told her she was "Now Entering the Central Time Zone." She had just lost an hour. She made a mental note to set her watch and clock ahead when she next stopped.

She kept her eye on the gas gauge and when the red needle reached the halfway mark, she stopped and got gas at a Quik Stop in Kennebec. When she went into the convenience store to pay for her gas she glanced at her watch and saw that it was lunchtime.

She had the clerk make up a turkey and swiss cheese sandwich at the deli counter, then picked up a Coke, a bag of chips, and two plain Hershey bars. One for her sweet tooth and the other for energy, she told herself.

She took the food with her to eat on the road. Inside the motorhome, she glanced at the atlas and decided she could make it to Sioux City, Iowa, if she continued at a steady pace.

She crossed the wide Missouri River at Chamberlain and kept on driving, not stopping at the scenic rest area that overlooked the Missouri. She let her gas tank fall below the half-full mark, and didn't stop again until she got to Hartford. She figured it would be easier to get gas there than in the big city of Sioux Falls, which was just a few miles ahead.

She looked at her watch as she stepped down out of her motorhome and was startled to see that it was already 4:50. And then she remembered the lost hour. She knew she'd never make it to Sioux City, Iowa, that night. She was already road weary from the long, hard, steady stretch of driving and she couldn't face another hour and a half on the road.

While she was inside the store paying for her gas, she bought three packages of cheese-and-cracker snacks, two twelve-ounce cans of V8 juice and a small package of chocolate chip cookies. She opened a can of juice and took a long drink. Then she tore open the cellophane wrapper on a package of cheese and crackers and ate one before she started the engine.

Thinking that she'd find a campground soon and call it a day, she drove on and ran smack dab into rush-hour traffic. And to make matters worse, she was trapped in the middle lane with no way to switch into the right-hand lane where she would be more comfortable.

She felt her shoulder muscles tense up as a rude driver cut in and out of traffic, causing an endless series of honking horns from irritable drivers making their way home from work.

She couldn't have picked a worse time of the day to come into the city. Not only was traffic heavy, but this was where she most needed to stay alert and watch for the junction where she would leave Interstate 90 and take Interstate 29 south.

She turned on her right blinker and checked her rearview mirror. Nobody slowed to let her change lanes.

She felt pressured beyond her ability to cope as her attention was suddenly divided three ways. She continued to glance in the rearview mirror, hoping for a chance to move to the other lane, while keeping her eye on the road ahead of her so she could keep the motorhome straight.

When she saw the big, green freeway sign that announced the turnoff for Interstate 29 one mile ahead, she knew she had to get into the other lane right away or risk missing her turn.

With her blinker still flashing, she

gripped the steering wheel and eased the nose of the motorhome to the right, prepared to swing back if the pickup truck coming up in the other lane didn't give her a break.

In her rearview mirror, she saw the red pickup slow down slightly as the driver motioned for her to cut in. Keeping her speed up with the flow of traffic, she eased into the right lane, straightened her wheels, and settled once again into the rhythm of the traffic.

A half mile later, she turned right on the off ramp, glad to leave the heavy traffic of I-90 behind her. She felt a sense of relief as she followed the curve of the off ramp, but she ran into more traffic on Interstate 29 than she'd had before. She slowed to match the pace of the bumper-to-bumper cars, relieved that at least she no longer had to maintain a high speed on a crowded freeway.

As traffic finally thinned out, she nibbled on the crackers. She drove on another twenty-five miles before she saw a billboard announcing the Windmill Campground in Beresford, South Dakota, three miles ahead. The colorful advertisement stated that the campground had a swimming pool, a game room hall, a playground, limited groceries, and ice. But Ruth didn't need any of these things. She just needed a place to spend the night. She'd been driving for eleven hours straight, with very few stops, and she felt like a mindless zombie.

It was a little after seven o'clock — six o'clock, the old time — but time didn't matter to her. She wanted nothing more than to change into her nightgown and climb in bed.

She plugged her electrical cord into the socket on the post a few feet from her Coachman, but didn't bother hooking up the water or sewer hoses. She had holding tanks in the motorhome and could get by for the night without going through the hassle of hooking up the hoses.

By the time she locked the door, she was so exhausted, she couldn't even think straight. She didn't turn on any lights. It wouldn't be dusk for at least another hour.

Once in the bedroom, she grabbed her nightgown out of a drawer, so tired she could barely stand up long enough to change into it. She her let her clothes fall to the floor in a pile, pulled her night-gown over her head, and sank down on the firm bed.

She fell asleep the minute she settled her head on the pillow.

Twenty-six

Ruth awoke with a start. Disoriented, she struggled to bring her brain up out of the fuzzy cobwebs of deep sleep. She couldn't think where she was, or what day it was.

She threw the covers back and blinked her eyes several times. The minute she moved, a sharp pain stabbed at the middle of her back and spread upward like shooting flames to her shoulder muscles. The pain was an instant reminder of the long day of driving she'd put in.

She slid her legs off the edge of the bed and sat up, then wiggled her bare toes on the soft carpet and tried to put her thoughts in order. Something tugged at her mind to be remembered, but she had no idea what it was.

She focused on the red digital numbers

on the bedside clock and saw that it was a few minutes after six o'clock. Had she slept for just a few minutes? Or had she slept straight through the night without waking? Was it dusk, or was it just beginning to turn light outside?

Confused, she glanced at her watch. It said 7:05. And then, it hit her. She'd changed into a new time zone. That's what she was supposed to remember: to set her bedside clock an hour ahead.

She stood up and rubbed her stiff shoulder muscles, promising herself that she wouldn't ever put in so many hours behind the wheel again. It took all the fun out of traveling.

After she showered and dressed, she stood in front of the bathroom mirror and turned on the blow dryer. She liked the way her hair fell naturally into place, but she definitely didn't like the new gray strands that seemed to have sprouted up overnight. She leaned closer to the mirror and swore that there were at least a dozen new wrinkles on her face, especially around her eyes. As she stared in the mirror, she still had the feeling that she was forgetting something. She squinted against the glare of the bright, early morning light that flooded through the eastern windows and spilled across the dinette table. The shaft of light that flowed through the living room glittered with floating particles of dust. She was once again glad that she would be driving south and not heading directly into the sun.

As she filled a cup with tap water, she glanced outside and saw that there were only a few recreation vehicles in the campground. She spooned a measure of instant coffee into the water, slid the cup into the microwave, and set the timer for two minutes.

When the buzzer rang, she retrieved the coffee from the microwave, and carried it and a bowl of cold cereal to the dinette booth. She knew she hadn't eaten anything last night except for the snacks she'd had while she was driving, but she didn't want to take the time to cook a hot breakfast. She chided herself for not eating right on the trip. The only decent meal she'd had since she left home was the one she'd shared with Jack Colby the first night out.

While she ate the cold cereal, she studied her atlas. She still had almost six hundred miles to go before she reached Branson.

She wished she were traveling across the country in her car, like that woman she'd met from Oklahoma. It would be so much easier.

She tried to shake her foul mood. Just a case of the grumps, she told herself as she washed her few dishes and put them away. Maybe the loneliness of traveling alone was getting to her.

"Oh, shoot," she said aloud, suddenly remembering Brenda. She'd been so exhausted when she pulled into the campground the night before, she'd forgotten to call. "She'll kill me."

She glanced at her watch. Seven o'clock, Billings time. Even though it was Saturday morning, Brenda would be up. She was an early riser.

Not able to recall where the office was located, Ruth stepped outside to get her bearings. The crisp morning air went right through her clothes and chilled her to the bone as she looked across the nearly deserted campground and spotted the red brick building that housed the office and small store on one end, the bathrooms and laundry room on the other. The public phone booth stood outside like a sentinel.

She rubbed her upper arms as she walked around to the other side of the Coachman and unhooked her electrical cord from the receptacle. With the cord coiled and tucked back into its small storage bin on the side of the motorhome, she went back inside and checked to make sure everything was in its proper place before she slid into the driver's seat and started the engine.

On her way out of the campground, she stopped near the office, shut off the engine, and walked over to the pay phone.

Brenda answered on the first ring, as if she'd been sitting next to the phone.

Ruth got chewed out for not calling the night before, as she knew she would. Because it was chilly outside, she kept the conversation brief, promising to call again that night after she got settled into a campground.

She kept her promise and called Brenda again Saturday evening from a lovely campground in St. Joseph, Missouri. After learning that everything was fine at home, she walked back and added two states, Iowa and Missouri, to the magnetic map.

Sunday morning, she made the loop around Kansas City and ended up on Highway 71 south, then took Highway 7 across to Clinton, where she headed south again on Highway 13, a two-lane road that would lead her to Springfield.

She stopped early that afternoon at the small town of Osceola, knowing that she was within a hundred miles of Branson.

Before she made her way to the campground on Truman Lake, she stopped at the Osceola Cheese Factory. Inside the store, the sharp, pleasant aroma of the various cheeses made her mouth water. She bought a carton of crackers and two pounds of cheddar. Then she arranged to send generous gift packages of cheese to her mother and all three of her children. Her total bill came to $96.82, and she wrote a check so she wouldn't have to dip into her cash supply.

After she checked in at the campground office and was assigned a site with full hookups, she walked outside and stopped at the pay phone to call Brenda before she drove on to her site.

"I'm in Osceola, Missouri, about a two or three hour drive from Branson," Ruth said after they'd exchanged greetings.

"You're getting close. I'll bet you're getting excited."

"Yes. The trees around here haven't started to change colors yet so I hope I'm not too early. But, I'm looking forward to the caravan through the Ozarks."

"I wish I were there with you."

"I do, too," Ruth said. "It would be a lot more fun to share the experience."

"Pretty lonely out there?"

Ruth could almost see Brenda's I-told-you-so expression. "Not really. I've met some interesting people and I'm sure I'll meet many more before I'm through. How are the kids?"

"Ornery as ever."

Ruth laughed. "I miss them. How's everybody else?"

"Well, for starters, Mama Murph's ticked off at me because I wouldn't take her grocery shopping yesterday. I figure if she can't help me out in a pinch, I'll be darned if I'm going to do anything for her."

"Brenda, you and your grandmother are both stubborn. You bicker like little kids."

"I know, you don't want to hear about it. Amy has a new boyfriend she met at college. She thinks she's madly in love, but that's nothing new. Next week it'll be someone else. Tony and his family are fine, but then everything's always hunky dory with Tony's perfect little family."

"Do I detect a bit of sarcasm?"

"Probably, but don't pay any attention to me. I'm just bitchy, as Danny constantly reminds me. He's turned into an old grouch."

"Brenda, what's the matter?"

"Danny wants me to quit work and stay home with the kids. I haven't been feeling good and he thinks I'm worrying myself sick over trying to find a new babysitter. God, I wish you were here."

Ruth ignored her daughter's hint for her to offer to babysit. "Have you been sick?"

"I'm just worn out and the flu keeps coming back. Nothing to worry about."

"Well, take care of yourself."

"I am. Oh, before I forget, guess who'll be in Branson when you are?" Brenda said.

"Who?"

"Meg and Scot Rodecker."

Ruth's heart sank. "You've got to be kidding."

"No, I'm not kidding. Meg called Friday night and said she'd gotten a magazine assignment to write an article on the Branson scene. I didn't realize there were so many country music stars there."

"So I've heard," Ruth said. She stared down at the ground, stunned at the thought of meeting up with Meg and Scot in Branson. She would be happy to have Meg there, but she just didn't want to see Scot. "Are you sure Scot is coming with her? I know at one time Meg talked about riding out to the Ozarks with me."

"I'm pretty sure Meg said they were both flying out there either Saturday or Sunday, which would be yesterday or today. In fact, Meg said that Scot wanted to fly on to Florida from there and take a Caribbean cruise."

"Well, they can afford to hop around the country."

"Meg wanted to know where you were staying, so I gave her the phone number you gave me for the Musicland KOA Kampground in Branson. She said she'd look you up."

"Thanks a lot, Brenda"

"What? Did I do something wrong?"

"No. I just don't feel comfortable around Scot."

"So ignore him. Don't let him spoil your vacation."

"I won't. Well, I'll talk to you after I get to Branson. Give my love to everyone."

As Ruth walked back to her motorhome, she thought about Meg and Scot visiting Branson. She realized that she should be happy to be with old friends in a strange place, but she knew that her vacation was already spoiled. The last thing she needed was a drunken Scot Rodecker looking over her shoulder.

Twenty-seven

When Ruth reached Interstate 44 near Springfield, she entered the eastbound lane. Five miles later, the big green exit sign for Branson loomed ahead. She turned onto Highway 65 south and coasted past Springfield without seeing much of the city. A smaller sign told her that she was just thirty-four miles from Branson.

Her blood tingled as she crossed the bridge over Lake Springfield and made the short climb to the flat prairie that was dotted with farms.

She gazed at the countryside through the big windows of the motorhome. The land was still green, the sky blue, dotted with flotillas of white clouds. Cars streamed by on the two-lane, which soon squeezed into single lane traffic in each direction. She drove behind a small car from Indiana. Ahead, motorhomes, trailers, pickups, eighteen-wheelers, and cars made a long snakelike line.

The land was still flat as she rounded the first curve. The highway was lined with trees whose leaves were turning. The sight took her breath away. The oaks and hickories burned like an artist's palette against the evergreen cedars. The sumac blazed bright red.

Then, the curved road dipped and she rounded the hill and plunged into the Ozarks, the trees rising above her on both sides. It was like entering an enchanted forest.

The road took her up and down blazing hills, past beautiful, towering bluffs blasted by time and the highway engineers. A majestic hill, the trees cleared off, grass still green, appeared out of nowhere like a giant park, and she saw a flock of turkeys fly from bluff to bluff overhead, their feathers shining in the late morning sun.

She began to notice the billboards for

Silver Dollar City and other Branson attractions. There was a huge photograph of Mel Tillis, another of Johnny Cash, and a beautifully designed one with Shoji Tabuchi wearing a burgundy-colored tuxedo, his violin tucked under one arm.

At each new hill, she saw more beauty as the thick stands of trees literally covered the gently rolling land, the dark green cedars interlaced with the golds, rusts, and magentas of their neighboring trees. She felt as if she were entering a magical world of fairyland kingdoms right out of a children's storybook.

Finally, she reached the Branson exit, right next to the huge Mel Tillis theater where, according to the marquee, Debbie Reynolds was performing. Shortly after she took the exit, she spotted a service station with a long, wide driveway. She pulled in, even though her gas tank was three-quarters full.

After she filled her tank, she went into the convenience store to pay for the gas.

"I'm looking for the Musicland KOA Kampground," she told the dark-haired clerk. "Am I headed the right way?"

The man plucked a map of Branson out of a small wire rack, unfolded it, and spread it out on the glass counter. He pointed to the map. "You're right here."

Ruth dug her glasses out of the side pouch of her big shoulder bag, slipped them on and leaned closer. "Okay."

"If you don't mind the traffic, it'd probably be easier for you to go out 76. Once you're on The Strip, you stay on it until you get to Gretna. Turn right at Gretna and the KOA is just around the corner."

"And, how do I get to 76 from here?"

The man grabbed a capped pen and used it as a pointer as he traced the route on the map. "Just go straight ahead. You'll pass Skaggs Hospital on your right and keep on going until you get to the traffic signal. At the signal, you'll see The Farm House Restaurant on your left and across the street, an ice cream parlor and The Fudge Shop. Turn right at the signal and you're on The Strip. From there on, it'll be slow going."

"I'd like to buy the map, too," Ruth said. "How much is it?"

The clerk folded the map back up and handed it to her. "It's free. Compliments of the Chamber of Commerce."

"Thank you." On her way out of the store, Ruth stopped at a rack and picked out a variety of colorful brochures that advertised the music shows and local attractions.

She stopped at the signal in downtown Branson and spotted The Farm House Restaurant on her left, The Fudge Shop across the street. She turned right onto 76 West, climbed a hill, and drove on the two-lane road.

Ahead, the cars were snailing up the hill, bumper-to-bumper. Even though she'd been warned about the heavy traffic, she couldn't believe that there were so many cars and recreation vehicles on The Strip at ten o'clock on a Monday morning. And she didn't even consider this the tourist season. She wondered what it had been like in July and August.

It seemed to take hours to reach the turnoff to the KOA. The famed Branson Strip had a center lane for vehicles turning left, but it was essentially single lane traffic, with cars feeding into her lane ahead of her at almost every place there was a driveway. But, she didn't mind. She was in no hurry and there was much to see.

Intermingled with motels, restaurants, and craft shops, there were music shows on both sides of the road, their marquees emblazoned with the names of the artists. There was Presley's, the Foggy River Boys, Roy Clark's Celebrity Theatre, Willie Nelson, Box Car Willie's, Moe Bandy, and a dozen others. Even driving at a snail's pace, she didn't have time to read all the signs.

Tourists walked on the sidewalks on both sides of The Strip, some clutching packages, most carrying cameras.

Traffic came to a standstill when she was directly across from The Grand Palace, a huge white building with tall columns across the front. It reminded her of a southern plantation. The marquee had the names of Glen Campbell and Loretta Lynn spelled out in big black letters.

Nearby was the Andy Williams Moon

River Theater, which was surrounded by beautiful, tall rock bluffs, much like those she'd seen along the highway. She wondered if they were real. Just beyond The Grand Palace was the Palace Inn and Sadie's Sideboard Restaurant. Two separate signs announced that the Wharf Restaurant and the Comfort Inn were located on Wildwood Drive, directly behind The Grand Palace.

Ruth knew this was a place where she could spend a month and not see everything she wanted to see. She saw the Osmond Brothers' Theater and just beyond that, the signal light with a sign that said Gretna Road.

She turned right at Gretna, spotted the entrance sign for the KOA, and drove through the gate into a hilly campground. It was woodsy and quiet, just a few hundred yards from the glitter and gaudiness of The Strip. When she saw the RVs tucked into every little cranny, she was glad she had reservations.

She shut down the engine in front of the office and went inside to register.

"Hi. My name is Debbie. Welcome to

Branson's Musicland KOA," said the young girl behind the counter.

"Hi. I'm Ruth Nichols and I have reservations."

The young clerk brushed her long, blonde hair back away from her face and sorted through a file index, withdrew a card. "Yes. Ruth Nichols." She grabbed a registration form from a stack near the cash register. "How many in your party?" she asked, her pen poised above the paper.

"One," Ruth said, still hating the question. She saw the girl glance at her wedding rings, as if to challenge her.

"Full hookups?" Debbie asked.

"Yes, please."

The girl made a check mark on the form, flipped her hair back out of her eyes, then slid the paper across the counter. "Will you please fill in your name, address, and license plate number?"

Ruth slid her glasses into place and filled in the information quickly. "I requested a pull-through site," she said as she pushed the form back to the clerk.

Debbie double-checked the information on the file card. "Oh, yes, I see we've already got you assigned to a site. And, we've got a couple of messages for you."

"You do?" Ruth thought about her family back home and hoped that nothing was wrong.

The clerk turned around, fished two identical pieces of yellow note paper out of a slot in the pigeon-hole message board, and handed them to Ruth.

"One of the notes is from a woman who called here three times yesterday to see if you'd checked in early," Debbie told her. "She's already called twice this morning and she stopped by the office and left this note for you not more than a half hour ago."

Ruth unfolded the first paper and recognized Meg Rodecker's flowery handwriting inside. "Dear Ruth. Guess what! We're here in Branson! Surprise, surprise," the note said. "Flew in yesterday. Anxious to see you. We're staying at the Palace Inn. Call as soon as you get in. Plan on having dinner with us tonight and maybe we'll take in a show. Love, Meg."

"She's a friend of mine," Ruth said.

"A persistent friend," the clerk answered with a smile. "She told me to make sure you called her just as soon as you arrived. It's a local call. You can use our phone if you want to."

"I'll wait until I get settled in," Ruth said. She had no intention of calling Meg right away. She'd stall as long as she possibly could.

She assumed the other yellow note was from Meg, too. She opened it and saw the flourish of the scrawled handwriting she didn't recognize. Puzzled, she read the short note. "Ruth. Gone fishin'. Be back in time to cook dinner for you. Love, Jack."

Ruth's heart soared. She stood there, totally stunned, as she stared at the note. She read it again. The tingle of excitement started in the pit of her stomach and shot straight to her heart.

Was Jack Colby really here in Branson? Had he come here merely because there were lakes to be fished, or had he come here specifically because he knew she'd be here? Would this be another brief encounter, like ships passing in the night, with poignant goodbyes at the end of the evening?

"Are you all right, Mrs. Nichols?" the clerk asked.

Lost in thought, Ruth had forgotten all about the girl. "Yes, of course."

"The gentleman who left that note checked in yesterday and insisted that we put you in the campsite next to his. He said you needed to be close to him because he didn't have an umbrella. Whatever that means."

Ruth laughed as she removed her reading glasses. "It's just a joke."

"I understand, Mrs. Nichols. A private joke." The young clerk glanced at Ruth's wedding bands again, then tossed her hair back and gave Ruth a knowing smile.

Ruth didn't like the insinuation in the girl's coy smile. She'd done nothing wrong and she didn't feel it was necessary to explain that she was a widow.

"Do I owe you anything?" she asked. She put her glasses away and stuffed the notes in the side pouch of her shoulder bag.

"No, your camp fee is included in the tour package," Debbie said. She finished filling out the registration form and handed Ruth a copy. "You're in space thirty-three." She drew directions on a campground map and circled Ruth's site, pushed the map over to Ruth.

"Thank you," Ruth said.

"And here's your tour packet," the clerk said as she handed Ruth a thick folder. "There's a copy of your tour itinerary inside."

"Oh, thanks." Ruth opened the folder, glanced through the packet. Besides the three-page, detailed itinerary of the tour, there were a few pages of instructions and suggestions, three or four maps, and a handful of brochures of local attractions.

"Your group is to meet at the recreation hall at eight o'clock tomorrow morning for a briefing before you leave for the Mark Twain National Forest. There'll be coffee and donuts at the rec hall. George and Sandy Barton will be your tour guides. They're in space ten if you have any questions. Enjoy your stay in the Ozarks."

"I'm sure I will. It's beautiful country."

Ruth found her campsite and pulled into her designated space. Her heart fluttered when she saw the familiar white and green Prowler sitting on the pad next door. She felt like a teenager and told herself she was being silly. Jack's battered Blazer was gone, as she knew it would be. After she parked, she got out and hooked up to the electricity, water and sewer.

When she walked back around the motorhome, she noticed that Jack had backed his trailer onto the paved RV pad so that their doors faced each other. A redwood picnic table and benches sat on the neatly trimmed grass between their two rigs. A stately pine grew a few feet away from one end of the picnic table. The tall oak that stood halfway between the other end of the picnic table and the edge of the campground road was just beginning to show its fall colors.

Acorns littered the ground. While she was standing there, a squirrel scurried toward her from across the road, snatched an acorn and scampered up the oak to a high branch. She watched the animal for a minute, then looked over at the Prowler.

Jack's striped awning was extended. Beneath it was his TV tray. She smiled when she saw that he had set out two folding lawn chairs.

"Mighty presumptuous of you, Mr. Colby," she said aloud as she turned and entered her motorhome.

Inside, she kicked off her moccasins. The thick, padded carpet massaged her stockinged feet as she walked up to the passenger seat. She retrieved the brochures she'd collected at the service station and the tour packet folder, tossed them on the couch on her way toward the back of the motorhome.

She had just settled down on the sofa to look through the packet and read the tour itinerary when she heard a knock on her door.

Her heart skipped a beat. It had to be Jack, home from his morning fishing trip. She slipped back into her moccasins and headed toward the door.

She had a big smile on her face when

she opened her door. The smile faded when she saw Meg and Scot standing outside.

She hoped her disappointment didn't show.

Twenty-eight

Framed by the thick, dark green pine tree behind them, Meg and Scot Rodecker looked the part of the colorful, well-dressed tourist. Meg wore an expensive pants suit, royal blue, silky crepe pants, a matching loose-flowing overblouse, and under that, a blouse the same color that was smooth silk. Several gold chains adorned the blouse and long golden earrings dangled from her pierced ears. Scot wore tight Levi's and a jade-green, short sleeved shirt. He wore a thick gold chain around his neck and a gold Rolex watch.

Ruth could see enough of the sleek silver car parked behind her motorhome to know that it was a Lincoln Town Car.

Backlit by the high noon sun, Meg's wild strawberry blonde hair looked like loose strands of spun gold. The bright sunlight highlighted Scot's hair and made him appear grayer than he actually was.

"It's so good to see you," Meg said as she started for the door.

Ruth reached over and flipped the switch that would keep the metal step in its extended position, then dashed out and hugged her friend. "I'm so glad you're here. Brenda told me you were coming."

"You didn't drive out here from Billings, did you?" Ruth nodded toward the Lincoln.

"No, we flew into Springfield and rented this," Meg said. "And guess where we're staying?"

"Your note said you were staying at the Palace Inn."

"Right, but we're staying in the very same room where President Bush and Barbara stayed when they came to Branson. Can you believe it?"

"Oh, may I touch you?" Ruth teased. "Come on in." She opened the door, held it open.

"No, we came to kidnap you," Meg said with a bright smile. "We came to take you to lunch."

Ruth hesitated. "Oh, I don't know. I just got in and I haven't had a chance to catch my breath."

"It's almost noon and you've got to eat, don't you?" Meg insisted.

Ruth laughed. "I guess so."

Scot stepped back, lit up a cigarette, and leaned against the end of the picnic table. Ruth was surprised. She thought he'd given up smoking two or three years ago.

"Good," Meg said. "We know your tour starts tomorrow so we want to spend all day with you today. We're going to have lunch, then drive you around to see the sights. We'll have an early dinner at a nice restaurant we found and then we've got tickets for the Mel Tillis show tonight."

Ruth thought about Jack Colby and his invitation to have dinner, "I can't," she said. "I've been on the road for nearly a week and if I don't do my laundry this afternoon, I won't have any clean clothes for the caravan."

"So, we'll eat lunch, take the scenic route back, drop you off and pick you up later in time for dinner and the show. Simple enough?"

"I can't go with you tonight," Ruth said. "I've got other plans."

Meg tipped her head and grinned. "You just got here and you've already got plans for tonight? You work fast."

"That's right," Ruth said with a teasing smile.

"Well, let's go to lunch. We're wasting valuable time." Meg, always the organizer, clapped her hands together.

"Do I need to change?"

"No." Meg turned around. "Scot, get the camera, will you? I want you to take a picture of Ruth and me by her motorhome."

Scot dropped his cigarette to the grass, ground it out with the toe of his shoe. He strolled over to the car and dug the camera out of the back seat. Meg and Ruth stood beside the motorhome, near the colorful map of the United States. Scot focused and took two pictures.

"Let me take a picture of the two of you," Meg said as she stepped away from the motorhome.

Scot checked the camera. "There's only one shot left."

"Good enough." Meg took the camera, looked through the viewfinder and instructed Scot and Ruth to smile. She clicked off the shot, then handed the camera back to Scot.

"Let me get my camera and take a picture of you two." Ruth dashed inside and came back out with her point-and-shoot camera. Using the same background of her motorhome, she took the last two pictures on the roll of film of Scot and Meg, after urging them to stand closer together.

"We'll drop the film off at Fast Photo and pick the pictures up after lunch," Meg said.

"Oh, good," Ruth said. "I've got another roll of film to be developed, too."

Although Meg suggested that Ruth ride in the front seat with Scot so she could see better, Ruth climbed in the back. The inside of the car smelled like stale cigarette smoke. She wanted to crack her window open, but didn't.

Scot turned left out of the campground driveway and drove the few blocks on The

Strip to the photo shop.

"Get double prints made," Meg said. She handed Scot her roll of film, reached back and got Ruth's two rolls.

Scot was only gone a minute and when he came back, he drove back to Gretna Road and wound around the back roads, ending up in downtown Branson. He parked the Lincoln in front of a gray building on a side road. The sign outside said Rocky's Italian Restaurant.

"We ate dinner here last night," Meg said as she got out of the car. "I think you'll like it."

When Ruth stepped inside the restaurant and smelled the aroma of herbs and spices, she realized that she was hungry. The room was full of old-time charm and atmosphere with its dark walnut tables and high-back chairs with upholstered seats, the polished hardwood floor.

A hostess greeted them and led them to a booth. Scot waited while Ruth and Meg sat down across from each other, then slid onto the seat next to his wife. Shortly after they were seated, a pretty, dark-haired waitress came to their table.

"Hi, I'm Bev. Can I get you something to drink?" she asked as she placed leather-bound menus in front of them.

Scot nodded to Ruth. "Ruth, what would you like? A glass of wine?"

"I'll have black coffee," she said.

"I'd like a glass of Piesporter wine," Meg said.

"A double Scotch on the rocks," Scot said.

Bev nodded and walked away from the table without writing anything down.

"I've got so much to tell you," Meg said as she picked up the menu.

"Brenda said you were talking about going on a cruise," Ruth said.

"Yes. Scot is taking three weeks off work and after we leave here, we're going to cruise the Caribbean for two marvelous weeks. I'd invite you to go along, but this is like a second honeymoon for us." Meg beamed when she spoke, then looked at Scot coyly. "Isn't that right, Scot?"

Scot shifted his weight, sat up straighter, and picked up his menu. "Yes, of course," he said without looking at either one of them.

Ruth sensed that something was wrong. She picked up her menu, glanced over the choices, but could barely concentrate on them. Away from the glare of the sunlight, Meg looked worn and haggard. She seemed too happy, as if she were putting on a good front for her old friend. And while Scot had appeared casual at the campground, and more relaxed than she'd ever seen him, he now seemed extremely nervous.

Ruth had noticed one change in the couple, however. While Meg used to bow to Scot's wishes, she now seemed to have taken charge. She had ordered Scot to get the camera out of the car. She had told him to take the film in and get double prints made. And she'd chosen the restaurant. Perhaps Meg had laid the law down to Scot. If so, maybe their marriage had a chance of surviving.

Bev brought the drinks, set them down. "Are you ready to order?" she asked.

Scot picked up his drink and took a healthy swig without taking his eye off the menu.

"I think I'll have that Italian sausage

sandwich," Meg said.

"That sounds good," Ruth said.

"Make it three of them," Scot added. "And I'll have a carafe of burgundy."

"Three glasses?" Bev asked.

"I'll stick to coffee," Ruth said.

"And I'll have another glass of Piesporter with my meal," Meg said.

"White wine with Italian sausage?" Scot asked.

"I prefer white wine," Meg said.

Scot closed his menu and looked up at Bev. "You'd better make that just a half a carafe of burgundy," he said.

After Bev walked away, Meg picked up her wine goblet, held it under her nose, and sniffed the delicate bouquet before she sampled it. "That's good wine," she said. She took another sip, then set it down. "So, how was your trip?" she asked Ruth.

"Good. I've seen a lot of beautiful country, but nothing to compare to the Ozarks. I'm really looking forward to the caravan."

"So are we," Meg said.

Ruth had just raised her cup to her lips.

She stopped before she took a drink. "Oh, are you going on the tour?"

"Yes," Meg said as she leaned forward and rested her elbows on the table, clasping her hands together. "Well, sort of."

"Part of it anyway," Scot said. He took a long drink of the Scotch, leaned back in the booth, and smiled at Ruth. "It'll be nice to spend some time with you, Ruth."

The look he gave her was not the kind of a look that an old friend would use. It was a leer. It was as if the belt of booze he'd just taken had given him the courage to be salaciously bold. Was he just teasing her? Being playful? Whatever it was, she didn't like it. She glared at him and turned her attention to Meg.

"Brenda said you were writing an article about Branson," she said.

"Yes, I am. I got an assignment to write about Branson for *Vacation World*. And then, I decided I could also write about the caravan tour, so I called the editor at *Trailer Life* and he said if I could write an interesting article about the fall trip through the Ozarks, they'd consider publishing it. I might also do a feature article for the Billings paper."

"That's great," Ruth said.

The waitress brought the drinks, setting the white wine in front of Meg, pouring a glass of burgundy for Scot, then leaving the small carafe on the table. She came back a minute later, balancing three plates in her hands.

The Italian sausage, formed into large meatballs and smothered with an herbed tomato sauce, was served on huge submarine rolls. It tasted as good as it smelled and although Ruth was hungry, she couldn't eat more than half of it.

Meg talked constantly during lunch. After three more glasses of the imported white wine, she was still picking her way through the thick sandwich.

Scot talked very little during the meal. He drank the half carafe of burgundy and ate most of his sandwich before he pushed his plate aside and ordered a brandy.

"So you're going on the caravan through the Ozarks with the tour group," Ruth commented after she took a drink of coffee.

"Like I said, sort of," Meg said between

bites. "I thought it would be fun to rent a nice, luxurious motorhome and camp out with everybody else, but Scott voted against it. He hasn't been feeling well lately. We'll meet up with the caravan every day and stay in motels at night."

When Bev brought the coffeepot around, Scot ordered another brandy and asked for the check.

"Scot," Meg said after the waitress left. "Your headaches have been bad lately and I'm concerned about you. That's why I've been trying to get you to go to a doctor."

"I'm not sick."

Meg shrugged her shoulders and looked across the table at Ruth. "Anyway, we'll follow the caravan during the day and stay at the Palace Inn at night. We've also made reservations at a hotel in Eureka Springs for the two nights you'll be camped there."

"Then you'll have the best of both worlds," Ruth said, trying to lighten up the conversation. "You'll see the beauty of the Ozarks during the day and sleep in a warm, comfy bed at night. I have a feeling the nights are going to be chilly."

Meg's laugh sounded forced. "That's right," she said. "And sometime during all this, I've got to write the articles and mail them off before we leave. We fly out of Springfield next Sunday afternoon for Florida. The cruise starts Monday, a week from today."

Bev brought Scot's brandy and presented him with the check on a small tray, then walked away.

"I'm sure you'll both have fun," Ruth said.

"And when we get back from the cruise, I'm going to start writing that novel I've been talking about. But you're going to have to help me come up with some outrageous, scandalous things for the hero and heroine to get involved in. We're in this together, Ruth. Co-authors."

Ruth laughed. "I never agreed to that. This is your book and you'll have to use your own imagination."

"Hey, come on, Ruth, it's got to be a joint effort. We have to come up with a sultry heroine, a hunk of a hero, and a real wicked villain."

"Oh, grow up, Meg," Scot said. "People

write books because they have something to say and obviously, you don't. I don't see why you're so hung up on trying to uncover some scandal in Billings. That's stupid."

"Because that's what sells," she argued.

Scot downed his drink in one swallow. He glanced at the check, stood up, dug three twenty-dollar bills out of his wallet, and plunked them down on the tray. "I'm going outside to have a smoke. I'll wait for you gals in the car. Take your time."

Ruth watched Scot march across the hardwood floor toward the front door, taking long strides, as if he couldn't wait to get out of there. Just before he walked out the door, he turned and glared at them.

A chill went up Ruth's spine. Scot Rodecker looked like a man who was on the verge of a mental breakdown.

Twenty-nine

Ruth was glad that Meg had her back to the door and couldn't see the hateful expression on Scot's face. When she looked over at her friend, she thought she detected a moist glistening in Meg's eyes that hadn't been there before.

"I hit a sore spot," Meg said, as if explaining her husband's rude behavior. "He just goes into a rage every time I mention that I'm going to work on the novel."

"Why would he care?"

"I think he's afraid I might be successful. I think Scot's got an inferiority complex because of my money," Meg said with a sigh. "He needs to feel like he's the man of the house, the breadwinner. Being a banker gives him that status in the community and the prestige that goes with the job."

"That makes sense."

"He just wants me to be a mousy, obedient wife who helps her husband's image by doing charitable work. Heaven forbid if I should happen to write a best-seller and draw a little attention to myself." She slapped her hand to her forehead, then laughed.

Ruth couldn't bring herself to even offer a smile. She could see that her friend's marriage was based on a sick dependency. Meg did pretty much what Scot expected of her because she didn't want to lose him and end up looking like a failure. And Scot stayed in line because he didn't want to lose his free access to her money, which was what would happen if Meg divorced him.

"So, what's really wrong, Meg?" she asked. "It's not just the novel and you know it. You're talking about going on a second honeymoon, but I sense that things aren't good between you and Scot."

"They're terrible," Meg admitted. "The cruise is just a final attempt to save our marriage. It was Scot's idea, but I don't hold out much hope for any miracle to happen on the high seas. His drinking just keeps getting worse and worse. The headaches he's having are nothing more than hangovers."

"Can't you get him some help?"

"I've tried, but unless he wants to be helped, it doesn't do any good. That's the real reason he won't camp out with the caravan. He doesn't want to be around other people when he's sloshed. He's become a real recluse. We don't even bother to argue anymore. The exchange you heard just now is the most we've communicated in more than a month."

"Oh, Meg, I wish I could help." Ruth reached across the table and patted her friend's hand.

"I don't think you can. Something is very, very wrong and I don't know what it is. God knows I've tried to be a good wife." Meg picked up her wine glass, stared down into it, then set it down. "I used to cry myself to sleep every night, but I've gotten to the point that I don't care anymore."

"You've got to take care of yourself, Meg."

"I will. And, on that happy note, I think we'd better leave."

As they slid out of opposite sides of the booth, Ruth wrapped her arm around Meg's shoulder. "I'm always there for you if you need me," she said.

"I know you are, Ruth, and I appreciate it." When they reached the door, Meg turned to Ruth. "I know tomorrow we'll both be busy with the caravan through the Mark Twain National Forest, but they've scheduled a free day in Branson on Wednesday, at least until the chartered bus ride to dinner that night. Let's have lunch that day. It'll be the only time we'll have a chance to be together without other people around before we leave for the cruise."

"Just the two of us?" Ruth asked.

"I can't exclude Scot. Not at this point."

Ruth thought about Jack Colby and wondered if he would still be around by then. "We'll try for lunch Wednesday, but we'll have to play it by ear."

"I know. Anything could happen between now and then."

The despair in Meg's voice worried

395

Ruth. "Keep your chin up," she said.

"I will," Meg said with a forced smile. "I'm fighting just to survive right now and I'm not going to let that s.o.b. ruin my life."

When they got back in the car, it was as if there were no problems between Meg and Scot as they continued the pretense of being happy in front of her. All the way back to the campground, Meg kept up a constant chatter about all the things she was going to write in her articles about Branson, and although Scot was quiet, he added a few comments and suggestions of his own.

"Would you like to come in?" Ruth asked when they pulled in behind her motorhome.

"No, I think we'd better go," Meg said. "We want to rest up for the show tonight and I want to work on my article if I have time."

"Well, I'll see you tomorrow morning, then. Thanks for lunch."

"Yeah, see you tomorrow," Meg said. "Oh, damn, we forgot to pick up our pictures."

"Oh, I did forget, didn't I?" Scot said. "My fault. I'll run over and get them. You gals can wait here."

Ruth and Meg were sitting at the picnic table when Scot got back. He walked up behind his wife with three white envelopes in his hand. He opened one of them, drew out a thin, blue folder, handed it to Meg. Ruth saw that it was a small, cardboard-covered photo album.

"The duplicate prints are in the envelope," he told Meg.

"Thanks," Meg said as she started turning the pages. "Oh, these turned out well."

Scot took the blue folders out of the two remaining envelopes and slid them across the table to Ruth, then tossed the white envelopes on the table.

"Who's your boyfriend?" he remarked.

"What are you talking about?" Ruth asked, resenting the fact that Scot had already looked at her pictures. She looked up at him and was stunned by the look of contempt on his face as he glared at her. His expression frightened her and she felt a sudden chill at the back of her neck.

Scot didn't answer. He just stood there

and stared at her as she started leafing through the pages of photos.

When she spotted the picture she'd taken of Jack Colby standing in front of his travel trailer with a full sack of food from the Chuck Wagon barbecue shack in Sheridan, she knew what Scot was referring to. She felt her cheeks flush.

"Who's your boyfriend?" Scot repeated, a cold edge to his voice.

"He's a friend who fixed the step on my motorhome," Ruth said.

"Oh, let me see," Meg said. She dragged the small photo album across the table and studied the picture. "Wow, he's nice looking, Ruth. Do we have a scandal brewing?" she said in a joking manner. "Are you keeping something from us?"

"No," Ruth said easily. "That was the first day of my trip and I haven't seen him since."

"That's his trailer behind me, isn't it?" Scot said, a cold edge to his accusing tone of voice. "Same one that's in that picture."

"Yes, it is," she said, feeling no need to explain.

"It figures."

"Scot, quit teasing her," Meg said.

But Ruth knew Scot wasn't teasing. She saw the flare of hatred in his eyes. She didn't understand why he was so angry, but she knew that the look on his face scared the heck out of her.

"Ruth's a big girl. She can take a little teasing," Scot said. "Are you ready to go, Meg?"

"In a minute. I want to give Ruth those extra copies of the pictures we took of her before lunch."

Scot lit a cigarette, walked back toward the Lincoln Town Car parked behind her motorhome.

"Let me give you copies of the pictures I took of you and Scot," Ruth told Meg. She shuddered when she heard Scot slam the car door.

After Meg and Scot drove away, Ruth took the packet of pictures inside, gathered up her tour folder and the loose brochures from the couch, and carried them to the dinette table. She slid into the booth and opened the first photo album, looked at the pictures that were sheathed in clear plastic.

As she turned the pages, the memories of her trip flooded through her mind. She took a closer look at the picture of Jack Colby holding the sack that contained their dinners. She tried to ignore the pleasant glow that came over her when she saw his mischievous smile. She was anxious to see him again, but she wouldn't allow herself to believe that their meeting would be anything but another brief encounter.

She flipped the page. The pictures of the city park in Spearfish, South Dakota, reminded her of the long hours of frustration she'd gone through waiting for her new fuel pump to arrive from Rapid City. When she saw the pictures she'd taken that evening from high atop the mountainside in the Piedmont campground, she got that same sick feeling in the pit of her stomach she'd experienced when she was up there, scared out of her mind.

Finished with one album, she set it aside, picked up the other blue folder, and started through the pages. When she came to the last two photographs in the album, the ones she'd taken of Meg and Scot, she picked up the three loose pictures Meg had given her and compared them. In the two photos Scot had taken of Meg and Ruth in their bright blue and softer lavender outfits, they looked like older versions of the happy, teenaged school chums they'd been so long ago.

But she was shocked when she studied the pictures with Scot in them. The body language told it all, she thought. In the photograph that Meg had taken of Scot and Ruth, she saw that Scot, who looked relaxed with his arm around her shoulder, had a big grin on his face.

There was a stark contrast between Scot's expression in that picture and the other two photographs. In the pictures Ruth had taken of Meg and Scot together, Meg had a forced smile, but Scot had a scowl on his face. With a gap of several inches between their shoulders, Meg stood with her hands at her side while Scot's arms were folded across his chest.

Ruth could almost feel the hatred that emanated from the cold, calculating expression in Scot's eyes.

She knew one thing for sure as she

closed the photo album. She never wanted to be in a position where she'd be alone with the husband of her best friend. She didn't trust Scot Rodecker one bit.

She got up, pulled the laundry bag out of the bottom of the tiny closet in the hallway, and headed toward the laundry room near the campground office.

An hour and a half later she stepped out into the fresh air, her oversized purse hanging by its long leather strap from her shoulder. She clutched six heavy hangers in one hand, each one holding either a clean outfit or a pair of slacks and a blouse. Her bath towels, washcloths, sheets, pillowcases, and lingerie, all neatly folded, were inside the cloth laundry bag she cradled in her other arm.

The breeze that brushed against Ruth's face had a chill to it that hadn't been there earlier when she'd strolled up to the laundry room. The woman she'd talked to while she was waiting for her clothes to dry told her that the weatherman on the noon news had said that it would get down to 38 degrees that night, but that the Ozarks desperately needed the cold snap for the trees to turn color.

Hollow acorns crunched under her moccasins as she walked along the left side of the campground road, the heavy hangers digging into her fingers. When she was within a hundred feet of her motorhome, she heard a slow-moving car coming up behind her. She stepped off the pavement and into the grass to let it pass. When the front of the vehicle was even with her, it stopped.

Out of the corner of her eye, she saw a flash of silver. Visions of the Lincoln Town Car with a drunken Scot Rodecker behind the wheel shot through her mind. Her throat constricted when she heard the brief toot of a horn. Afraid that it might actually be Scot, she didn't turn her head to look, but kept on walking.

"Want a ride, lady?" the driver called out in a low, husky voice.

Thirty

The car snailed along beside her as she walked in the grass and finally, when Ruth didn't respond to the second toot of its horn, it drove on by.

When she saw the van turn into the parking space behind Jack Colby's travel trailer, she was confused. By the time she reached her motorhome, the driver was out of the van and waiting for her at the picnic table. She couldn't see who it was until she rounded the corner of the van.

"Still not speaking to strangers?" Jack Colby asked, a big grin on his face.

"Jack. I didn't know that was you," she said, returning his smile. "How are you?"

Ruth was glad her hands were full, because if they hadn't been, she knew she would have instinctively rushed up and hugged him.

It was odd, she thought. She hadn't known him very long, and yet she felt closer to Jack than she did to her friends back home. Maybe it had something to do with time and place. She didn't know. Maybe it was something as simple as the way she felt when she was around him: comfortable and secure, happy.

"Great," Jack replied. "Here, let me help you." He reached out his hands.

She gladly let him take the heavy hangers from the crook of her hand. Balancing the laundry bag on her other arm, she dug her keys out of the shoulder bag hanging waist-high at her side.

"So you bought a new van. It's beautiful." Ruth looked over at the glistening van, then turned and unlocked her door.

"Yep. I had trouble with the old Blazer all the way out here, so when I got to Springfield on Saturday, I traded it in for the van. The car dealer is a friend of my daughter's so I got a good deal on it. And he threw in a free set of luggage with the deal. Can't beat that," he laughed.

"Well, it's better than nothing." Ruth opened her door, waited until the step swung down into place.

"It still works," Jack commented as he watched the step.

"Yes, thanks to you. Come on in." Inside, she set the laundry bag down on the kitchen table, slid her shoulder bag off onto the bench seat, then took the clothes hangers from Jack and hung her clean outfits in the cramped closet.

Jack stood near the door and ran his hand across the top of the nearby recliner chair. "I like the color scheme."

"It's like a home, isn't it?" Ruth said.

Jack smiled. "Home is where the heart is." He looked toward the bucket seats in the front, glanced at the couch and chairs, turned his head and studied the kitchen, then looked down the hallway at the bed in the back and the window above the bed. "This is nice and roomy."

"My daughter thinks it's small and cramped."

"I like it. And I like the fact that you have a permanent, fixed bed in here. My sleeper sofa goes across the front of my trailer and I have to fold it out into a bed every night and fold it back up in the morning. Yes, it's very nice in here, very cozy and comfortable."

"That's right, you haven't been in here before, have you?"

"I haven't been invited before," he said with a grin.

"Well, sit down, please."

"For just a few minutes," Jack said as he eased into a recliner. "I've got a dinner engagement in a little while."

Ruth's heart sank. She sat down on the couch across from him. "So, how'd the fishing go today?" she asked, hoping her disappointment didn't show. His note had said that he'd be back in time to cook dinner for her, but if he had a dinner date, he'd obviously forgotten about the note.

"Lousy. The fish just weren't biting." He leaned back in the chair and looked totally at ease.

"Well, there's always tomorrow, if you're still here."

"Oh, I'll be here for awhile. I've signed up to take the caravan tour through the Ozarks."

"You have?" Ruth smiled, pleasantly

surprised by his announcement.

"I've been coming here every year to fish the three lakes, but I've decided to do the tourist thing for a change. After looking at their jam-packed schedule, I guess we'll get our money's worth."

"I know," Ruth said. "I looked at the itinerary while I was doing my laundry and I saw that they've got every minute of the tour planned out for us. The only free time they've allowed is during the day Wednesday."

"And that's the day I have to take my van back up to Springfield to have my new CB installed. The fellow got my mobile phone transferred over from the Blazer, but he didn't have time to put in the new CB."

"Will you be back for the festivities Wednesday night?" Ruth asked. "I think that's the night they're going to drive us around in a chartered bus."

"It is, but I'll probably have to miss it. I told my daughter I'd stop and see her again while I was up there and she doesn't get through teaching until late afternoon. By the way, would you like to have those suitcases I got with the van?"

Ruth laughed. "No, I don't need any more suitcases," she said. "When I retired last June, my three kids bought me a nice five-piece set. I used one of the suitcases once, when I camped out with my son and his family in Big Timber." Ruth watched Jack's face, but his expression didn't change at the mention of the Big Timber campground. He didn't remember her at all.

"That's the nice thing about living in my travel trailer," he said. "I don't have to live out of a suitcase. I've got a set of Samsonite bags sitting in my closet in Livingston that I seldom use."

"How long have you had the place in Livingston?" Ruth brought her feet up on the couch and leaned into the padded armrest.

"More than twenty years now. Actually, the house is in Paradise Valley, way back in the hills."

"Oh, where the celebrities live. Peter Fonda and his friends."

"And Russell Chatham, the artist," Jack added. "Over the years, I've run into him a few times fly fishing the Yellowstone."

"Really? I've got one of his lithographs hanging in my living room at home."

"I've got one of Chatham's originals hanging in my living room," Jack said with a smug smile.

"You're kidding. I couldn't afford an original."

"Neither could I. I bartered my services for it a long time ago, before he became famous."

"How'd you manage that?"

"He was building his studio and needed some electrical work done. Since that was my field of expertise in the Navy, I did the work for him. He didn't have any more money than I did at the time, so I traded him my services for a painting."

"You lucky guy."

"Believe me, I got the best end of the bargain. Do you believe in fate, Ruth?"

It was an odd question and one that Ruth hadn't thought about for a long time. "I don't know," she said. "I guess I used to, but I'm not so sure anymore."

"Well, I do." Jack sat forward in the chair, a serious look on his face. "I was meant to have that painting. It's almost as if Russell Chatham had been sitting in my living room when he painted it because it shows the same view I have of the snow-capped mountains and the Yellowstone when I look out my front window. I've got an 8x10 color photo of the painting in my trailer."

"I'd like to see it sometime."

"You shall." Jack looked at his watch, then stood up. "Well, I'd better go get cleaned up and changed for dinner. Can you be ready to go by 5:30? I made the reservations for 6:00."

Ruth's heart leaped up into her throat. "Me?" She slid her feet to the floor and stood up.

Jack laughed. "Of course, you. Didn't you get my note?"

"Well, yes, but I thought . . ."

"I know, I said I'd cook dinner for you, but since I didn't catch any fish, I thought I'd take you to a real nice restaurant my daughter recommended. The Candlestick Inn. Jenny said it sits on a hill overlooking Branson and that the view from there is fabulous. Is that all right with you?"

"Yes, of course." Stunned by his invitation, she just stood there, her arms limp at her sides. She knew she had a blank look on her face.

Jack grinned at her. "I told you I believed in fate. The very first time I saw you, I knew I'd see you again. Think about it. I'm supposed to be fishing in Colorado right now and because of a freak storm, here I am. I'll see you in a little while."

Ruth was so flustered, she didn't know what to do first. Knowing that she only had a half hour to get ready, she opened her closet, sorted through her clothes. She couldn't decide what to wear.

She pulled out her good black pants suit, stepped over to the full-length mirror on the closet door, held it up in front of her. Even if she added a bright scarf, it was too dark, too somber. She held up a bold, flowery-print dress, but didn't like that either.

She tried several more outfits and finally brought out the jersey Wedgwood-blue dress she'd bought to wear to her retirement party. It was high-necked, with a straight skirt that fell just below her knees, and had a matching sweater-jacket with beading across the front. When she held it up and looked in the mirror, she knew it was the perfect thing to wear.

After she showered, dressed, and dabbed perfume on her neck, she put on her delicate gold-chain necklace. Feeling elegant in her special-occasion dress, she stepped over and looked in the full-length mirror. The gold chain was all wrong for the outfit. It clashed with the beading of the jacket.

She reached up to unfasten the necklace and stopped when she saw the reflection of her sparkling diamond wedding rings in the mirror. She brought her hand down and stared at the rings, suddenly feeling guilty. She knew she had nothing to feel guilty about, and yet, it just didn't seem right to wear her wedding bands on a date with another man.

She hesitated a minute, then slid the rings off her finger. Her hand felt strangely naked. She placed her wedding bands in her small jewelry box, picked up the star sapphire ring that she seldom wore and slipped it on the finger where her wedding rings had been. The pure deep blue of the sapphire was the perfect match for her dress.

As she took one final check in the mirror, she wondered if there was such a thing as fate.

Thirty-one

Even though the overhead lighting in the Candlestick Inn was subdued, the elegant dining room glittered with its own ambience. Flickering light from the fat, round candles, on each table reflected off of sparkling crystal goblets and white linen tablecloths.

Ruth and Jack sat at a small table facing the window that overlooked Branson and the surrounding hills, their dinner plates and empty wineglasses already cleared away. Below, the waters of Lake Taneycomo shimmered in the last light of the disappearing sun.

Ruth paid no attention to the other diners. She listened to Jack talk about his home in Montana, fascinated by the way the wavering light of their candle threw dancing shadows across his face, exaggerating his rugged features, softening them at the same time. He looked casual, yet handsome, in his dark blue slacks, gray tweed sport jacket, and white shirt, unbuttoned at the collar.

"We moved around so much when Jenny was little, I decided that we needed a place to call home, a place where I could go after I retired from the Navy," Jack explained. "I bought the fishing shack when Jenny was five."

"The sprawling, three-bedroom, fishing shack," Ruth reminded him in a teasing manner. She wrapped both hands around her coffee cup and felt the warmth come through the clear glass.

"A nice home with live-in caretakers," Jack said, "but to Jenny and me, it was always our fishing shack. Every time I got leave, we headed for Montana. And with Charlie and Rosie there to do the cooking and the chores, it was like having our own private resort."

"It sounds like an ideal situation," Ruth said, trying to picture Jack's remote cabin in the foothills.

"It really was, for both Jenny and me," Jack said with a faraway look in his eyes.

"I give Rosie and Charlie full credit for the way Jenny turned out."

"What do you mean?"

"Jenny went through a rough time after the divorce. She was only two and in those first few years she thought the divorce was her fault. She felt rejected. She thought there was something terribly wrong with her if her own mother didn't want to see her. She broke my heart with all her questions."

"Poor little thing," Ruth said.

Jack looked across the table and smiled. "All that changed after I bought the cabin in Paradise Valley. Rosie and Charlie treated Jenny like their own granddaughter. Over the years, Rosie taught Jenny to cook and sew and all the other things a mother would teach her daughter. I can still remember the bouquets of blue flowers Jenny and Rosie picked for me every time we were there."

"And you taught her to fish, I'll bet," Ruth said.

"I did. Jenny loved the outdoors as much as I did and Charlie taught her to ride a horse and chop wood. They gave her love and a sense of stability, but they didn't spoil her. They were like family to Jenny and me. Still are."

"Are Rosie and Charlie still living there?" Ruth sipped her coffee and watched the intensity in Jack's blue eyes when he talked about the older couple.

"No, they moved to Livingston five years ago, when I moved in after I retired from the Navy. Jenny was in college and on her own by then. But Rosie and Charlie had lived there for seventeen years."

"So you were all by yourself when you moved in," Ruth said.

"Yes and after living with the regimentation of Navy life for thirty years, I loved the freedom. It was so quiet and peaceful out there. I fished all the time. I bought my Blazer and sometimes I'd throw my tent and fishing gear in the back and take off for Colorado for a week or so. Did you know that God doesn't subtract from a man's life those days he spends fishing?"

Ruth laughed. "No, I didn't know that."

"Well, it's true. I bought the Prowler travel trailer that first winter I lived there so I could head south and fish all winter. But before I could get out of town, a blizzard hit. There were snowdrifts six and seven feet high. The storm knocked my electricity out and I'd already had my phone shut off because I'd planned to leave that day. I was stranded out there for a month."

"Without electricity or a phone?"

"My electricity was restored after a week, but I had no way to let the phone company know that I wanted my service turned back on. I couldn't get to town. I didn't see another human being. I didn't talk to a soul for more than a month."

"Wasn't it lonely?"

"Yes, but I didn't mind. You can't imagine how beautiful and silent the woods were with all that snow. I fed the birds and the animals, and after the electricity came back on, I had television and radio. I had plenty of food and wood for the fireplace. I had books and music, and during the long, dark evenings, I brought out my maps and studied the lakes and rivers, and dreamed of fishing. I think everybody should spend a whole month alone."

"What do you mean?"

"I needed that time alone, Ruth. It made me realize that I wanted other people in my life, but more important, it made me realize that I wanted to do something more with my life than just fish my days away."

"But that's what you're doing, isn't it?" Ruth asked.

Jack's eyes sparkled in the candlelight when he laughed. "Fishing is my hobby now. Four years ago I joined a small organization of volunteers called RORP, Reach Out Retired People. Since then, I've been a volunteer consultant for a couple of big firms. I've given motivational seminars across the country, and here in Missouri, I've helped build houses for Habitat for Humanity, a group of people who volunteer their services to build houses for those less fortunate. It's a great life."

"So that's why you live full-time in your trailer," Ruth said.

"And you thought I was a bum. Well, I am at heart. I live in Paradise Valley four or five months out of the year. The rest of the time I travel around and volunteer my services through RORP, but only in places where the fishing's good."

Ruth turned when she saw their waiter walk up to their table. Her eyes widened when she saw the big, round tray of pastries he held out for their consideration.

"Would you care for some dessert?" asked Ron, their tall, neatly groomed waiter.

Ruth stared at each appetizing dessert as Ron named them. Caramel cheesecake, chocolate torte sprinkled with walnuts, apple dumpling, devil's food cake, pecan apple crisp with a rich vanilla sauce, and Key lime pie.

"That chocolate cake looks delicious," she said. "But, I can't. I'm stuffed."

"Could you wrap up two pieces of the chocolate cake so we can take them with us?" Jack asked the waiter.

"I sure can," Ron said with a smile.

"Then, I guess we're ready for the check," Jack said.

Ron nodded. "I'll be right back." He disappeared for a few minutes, then returned with two small, white plastic containers. He set them down on the table, presented Jack the bill on a small tray. Jack dug into his wallet, paid in cash, and told Ron to keep the change.

"It's going to be a beautiful sunset," Jack said as he stood up.

Ruth glanced out the window and saw the pink underbellies of the white, billowy clouds. "Yes, it is.

"Would you like to go out on the deck for a few minutes and watch it?" he asked.

"Yes, I would."

Ruth felt the chill of the evening as they stepped out onto the deck and was glad that she'd worn the dress with its matching sweater jacket.

"I never miss a sunset or a sunrise if I can help it," Jack said as they walked over to the railing.

"I don't think anything can beat a Montana sunset, but this one should come close," Ruth said. The edges of the clouds blazed with bright pinks and streaks of salmon.

"Look at that river down there. They call it a lake, Lake Taneycomo, but it's part of the White River."

Ruth looked down and felt dizzy. For an instant, she had the sensation that she was going to tumble over the waist-high railing and fall off the cliff as her old fear of heights came back on her. She gripped the railing and then was able to see the reddish clouds reflected in the shimmering water. "It's beautiful."

"And look at that campground over there, just across the river." Jack pointed to his left. "We couldn't see that from inside."

"No, I didn't notice it before," Ruth said. "It's full."

"And over there. The lights of the city are starting to come on." Again Jack pointed. "I think that's The Strip. Look at all those red tail lights."

A cold breeze whipped across the deck, flapping the edges of her open sweater. Ruth shivered as the chill penetrated her jersey dress.

"Are you cold?" Jack asked. He put his arm around Ruth's shoulder, drawing her close.

"It's chilly," Ruth said, feeling the warmth of his body. At that moment, her world was perfect. She had no worries about family or friends. With Jack holding her, she had no fear of heights as she stood at the railing high above the river. She felt only the beauty of the evening and the warm security of Jack's embrace.

"Do you want to leave?" he asked.

"No," she said as she snuggled in closer to him. "I want to stay here forever."

Thirty-two

Jack and Ruth walked over to the recreation hall together that morning at a few minutes before eight. The night before, they'd driven back to the campground by way of the busy Strip so they could see the glittery neon lights of the various music shows. They had eaten the chocolate cake at Ruth's dinette booth and talked for another half hour before Jack went back to his own trailer. Contented, Ruth had no trouble falling asleep, even though she'd had three cups of coffee after dinner.

"You look cute in jeans," Jack said as he reached to open the door of the rec hall.

Ruth smiled. She had decided that since this was to be a day of driving through the Ozark hills and eating lunch and dinner at dusty picnic tables, it would be the perfect time to try out her new stretch jeans. She was surprised at how comfortable they were, even though she knew they clung to her rear end like a glove.

"Thanks," she said. "So do you."

Jack laughed. "I look cute in jeans?"

"Why not?"

Jack opened the door to the big recreation room and they were greeted by a balding, jovial man who was on the plump side. He wore faded jeans, red suspenders, and a blue shirt that didn't hide the thick stomach that hung over his pants at the waistline.

"Come on in. I'm George Barton," the fellow said, "and this is my wife, Sandy. For better or worse, we're your tour guides."

"Your names, please," Sandy said. She was on the plump side, too, and wore jeans and a loose-fitting white blouse. Her blonde hair was pulled back from her face and tied with a ribbon.

"I'm Jack Colby and this is Ruth Nichols," Jack said.

Sandy looked down at the list on her clipboard. "Jack Colby," she repeated. "Here you are. And Ruth Nichols. The two singles. Okay, I got you." She made a check mark by each of their names. "Help yourself to the coffee and donuts and then find a seat at one of the tables. Pick up a tour packet if you didn't bring yours with you."

"I brought mine." Ruth patted the side of her large shoulder bag.

Ruth heard her name called out as she was putting two donuts on a paper plate. She turned around and saw Meg Rodecker waving to her from across the room. She acknowledged her with a nod.

"That's the couple I was telling you about last night," she said to Jack. "My friends from Billings."

"They look happy enough to me," Jack commented. He drew two cups of coffee from the urn, handed one of them to Ruth and selected two donuts from the tray.

"Scot's probably sober this time of morning, but I'd be willing to bet that he's hung over."

On the way over to Meg's table, Ruth stopped to say hello to Bill and Clara Letterman, the older couple she'd met at the rest area the first day of her trip. After she and Jack sat down across the table from Meg and Scot, she made quick introductions and was relieved to immediately hear George Barton begin his welcome speech.

"We're glad you're all here. What a fine bunch you are," he said, standing at the front of the room. "Now, you all know that I'm George, your wagon master on this here trail ride, so if you've got any questions, you come to me. If you got any complaints, you talk to my purty little wife, Sandy." He patted Sandy on the head. "Living with me, she's used to complaints." Nervous laughter floated across the room.

"That's right." Sandy nodded, agreeing with him.

"Look around at the other people in the room," George said. He paused while the people did what they were told. "Now, these are the people you're going to be eating, sleeping, and breathing with for the next nine days, so I suggest you get to know each other. Shall we start by asking the women their ages?"

"No," Sandy said. "Your mama taught you better than to ask a woman her age."

A gray-haired woman near the front of the room stood up and held her hand up. "We don't mind telling our age, do we, Ida?" she said. She tugged on the arm of her female companion and forced her to stand up. "I'm Ada and this is my twin sister, Ida, and we're seventy-nine years old," she said with obvious pride. "And if there's any hiking to be done, we'll be at the head of the pack."

The people in the room began to applaud. Ada took a bow, then the two women sat down.

"Well, congratulations, ladies. I won't be picking any fights with you," George said. "Now, let's go around the room. I want everyone to stand up and tell us your name and where you're from. If you're traveling together, stand up together so we can get an idea who belongs to whom. We'll start with Ada and Ida."

The two women stood up again and stated their full names, and said they were from Fayetteville, Arkansas. They sat down and two couples stood up together, stating they were all from Jupiter, Florida. As they went around the room, Ruth and Jack were the only ones who stood up separately. After the ritual of introductions was over, George turned the briefing over to his wife.

"We have eighteen people signed up for the caravan," Sandy stated, referring to notes on the table in front of her. "Counting George and me, that makes twenty of us and I assure you we're going to have a good time."

"There'll be a total of seven rigs and one car in our caravan," George said. "So, when we're driving from place to place, we'd like you to leave several car lengths between vehicles so other motorists can pass."

"That's right," Sandy said. "All of your campgrounds fees are included in the tour package, and so are most of your meals and two music shows. There are several maps in your packet, which you'll be using during the tour. We'll be visiting each of the three lakes, Lake Taneycomo, Table Rock Lake, and Bull Shoals Lake. Actually, they're all part of the White River, but they were dammed up years ago to control the water."

"Save the history lesson for later, Sandy," George said. "These people paid good money to see the sights, not to listen to you spout facts."

George's remark brought roaring applause from the small audience.

"See, Sandy, I told you these people were anxious to get on the road," George said with a grin.

"Don't pay any attention to George," Sandy said. "You'll get used to him, just as I have after twenty-five years of marriage."

Everyone laughed and Ruth could see that George and Sandy were setting the tone for the trip.

"Now, let's go over our itinerary briefly,"

Sandy continued. "Does everybody have a copy?" She looked out at her attentive audience. A rattling of papers rippled through the room. "Good. Now, today we're going to loop through the Mark Twain National Forest. There's a small map of the area in your packet. We'll go through Hercules Glades Wilderness, across Gladetop Trail, and we'll have a catered lunch at the campground at Camp Ridge."

"This will be one of the prettiest parts of the entire tour," George added. "Three days ago we were holding our breath because the leaves hadn't started to change. Luckily we had a cold snap and the trees are brilliant with color now. Hope you've got cameras."

"After lunch, we'll swing back through Forsyth and Hollister," Sandy continued. "We'll take Highway 65 south to 86, and we'll camp at the Table Rock State Park tonight. It's right on Table Rock Lake. We'll barbecue hamburgers there tonight. Look at the bigger map of the Branson area and you'll see where the campground is."

Ruth leaned toward Jack. "It's exciting, isn't it?" she whispered.

"It's going to be fun," Jack whispered back.

Ruth glanced over at her friends, she didn't

431

like the way Scot was glaring at her.

"There's good bass fishing there," George said. "And you can swim at Sunset Beach if you don't mind freezing your butt."

"George, hush," Sandy said. "Tomorrow, Wednesday, we'll come back here and you'll have a free day in Branson. You'll be responsible for your own breakfast and lunch. We'll have a shuttle bus and a driver here at the campground all day if you want a ride anyplace. We'll all meet at five o'clock at the office and we'll take the shuttle bus to dinner at The Wharf. Then we'll drive around and show you the sights at night."

George interrupted. "If any of you want to stay at Table Rock Park during the day tomorrow, you can rent a boat or fishing gear. Just be back here by five o'clock or you'll miss dinner."

"Thursday, we'll caravan to Eureka Springs and stay there two nights," Sandy continued. "Friday night you'll see the Great Passion Play. Saturday night we'll stay in a state park campground and have another cookout. We'll return to Branson Sunday afternoon and then we've got three full days of fun scheduled for you, including two music shows, a trip to Silver Dollar City, and a boat ride on the Lake

Queen. I'll fill you in on the details as we go along. Any questions?"

"Yes," George called out. "Can we get going now?"

Again, the people laughed.

"Let's go, then," Sandy said. "Line your rigs up behind our Holiday Rambler motorhome near the office." She glanced at her watch. "It's 8:30 and we'll pull out in fifteen minutes. When we get out on the highway, we'll probably get separated by traffic, but you've all got your maps. You'll catch up when the traffic thins out, so don't worry about it."

"Let's hit the road," George said. "It's now 8:31."

The room erupted in laughter, which was quickly replaced by the sound of scuffling chairs scraping against the hardwood floors and the din of excited voices as the tour members got up to leave.

In the crush of things, Ruth ended up next to Meg as they walked toward the door.

"We've got to run back over to our hotel first," Meg said as they walked out together. "I forgot my tape recorder. But we'll catch up to you along the way."

"See you at the lunch stop, then, if not before," Ruth said.

"See you later," Meg called as she caught up with Scot and headed toward the visitor's parking lot near the front office.

Jack waited for Ruth just outside the door and they walked back to their respective rigs together. They had both already unhooked their cords and hoses from the outlets and Jack had hooked his new blue and silver conversion van up to his travel trailer and was ready to pull out.

"You go ahead," Jack said, "and I'll fall in right behind you."

Ruth climbed into the driver's seat and cracked her side window open. She fastened her seat belt, slid her driving glasses into place, and assumed a comfortable driving position.

When she turned the ignition key, her engine made a funny clunking noise. "What the heck?" she said aloud. She tried it again and there was no noise at all. The engine didn't even turn over.

Ruth's heart sank to the pit of her stomach.

"What's the matter?" Jack asked as he strolled back over to her motorhome.

"I don't know." She tried it again. Nothing. "It won't start."

Jack propped open the panel below the wide windshield that exposed the motor. "Try it again," he called from the front of the motorhome.

Ruth turned the key several more times. Nothing happened.

Jack walked around to the driver's side, shook his head. "I don't know what it is," he said. "I don't think it's your starter or your alternator, though. How old is your battery?"

"I had a new one put in just before I left home."

"Then it should be all right." Jack frowned and stared down at the ground for a minute. "That loud clunk I heard didn't sound good. I think you're going to have to call a mechanic."

Ruth looked at her watch and saw that it was already ten minutes after eight. "Oh, no, why does this have to happen right now?" She lowered her head and rubbed her forehead with her fingers.

"Don't worry. We'll get it fixed."

"But the caravan's not going to wait for me. You'd better go on with them."

"I'll stay with you until you get it fixed," Jack assured her. "We can catch up to them, even if we're an hour behind. I'll run up to the office and tell George that we'll be a little late

435

in starting out. Maybe he can recommend a good mechanic."

Ruth watched helplessly as Jack took off at a trot. Totally frustrated, she pounded her fist against the steering wheel and muttered an oath under her breath.

After a minute, she pulled the key out of the ignition and checked to be sure she was using the right one. That's stupid, she thought. If it were the wrong key, it wouldn't even turn in the slot. But she was desperate.

She slid the key back in, turned it just enough to check the fuel tank meter. The red needle slowly swung over to just above the three-quarter mark. She had plenty of gas. Then what was wrong? Her friend, Glen Amos, had checked everything thoroughly before she left home. But he had also cautioned her that since she hadn't driven the motorhome for so long, she was likely to develop problems that he couldn't detect.

She took her driving glasses off, set them in the console between the seats, and unfastened her seat belt, then climbed out of the motorhome. She walked around the front and stared into the maw of the engine for several minutes. It was a jumble of wires and hoses and metal parts she didn't understand. Nothing looked loose. Nothing looked broken. But she had no idea what she was looking for.

She looked up and saw Jack running back from the office. He was out of breath by the time he reached her.

"A mechanic is on his way," he said with a reassuring smile. "If traffic is in his favor, he'll be here in ten minutes. If not, then it could take him a half hour to get here."

"What about the caravan?"

"They were just pulling out. George said we'd have no trouble catching up to them. They plan to make a couple of stops at scenic spots along the way so people can take pictures. We'll catch them before lunch, I'm sure."

"And, what if the mechanic can't fix the motorhome right away?"

"We'll just have to wait and see." Jack sat down at the picnic table between their two vehicles.

Ruth looked once more at the maze of wires and hoses, then walked over and sat down across the table from Jack. She checked her watch every few minutes. It took the mechanic the full half-hour and five minutes more to get there.

Her hopes soared when she saw the white

and blue tow truck drive up the paved lane. She jumped up and waited for the truck to pull up in front of her motorhome. Jack followed her.

A middle-aged man with a dark, wiry mustache hopped out of the driver's seat and walked over to the open hood. He wore a blue, grease-stained jumpsuit.

"Hi, I'm Kenny," he said with a friendly smile. "What have we got here?"

Ruth explained her problem, told him about the loud clunking noise.

"Hmmm, that doesn't sound good. Let me have a look."

Ruth watched as the mechanic jiggled a few wires, tested the spark plugs to be sure they were secure.

"Let me try to jumpstart it," he said after a few minutes of checking hoses and wires more thoroughly and tapping on metal parts with a screwdriver.

Jack climbed up in the driver's seat of the motorhome. Ruth gladly allowed the men to take over. She didn't even want to think about her problems. She stood there and watched the mechanic hook up the jumper cables to both vehicles.

Kenny got in the truck, started the engine.

"Okay, try it," he hollered above the roar of his whining engine.

Jack turned the key then shook his head. Kenny revved the truck's motor for a minute, called out for Jack to try again.

Jack turned the key. "Nothing," he told Ruth through the open window. "It's not going to start."

Ruth put her hand to her mouth and felt a nervous fluttering in the pit of her stomach.

The mechanic swung down from the truck's bench seat and unhooked the jumper cables, careful that the clip ends didn't touch each other.

"We're going to have to tow it in," he said as he tossed the jumper cables into the cab of the truck.

"How long will it take to fix it?" Ruth asked.

"There's no way of knowing until we check it out. If it's nothing serious, it would be late this afternoon at the very earliest."

Ruth tried not to let her disappointment show. "You think it's something simple to fix, then?" she asked, exercising her last shred of hope.

"We won't know until we check it out," he said patiently. "But, from the clanking noise you described, I'd say you've got major problems."

"And what does that mean?"

"If we have to tear your engine apart, it'll take us three or four days. If we have to replace your motor, it'll take at least a week."

Ruth clapped her hands to her cheeks and tried to quell the sick feeling in her stomach. "Oh, no. I'm part of a tour group," she said. "What am I going to do?"

"I don't know, ma'am." The mechanic handed her a business card. "Call us about 5:00 this afternoon. We should be able to tell you what's wrong by then."

Ruth took the card but didn't reply for fear of bursting into tears.

There went the first day of her trip through the Ozarks, she thought. And with her luck, she figured she'd miss the whole damned tour. She repeated the serenity prayer in her mind, but it didn't do one bit of good.

Thirty-three

The mechanic backed his tow truck up to the motorhome, then got out to check the distance between the two vehicles.

Ruth stared at his business card as the impact of her situation hit her full force. "I guess I'll have to miss the tour," she told Jack. "At least today's trip."

"No you won't," Jack said. "You can ride with me."

"That's fine, but where do I sleep tonight? On the ground? Which I wouldn't mind doing if I had a warm sleeping bag."

"I've got a brand new sleeping bag, but you're welcome to stay in my trailer. My couch makes into a bed and so does my dinette booth, same as yours. And I've got a privacy curtain I can pull between the two sleeping areas. I don't bite, Ruth."

Ruth struggled with her conscience. Even if Meg and Scot weren't around to monitor her actions, she didn't think she could bring herself to spend the night in Jack's trailer, no matter how innocent.

When they had stood on the deck of the Candlestick Inn watching the sunset together, his arm wrapped around her, Ruth hadn't wanted the moment to end. After she went to bed, she'd fantasized about spending the rest of her days with him, sharing other quiet sunsets and walking through the woods together, hand in hand. But in the reality of the morning light, she'd realized that it wasn't to be. Jack was basically a loner and she was tied to family obligations.

Now that she had the opportunity to share the overnight camping trip with him, she couldn't do it. She trusted Jack completely, but she didn't know if she could trust her own feelings of vulnerability. And she didn't want to do anything that would eventually spoil the close, comfortable friendship they'd developed.

"As much as I'd like to take you up on your offer, I just can't, Jack."

"I'm disappointed," Jack said. "It would be fun to share the drive through the countryside. It's not as much fun when you have to drive it alone."

"It would be fun, Jack." For a minute, Ruth reconsidered.

The mechanic strolled over to them and broke the spell. "Ma'am, do you need to get anything out of your motorhome before I hook it up to the tow truck?"

"Yes, my purse. Just a minute."

"Let me know when you're ready." Kenny walked back over to his truck.

Ruth made a quick decision. She wanted to share the trip with Jack and she wasn't going to let this rare opportunity slip through her fingers. Besides, she really didn't care what anyone else thought.

"Jack, I'm going with you. What do I need to take with me?"

"Not much. Just whatever you'll need for tonight. A nightgown, pajamas, whatever you sleep in. We'll be back here in the morning and if your motorhome isn't ready by then, I'll drive you to the repair shop and you can get whatever you need for the rest of the trip."

"Oh, that's right. If they don't get it fixed right away, I won't have a home to come home to, will I? I'll have a vacant campsite and no place to sleep. I'll have to find a motel somewhere. Oh, shoot. Life does get complicated, doesn't it?" But Ruth wasn't going to let anything ruin her good mood. She'd face that problem when she had to.

"Mi casa es su casa," Jack said with a smile. "For as long as you need it."

She laughed. "Seriously, I may need it. Let me get my things. Oh, I don't have a suitcase. Well, I'll use my laundry bag," she said, expressing her thoughts out loud.

"You need a suitcase? Well, I just happen to have a whole set of luggage I'm trying to give away. Take your pick."

"What a handy person you are to have around," she teased.

"I think so." Jack had a playful twinkle in his eyes when he looked at her. "I fix broken steps. I offer free shuttle service to lovely ladies, free lodging. What more could you want?"

"Not much. If you do cooking and laundry, I might be interested."

"Don't push your luck, lady." He walked over to his van, stepped through the tow bars that linked it to the travel trailer, and opened the back door far enough to reach inside and grab one of the new suitcases.

"Thanks," Ruth said when she took the gray, soft-sided bag from him.

"You'd better hurry," he said. "Your free shuttle service leaves in two minutes."

"Yes, sir," Ruth said with a smile.

Inside her motorhome, she set the piece of luggage on top of her bed and opened it. Rushed for time, she opened her top dresser drawer, pulled out a pink nightgown and clean underwear. Then she stared at the thin, frilly gown, put it back in the drawer. She wasn't going to parade around in Jack's trailer in a nightgown.

She opened another drawer, picked up her old gray sweat suit with the pink trim. That was as sexy as she was going to be that night, she thought, as she placed the baggy outfit in the suitcase.

She opened her sweater drawer, took out her warm, pink, button-down sweater. She packed a light blue blouse for morning, and another complete outfit, just in case. She added a clean washcloth and towel, her old slippers, and her small jewelry case to the other things in the suitcase.

She went to the closet, stripped a dark blue windbreaker jacket off its hanger and set it in the bag in case the sweater wasn't enough. She zipped the suitcase closed, carried it to the door, and set it down.

She paused and closed her eyes, cupped her forehead in her hand, and tried to think of anything else she might need for the overnight jaunt. Her toothbrush, toothpaste, and a bar of soap, which she stuck into her oversized shoulder bag.

She checked to make sure she'd left the keys in the ignition. She had, but all of her other keys were there, too, and she didn't want to leave them on the key chain. She walked up to the driver's seat and removed them from the key chain, leaving only those that belonged with the motorhome. She stuck the extra keys in a coin purse in her shoulder bag.

Jack was right. If she needed anything else, she could pick it up at the repair shop in the morning. Hopefully, she'd have her motorhome back by then.

Just before she left, she looked in the refrigerator. She took out the clear plastic bag that held four apples and the block of cheddar cheese she'd bought at the Osceola Cheese Factory. She put those items into a paper sack, and added an unopened box of saltine crackers.

"I think I've got everything I need," she said as she carried the light suitcase and the paper sack outside. Her bag and her camera hung from their straps over her shoulder.

"I'll put the suitcase in the van," Jack said as he took the gray tweed bag and the paper sack from her.

"I've got some apples and cheese in that sack. Do you have room for them in your refrigerator?"

"I'll make room, but you didn't need to bring any food."

Ruth smiled. "I don't know what I'd do without you, Jack."

"You'd probably bum a ride with those little old twins, Ada and Ida."

"Heaven forbid. They'd talk your leg off."

"You know, I got that same impression."

Kenny, the mechanic walked over. "Are we ready to hook you up?"

"Yes," Ruth said. "I sure hope you can get it fixed by tomorrow morning. That's not just my transportation, it's my home."

"We'll do our best, ma'am."

Ruth and Jack stood together and watched Kenny go through the various steps of attaching the heavy towing bar to the bulky Coachman.

"I don't think I can watch," Ruth said as

Kenny got into the tow truck and started the engine.

Jack put his arm around her. "You'll get it back."

Ruth got a sick, empty feeling in her stomach as she watched her motorhome being towed away.

"Well, there goes my home," she said as it disappeared from sight. "I feel so . . . so lost, so disoriented. Stranded." She turned in Jack's arm and buried her head on his chest. She welcomed his support when he wrapped both arms around her and held her tight.

It wasn't just that her motorhome was being towed away that bothered her. It was that her memories were being towed away with it. It was a preview of the feelings she'd have to face when she returned to Billings and sold the motorhome.

Maybe those were the feelings she'd have to face before she'd be free to accept new emotions into her heart.

Thirty-four

Even though they were nearly two hours behind the rest of the caravan, Jack and Ruth drove the loop through the Mark Twain National Forest at a leisurely pace.

The narrow country pavement snaked through the thick autumn woods for miles and each curve of the road brought a new breathtaking view of the brilliantly colored oak and hickory leaves. On both sides of the road, flame-red, golden-ocher, royal purple, lemon-yellow, and bright orange leaves flamed against the green of the hearty cedars and the tall Missouri pines.

Ruth was awed by the spectacle of what the Ozarks chambers of commerce called the "Flaming Fall Revue." Each far hill and distant glen presented a new painting, each more vivid than the last, each a dazzling feast for the senses. It was as if Mother

Nature was proclaiming a wondrous beauty in each dying leaf.

By the time they reached the designated lunch stop area, they were too late to take advantage of the catered lunch that was included in the tour. They stopped there anyway, even though the others were long gone.

They ate sandwiches made from Jack's bread and lunchmeat, and cheese sliced from Ruth's block of cheddar. They ate two of the apples, then strolled through the nearby woods so Ruth could take pictures of the spectacular fall colors.

They didn't catch up with the other sixteen members of the caravan until they arrived at the overnight campground on Table Rock Lake late in the afternoon.

Jack eased his rig to a stop at the tiny Corps of Engineers registration booth at the entrance to Long Creek Park. When he didn't see anyone inside, he got out of the van.

A woman came out of a nearby travel trailer and headed toward them. "Hi, can I help you?" she asked.

"We're part of the caravan tour," Jack said. "Where are we supposed to park?"

"You can park in any site you want to.

The others in your group wanted to be close to the covered picnic area, so they're camped down near the lake. Just follow this road on down and you'll run into them," she said, pointing.

"Thanks. We'll find them."

Jack got back in the van and pulled away, keeping his speed below the park's posted fifteen-miles-per-hour speed limit as he drove through the wooded campground.

Ruth spotted the small cluster of familiar motorhomes and travel trailers nestled among the trees near the end of the road. Beyond the trees, the blue, shimmering lake stretched out around the peninsula of land. Off to the right of the parked RVs, the tin roof of the covered picnic area glinted in the late afternoon sun.

"There they are," she said. "Like birds of a feather." When she noticed the silver Lincoln Town Car parked in the shade, she felt herself tense. She had hoped that Meg and Scot would have gone back to their hotel. She didn't want them to know she was spending the night in Jack's trailer, but she wouldn't hide the fact if it came up.

Jack slowed down long before he reached the others and backed his travel trailer into a paved site that overlooked the lake. The ground was covered with dry, brittle leaves that had blown off the trees surrounding the campsite. The leaves that remained on the trees were at the peak of their color.

"How's this?" he asked.

"It's perfect," Ruth said. "Look at the view of the lake we've got from here. You couldn't ask for anything better."

Jack started to open his door, then hesitated. "If you want to call and check on your motorhome, you can use my car phone."

"No, I don't even want to think about it tonight. I'll wait until we get back to Branson in the morning."

"Do you want to call your daughter?"

Ruth laughed. "No, not tonight. I told her we'd be camped in the wilderness and I probably wouldn't have access to a phone. Besides, I don't want her to worry about the motorhome. I'll wait until I know what's wrong with it."

"I guess we'd better walk down there and join the others as soon as I hook up or we're going to miss the barbecue."

Ruth opened her car door and immediately felt the chill in the crisp autumn air.

"I'd better take a sweater."

"A good idea." He got the suitcase out of the van, set it on the picnic table for her. "It'll probably be dark by the time we get back. I'll take the flashlight and leave a light on in the trailer."

While Jack took care of the hookups, Ruth dug her heavy pink sweater out of the suitcase and put it on. She retrieved her shoulder bag and camera from the floor in front of her seat.

With the hookups done, Jack picked up the suitcase and carried it into the trailer. He closed the drapes, turned on an overhead light and when he came out, he was carrying a bulky, down jacket and a big black flashlight.

They walked down the hill and as they neared the covered picnic area where everyone was gathered, Meg was the first one to spot them coming. She rushed up to greet them.

"Ruth, I'm so glad you made it. George told us you had car trouble and we were worried about you when you didn't show up for lunch. Hi, Jack," she said, acknowledging his presence, then turning her attention back to Ruth. "What happened to your motorhome?"

Scot ambled up and stood by Meg's side. He nodded to both Ruth and Jack, but didn't speak.

"It just wouldn't start," Ruth said.

"Where are you parked?" Meg asked.

"Back up the hill a ways."

"So, what was wrong?"

"I don't know yet. It's in the shop and I won't know until morning."

Meg looked surprised. "So, you rode out here with Jack?"

"Yes. It was a beautiful drive through the Mark Twain Forest, wasn't it?"

"Yes. Scot and I were just ready to head back to Branson. I'm glad you got here before we left."

"Oh, have they already eaten?" Ruth smelled the woodsmoke as she leaned sideways and peered around Meg. Most of the people were sitting in the shade of the high tin roof that covered the three long, cement picnic tables. George Barton, wearing a chef's hat and apron, hovered over the smoking barbecue grill beyond the tables, a spatula in his hand. At least two dozen thick hamburgers sizzled on the grill. Sandy Barton and a couple of the other women were busy setting the food out on the tables.

"Not yet," Meg said. "Scot and I are going to eat at Dimitri's Floating Restaurant near downtown Branson and then we're going to see some of Branson's nightlife. Would you like to ride back into town with us, Ruth?"

"I just got here," Ruth said.

"But you'll need a ride back to town."

"No, I'm staying here tonight. I paid good money for this tour and I'm going to enjoy every minute of it."

"But where will you sleep?"

Ruth glanced up at Jack. "Jack was kind enough to offer me one of the beds in his trailer."

"Oh, that was nice of him," Meg said.

"That ought to be nice and cozy," Scot said sarcastically. He crossed his arms and gave Ruth a dirty look.

She wanted to slap him for his blunt remark, the insinuation in his expression. She felt Jack's arm slide across her back, his hand settle on her upper arm as he pulled her to his side. Although she was embarrassed by the gesture, she appreciated his show of protection.

"I haven't been inside Jack's trailer yet,"

Ruth said, leveling a cold look at Scot, "but I certainly hope it's cozy in there. It's supposed to get down to thirty-six degrees tonight."

"Ruth, let's have lunch tomorrow," Meg said, paying no attention to her husband's crude remark. "It'll be the only chance we'll have to get together before Scot and I leave for the Caribbean on Sunday. Jack, you're welcome to come along."

"Thanks anyway," Jack said, "but after I get Ruth squared away, I have to drive up to Springfield."

"It'll have to be an early lunch, Ruth," Meg said. "I've got an interview with Andy Williams at one o'clock and then we're going to his matinee at three o'clock. Isn't that exciting? I'll get an extra ticket for the show so you can go with us."

"It sounds like fun, but I really want to wander through some of the craft shops tomorrow afternoon and buy some souvenirs for my grandchildren."

"Well, at least you can have lunch with us," Meg insisted.

"I think I'll pass on lunch," Ruth said.

Scot glared at Ruth. "Meg, don't beg," he said. "Can't you see that Ruth no longer has time for old loyal friends like us?"

"That's nonsense, Scot," Meg said. "I can understand her wanting some time alone to shop, but she'll have lunch with us. Ruth, we'll pick you up at the Branson campground at 11:00 tomorrow morning."

"Okay. Lunch only." Ruth said.

"Good. Come on, Scot. Let's get back to town. I'm hungry." Meg grabbed Scot's arm and led him to their rented car.

Jack didn't take his arm away from Ruth until after Scot and Meg had driven away.

"I know Scot's a friend of yours, but I don't think I could spend more than five minutes around that man without punching him in the nose," Jack said. "There's just no excuse for his rudeness and you don't deserve to be treated that way."

"I really don't want to have lunch with them tomorrow. Oh, why do I get myself into these things?"

Jack smiled at her. "You just haven't learned to say no."

Thirty-five

Ruth was stuffed from eating a thick hamburger and sampling all of the salads and desserts that were offered, but she enjoyed sitting around the table after dinner, talking to Bill and Clara Letterman and the others she'd met on the trip.

Once the sun dropped below the horizon, the cold nip of evening set in quickly. When the older tour members retired to their trailers and motorhomes to watch television or play cards, she and Jack strolled back up the hill, pausing halfway up to watch the glorious sunset over the water. By the time they reached Jack's trailer, it was totally dark outside.

When she stepped up into the softly lit trailer, she was surprised at how neat and homey it looked. "It's cozy in here. And warm."

He followed her inside. "I turned the

heater on low before we left. It's a lot smaller than your motorhome, but there's plenty of room for me. This is my closet," he said, tapping the sliding wood panels just inside the door. "And the bathroom next to it."

Ruth stood near the kitchen sink and glanced around the small open area. The beige and brown upholstery of the padded dinette cushions matched the fabric of the sleeper sofa at the far end of the room. "I really like your trailer," she said. "You keep it so neat and clean."

Jack laughed. "I live by the motto, 'A place for everything and everything in its place.' As you know, when you live in cramped quarters, you have to keep things put away or before you know it, you won't have room to move."

"That's true. I don't even save magazines like I do at home."

"Oh, take a look at that copy of my Russell Chatham original. It's right there on the wall above the dining booth."

Ruth stepped across the aisle and looked up at the framed color photo of the painting. She felt the hairs on her arms stand straight up. "Oh, Jack, I've got goosebumps all over."

"It's a beauty, isn't it? The mountains on a misty morning, the Yellowstone. Chatham captured it all."

"No, I mean, my Chatham lithograph is of that exact same painting. I'm sure of it."

"Really?" Jack looked at her and smiled. "Then you know what I see when I look out my front room window in Paradise Valley."

"That's eerie that we'd have the same paintings. You don't know how many times I've stared at my copy and wished I had a little cabin on the Yellowstone with that kind of a view of the mountains."

Jack grinned. "Maybe it's fate," he teased.

"I don't believe in fate. At least, I didn't before."

"What does that mean?"

"I think things happen because of one's own actions. I believe that people have control over their own destinies and over the lives they create for themselves."

"And sometimes people create comfortable little lives for themselves and then they're afraid to grow and make the changes that might make them happier."

Ruth cocked her head and looked up at Jack. "Are you talking about me?"

"No. Just making a comment. Come on in

and sit down in my humble living room. Would you like some coffee?"

"Sounds good." Ruth walked up front and started to sit down on the long sofa when she noticed a picture hanging on the wood paneled wall at the opposite end of the couch. She saw that it was actually two pictures, side by side, within one frame, but from that distance, she couldn't make out the features. "Is that your daughter?" she asked.

"No," Jack said as he drew two cups and a jar of instant coffee from a kitchen cupboard.

Ruth strolled over to the wall and was startled when she saw the double photographs. One of them was of Jack in rumpled clothes, standing beside the fishing pond at the campground in Big Timber, showing off his fish. She was positive that it was the picture she'd taken of him that day.

The other picture was even more of a shock to her. It was of her, taken that same day in Big Timber by her son, Tony, with her own camera. She held a fishing pole in her hand and wore that silly white seaman's cap with the brim pulled down to shade her eyes from the bright sun. Directly beneath the two photographs, Jack had printed the words, "Two Old Fishing Cronies."

Ruth whirled around. "Jack, where did you get these pictures?" she asked, not caring that there was a tone of accusation in her voice.

"From your son," he said casually. He filled the two cups with water, added instant coffee, and setting both cups in the microwave oven, pushed the timer buttons.

"You know Tony?"

"Sure. I've fished with Tony on several occasions. He gave me those pictures the last time I saw him, over the Labor Day weekend, when we were both camped at the Spring Creek Trout Ranch in Big Timber. He said you'd sent him an extra set of prints. That's a cute picture of you," he said with a smile.

"Cute? I looked awful that day. It was so hot."

"Well, look at me. I look like an old wino with my missing teeth. That was when I'd chipped a tooth on my partial plate and had to leave it with the dentist to be repaired."

He set up a TV tray in front of the couch, then put both cups of hot coffee on it.

Ruth sat down, picked up a cup and blew

462

on it. "So, you've known who I was all along."

"Yes."

"Did you recognize me that first day at the rest area when you offered to fix my step?" She took a sip of coffee, set the cup down.

Jack grinned. "Sure, I recognized you. After all, there aren't too many short, stubborn women around."

"Thanks a lot."

"I remembered meeting you at the fishing pond. I knew you were Tony's mother, but I didn't know your name until you told me."

"Well, what a coincidence that we ran into each other again at the rest area."

"I thought so."

They talked for more than an hour, until Ruth began to get sleepy. "I think I'll get changed for bed," she said.

"I'm sleepy, too," Jack said. "You can change in the bathroom while I make up the beds."

"I think I'll walk over to the restroom." She opened the suitcase and took out her old gray sweat suit and a clean, blue blouse for morning. "Be back in a few minutes."

In the public restroom, she changed into the sweat suit, removing her bra and panty hose, wrapping them inside her jeans and blouse. She thought about their chance meeting at the rest area and wondered if it were more than a coincidence. When she got back to the trailer, Jack was standing outside, looking up at the stars. She could see by the light of his porch light that he'd changed into a dark blue jogging suit.

"Jack, tell me something. Are you part of a conspiracy?"

"A conspiracy?" Jack turned to look at her. "What are you talking about?"

"Did Tony ask you to follow me out here and keep an eye on me?"

Jack laughed. "No, but it wouldn't have been a bad idea. I think you need a keeper."

"I can take care of myself."

"Sure you can. I'll guarantee you, I wasn't appointed to watch over you. I told you I come out here to the Ozarks every year to fish and to visit my daughter."

"I know."

"When I saw Tony over the Labor Day weekend, he told me you were coming out here for the caravan. I had already decided to head this way and I planned to look you up while I was here. But it wasn't until we spent that wonderful, rainy evening together in the Sheridan campground that I decided to join the tour so I could spend more time with you."

Ruth was surprised and pleased by his words. "I'm glad you did," she said, hoping the huskiness in her voice wasn't obvious. "The stars are pretty, aren't they?"

Jack turned off the porch light, then walked over and stood behind her. "Now look at them. Without the light, you can see so many more stars." He put his arms around her and pulled her against him.

She tipped her head back against his shoulder and looked up at the velvet sky. "And they look so much closer." When she felt the warmth of his body through the fabric of her sweat suit, she wanted to stay in his arms for a long time. She shuddered, but not from the cold.

"I guess we'd better go in," Jack said. "It's cold out here."

"Yes, we'd better." She stepped away and turned to face him. "I really enjoy being with you, Jack. You're a very special person."

Even though it was dark, she could see the shadow of his smile.

"You're very special to me, Ruth. I think you must know that I'm very fond of you."

Ruth felt her cheeks flush and was glad it was dark outside.

Once they were inside, she saw that he'd already made up both beds. There was a sleeping bag and a pillow on each.

"You've got your choice of beds. I put the new sleeping bag on this one," he said, indicating the converted dinette booth, "but I can switch them around if you'd rather sleep on the couch."

"This is fine," Ruth said. She sat on the edge of the thick cushion and removed her shoes.

"Are you ready for lights out?"

"I'm ready."

Jack turned the light off. The room was instantly dark and Ruth's eyes gradually adjusted to the dim light of the two night lights that were plugged into wall sockets, one near the kitchen sink and the other close to the floor, near the door.

"Well, goodnight, Ruth. Pleasant dreams," he said as he pulled the curtain between them.

"Goodnight, Jack. Thanks for everything." As she climbed into the sleeping bag, she heard him kick off his shoes. After he settled into his bed, the only sound she heard was the distant barking of a dog, or perhaps a coyote. She didn't know.

Feeling peaceful and secure, she fell asleep almost immediately and when she awoke, she saw the pale light of morning showing through beneath the drapes over her bed. She glanced around and saw that the curtain between the two beds was still closed.

Not wanting to wake Jack, she slipped into her shoes and gathered up her jeans, bra, pink sweater, and the clean blouse she'd set out the night before. She picked up her shoulder bag and quietly made her way out of the trailer, walking over to the restrooms where she changed clothes and put on her sweater. Since there was no sink or running water in the bathroom, she brushed her teeth outside, using the water from a nearby faucet.

Back at the trailer, she sat at the picnic table and watched the gray, eastern sky begin to take on the pink tinge of sunrise. A few minutes later, she heard someone walking up the lane. She stood up, turned around and was surprised to see Jack walking toward her. He wore jeans, a clean, blue chambray shirt, and his bulky jacket.

"Oh, I thought you were still asleep," she said.

"No, I've been awake for an hour. I didn't want to wake you up so I walked down to the lake."

"You made it back in time so we can watch the sunrise together. It's going to be just as pretty as the sunset was last night."

When Jack walked over to her, she smelled the fresh, delicate scent of his aftershave.

"Oh, Ruth, you're so beautiful. I wish you could see how radiant you look in the morning light." He cupped her face in his hands, then lowered his head and kissed her.

It was just a light brush of his lips, but Ruth wanted more. She followed his lips with her own, not letting him go. He came back to her with a full, warm kiss that melted her insides. Without breaking the kiss, he wrapped her in his arms and drew her close to him.

She felt the warmth of his body, the stiff bulge of his jeans as he pressed against her. She pushed against him and felt the tingle of arousal in her breasts, her veins, her whole body.

When they finally broke the kiss, she backed away and caught her breath. "Wow, you do things to me, Jack. You make me warm all over."

"And you've warmed me up, Ruth. Your lips are so soft and sweet."

"I'm glad you didn't kiss me like that last night. I wouldn't have been able to resist you."

"That's why I didn't kiss you last night when I wanted to so much. I knew that if I took you in my arms, all my promises to be a gentleman would be shot to hell."

Ruth sighed. "We're a couple of old fools, aren't we?"

"We're a couple of old cronies who are still young at heart."

Thirty-six

The hood of Ruth's motorhome yawned open. Greasy parts of her engine lay strewn on the concrete floor around the front of the vehicle like a child's broken toys.

"The news isn't good," Kenny Price told her. "You're going to need a new motor. The only used motor we could locate had too many miles on it. We could rebuild your engine, but by the time you pay for parts and labor, it would cost you nearly as much as a new one and you'd still have a used motor."

"Then I guess I'll have to go with the new engine," she said. "How long will it take?"

"It'll take two to four days to get a new motor shipped in. This is Wednesday. We'll probably have it by next Monday. We'll need a day or two to install and check it out. I'd say it'll be ready a week from today."

"The tour will be over by then. I know

this is going to cost a small fortune. Dare I ask how much?"

Kenny Price picked up a sheet of paper, looked at the figures. "It'll cost $3,750. That includes $200 labor."

"Ouch, that hurts," Ruth said. "Do you need a deposit?"

"No. Just your signature on the authorization sheet."

"Do you take personal, out-of town checks?"

Kenny smiled at her. "If they're good."

"I'll have to arrange to transfer funds into my checking account."

"Just pay for it when you pick it up."

"Ruth, do you want to get some of your clothes out of the motorhome?" Jack asked.

"Oh, yes. Thanks for reminding me."

Jack walked to the van and got out the suitcase he'd given her to use.

Ruth selected a couple of pants suits, a simple blue dress, clean underwear, three nightgowns, the pink duster to wear over her gown, and a pair of black heels. Enough clothes to last that day and the two days in Eureka Springs. She put them in the suitcase with her other clothes and at the last minute, she grabbed her album of family pictures and stuck it on top of her clothes.

By the time they got back to the KOA Kampground in Branson, where Jack had unhooked his trailer earlier, it was almost 11:00 A.M. and she knew she didn't have time to shower and change clothes. She'd have to wait until after her lunch with Meg and Scot.

"Here's a key to my trailer," Jack said as they got out of his van.

Ruth took the key. "Oh, you're not taking your trailer to Springfield?"

"No. I'm just going to get my CB hooked up in the van and visit my daughter. I'll be back sometime this evening, but you'll need a place to stay this afternoon."

"Are you leaving now?"

"Not for Springfield. I'm going to drive out to the lake and see if the fish are biting and I'll probably stop at a couple of tackle shops along the way. I'll leave for Springfield about 2:00 this afternoon."

"I'm going to browse through the gift shops after lunch."

"Then I probably won't see you until after the tour bus brings you back from your night on the town. Have fun, and you know you have a place to sleep tonight."

"I really appreciate it, Jack."

After Jack left, she went into the trailer and brushed her hair and put fresh lipstick on. She had just gone outside to wait at the picnic table when the Lincoln drove up, music drifting out of the open window. Scot was driving, but Meg wasn't in the car.

Ruth strolled over to the open window. "Where's Meg?"

Scot turned down the radio. "She's waiting for us. Climb in."

Ruth felt uncomfortable riding alone with Scot, and she was glad that he turned the radio back up after she got in. At least she didn't have to carry on a conversation with him. A few minutes later, he pulled into the parking lot of the Palace Inn.

Scot got out of the car, walked around and opened her door. "Let's go," he said.

"I'll wait in the car."

"And disappoint Meg? She wants you to see our room because President Bush slept there. You know how star struck Meg is."

Reluctantly, Ruth got out of the car and followed Scot inside the hotel. They took the elevator up to the fifth floor and walked along the brightly lit hallway. Scot unlocked the door to his room, pushed the door open, and invited her in. He closed the door after they were both inside.

Ruth slipped her heavy shoulder bag off and set it on the small entrance table near the door and glanced around. She saw that the room was more plush than most hotel rooms.

The desk where Meg's laptop computer and printer were set up was littered with colorful brochures and scattered notes. The bathroom door was closed, but Ruth could imagine that it was big and roomy.

"When President Bush was here, he had this room and the one next door," Scot said. "Meg wanted to rent the adjoining room too, but I convinced her it was a waste of money."

"Where's Meg?" Ruth glanced toward the bathroom door, but didn't hear any sounds coming from there.

"She's doing the interview with Andy Williams."

"Right now?" Ruth felt her knees go weak when she realized that she was alone with Scot in the hotel room.

"Yes. His office called this morning and

rescheduled the meeting for 11:00. We're to pick her up in front of his theater at 12:30. We've got an hour and a half to ourselves."

"Then what in the hell are we doing in your hotel room?" she said, her voice laced with outrage. She turned and headed for the door.

Scot reached out and grabbed her arm, spun her around. "You know damned well what we're doing here," Scot said with a smug grin.

Her throat constricted with fear when she saw the crazed look in his eyes. "I don't know what you're doing, but I'm leaving." She jerked her arm away from his grip.

Scot stepped around her with lightning speed, blocking her path to the door. "Don't pull that innocent shit with me, Ruth," he roared. "Everybody knows you're sleeping with that jerk who's running a private escort service just for you. You and Jack aren't fooling anybody with that phony sob story about your broken-down motorhome."

Ruth's fear turned to anger. "It's nobody's business what I do," she said, refusing to dignify his crude remarks with a denial. "Now get out of my way, Scot."

"Not so fast, Babe. You took your wedding rings off, a surefire sign that you're available, and I aim to take advantage of your open invitation. You want me, Ruth. Admit it." He reached out and tried to touch her breast. She ducked away from his outstretched hand.

She saw the glaze of lust in his cold eyes and her stomach knotted with a deeper fear. "Please move out of my way, Scot. I want to leave," she said in a calm, even voice, trying to reason with him.

"You're not going anywhere, Ruth. You're not leaving this room until you give me what I want, and we both know what that is." He grabbed her arm again and jerked her toward the bed.

She felt his fingers dig into the soft flesh of her arm. "Let go of me," she demanded. She wrenched free of him and slapped him hard across the face.

Stunned, Scot raised his hand to his cheek. "Why you dirty little bitch. If you want a struggle, that's what you'll get." He reached for her again.

Ruth drew her hand back and slapped him again. "That one's for Meg," she said. Before he could recover from the second blow, she dashed across the room, snatched her purse from the entry table and ran out of the room, not taking the time to close the door. She reached the elevator and pressed the button.

"Ruth, you come back here," Scot called from his open doorway.

"You step one foot out in the hall and I'll scream loud enough to draw a crowd," she threatened.

The elevator doors opened and Ruth stepped in and pressed the button. The doors closed, shutting out her vision of Scot.

She held her breath all the way down and when she walked out into the bright sunlight, she ran across the parking lot, fearing that Scot would follow her. When she got to the sidewalk of the busy Strip, she turned left and walked fast, knowing that she was only three or four blocks away from Gretna Road.

A uniformed policeman stood in the middle of the crossroads of The Strip and Gretna Road, guiding the heavy traffic through the busy intersection.

Ruth felt safer after she'd crossed the congested highway. She slowed her pace as she walked the long block to the campground entrance. Once inside the campground, she began to tremble and wondered if her wobbly legs would carry her the rest of the way. When she spotted Jack's van parked beside his travel trailer, she burst into tears.

Jack was just getting out of his van when she got there.

"Ruth, what's wrong?" he asked, rushing up to her.

Ruth buried her face in her hands. "Oh, God. Scot . . . he tried . . . he tried to . . ." She was sobbing and couldn't speak.

Jack took her in his arms, patted her shoulder. "He tried to rape you, didn't he?"

"Yes." Ruth shuddered. "Oh, Jack, I'm afraid to stay here by myself," she said between sobs.

"I'm not going to leave you here by yourself, Ruth. You're going to Springfield with me." He walked her to the van and settled her into the passenger seat.

Ruth didn't feel safe until they were well away from Branson, and she didn't begin to relax until they entered Burr's Restaurant in Springfield for lunch.

Thirty-seven

With time to kill between lunch and his three o'clock appointment to get his CB installed, Jack took Ruth to the huge Bass Pro-Outdoor World store. She was overwhelmed by the massive size of the store. He showed her the aquarium near the entrance where large fish swam back and forth. In another room, he pointed out a monstrous stuffed bear. In still another section, they stopped to stare up at a cascading waterfall. Jack said something to her in front of it, but she couldn't hear him because of the roar of the crashing water.

She knew they could spend a whole day in the store and still not see everything, but she was grateful that she was able to purchase two shirts for her son for Christmas presents.

After they left Bass Pro, they spent the

next hour sitting in the reception room of the Dodge dealership, waiting for Jack's CB to be installed.

"I'm glad you're with me, Ruth," Jack said when they drove away from the car lot. "I want you to meet my daughter. I think you'll like Jenny."

Ruth smiled. "If she's anything like her father, I'll like her."

A few blocks later, Jack pulled into the parking lot of an apartment complex. They got out of the van and she followed him up a flight of stairs. He rang the doorbell of a corner apartment.

Jenny opened the door and her face immediately lit up with a big smile. Ruth saw that the girl had her father's bright, blue eyes and the same ingenuous smile, complete with dimples. Her dark brown hair fell in soft curls around her face.

Jenny's graceful hands flew into action as she began gesturing in sign language.

"It's good to see you, too, Jenny. This is my friend, Ruth Nichols," Jack said, using sign language too as he spoke.

Ruth was impressed. Jack had obviously taught his daughter sign language and apparently, this was the way they greeted each other. She wondered if Jack had also taught Jenny to speak Spanish and French.

Jenny smiled at Ruth and again gestured with her nimble fingers.

"Come on in," Jack said.

Inside the apartment, Jack and Jenny continued to smile at each other and speak with their hands. Ruth watched in fascination and it came as a shock when she finally realized that Jack's daughter was actually deaf. Jack had never mentioned it.

Jenny smiled at Ruth, spoke in sign language, and gestured toward one of the comfortable chairs. Ruth didn't know exactly what Jenny had said, but she knew the girl had just invited her to sit down in the chair.

Jack sat down in the other overstuffed chair and Jenny sat on the couch directly opposite them. Ruth didn't feel awkward or left out. Jack translated and drew Ruth into the conversation.

As she watched them, her curiosity brought several questions to mind. If Jenny was deaf, how had she known that Jack had rung the doorbell? How did Jack talk to her on the phone? Jenny was a schoolteacher, but whom did she teach? Hearing impaired children?

Ruth glanced across the room and saw a computer, a printer, and a fax machine on a desk. There were three other machines on the desk, each one with an unlit red bulb built into it. She supposed that one of them was connected to the doorbell and that the red light flashed whenever someone rang the bell. She knew that Jack could communicate instantly with his daughter using either a computer modem or fax machine.

Jack and Jenny stood up at the same time. "Jenny has to leave for a meeting," he explained. "She's sorry she has to go, but she wants you to come back and visit again."

"It was a pleasure to meet you, Jenny," Ruth said, looking directly at the young woman. Jack translated with sign language.

Jenny smiled at her. "It was a joy to meet you, Ruth," Jack said, translating his daughter's rapid hand gestures.

Jenny looked at her father and spoke in sign language. They both laughed and looked over at Ruth.

"What's the joke?" Ruth asked.

"Jenny said you're a very nice lady and that I should marry you. I told you she was smart."

"I think it's time to go before you both embarrass me."

All three of them walked down to the parking lot together. Jenny waved to them, then got into her car. Jack unlocked Ruth's door and opened it for her.

"Jack, you didn't tell me your daughter was deaf," Ruth said when he got into the van.

"Probably not. I don't think of her as being different."

"I can see why. She's absolutely delightful."

"I knew you'd like her. And I knew she'd like you."

"How does Jenny drive a car?"

Jack looked over at her and grinned. "She's deaf, Ruth, not blind."

"That was a dumb question. I meant, what about sirens?"

"She has a special device in her car that recognizes sirens. A red light flashes. It's the same with her doorbell."

"That's what I figured. You must be proud of her."

"I am. It was a struggle for her to get through college, but now she teaches deaf children. At night she teaches sign language to parents with hearing-impaired children. Yes, I'm very proud of her." He started his engine and glanced at his watch. "It's almost 5:00. Do you want to drive back to Branson and see if we can find the tour bus?"

Ruth shuddered. "No. I couldn't bear to see Scot tonight."

"Why don't we stay at a hotel up here tonight and drive back in the morning?" he suggested.

"I'd like that, but only if I can buy you dinner and pay for the room."

Jack tipped his head and looked at her. "Just one room?"

Ruth smiled. "With two beds. Why waste money on two rooms? After all, we slept in your trailer last night."

"That's true. I like your spunk."

"Oh, I don't have any clothes except the ones I'm wearing."

"Yes, you do. The clothes you took out of your motorhome this morning are still in the suitcase in the back of the van. That's why I drove back to the trailer. I forgot to give you the suitcase."

"Oh, good. I need to take a shower and change out of these jeans I've been wearing for two days."

"I'm the one without any clean clothes, but I'll stop at a store along the way," he said as he eased out into traffic.

"How long has Jenny been deaf?"

"Since she was born. That's what caused the problems in my marriage. My wife just couldn't handle the frustration of raising a deaf child. She wanted to put Jenny in an institution and forget about her."

"I don't understand how a mother could feel that way."

"I never understood it either, but I knew I couldn't let Jenny be put in a home. When Jenny was two, my wife just walked out one day and told me if I wanted Jenny so bad, she was all mine. June filed for a divorce the next day and never came back."

Ruth leaned her head back against the seat and thought about how lucky she'd been in her own marriage. She stayed in the car when Jack went into a men's store to buy the clothes he needed, and again when he went into the Ramada Inn to register.

When they got to their luxurious room, Ruth saw that there was only one bed, a king-sized one. A couch, a matching chair and a coffee table sat in one corner of the room. There was also a big round table with four chairs around it.

"This really is a nice room," she said, "but I wish you'd let me pay for it."

"It was my idea." Jack set the suitcase down next to the wall, placed the sack from the men's store on the dresser and glanced around the room.

"Well, I'm paying for dinner," Ruth insisted. "Do you know what I'd like to do?"

"What?"

"I don't feel like going out to dinner. I'd like to order from room service and just relax tonight. Maybe watch a movie on television."

"Sounds good to me. They didn't have any vacant rooms with two beds," he said, "but the couch converts into a bed and I'll sleep there."

"Always the gentleman."

"Not always," he said with a mischievous smile.

Thirty-eight

While they waited for their club sandwiches, bowl of fresh fruit, and bottle of chilled white wine to be delivered by room service, Ruth sat on the edge of the bed and dialed Brenda's number. When a recorded voice came on the line, Ruth entered her calling card numbers.

"How are things at home?" she asked after Brenda answered.

"We miss you, especially the kids. Lori loves school. She's been chosen to play a pumpkin in the kindergarten Halloween play. You'll be back by then, won't you?"

"I'm sure I will be."

"A neighbor lady is watching the kids after school, but I still haven't found a permanent babysitter."

"You will."

"Oh, we got the cheese you sent from Osceola. Thanks. Mama Murph called to say she'd gotten her's too."

"Good. How's she doing?"

Brenda sighed. "You know Mama Murph. She's still grumbling about her sore hip but she won't go to the doctor."

"Ha, she should meet the twin sisters who are traveling with us. They're seventy-nine, two years older than Mother, and they take turns driving a motorhome that's just as big as mine. And they're shorter than I am."

Ruth glanced over and saw that Jack was leaning forward on the couch, watching the weather report on the local news.

"Can't you see Mama Murph doing that? I wish you'd hurry home so she'd stop bugging me to do things for her. Stupid things like straightening the picture on her living room wall."

Ruth laughed. "Did you do it?"

"No, I didn't. She wouldn't watch the kids the other day when I was in a pinch so I'm not about to do anything for her."

"Nothing's changed since I left. How's Danny?"

"He's still trying to get me to quit my job and stay home with the kids. And right now, I'm tempted to, but I'm not going to tell him that."

"Why? Did something happen at work?" Ruth picked up the pen from the nightstand and started doodling on the hotel notepad.

"As part of the secretarial pool at the college, I've had to serve as Dr. Norman Rogers' personal secretary for the past two days. What a pompous pain he turned out to be."

"I tried to tell you that, but you thought he was Mr. Wonderful. Now you know why I didn't cotton to him."

Jack, obviously listening to her end of the conversation, looked over at her and smiled.

"Where are you?" Brenda asked. "In Branson?"

"No, I'm spending the night in Springfield, thirty-five miles north of Branson."

"Is that part of the tour?"

"No, we're on our own today, so I decided to stay in a luxurious hotel and pamper myself with room service."

"All alone? What a pity," Brenda teased.

"What makes you think I'm alone?" Ruth said in an equally joking manner.

"Because I know you, Mother."

"Well, I'm not alone. I'm sharing the room with a handsome, virile man. A younger man, at that."

"A studmuffin?" Brenda said, continuing their banter.

Ruth glanced over at Jack's profile. "Yes, I think you could call him a studmuffin."

Jack looked over at her and grinned.

Brenda's laughter floated over the phone lines. "Well, I hope you enjoy your fantasy, Mother."

"Oh, I plan to enjoy it. There's only one bed in the room."

"Seriously, Mother, are you having fun on the tour?"

"I'm having a blast. By the way, the engine went out on my motorhome this morning, but not to worry. It's in the shop and they're putting a new motor in it."

"Really? That's too bad," Brenda said, her tone serious. "Well, that explains why you're staying in a hotel tonight."

"Yes, I can't very well sleep in my motorhome while it's locked up inside the repair shop." Ruth heard the knock at the door. "I've got to go, Brenda. Room service is here with my dinner."

Jack got up and walked toward the door.

"Dinner for two, I presume," Brenda teased. "Complete with an expensive bottle of wine. And candlelight. Don't forget the candlelight."

Ruth laughed. "Chilled white wine. Chablis, to be exact." She looked up and watched the uniformed waiter roll a cart into the room. She smiled when she saw that there was a white tapered candle on the tray. "Yes, Brenda. Studmuffin and I will dine by candlelight."

"Somehow I can't quite picture it, but as long as you're having a fantasy, you might as well make it a romantic one."

"That's right. Got to go. I'll call you in a day or two."

"Seriously, Mom, I hope you're not lonely. I know how cold and impersonal hotel rooms can be."

"I promise you, I'm not lonely."

Ruth hung up just as the waiter was lighting the candle. He'd already transferred the dome-covered plates to their table and leaned the empty tray against the wall. She reached for her purse.

"Thank you, sir," the waiter said. He turned and rolled the cart out of the room, closed the door behind him.

Jack pulled her chair out from the table and made a sweeping gesture with his hand. "Dinner is served, Madame."

Ruth slid into the padded chair, unfolded the blue linen napkin, and put it across her lap.

Before Jack sat down, he removed the silver domes from the two plates. He draped a napkin over his arm and made a dramatic production of pouring the white wine into sparkling goblets.

"It looks good." Ruth dished up a portion of fresh fruit, then handed the bowl to Jack.

"It does, and I'm starved," he said. "A studmuffin?"

Ruth laughed. "That's what Brenda calls hunky men."

"So, what did your daughter say when you told her you were spending the night with one?" Jack set the bowl down and looked over at Ruth.

"She didn't believe me." Ruth removed the fancy red toothpick from a section of her club sandwich and took a bite.

"What would she think if she knew it was true?"

Ruth smiled. "She'd probably approve. Brenda's always trying to fix me up with a lifetime companion. I think she's afraid she'll have to take care of me in my old age."

"I wouldn't mind taking care of you when you're old and gray."

Ruth saw the serious expression on Jack's face and wondered if he meant it. She knew she'd been wondering what it would be like to grow old with Jack.

"Gray, yes, but I'm not going to get old. I'm going to stay young forever."

"Me, too."

Except for that brief exchange, Ruth and Jack ate in silence.

When they were through eating, Ruth placed the dirty dishes on the empty tray. Jack set the tray in the hallway and bolted the door when he came back in.

"I'm going to take a shower," Ruth said. "And if you don't mind, I'll go ahead and put on my nightgown and robe so I can be comfortable. Maybe there's a good movie on television."

"I don't mind. In fact, I plan to do the same thing."

"You wear a nightgown?" Ruth teased.

"No. Usually I sleep in my shorts, but in deference to you, I actually bought a pair of pajamas today. It'd be nice to sit around and watch a movie together. The tour is nice during the day, but I'm basically a loner. I'd rather spend a quiet night at home than mingle with a group of people."

"I'm the same way." Ruth set her suitcase on the bed, opened it, and took out the photo album that was on top of her clothes. "There are some pictures of my kids and grandchildren in here. Would you like to look at them while I'm in the shower?"

"Yes. I know Tony, but I'd like to see your daughters."

Ruth dug her pink nightgown and the duster out of the suitcase. She grabbed her shoulder bag because it contained all of her toiletries. On her way to the bathroom, she dropped the photo album on the table.

When she came out of the bathroom, Jack looked up from the open photo album. "So I'm an old reprobate," he said.

Ruth frowned, then remembered the picture of Jack that was in the album. "Oh, I forgot that was in there," she said, thoroughly embarrassed that he'd seen what she'd written.

"Well, you called it right. I did look like an old reprobate that day, especially with my missing teeth."

"Yes, you did." While Jack showered, Ruth flipped the dial on the television and was delighted when she saw that "The Sound of Music" was playing. She turned off all the lights except the lamp on the end table between the couch and chair. She walked over to the window, pulling the heavy drapes aside. The view of the city lights from their sixth-floor room was magnificent.

She was still standing at the window when Jack came out of the bathroom wearing his new, dark blue pajamas.

"Look at the view from here," she said.

Jack turned out the light on the end table, then stepped over and stood behind her, looking over her shoulder as he gazed out the window. "It's pretty out there. Oh, you smell so good, Ruth."

Ruth turned her head and looked up at him. "So do you, Jack. After wearing those jeans for two days, it feels good to be clean again."

He put his arms around her, as he'd done before, and they stared out at the night. For several minutes, neither one of them spoke.

"I'm glad we're here, together," Jack said. "I can't tell you how much I enjoy being with you. I feel so . . . so comfortable around you." He brushed his lips across the back of her neck.

His hot breath on her neck caused her to shudder. When she felt the warmth of his body through their thin garments, a burning heat of desire flooded her loins. She heard herself gasp and spoke to cover the sound. "I feel very comfortable with you, too. We seem to enjoy the same things in life."

"Oh? Do you fish?"

"I've been known to catch a few in my day." She tried to keep the tone light-hearted, but she heard the huskiness in her own voice.

"Maybe we can fish the Yellowstone together some day."

"Maybe." Ruth let the drapes fall together, shutting out the rest of the world. The only light in the room came from the screen of the television set. She turned in his arms to face him, slipping her arms around his waist, and buried her head against his chest. She breathed in his scent, a mingling of soap and aftershave.

His hands slid down across the fabric of her duster. He pulled her tight against him.

They remained in that position, motionless, for a long moment. It was as if they were each afraid to move, to either pursue their feelings for each other, or to back away from them. Or maybe they stood there, locked together, because they wanted to be close. Ruth didn't know. Her thoughts were clouded with desire, and she knew that they were both experiencing a mutual desire, a need.

She knew she had a choice. She could step away from him right then and he wouldn't push his attentions on her. Or she could stay in his arms and let things happen the way they were supposed to.

She'd been the one who'd suggested sharing a room. Had she known then that at some point during the evening they would be in each other's arms?

Jack drew his hand up and cupped her under the chin, raising her head. He kissed her full on the lips, pressing his body tight to hers.

His mouth was soft and gentle. The tip of his tongue probed her slightly parted lips, sending shoots of heat through her body. When she felt the hard bulge of his desire press against her, she knew it was too late to turn away from him. Her need was so strong that even if he walked away, she knew she would cling to him.

She felt his hand slide up and cover her breast. He kneaded it gently until the nipple raised to a hard nub.

Jack broke the kiss and rested his smooth, freshly shaved cheek against hers. "Oh, Ruth, I love you so much."

"I—I think I love you, too, Jack," she breathed. And, in saying it, she knew it was true. There was the desire, yes, but something deeper, too, more than need, more than lust, gripped her. She felt a bonding with Jack, as if they were destined to be together, to become one.

"I want you," he said, his voice husky.

"I want you, too," she answered, surprised that she still had breath enough to speak. "So much."

He kissed her on the neck, then behind her ear, and the last wisp of resolve melted like candlewax. Her body seemed to blossom, become youthful, flame with his gentle warmth.

"Come to bed," he whispered.

"Yes, oh, yes," she murmured.

It seemed to her that they glided to the bed, and then he was beside her and his hands were on her flesh and she felt that growing again, that melding sensation, and when he kissed her again, she wanted to open to him like a flower to the sun.

His tongue probed the warmth of her mouth and she tantalized him with probes of her own until she thought she would melt with his heat.

He slid off her duster, then removed her nightgown. It crackled with electricity as he pulled it over her head. In a moment, he, too, was naked beside her and she looked at him with the wonder of a woman in love for the first time.

His touches brought the desire in her bubbling to the surface. His hand slid across her stomach and down between her legs. His gentle caress as he cupped her nest, kneading it gently, heightened her rapture. She felt the sudden warmth as her loins flushed with the oils of love.

"I want you so much," she whispered into his ear, and he kissed each of her breasts, sending needles of pleasure and pain through each nipple until they stood taut and hard. She felt him enter her so slowly she thought he would never fill her, and it felt wonderful and full of sweetness, like sugars flooding her bloodstream.

He was slow and gentle and she surged to him, swelled beneath him until stars exploded in her brain and comets streaked through her senses and she was afire with pleasure. She was almost senseless with the wonder in him and in her, the exquisite feel of him inside until they were just one person, joined together across an eternity that had no beginning, no end, and was, finally, just a brief flash that felt like creation itself and could not be remembered entirely, but could only be treasured and tasted like the last drink of fine wine.

There was finally, just that one tiny moment in eternity, and it was itself eternal and would forever linger in their hearts.

Thirty-nine

Jack and Ruth arrived back at the KOA Kampground in Branson at ten o'clock in the morning, just as the others in the group were lining their rigs up on the wide section of pavement near the office.

"Right on time," Ruth commented as they drove through the entrance. Their itinerary called for them to have a late breakfast at The Wharf restaurant near the Grand Palace, then caravan through the scenic hills to the quaint town of Eureka Springs in the northwest corner of Arkansas.

George Barton, their jovial tour guide, waved to them from the driver's seat of his Holiday Rambler motorhome. His wife, Sandy, stood outside, guiding a travel trailer into the line.

When Jack eased the van by her, Sandy

looked over at them, then held her hand up for them to stop. She walked over to Ruth's side of the van.

"Your friend, Meg Rodecker, wanted me to give you a message. Last night she told me that she and Scot were going to skip breakfast and lunch with the group today."

"Did they both go on the tour bus last night?"

"Yes," Sandy said. "They were a lot of fun. Too bad you missed it. Anyway, they planned to drive over to Eureka Springs early this morning and rent a motel room. Meg wanted to spend the day researching the town for the travel articles she's writing. She said to tell you that they'd see you at the campground in Eureka Springs sometime this afternoon."

"Okay. Thanks."

"You two are going to Eureka Springs, aren't you?"

"Yes, we wouldn't miss it," Ruth said.

"We're ready to drive over to The Wharf for breakfast. We'll be there for about an hour before we start the caravan to Eureka Springs."

Jack leaned over toward the open window. "We'll drive over to The Wharf as soon as I hook the trailer up to the van. It'll take about five minutes."

"Good. We'll see you over there." Sandy turned back to the line of rigs. She counted the vehicles, then signaled that they were ready to head out. George started his engine as soon as she was settled into the passenger seat.

Jack drove down the shaded lane and backed his van up to his travel trailer. When he stopped, Ruth got out and checked to see how close he was to the trailer hitch. She walked around to Jack's side of the van. "You're straight on. Just back up another three inches." She watched as he eased back and shouted, "Whoa!" when the chrome ball on the back bumper of the van was directly below the hitch on the trailer.

While Jack connected the two vehicles and removed the metal hitch blocks, Ruth unhooked the electrical cord from the socket and tucked it away in a side bin on the trailer. She did the same with the water hose. Jack took care of the sewer hose and working together, they were ready to go in five minutes.

Jack and Ruth had just gotten into the van when they saw the campground golf cart driving up the lane toward them. A young woman, wearing the campground uniform, was steering it. Jack waited for the cart to pass in front of them before he started the engine.

But the cart didn't pass them. It pulled in next to the van. The young, blonde desk clerk hopped off the cart, clutching a yellow note in her hand. She looked inside the van, then walked around to Ruth's side.

"Mrs. Nichols?" she asked.

"Yes. I'm Ruth Nichols."

"I have a message for you to call home."

Ruth glanced over at Jack and sighed. "Now what's Brenda up to?" And then a prickling sense of apprehension came over her. "Maybe my mother fell and broke her hip again."

"Maybe you should find out," Jack said, his expression serious.

"Call home," Ruth said to the girl. "You mean my daughter's house?"

"I'm not sure. I've got the number right here." The clerk handed the small yellow sheet of paper to Ruth.

Ruth glanced at the number written at the bottom of the page; it was Brenda's. Then she read the rest of the brief, scrawled note. "Ruth Nichols—Space #33. Call home immediately. Emergency." The word "Emergency" was underlined twice.

Ruth went numb. Tears welled up in her eyes immediately. "Oh, God, something's happened! When did you get this message?"

"The time's written right there in the top corner." The clerk pointed to the time that had been noted when the call came into the office.

"Nine thirty-five," Ruth said. "Was that last night or this morning?"

"This morning." The clerk looked at her watch. "The call came in a half hour ago. I drove down here right away, but you weren't here."

"Nine thirty-five," Ruth repeated, trying to think clearly. "That would be 8:35 Montana time. Who called? A man or a woman?"

"I don't know. My boss took the call. Do you want to ride up to the office and use the phone?"

"No," Jack said. "I've got a car phone. Thanks for delivering the message."

"If there's anything we can do, let us know." The clerk got back on the golf cart and drove away.

Jack handed Ruth the receiver.

Ruth looked at the note and stared blankly at Brenda's number. "God, I can't even remember my calling card number."

"You don't need it," Jack said. "Let me dial the number for you." He took the receiver from Ruth and punched in the numbers that were written on the note. When he heard the call ring through, he handed it back to her.

"Hello. Parker residence."

Ruth didn't recognize the woman's voice. "Who is this?" she asked.

"This is Helen Tucker, Brenda's neighbor. Her babysitter. Is this Brenda's mother?"

"Yes. What's wrong?"

"Well, I hate to be the one to tell you, but Brenda was in a car accident this morning on her way to work."

"Oh, no," Ruth cried. "How bad is it?"

"I really don't know. The last time I talked to Danny, Brenda was still in the emergency room. Danny's at the hospital with her now and I've got the children here with me."

"Oh, God, I'm so far away." Ruth was shaking so badly, she had to hold the phone with both hands to keep it close to her ear.

"I'll give you the phone number of the hospital so you can talk to Danny. He said

506

that if you called to tell you that he'd already called your other two children. Tony is on his way here from Big Timber and Amy will probably drive over from Missoula this afternoon. Your mother's also been notified."

If Tony and Amy were coming, Brenda's injuries must be really serious. The tears flowed down Ruth's face. Jack reached over and patted her on the shoulder. "What happened?"

"Apparently, a pickup truck went out of control and hit Brenda's car almost head-on. The accident happened at 7:45 this morning, an hour and fifteen minutes ago. Danny was just leaving for work at 8:00 when he got the call from the hospital. I was here at the house to get the children off to school, but Danny wants them to stay home today. Let me give you the phone number of the hospital. Have you get something to write it on?"

"Just a minute." Ruth grabbed the yellow note and turned it over. She fished a pen out of the side pouch of her shoulder bag. "Okay, go ahead." She tried to write the number down, but couldn't steady her trembling hand. She handed the phone to Jack. "Get the number, will you?"

Jack picked up the pen and wrote the number down on the note. "Okay, we'll call the hospital right away." He pushed the disconnect button on the receiver, then dialed the hospital. When he finally got Danny on the line, he handed the receiver to Ruth.

"Danny, is Brenda all right?"

"She's alive, but we don't know how bad her injuries are yet. The doctors rushed her to surgery a half hour ago and she's still there."

"Oh, God, *no*."

"Calm down, Ruth, and let me tell you what I know so far. Brenda hadn't regained consciousness when they took her to surgery."

"What are they doing to her in surgery?" Ruth asked, her voice shaky.

"She was bleeding pretty bad, so they wanted to stop the bleeding before they did anything else. We know she's got a broken leg and a broken wrist, but they'll wait on that. The doctor said their first priority is to get her stabilized. They'll do a full set of X-rays when she comes out of surgery. You'd better fly home as soon as you can."

When she heard the somber tone of his

voice, she felt as if her breath had been cut off.

"Is there something you're not telling me, Danny?"

"No, except that Brenda stopped breathing in the emergency room and they had to resuscitate her. The bones can be fixed, but the doctors still don't know the extent of her internal injuries. If they can bring her out of the coma, they think she'll recover. If not, well, I just don't know. I won't let myself think about it. But I think you should be here."

Ruth felt numb all over. "I'll get there as soon as I can. I'll take the earliest flight out, but the Springfield airport isn't one of the major terminals, so it may be tomorrow morning before I can leave. I'll let you know."

Ruth handed the phone to Jack, then buried her head in her hands and cried, her shoulders shaking with wracking sobs.

Jack came around to her side of the van and held her up as he led her into his travel trailer. "I'm really sorry, Ruth," he said.

"Oh, Jack, how am I going to get to Montana? I should be there with Brenda right now. I wonder if there's a travel agent in town." Ruth's legs turned to rubber and gave up their support. She held onto the table and eased into the dinette booth.

Jack handed her a box of Kleenex. "Let me see what I can do."

Ruth didn't even hear him. Her mind blotted out everything but the terrifying images of her injured daughter. She tried to think of the things she needed to do, but the thoughts flitted through her mind so fast, she couldn't remember any of them.

"I can't think straight. Do you have some paper?" she asked. "I have to figure out what to do."

Jack gave her a pen and a spiral notebook, turning to a blank page. "Let me take care of it, Ruth. I'll see if I can get you a flight out of here today."

She looked up at him, the expression in her eyes pleading for his help. "Do you think you can?" she asked.

"I'll try my damndest. I'm going to run up to the office and borrow their phone book. I'll be right back."

While he was gone, Ruth tried to sort out her thoughts.

The only things she jotted down on the notepad were the things that she could remember of what Danny had told her about Brenda. She couldn't think beyond that point. The image of Brenda lying motionless in some hospital room kept intruding on her thoughts.

Jack came back into the trailer ten minutes later. "Okay, I called The Wharf Restaurant and told Sandy Barton what had happened. She'll tell your friend Meg when she sees her this afternoon."

"Oh, thanks. I didn't think of that." Ruth dabbed the tears from her cheeks with a fresh Kleenex.

"Now, I've got us booked on a flight out of Springfield at 1:17 this afternoon. That's only three hours from now, so we've got to hustle. The airport is north of Springfield, so it'll take us an hour and a half to drive up there."

"You're going with me?" she asked.

"Of course I'm going. Under the circumstances, I'm not going to let you fly out there by yourself. You need my support right now."

"Yes, I really do, Jack." She reached up and squeezed his hand. "What time will we get to Billings?"

"About six o'clock, Montana time. We

have to change planes somewhere, but I can't remember what the travel agent told me. We have to pick up the tickets at the airport thirty minutes before departure time, so we'd better get going. I have to stop and get gas on the way and we'll have to grab something to eat. Do you need to get anything out of the motorhome?"

"No, I have enough clothes in the suitcase. I should change into a dress."

"You look fine. Let me throw a few things in a suitcase and we'll be on our way."

"It looks like your free set of luggage came in handy," she said with a weak smile. "I'll wait in the van." She was grateful to Jack for his help and felt even closer to him now than she had the night before when they'd made love.

They were on the road in ten minutes and after stopping for lunch, which Ruth could barely eat, they arrived at the Springfield airport forty-five minutes before their plane was scheduled to leave. Jack insisted that Ruth sit in the airport lobby while he took care of picking up their tickets and checking their bags through.

"I've got the tickets," he said when he returned from the counter. "Do you want to call the hospital again before we leave?"

"Yes, I do. Oh, I wasn't even thinking. Did you pay for the tickets?"

"I charged them on my credit card."

"I'll write you a check."

"We'll settle it later, Ruth. Let's go call the hospital."

They walked to the pay phones and Ruth used her calling card number this time. Tony was the one who took the call at the hospital.

"Hi, Mom. How're you holding up?"

"I'm okay, Tony. I'm so glad you're there. How's Brenda doing?"

"She's holding her own. They were able to stop the bleeding without operating, so that's good news. She's still facing surgery to set her broken bones, but they've stabilized her vitals. So things are looking better than when I first got here an hour ago."

"Oh, good. The broken bones will heal."

"Are you going to fly home?" Tony asked.

"Yes. We were able to get a flight out of Springfield this afternoon. We're at the airport now and our plane leaves in thirty minutes. We'll arrive in Billings about six o'clock your time."

"Who's coming with you?"

"Jack Colby. Do you remember him?"

"Sure I do. He's there with you?"

"Yes, he insisted on flying back with me."

"Well, that pleases me. I know this is hard on you, Mom, and I've been worried about you. But if Jack's with you, I know you're in good hands. Do you want me to pick you up at the airport?"

"No. We'll rent a car when we get there. We'll go directly to the hospital. What room is Brenda in?"

"She's in intensive care. There's a small waiting room nearby and that's where Danny and I will be."

"Okay, we'll see you when we get there." Ruth started to hang up, then asked the question she didn't want to ask. "Tony, is Brenda . . . is she still in a coma?"

"Yes, Mother," Tony said sadly. "I wish I could tell you differently, but I can't. We're all very worried about her and I know you are, too. All we can do now is wait, and pray for the best."

Forty

Ruth and Jack went directly to Intensive Care and looked into the small waiting room. Tony and Danny weren't there. Ruth stopped at a nursing station just outside the closed doors of the Intensive Care Unit.

"I'm Brenda Parker's mother," Ruth told the nurse behind the counter. "Can we see her?"

A doctor stood near the rack of charts inside the nurses' station. He looked up, then strolled over to the counter.

"You're Brenda's mother?"

"Yes. Are you her doctor?"

"Yes, I'm Dr. Peterson. Tony and Danny went to get a bite to eat. You can see your daughter in a minute, but I'd like to talk to you first. Come on into my office." He grabbed Brenda's chart out of the rack, then stepped around the end of the counter.

Ruth followed him down the hall toward a closed door. When Jack didn't come with her, she reached back and grabbed his hand. She didn't like the somber look on the doctor's face and she needed Jack by her side for support.

"Sit down, please," the doctor said when they entered the small room. He closed the door, set the metal folder on the cluttered desk, and sat down in a swivel chair. Jack and Ruth sat in chairs facing him.

"Is Brenda going to be all right, Doctor?" Ruth asked, almost afraid to hear the answer.

"It was touch and go there for awhile this morning, but she made it through the worst of it. I just wanted you to be prepared for what you see when you go in there. It's not a pretty sight."

"How bad is it?" Ruth asked, sitting on the edge of the chair. She felt her heart pounding in her chest.

The doctor glanced down at his desk, as if trying to find the right words, then looked back at Ruth. "Well, actually, she looks worse than she is. She's hooked up to monitors and IVs so she's got wires and tubes all over the place."

"I guess all those tubes would scare a person," Ruth said nervously. Why didn't Dr. Peterson mention the coma? That's what really concerned Ruth. But she knew that doctors had a gentle way of delivering bad news. She didn't think she could take it if he told her that Brenda would be a vegetable the rest of her life.

"I don't know how much you know about her injuries," the doctor said.

"I talked to Danny before I left Missouri. He said she had a broken leg and a broken wrist."

"We put temporary splints on her leg and arm," the doctor continued in his gentle voice, "and we bandaged some of her lacerations. She got a pretty bad cut on the top of her head, so there's still a lot of blood in her hair. And she looks very pale because she lost a lot of blood."

"I understand she's . . . she's in a coma." Ruth had to know.

Dr. Peterson finally smiled. "Brenda came out of the coma about fifteen minutes ago, just after Danny and Tony left."

Ruth sighed with relief. "So they don't know yet?"

"No, but they'll be just as pleased as we

are. Now, the bad news is that she'll have to have surgery early tomorrow morning. We've got the X-rays, but we're still waiting for the results of some lab tests."

"What kind of surgery?" Ruth asked.

"Repair work. Her left leg is broken between the knee and the ankle, so we have to set that. Her left arm is broken at the wrist where she tried to brace herself, so that'll take some work. She's got two fractured ribs and we've got those bound up. Did you know that Brenda was pinned in the wreckage?"

"No, I didn't know."

"They had to cut her out with the Jaws of Life. Her left arm, the one that's broken, was pinned against the door. So far her entire arm isn't showing any response to stimulation."

"Does that mean her arm is paralyzed?"

"Right now it is, but we're hoping that eventually, she'll get the full use of it back. The pickup broadsided her on the driver's side, so Brenda got a pretty good jolt. She's going to be mighty sore for awhile, and the healing process might take longer than she wants it to, but unless something unforseen shows up, she should have a full recovery."

Ruth couldn't find words to answer him, so she only nodded.

"I want to caution you that the next twenty-four hours are critical."

"So, she's not out of the woods yet?"

"No, but once she's passed that twenty-four-hour mark, you can start to breathe a little easier. Luckily, she was wearing her seat belt."

"So is there any good news?" Ruth asked with a nervous laugh.

Dr. Peterson grinned. "Yes. The baby's fine. That was one of my major concerns."

Ruth frowned. "Was Lori in the car with her?"

A puzzled look came over the doctor's face. He raised the metal cover of Brenda's chart and flipped through the pages. When he found the one he was looking for, he scanned the handwritten information that had been entered on the form.

"Lori's her five-year-old daughter. Right?"

"Yes." Ruth waited anxiously.

"No, Lori wasn't with her. I was talking about the baby Brenda's expecting."

Ruth's jaw fell open. "I didn't know she was pregnant. Are you sure?"

Dr. Peterson turned to another page. "Yes. That's what the lab report shows. We figure she's ten weeks into her pregnancy. She's two and a half months along."

"She never mentioned it to me. She didn't say a word about it when I talked to her last night." Ruth glanced at Jack. "Was it just last night when I talked to her from Springfield? It seems so long ago."

"It was last night," Jack assured her.

Brenda looked at the doctor. "I wonder if Brenda knows she's pregnant."

Dr. Peterson leaned back in his chair and ran his fingers through his hair. "I wouldn't know. But come to think of it, Danny never asked about the baby. You'd think he would have been concerned about the baby's condition if he knew."

"Oh, boy," Ruth sighed. "I'll bet neither one of them knows."

"Before you go in to see her, let me go talk to her. If she doesn't know about the baby, this might not be the best time to break the news. I'll do what I think is right." He picked up Brenda's chart and dropped it off at the nurses' station.

When he came back a few minutes later, he had a smile on his face. "Well, she knows now. I just told her."

"And?"

"She's happy about the baby." He sat on the corner of his desk. "She said about a month ago she thought she might be pregnant, but she started spotting and assumed that she wasn't. Danny doesn't know. She never told him of her suspicions."

"He'll be pleased," Ruth said. "He's been trying to get her to quit her job and stay home with the children. Now, I guess she'll have to. The baby might be just the thing to save their marriage."

"Their marriage is rock solid, with or without a new baby. You should see Danny's loving devotion to your daughter. But the baby might be the medicine we need to pull her through this ordeal. Now she's got something to live for."

"Is Brenda's condition that critical?"

"Right now it is. She's very weak and she's in a lot of pain. Since she's pregnant, we can't give her as much pain medication as she's going to want. She'll have to fight a lot of the pain by sheer guts. When she comes to realize the extent of her injuries, she might want to give up. We'll do everything we can for her, but she's got to have the will to live."

"Brenda's a strong person. She'll make it."

The doctor smiled. "You can go in and see her now. I told her you were here."

"Can Jack go in with me? I'm so nervous."

"Yes, but don't stay long. She was alert when I went in, but we just gave her some pain medication and it works pretty fast. She'll be groggy, and as the medication works through her system, she may fade out on you. Don't be alarmed if she does."

Even though Dr. Peterson had warned her about what to expect, Ruth was shocked when she saw Brenda lying in the hospital bed, tubes and wires stretching out from her body to the bank of strange-looking machines lined up behind her on either side of the bed.

Brenda's hair was matted with dried blood. A big gauze bandage covered the large cut on the top of her head. With her eyes closed, she looked so pale and fragile, Ruth didn't know how she had the strength to breathe on her own.

Ruth walked slowly over to the bed. When she looked down at her bruised, bandaged daughter, she felt totally helpless. Fighting back tears, she motioned for Jack to come and stand beside her.

"She looks so sick," she whispered.

Jack squeezed Ruth's hand, then let it go.

Ruth wanted to reach out and touch Brenda, but she was afraid she'd hurt her.

"Hi, Brenda. How are you doing?" she said in a hushed voice.

Brenda's eyes fluttered open. A tiny smile formed on her pale lips.

"Hi, Mom. I spoiled your vacation, didn't I?" Her voice was weak, her speech slow and slightly slurred.

"No you didn't. I'm just grateful you're okay. Do you hurt?"

"No. I feel woozy. Dizzy. Too much to drink."

"It's the medication, Brenda." Ruth leaned closer.

"I know. I'm having a baby today," Brenda said with a thick tongue.

"Not today, Brenda."

"The doctor told me." Brenda's eyes closed.

Ruth ran her fingers across Brenda's forehead. "Don't talk anymore, sweetheart. Just rest." She waited a minute, then backed away from the bed. She knew that Brenda probably wouldn't even remember that she'd been there.

When she stepped out into the hall, she felt limp all over.

"It's a shock to the system to see her like that," Ruth said.

"I know." Jack led her down the hall to the small waiting room, where they sat down on a couch together.

"We'll wait a few minutes to see if Danny and Tony come back, and then I think we'll go on out to the house. There's nothing I can do for Brenda tonight, and I'm emotionally drained."

"I'll drop you off at your house and then I'll find a motel for the night."

"You'll do no such thing, Jack. You'll stay at my house."

"But Tony will probably stay with you, and if your daughter, Amy, comes in from Missoula, I'm sure she'll stay at your house."

"I don't know what difference that makes. It's my house and I'd already planned to put you up in the bedroom that I converted into an office. It's got a comfortable sleeper sofa in it."

"We'll see."

Several minutes later, Danny and Tony walked into the room, followed by Amy. Ruth jumped up and ran to greet them.

"Hi, Mom," Tony said. "Look who we dragged in from the parking lot."

"Dragged in is right," Amy said. "I hope you've still got a bed for me, Mom. I've been driving for eight hours and after I look in on Brenda, I'm going home to crash."

Tony shook hands with Jack, then introduced him to Danny and Amy. There was a mass confusion of hugs and kisses, handshakes and warm greetings.

"We just came from the sheriff's office," Tony said. "They found out who smashed into Brenda's car."

"What do you mean?" Ruth asked. "I assumed they already knew."

"No, it was a hit and run. But there were witnesses who saw the accident and one of them wrote down the license number of the pickup as it drove away. As badly smashed as it was, it's a wonder it still ran. The witnesses said the driver was drunk."

"Oh, that rotten sonofagun," Ruth said. "Have they arrested him?"

"No. They found the pickup, but the bastard's hiding out."

"Well, I hope they find him and lock him up forever."

"We all do," Tony said. "Did you see Brenda?"

"Yes, she doesn't look good, but she's sleeping now."

"Well, the doctor just told us the good news," Danny said with a broad grin.

"You probably heard the big cheer when he told us that Brenda came out of the coma," Tony added.

"Did he tell you anything else?" Ruth asked.

"You mean about the baby?" Danny grinned. "I'm so excited about it, but what a shock. The only bad part is that the doctor said Brenda would have to quit her job. Isn't that great?"

"I'm happy for you both," Ruth said. "And I'm glad Brenda's going to be okay. Since Brenda's sleeping, Jack and I are going to go on out to the house. Amy, come on over whenever you want to. Tony, you'll come too, won't you? Jack will be staying with me, but there's plenty of room."

"No, I'll stay over at Brenda's house tonight," Tony said. "Danny wants to stay at the hospital, so I'll go over and help Grandma take care of the kids."

"Grandma? Is she there with the kids?"

"Yes," Danny said. "She came over this afternoon and she says she won't leave until Brenda's able to walk on her own. Mama Murph's quite the little trooper. She's been cooking and cleaning and baking. The kids adore her and they mind her better than they do me or Brenda."

Ruth shook her head. "Well, talk about miracles."

"I know," Danny said.

"Well, let's go, Jack. It's been a long, emotional day."

"I'll walk you out to the parking lot," Tony said.

"Mom, I need to talk to you for a minute," Amy said.

"Okay. You men go on. I'll be along in a minute." After the men walked out of the room, Ruth turned back to Amy. "What is it, Amy?"

"Mother, you can't let that man stay at our house tonight. It's . . . it's immoral."

Ruth looked at her youngest daughter and smiled. "And this from my sweet, innocent daughter who brought a young college man home to share her bedroom during the last spring break?"

"I was old enough to make that decision," Amy said defensively.

"And how old do you think I am?"

"That's not the point. You're my mother."

"And mothers aren't supposed to sleep with men?"

"Oh, no, Mother! You're not . . ." Amy plunked her hand on her forehead. "I don't even want to think about it."

"Then mind your own business and you won't have to." Ruth smiled and patted Amy on the shoulder as she walked out the door. "See you later, Amy."

Forty-one

Ruth and Jack were at the hospital early enough to talk to Brenda for a few minutes before she was rolled away to surgery. Tony and Amy arrived at the same time, and Danny had been there all night.

The waiting was the hardest part, the pacing back and forth, the attempts at mindless conversation. During the long hours of the operation, they took turns going down to the cafeteria for coffee, just to get a break from the oppressive atmosphere.

"Did you know that Barbara and Glen Amos's daughter is one of Brenda's nurses in Intensive Care?" Danny said.

"Diane? No, I didn't know," Ruth said.

"I knew she was a nurse here, but I didn't realize she worked in Intensive Care."

"She came on at eleven last night and left a little while ago, at seven o'clock."

"I'm sorry I missed her," Ruth said.

"Diane told me she'd come back as soon as Brenda gets out of surgery and she'll stay with her around the clock tonight, even though it's her day off."

Tears welled up in Ruth's eyes. "That's so sweet of her."

"Well, she was really a big help to me last night. She got me a blanket and pillow and insisted that I sleep on the couch in here. I didn't think I'd be able to sleep, but knowing that Diane would let me know if there were any changes in Brenda's condition, I was able to get a few hours of rest."

A nurse in a crisp, white uniform came through the open door. Ruth's heart skipped a beat.

"The doctor wanted me to tell you that the operation is going as expected," she said, addressing the small group.

Ruth glanced at her watch for the hundredth time that morning. "Brenda's been in surgery for more than two hours now. Should it take this long?"

The nurse smiled. "Yes. Operations take as long as they take. The doctor said that they're about halfway through, so it'll be at least another two hours. If you want to go down to the cafeteria to get something to eat, or walk around outside, go ahead."

"What are they doing to Brenda?" Ruth asked.

"I'm not allowed to give you that information. The doctor will explain everything following surgery."

Tony stood up. "Since it's going to be so long, I think it's a good idea if we all go for a walk."

"If you all leave at the same time, just stop by the nurses' station and tell us where you'll be so we can find you if we need to," the nurse said. She turned and walked out of the room.

The five of them walked around the hospital, making three complete loops before they came back to the room to begin the waiting game again.

Ruth practically wore out her watch looking at it so often. Another half hour passed when Danny went out in the hall to pace back and forth again. He was still out there when Barbara Amos entered the room, carrying a tray covered with plastic wrap.

"I brought you some fresh-baked cinnamon rolls," Barbara said. She set the tray on the coffee table and then rushed over and hugged Ruth. "I'm so sorry about Brenda. I want you to know that we're praying for her."

"Thanks."

"So, how're you doing?"

"I'm hanging in there," Ruth said, the tears coming again.

"Well, you'd better be. You're a tough old bird, you know."

"I know. Barbara, I'd like you to meet my friend, Jack Colby."

Barbara extended her hand. "Nice to meet you, Jack 'Big Cheese' Colby."

Jack laughed. "Nobody's called me that since my Navy days. Pleased to meet you, Barbara. I've heard a lot about you."

"All good, I hope."

Jack smiled. "Well, Ruth has bragged about your famous cinnamon rolls."

"Ruth, you did all right for yourself with this one. Where'd you find him?"

"Oh, I picked him up along the way." Ruth looked up at Jack and was sure he was blushing.

"Well, I'd hang onto him. He's a real . . . no, I'd better not say it. I'll wait until I get to know him better."

"A studmuffin?" Jack said with a grin.

That broke Barbara up. She slapped her leg and doubled over with laughter.

Despite her apprehension about Brenda, Ruth laughed through her tears. Tony and Jack joined in the merriment. Amy didn't think it was the least bit funny and she went out in the hall to join her brother-in-law.

Ruth knew that Barbara wasn't being irreverent. She was simply trying to help all of them get through the difficult time.

"I know there's going to be a lot of people at your house this evening, Ruth," Barbara said. "So I'm cooking up enough food to feed a small army."

"You shouldn't, but I appreciate it. I hadn't even thought about cooking."

"Glen and I will come over to the house and serve it up. I've got to go now." She hugged Ruth again.

Ruth fought back the tears after Barbara left. "You don't find many friends like Barbara and Glen and Diane."

Another hour passed before the doctor came into the room.

"Everything went as we expected it to," he announced. "Brenda is doing just fine. We kept a monitor on the baby during the surgery and the baby is all right."

"What did you do to Brenda?" Ruth asked.

"We set her broken bones. She had multiple fractures in her wrist and hand, so that took quite a while. There was still bleeding from her head wound, so we took care of that. The lab tests showed that there was internal bleeding, so we did exploratory surgery and did a lot of stitching up while we were in there. Her prognosis is good."

"How long will she be in the hospital?" Danny asked.

"At least a week, but she'll probably have to have physical therapy to regain the use of her left arm. Brenda is in the recovery room. The nurse will let you know when you can see her."

"Thanks, Dr. Peterson," Ruth said.

"I know you're all anxious to be with Brenda, but right now she needs complete rest. When she wakes up, I'll allow you to visit her two at a time for a very short period. After that, you'll have to keep your visits very brief for a few days."

After the doctor left, Amy decided to go back to the house. The rest of them waited until Brenda woke up.

It was four o'clock in the afternoon when Ruth and Jack left the hospital, after looking in on Brenda, who was still too groggy to talk.

"I'd like to stop at the post office and pick up my mail," Ruth said as they got into the rented car. "And then I'd like to swing by the bank and cash a check so I can pay you back for the airplane fares."

"You don't need to do that," Jack said.

"Yes, I do."

Ruth dashed into the post office and gathered a stack of mail from her box. As they drove to the bank, she looked through the mail. She pulled a window envelope out of the stack and stared at it. The letter was from her bank and the slip that showed through the window was pink. She knew what the pink slip meant. A bounced check notice. But she'd never had a check bounce in her entire life. It had to be a mistake.

She tore the envelope open. The check that had bounced was for $96.82. It was the check she'd written at the Osceola Cheese Factory.

"That doesn't make sense," she said aloud.

"What's that?" Jack glanced over at the envelope.

"A check I wrote at the Cheese Factory in Missouri bounced, according to this. But there's a foul up somewhere. I had almost $3,000 in my checking account when I wrote this and I've only written two small checks since then."

"Well, banks do make errors sometimes."

"I'd better hold off on writing you a check until I get this straightened out."

Jack laughed. "Good idea."

"Oh, darn," Ruth said when they got to the bank. "We'll have to go through the drive-thru window. The lobby closed an hour ago."

Jack drove the car around to the side of the bank and waited his turn in line. When they got to the drive-thru window, Ruth got out so she could talk to the teller behind the window. She slipped the pink slip into the tube and pushed the button to send it into the bank. "Would you check my account?" Ruth asked. "This check shouldn't have bounced."

The teller punched in Ruth's account number on her computer, waited for the figures to appear. "Your account shows a negative balance," she said.

"There's been a mistake," Ruth said. "Would you please arrange for me to go inside so I can talk to the bank president or the accounting department?"

"I'm sorry, Mrs. Nichols. Everyone's gone for the day and I don't have access to your records."

"This is Friday. Do you mean I have to wait until Monday to get this straightened out?"

"The drive-up window will be open tomorrow morning and a bank official will be here. Come back then and we'll see that you get inside."

"One more worry," Ruth said as they drove away.

An hour after they got to Ruth's house, Barbara and Glen Amos arrived with several trays of food and more casserole dishes than Ruth could count. Shortly after the food was set out, people began arriving. Danny and Tony came from the hospital. Ernestine arrived with Hank and Lori. Norman Rogers stopped by long enough to convey his concern for Brenda. Several of Ruth's friends from school came by and stayed just long enough to eat.

Ruth appreciated the concern of her friends, but after an hour of talking to well-wishers, she was exhausted. Ernestine took the children back to Brenda's house and after the other company cleared out, Amy went back to the hospital with Danny. Finally, there were just the three of them. Ruth, Jack, and Tony. Ruth turned the television on in the family room so they could watch the news.

When she heard the knock on the side door, she didn't think she could take anymore company. Tony answered the door.

Meg Rodecker came into the room, her eyes red from crying. She ran over to Ruth and put her arms around her.

Ruth was stunned to see her.

"Ruth, I'm so sorry about Brenda. We didn't find out until late yesterday afternoon. We couldn't get a flight out of Springfield until this morning."

"Oh, you shouldn't have flown back and spoiled your trip," Ruth said.

"What are friends for?"

Tony turned the television up. "Listen. They're talking about the man who hit Brenda."

They all crowded around the television.

"The man was arrested shortly after noon," the television reporter said. "According to witnesses, he was drunk at the time of the accident. Several charges are pending. Mrs. Brenda Parker remains in critical condition at Mercy Hospital."

"I knew they'd get him," Tony said.

"Also arrested this afternoon was a local banker," the news reporter continued. "Scot Rodecker, Senior Loan Officer at the Citizens National Bank in Billings, was taken into custody at the airport."

Ruth stared at the screen in disbelief.

"Rodecker has been charged with embezzlement, following an extensive bank audit," the newscaster said in a staccato voice. "Details have not been released, but one bank official indicated that the amount embezzled could exceed a million dollars."

Ruth turned to Meg. Now she knew why Meg's eyes were so red and puffy. "Oh, Meg, I'm so sorry."

"I should have known," Meg said as the tears flowed down her cheeks. The two friends hugged each other for a long time.

"When did you find out?" Ruth asked.

"Not until we stepped off the plane and entered the terminal. There were a dozen cops there waiting to arrest Scot.

Ruth, he took me for everything I had. I don't have a penny left. Not a penny."

"I assumed it was bank money he embezzled."

"That's where my money was. My money *was* bank money. I never thought to check on my funds. Scot was the banker in the family. I don't have any money left."

"Oh, I'm so sorry, Meg."

"After they arrested him, the police gave me all of his personal things and drove me home. When I got the cruise tickets out of his jacket, I discovered something else. Scot had bought an airline ticket for himself from the Caribbean to San Diego. He had planned to leave me at the first port of call and fly to San Diego alone. I have a hunch he planned to hide out in Mexico. And I think that hurts as much as losing my money. Knowing that he planned to dump me after he'd stolen everything I had."

"Meg, is there anything I can do?"

"I don't know. I'm just numb. Yes, I know one thing you can do."

"What's that?"

"You can help me write that novel. We finally have a scandal worth writing about." She laughed through her tears.

Ruth stood there for a long time after Meg left, unable to believe how terrible Scot had been.

And then a thought occurred to her that disturbed her very much. Scot had embezzled his own wife's accounts. Ruth had several accounts at the same bank. A checking account. A savings account, and several CDs and other investments. And Scot had been all too helpful in changing her accounts to her name after Henry died.

Ruth knew she'd signed her name to dozens of papers when she was settling Henry's estate. Overcome with grief, she'd signed every paper that Scot had put in front of her. And she hadn't read the fine print because she'd trusted Scot.

And now, she had the first bounced check notification she'd ever gotten in her life. Everything was coming together. Scot had planned everything down to the last detail. He'd known when she was

542

leaving on her trip to the Ozarks and if it hadn't been for Brenda's accident, Ruth wouldn't have come home for another two weeks.

Ruth felt an icy chill down her spine. Had Scot embezzled from her accounts as well as Meg's?

"Don't let it be true," she said aloud.

But the sick feeling in the pit of her stomach wouldn't go away.

Forty-two

Ruth didn't have to wait until the following morning to find out about her insufficient funds account. William Conway, the president of the bank and longtime friend, stopped by Ruth's house at eight o'clock that evening.

"I hate to talk business at a time when you're so concerned about Brenda, but this can't wait," Bill Conway began.

"It's not good news, is it, Bill?" Ruth asked.

"No. Do you want to talk in private?"

"No, whatever you've got to say, I want Tony and my friend to be in on it. Let's sit down at the dining room table."

"I assume you know that Scot Rodecker has been arrested for embezzlement."

"Yes. Meg was here when I heard the

544

news on the television. Needless to say, I was shocked."

"Did she tell you that Scot embezzled all of her funds and left her penniless?"

"Yes."

"I don't know how to tell you this, Ruth, except to say it right out."

"Go ahead." Ruth held her breath.

"Scot Rodecker has done the same thing to all of your accounts."

Ruth's heart sank. "You mean I have nothing left?"

"Nothing at all, Ruth. Scot took everything."

"But how could he do that? I don't understand."

"Do you remember when Henry died and I promoted Scot to the position of Senior Loan Officer?"

"Yes."

"Well, we've just finished an extensive audit at the bank and we've traced the paper trail. Scot had you sign a lot of papers, including a legal form granting him power of attorney over your affairs."

"No, I didn't," Ruth said. "I signed a form giving power of attorney to my

545

son, Tony. I remember that distinctly."

"Scot was a very clever, deceitful man. He manipulated you and got you to think that you were assigning power of attorney to Tony, but when he got through with the paperwork, it came out differently. He did the same thing with all of your accounts."

"You mean he took my money *legally?*"

"Technically, yes, but he will be charged with intent to commit fraud, among many other charges."

"Is my money gone forever?" Ruth asked. "Or is there a chance of recovering any of it?"

"If we can find it, you'll get it back. Or if we can get Scot to tell us where it's stashed. We're working on it."

"Well, I knew something was wrong when I got a bounced check notice today. What am I going to do about that?"

"We'll arrange a temporary loan for you," Bill said. "In tracing Scot's recent actions at the bank, we discovered that he had cleared all of your accounts out except your savings and checking accounts. The day after you left for the Ozarks, he did the paperwork to clean out both of those accounts. That's why the check bounced. If you've written any others, they'll bounce, too."

"I'm facing almost four thousand dollars in repair bills for my motorhome. How can I take out a loan if I won't have the money to pay it back? All I've got left is my retirement benefits."

"We'll try to work with you, Ruth. There's one thing more. As of this moment, Scot Rodecker owns this house."

"No!" Ruth cried.

"Ruth, if we can find the money, you'll get it back. Meg will get hers back, too. We just hope he hasn't spent it all. Meg thinks Scot was heading for Mexico, so we've got investigators down there checking every single bank, looking for certain large deposits. Scot probably didn't use his own name."

"What about San Diego?" Ruth suggested. "Wouldn't it be easier for him to funnel the money through an American bank?"

"You know, I don't know if the investigators have checked the banks in San Diego, but we may be looking in the wrong place." William Conway stood up. "We'll keep you informed, Ruth. Meanwhile, I wish the best for your daughter."

Forty-three

Brenda had recovered nicely in a week's time, and although she still couldn't walk or use her left arm, she was due to be released from the hospital the following morning.

Jack and Ruth had taken a day away from the family to drive to his home in Paradise Valley. They would fly back to Branson the following Monday, the first flight they'd been able to get on such short notice.

"Thank God, I got the loan through," Ruth told Jack as they drove the last miles to his place in the hills. "At least I can get my motorhome out of hock and stay afloat for a while. I'm dreading the drive back here from Branson."

She'd lost all hope of getting any portion of her money back and she wasn't sure that she would be able to keep her house. William Conway had told her that Scot had sold it out from under her.

"Maybe you can find a buyer for your motorhome out there and ride back to Montana with me," he suggested.

"Maybe."

They drove down the autumn lane. The trees had lost all their color and the leaves that still clung to the bare branches were dead and brown. It was much the way Ruth felt about herself, her life.

As they drove up to Jack's house, Ruth decided to put her troubles aside. Brenda was going to fully recover and that was all that really mattered.

They stood in his living room and looked out the window at the view of the mountains. Ruth was awed by the sight and felt a chill when she remembered her Russell Chatham lithograph. The view was so familiar to her, she knew it by heart.

"How would you like to have a view like this for the rest of your life?" Jack said as he stood with his arm around her.

"I'd love to. I have my lithograph and now when I look at it, I'll know where it came from."

"Do you believe in fate?"

"I'm not sure."

"I know I'm stumbling all over the place, but I love you Ruth. I'm trying to ask you to marry me. Will you be my wife forever?"

Ruth's heart soared for the first time in days. She wanted so very much to tell him she would. "If you'd asked me a week ago, I would have said yes. But now I don't have anything to offer. My money is gone and I'd be a financial burden to you."

"Ruth, you've got everything to offer. I don't want your money. We both like the simple life and I can support us. Please, Ruth. I love you so much."

"I love you, too, Jack." And when he took her in his arms and kissed her, she had no defenses. She just melted into him.

"Ruth, will you marry me?" he asked again.

"Yes, Jack. I want very much to marry you."

"*When* will you marry me?"

"When we get back from Branson?"

"I've got a better idea. How about getting married next Saturday and spending our honeymoon in Branson?"

"I'd like that. Branson would be a lovely place for a honeymoon."

"We agree on everything."

"You know where I'd like to get married?" Ruth said, a dreamy quality to her voice.

"Where?"

"Right here in your living room where we can see the mountains."

Jack smiled. "That can be arranged."

They headed back to Billings to announce the news to the family, discussing their plans for the future all the way there.

Brenda and Tony were delighted when Ruth told them the news. And when they called Amy, who had returned to college after the weekend, she was happy for them, too.

"I feel like I should stay here and take care of Brenda's kids," Ruth told Tony as the three of them shared a pizza that night. Tony had bought the pizza to celebrate their engagement and they sat at Ruth's dinette booth talking about the future.

"You can't allow yourself to feel guilty anymore," Tony said. "You've got your own life to live and so does Brenda. And now, Mama Murph's got something to live for."

"She's really surprised me," Ruth said.

"She's surprised herself, I think." Tony laughed. "She loves taking care of the kids. She works like a Trojan cleaning and cooking for Brenda's family. She's even given up her bridge club. She says that what she's doing is a lot more fun than sitting around with the little old biddies."

"Miracles do happen," Ruth said.

"Yes, they do," Jack said as he squeezed Ruth's hand. "Look at us."

"Please, Jack, you're embarrassing my son."

"Not me," Tony grinned. "Speak for yourself. I think you two deserve each other."

"I'm not sure how to take that," Ruth smiled.

Ruth jumped when the phone rang on the ledge behind her. "I don't want to talk to anyone tonight," she sighed.

"Do you want me to answer it?" Tony asked.

"No, I'll get it." Ruth turned and picked up the receiver.

"Mrs. Nichols?"

Ruth didn't recognize the caller's voice.

"Yes, I'm Ruth Nichols." But not for long, she wanted to add.

"This is Kenny Price out here in Branson, Missouri."

"Oh, yes, the mechanic," Ruth said. "I forgot to tell you that we had left town. We had a family emergency."

"Yeah, I know. I talked to the lady at the campground and she told me about your daughter. Is your daughter okay now?"

"Yes, she'll be okay. Did you get my motorhome finished?"

"Well, no, not really."

"Well, we won't be back for about a week. Will it be ready by then?"

"I reckon so, but what I'm calling about is that I've got a fellow here in the office who wants to buy it. I was wondering if you wanted to sell it."

"Yes, I do." Ruth glanced at Jack and smiled.

"How much are you asking for it?"

"Well, I don't know. I'll have to check with the fellow who sold it to me. I can call you back tomorrow."

Ruth saw Tony gesturing to her. She covered the handpiece.

"Don't take less than $25,000," Tony whispered. "Glen Amos can get that much for you."

Ruth nodded.

"Well, the fellow wants to make you an offer," Kenny Price said.

"What kind of an offer?" Ruth asked.

"He's been checking around and he knows his prices for used motorhomes. He knows you paid $65,000 for it new and he's willing to offer you half that amount. $32,500."

Ruth was pleasantly surprised by the offer. "That sounds like a fair offer," she said. "I still owe you for the repairs."

"I know. I told the man that since your motorhome is so clean, he'd have to pay you $35,000. He agreed. So if you agree, you've got yourself a deal."

"I'll let you talk to my son. He handles all of my affairs."

Tony took the phone and by the time he hung up, he'd made the deal. "I accepted the $35,000. After paying for the repairs, you'd end up with $31,250, so I told Mr. Price that you'd give him a $1,250 commission. You'll still end up with $30,000, which ain't peanuts."

"That'll certainly help make up for some of the money I lost," Ruth said.

The phone rang again almost immediately. "You answer it this time, Tony." She slid the phone across the table.

Ruth listened to Tony's side of the conversation, but she couldn't tell who he was talking to or what was being discussed. Tony talked in one word sentences. "Yes. Yeah. Okay. When?"

"Keep 'em coming," Tony said when he hung up. He had a big grin on his face.

"What was that all about?" Ruth asked.

"That was the bank president, Mr. Conway. First of all, he said that Scot Rodecker had agreed to sign the house back over to you."

"That's a relief."

"And second, he said you were right. They found the money in San Diego. It'll take time to go through the legal system, but you'll get back every dime Scot embezzled from you. They got Scot to talk and he said he'd put all the money in a bank in San Diego and had planned to pick it up on his way to Mexico. Conway said that all of Meg's was money recovered, too."

"I can't believe it," Ruth said. "Well, Jack, it looks like I can pay you back for the airline tickets."

"Keep it, Ruth. You can pay for the honeymoon," he teased.

Ruth sat there for a minute, thinking over her good fortune. "Tony, I've got an idea. Let me bounce if off you."

"I'm all ears."

"Brenda's going to need a bigger house now that she's having another baby."

"That's true. Her house is a cracker-box."

"Well, Jack and I are going to spend a lot of time living in his travel trailer. Right, Jack?"

"I hope so." He took Ruth's hand and held it. "I might even buy you a new travel trailer for a wedding present."

"Maybe we'll buy one together."

"Still trying to prove your independence," Jack teased.

"That's right. Anyway, I'm not going to need this house, but I don't want to sell it."

"So what are you going to do?" Tony asked. "Rent it to Brenda?"

"No, I'm going to give the house to all three of you children. I've been thinking about this ever since I found out Brenda was pregnant. I thought I'd have papers drawn up giving legal title to Brenda and Danny with the stipulation that when and if she ever sells it, the profits are to be divided equally between all three of you. Does that sound fair?"

"It does to me. Brenda's the only one who needs this house and you know how much she loves it."

"I know. That's why I made the decision. I love the house, too, but once Jack and I are married, I'm going to be extremely busy."

"Taking care of Jack?" Tony grinned.

"No. Following him all over the place so we can fish every lake, stream, and creek in the country."

"That's exactly right," Jack said. "I'm going to have it written into our marriage vows." He leaned over and kissed Ruth tenderly, lingering for a long moment.

Tony stood up and cleared his throat. "I think it's time for me to go."

"I think so, too," Ruth said with a huskiness in her voice. "I think Jack and I need time alone to talk about our wedding."

"Or practicing for it," Jack said, his huskiness equalling hers.

"I didn't hear that," Tony said with a laugh.

Ruth closed the door behind her son and

when she turned around, Jack swept her up into his arms. He kissed her and it was like the first kiss. She felt warm and sheltered in his arms, blossoming once again with a radiance that buffed away the years, made her feel young and hopeful. Jack kissed her on the neck, behind the ear. She melted.

"Now?" she whispered.

"Now," he said.

They walked hand in hand toward the bedroom, through the soft darkness, Ruth leading the way, her stomach fluttering with butterflies, her pulse racing like a young girl's. She squeezed his hand as they entered the bedroom.

Jack closed the door and they moved through the bars of light streaming through the windows, splashing their shadows on the bed until they blended together and were a single graven shape. Their eyes were full of stars burnished to a diamond shine as they made love, discovered each other's wonders and secrets once more, sealing the bond between them for all time to come.